BLACK SEAS

T.K. Blackwood

Chromatic Aberration

Chromatic
Aberration

In memory of Lieutenant Colonel Dan Barber, USMC, Retired.

*You were one of the bravest, kindest and most
honorable men I have ever had the pleasure to know.
We all miss you and will never forget you.*

FOREWORD

As with everything I do, this novel is the product of many other people working (mostly) thanklessly behind the scenes. It was made possible with gracious assistance from many readers including Pax, Alex Aaronson, James Houser of the Unknown Soldiers Podcast (https://www.unknownsoldierspodcast.com/), and my parents. What I got right, I did with their help, and where I went astray I did so on my own.

Cover illustration by Matthew McEntire

(https://matthewmcentire.com/)

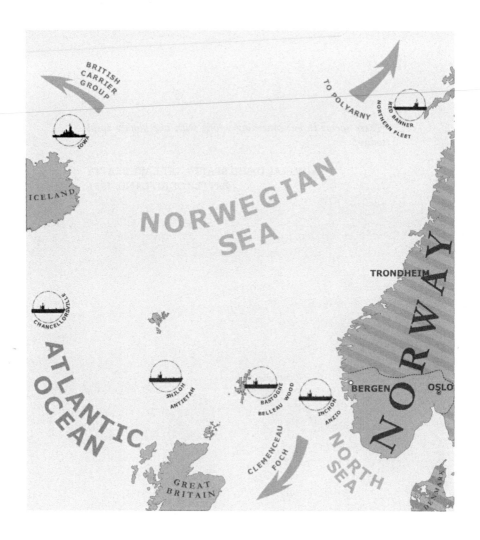

Norwegian Sea, October 1992

"There seems to be something wrong with our bloody ships today."

ADMIRAL DAVID BEATTY, 1ST EARL BEATTY
BATTLE OF JUTLAND, 1916

1

Late October 1992

A soft breeze rustled the branches of the birch trees overhead, sending dappled sunlight dancing across the forest floor, creating patterns of shadows which Corporal Ingrid Karlsdotter followed with a predator's lethal grace. The tall grass whispered against her boots and trousers, the black muzzle of her rifle trained unerringly ahead. She was grateful for the breeze, keeping the ambient noise of the forest just loud enough to partially drown out some of her movements as she crept slowly uphill, step by careful step. In peacetime she'd been an avid hiker, trekking up and down trails across Sweden. The weather was picture perfect, especially for this time of year, though Karlsdotter couldn't allow herself to properly enjoy it. She wasn't out here for pleasure.

Her platoon moved with her, fanned out in combat deployment, weapons ready. Just weeks ago they had been weekend warriors, soldiers in name only. Now, the platoon's survivors had seen enough combat to truly *be* soldiers.

Karlsdotter paused in cover behind a narrow birch tree. Its white, papery bark rasped on her fatigues. She peered around the trunk and up toward the gravel road just ahead. Her heart beat a steady rhythm in her chest, the sound like war drums in her ears. The rising thrill within her was shadowed by mounting fear in her gut but above it all was the smoldering furnace of anger in her heart.

She tightened her hold on the grip of her rifle and resisted the urge to wipe the sweat from her face. It wasn't hot, if anything the opposite, but nerves always got the better of her just before combat. She couldn't help but think about all the times she had gone hunting with her father when she was a little girl. It wasn't so different from this; in better times she had crept through the woods in the mountains hunting for deer, or hares, or moose, all that had changed was the prey.

She rested her rifle in the crook of a branch to steady it, drawing a bead on her target.

Her prey stood fifty meters distant, a Soviet infantryman standing watch at the edge of the road beside a BTR armored personnel carrier. His sentry keeping was sloppy. Karlsdotter watched as he smoked and scanned the treeline anxiously. He was jittery and on edge, but his fear wasn't making him more observant. His gaze jumped around at random. He was tense, afraid, probably thinking every tree hid a Swede with murderous intent.

In this case, he was right.

The rustling of the trees hid the movement of Karlsdotter's platoon, allowing them to get dangerously close. They'd painstakingly swept these woods looking for stragglers and once they picked up the scent it was just a matter of enveloping them and closing in to range. If they had just wanted to wipe them out, it would have been trivial work. Instead, they had a higher purpose for these enemies.

It was clear that this particular Soviet detachment wasn't expecting any real danger. They'd been clashing off and on with Swedish forces, but these Soviets had fled from where the front had been. As far as they knew they were safe this far out. The sentry was perfunctory. They hadn't yet realized they were very wrong.

The sentry had an RPG launcher slung on his back and a Kalashnikov in his hands. Even from this distance, Karlsdotter could see the telltale yellow headphone cable of a Sony Walkman cassette player. She knew that they didn't make Walkmen in the Soviet Union. She wondered what unfortunate soul he stole that bit of loot from as she pulled the trigger twice.

The gunshots were deafening.

The sentry jerked in surprise and dived away, going for cover even as his body betrayed him by going limp.

Karlsdotter managed to put a third shot into him before he hit the ground.

Her platoon surged forward and up the hill with a smattering of gunshots to suppress the enemy and she followed swiftly behind them, her boots digging into the soft earth as she climbed the shallow hill.

"Take prisoners!" Sergeant Hellström shouted over the gunfire. Living prisoners meant the possibility of gathering intelligence. It was an unwelcome order, but one she intended to obey.

Karlsdotter crested the hill and reached the flat plateau of the road. She reached the downed sentry first and knelt by him as the rest of her platoon paired off and secured the remaining Soviets with gunfire and shouted Russian commands to surrender.

The sentry flopped limply on the ground, his eyes wide, wild, and searching until they found hers. He gaped his bloody mouth at her, trying to speak, maybe to plead, beg for help. The raw gash her round had torn across his throat precluded any of that. It foamed with red fluid which spilled down his neck and collar.

He was young—maybe just a few years older than her—but the dirt and blood made that hard to tell for sure.

Karlsdotter kicked his rifle out of reach as his blood, bright crimson and thick, spurted with surprising intensity from the gash in his neck across the gravel road. His struggling grew weaker, his eyes becoming glazed. She watched him as he died bit by bit, waiting until his kicking legs stopped moving completely. His stolen Walkman sat in a spreading pool of blood, dark venous mixed with bright red capillary. One less invader to pollute, rape, and pillage her home.

She set to work checking the body for intel, tossing

his pockets. A half empty packet of Soviet-made cigarettes followed a military ID into the dirt. She pulled a small wad of Swedish krona from his pocket. The bills were ruined, stained with dark blood and pieced with a bullet. She let them fall and scatter in the wind around his body.

With a grunt and a heave, she rolled him face down into the blood pool and checked his remaining pockets. In one she found a small notebook. She fished it out and flipped it open, hoping to see notes, maps, orders, anything of value.

Instead the notepad was filled with sketches, drawings and doodles, a mixture of cartoon characters she recognized, and some she didn't. Prominently among them was a roguish wolf with long, unkempt hair and dressed like a Russian sailor.

"A wolf," she said, eyeing the soldier's body. "It suits you." Karlsdotter dropped the sketchpad on the dead man and stood back up.

The rest of the enemy had been rounded up by her platoon, those that had surrendered quickly enough anyway. She circled the silent BTR to find Hellström gathering the Soviet POWs on the side of the road, their hands on their heads.

Another soldier in her platoon, Bergman, came to stand beside her as they stared at the POWs.

"Wolves," Karlsdotter said.

Bergman nodded. "Looks that way." He thumped the APC with a hand. "No gas if you can believe it. I don't see any officers or NCOs with them either."

"Deserters?" Karlsdotter asked. In truth, she didn't care either way. An invader who followed orders was no different to her than one who didn't.

Bergman shook his head, "I don't think so. I think they were trying to get back to their lines. Who knows."

Karlsdotter stepped closer to the POWs, eyeing each one of them in turn. There were a half dozen in total and none of them met her gaze. Each was disheveled, dirty, and tired. Their uniforms were stained and torn, a state made worse by the search they were being subjected to as each one was checked for weapons and documents. Flak vests, helmets, bandoliers, and webbing—the accouterments of war were removed with surgical care before being tossed into a growing pile. As the search continued, Karlsdotter watched as military IDs, looted krona, and knick-knacks like cigarettes and chewing gum fell around them.

A captive soldier at the end of this line of prisoners looked up at her. The hate and fear in his eyes came close to matching her own. She looked at his hands clasped on top of his head and jerked his sleeve down to his elbow, revealing a string of watches decorating his arm, four total. Gold and silver, digital and analog. More stolen loot from other Swedes no doubt.

He flashed her a toothy smile that she longed to break with the butt of her rifle. Instead she pressed the muzzle of the weapon against his belly, pushing hard against his gut as her finger looped the trigger.

The Soviet's face drained of color, his confident smile turning to shock in an instant.

"Karlsdotter!" Hellström shouted.

She kept the weapon against the Russian's stomach, hot metal on warm flesh. One trigger pull and she could send another one straight to hell. God knew that these thugs deserved it.

God.

She thought of the Soviet soldier she'd gunned down in the ditch days prior. She thought of the way he'd gripped his cross necklace like a drowning man gripping a life preserver. She thought of his limp body and lifeless eyes after she'd finished him off.

Hellström stopped a short distance away. "Ingrid."

She didn't take her eyes off the Russian she held at gunpoint. Sweat beaded down his face, his once smarmy smirk was now a rictus grin, his teeth were clenched tight as could be.

Karlsdotter lowered her rifle, the barrel coming away from the Russian's gut only reluctantly. "Contraband, Sergeant." She nodded toward the watches.

Hellström half-turned his head, not taking his eyes from Karlsdotter. "Bucht, take him."

The trooper stepped forward to strip the looter of his ill-gotten wealth.

Hellström laid a hand on Karlsdotter's arm and steered her away from the POWs.

She waited until they were out of sight of the others before speaking. "I saw the watches. The way he smiled at me," she said. "I just couldn't—."

"I know," Hellström cut her off. "But this isn't our job. We aren't barbarians. We aren't animals."

"So we let them do whatever they want?" she retorted. "God only knows what they've done to our families! To our homes!"

"Then we make the bastards pay," Hellström said. "But not *these* bastards. Their war is over. We log them as looters and send them back for processing. But this war is far from over for us. I need to know I can count on you. I don't need a Viking, I need a soldier."

Karlsdotter exhaled a shaky breath. "You have one."

Hellström's gaze didn't waver. "Do I?"

She met it evenly. "Yes."

Hellström looked unconvinced. He ran his hand over his braided beard and sighed. "You're a fighter, Ingrid. A killer. We're going to need people like you. I recommended you for promotion for a reason, but I need to count on you."

She said nothing.

"Do not get yourself wasted on a court martial. We have rules—even if they don't, *we* do. Understand?"

"I understand."

Hellström thumped her arm, a show of solidarity. "Let's beat them first, then we can make them pay. Yes?"

Ingrid thought of her family, wherever they may be, she thought of her boyfriend Johann, wondering if he was facedown dead somewhere. She took a deep breath and let it out. "Yes," she said. "One at a time."

***

2

Many of the ships in the NATO convoy gathering off Edinburgh had come a long way to be here. For the American vessels in the convoy, they'd traveled across the breadth of the Atlantic ocean. For the men of HMS *Somerset*, although Britain was their home, they'd had to sail from their station in the Adriatic to join the growing fleet here. *Somerset's* closeness to Britain made her mission feel all the more pressing, positioned directly between their home and the war. As a Type-42 guided missile destroyer, *Somerset* was broadly used for surface warfare, though it also possessed submarine detection equipment. One hundred and forty meters long and displacing around 5,000 tons at combat loadout, *Somerset* held three hundred souls in her metal confines.

Captain Seymour walked the length of *Somerset's* operations room—the warship's nerve center. Windowless, cold, and dark save for the light of the multitude of computer monitors at each station, the operations room was more akin to a computer lab than what most people thought of when they imagined the control center of a ship. It reminded Seymour of the bridge of the starship *Enterprise* more than anything else. As he walked he pretended not to notice the men hunched over their consoles hard at work—the murmurs of officers speaking into microphones, gathering and providing information necessary to the functioning of the ship. It did a captain's image good to remain aloof, detached, almost mythical. Seymour found that too much meddling and micromanagement undid that picture, it reminded the men that he was only a man like they were.

Seymour was a navy man from a navy family. That was to say he was the child of a naval officer who was also the child of a naval officer. At least four consecutive generations of Seymour's family had served in the Royal Navy. It was a tradition his own son was carrying on as a midshipman aboard the HMS *Sovereign*, though his son had bucked the family tradition somewhat since *Sovereign* was a submarine. Seymour used to tease his son about that fact, but right now he found nothing funny about it. He could only hope his son was safe.

Outside, the sea was calm enough for *Somerset*'s kitchen to be serving food, which was often all that could be asked for from the temperamental waters of the North Sea. In times like this, when the crew was busy with their work and there was no immediate threat, it was easy to forget there was a war on. Their compatriots in the anti-submarine arm were busy cruising up and down the Atlantic hunting for the submarines that still threatened the vulnerable lifeline between Europe and America, as their fathers and grandfathers had done. The weapons were more advanced and the enemy was different, but the battlefield was the same. Seymour had grown up listening to tales of German submarine and surface raiders hunting defenseless transport ships in the dark. He'd heard the stories of ships going down with all hands and stricken U-boats vomiting up roils of dark oil. His father had lived that nightmare.

And now Seymour was about to partake in his own small slice of it.

As *Somerset* and the other frigates and destroyers of the escort group patrolled the mouth of the Firth of Forth, a growing collection of civilian and merchant marine ships gathered in the relative safety of the estuary.

Despite all the obvious dangers, Seymour envied the men tasked with patrolling the GIUK gap and North Atlantic in some ways. Their fight had begun in earnest and they were free to act—to fight—striking back at Soviet submarines and doing their damnedest to get allied shipping across the Atlantic intact. Here, Seymour felt like he was little more than a prisoner of circumstance. There was a war going on and he was missing it. He and the ship had seen some action near the Straits of Taranto during the Yugoslav Invasion, firing salvos at Soviet aircraft that dared to risk attack runs on the Adriatic and probing for submarines, but since then there had been little in the way of combat—certainly nothing that could compare to the intensity of the fighting in the Adriatic.

"Captain Seymour, sir," an ensign said, crossing the operations center. "You're wanted on the bridge."

Seymour kept his face stony and impassable, but the prospect of *something* happening was appealing nonetheless. "Word from *Nauls*?"

The American *Oliver Hazard Perry*-class frigate *Thomas Nauls* was the designated convoy leader, it was only on her go that they would weigh anchor.

The ensign gave a slight shake of his head. "Didn't say, sir."

Seymour hid his disappointment. "Very well." After turning control over to the duty officer, Seymour left the dark confines of the operations center, heading up for the bridge.

The Soviet Northern Fleet—the surface component anyway —had chosen not to sortie in grand style alongside their submarine forces and instead remained bottled up beyond the northern tip of Norway in the Barents Sea. The reasons for that choice were innumerable, not the least of which was the Soviet Navy's relative weakness when compared to their NATO counterpart. A fleet was not like an army, it was not a weapon to be handled roughly and rebuilt by packing it with conscripts. Sailors were not cannon fodder; they were technical specialists and equipment operators. Ships could take years to build and were not easily mass produced like rifles or tanks.

In denying NATO a swift surface engagement, the Soviets maintained a "fleet-in-being," a concept nearly as old as national navies themselves. Rather than throwing a weaker fleet away in a futile engagement, it could be kept around in order to force an opponent to dedicate resources to containing it.

There was that and Norway.

Seymour arrived on *Somerset*'s bridge and gazed briefly out at the expansive view the forward windows offered. From here he had an excellent view down the ship's nose including the Sea Dart launcher just forward of the bridge, its two arms each holding a waiting anti-air missile. Small windscreen wipers which kept the windows free of sea spray in rough seas currently sat motionless. Aside from a lovely view of the ocean, he couldn't see much of the task force with the naked eye as it was so far spread out.

"Captain on the bridge!" a sailor called, drawing everyone to attention.

"As you were," Seymour said. "Where's Mr. Smith?" Seymour asked.

The ensign gestured toward the other side of the compartment. "The XO wanted you to know he'll be with you in a minute, sir, still talking with the *Nauls*."

Seymour nodded patiently and moved to the forward section of the bridge where he took an offered pair of binoculars from a sailor. Gazing out over the ocean, he studied the distant gray form of HMS *Gloucester* conducting her own patrol, sweeping for enemy submarines. As he watched, movement overhead caught his eye, a P-3 Orion anti-submarine aircraft on patrol. This close to NATO air bases, friendly air cover would provide a welcome umbrella of protection against two prongs of the Soviet anti-ship force, submarines and aircraft. Once the convoy got further out, they would be more reliant on carrier-based aircraft.

Carriers could provide a measure of air cover, but carrier-based fighters generally struggled to compete with their more numerous and more heavily-armed land-based counterparts. In that sense, the air bases that dotted Norway gave the NATO allies a huge degree of control over the Norwegian Sea, making any Soviet sortie out of the Barents Sea a risky proposition. So long as those bases stood, the Soviets couldn't safely enter the Norwegian Sea, let alone the North Sea.

"Captain," Seymour's XO, Smith, came to stand beside him.

"Word from *Nauls*?"

Smith's professional facade cracked just enough to show the hint of a smile. For as long as he'd served with Smith, Seymour rarely knew him to speak or act casually. Some officers might have found him overly stiff, but Seymour actually appreciated the formality. Smith wasn't afraid to speak his mind or challenge Seymour when necessary, but he always did so with a strict professionalism.

"We're waiting on one last ship to finish loading. *Million*."

"*Million*," Seymour repeated. "Which one is that?"

"Cruise ship, sir."

"That's right."

Seymour had seen it when arrived in Edinburgh the day prior. *Million*'s hull was a pristine, gaudy white. Recently nationalized by an act of Congress, it carried humanitarian and food aid intended for Norway like the other ships of the convoy—meals, blankets, heaters, warm clothes, medicine, the bulk of America's plenty, directed to help people in need. Once unloaded it would assist with evacuating civilians to Britain, shuttling back and forth with as many as it could hold.

"Quite a motley collection of ships we've got here," Seymour said.

"Yes, sir."

"And the escorts. Us, *Gloucester*, *Nauls*, *Fuchs* ... who am I forgetting?"

"*Callenburgh*, sir."

"*Callenburgh*. Yes."

Callenburgh was a Dutch *Kortenaer*-class. Like *Gloucester* she was built for anti-submarine action.

"Did *Nauls* give any indication of when they expected we would be moving out?"

"None, sir."

"Americans," Seymour muttered. "Expect us to jump on command, don't they?"

"Yes, sir."

"It's seventeen hours from here to Bergen at good speed." Seymour grimaced. "God knows what the merchant ships can maintain."

"Yes, sir."

With Norway's capital of Oslo a straight shot from occupied Denmark and the mouth of the Soviet-controlled Baltic Sea, it was vulnerable to both aerial and naval attack from Soviet forces. As such, Bergen—their destination—had become the harbor of choice for delivering supplies to Scandinavia.

"It's going to be a long day."

"Yes, sir."

Seymour spared a glance at Smith, frowning. "Well we ought to show them how it's done. Let's make ready to depart by tomorrow morning at the latest. Shouldn't be long, and I'll be damned if we'll be the ones to hold up everything."

"Yes, sir."

Seymour half-nodded, dismissing Smith, and turned back to the forward windows. Seventeen hours to Bergen. Seventeen hours for the Soviets to make it hell for them if they chose to.

With Danish airfields now in Soviet hands it meant the whole North Sea was vulnerable to attack. Over-the-horizon missile attacks would steadily eat away at unarmed merchant ships unless anti-aircraft vessels like *Somerset* stayed to protect them.

For all the combined might of NATO, their position in Scandinavia was perilous. How many missed supply runs would it take for resistance to crack and fold? It was a question Seymour would rather never know the answer to. The supplies in this convoy were absolutely essential to continuing the fight. Food, fuel, ammunition, bandages, medicine, boots, uniforms, weapons, spare parts, and warm clothing.

Seymour forced the dread from his mind. He wasn't accustomed to losing and didn't intend to start now. He'd faced the Soviets in the Adriatic and it would be no different now.

Let the Soviets hide in their naval bastion. They would grow weaker by the day while the allied fleets gathered in strength. Until the enemy was ready to run the gauntlet of Norwegian air support, they could do nothing.

Battered and bruised, but unbowed, the Scandinavians fought on. So long as Norway still stood, the Soviet Navy was trapped.

***

3

The high-pitched howl of jet engines and the lingering scent of aviation fuel were welcome changes for Major Ken Morris. He'd spent the better part of a week wandering around the Swedish woods, desperately avoiding capture at the hands of Soviet patrols in what had become occupied Sweden. Morris stepped from the idling helicopter and onto the tarmac. In the distance he could see the enormous main terminal of the Oslo Gardermoen Airport, currently servicing a veritable flock of passenger aircraft which were taking off and setting down with clockwork regularity, shuttling civilians out of the country and bringing military personnel and supplies in.

"Back from the dead."

Morris turned at the sound of the voice and lowered his sunglasses, a grin spreading across his face. "Just a little vacation," Morris said.

His wingman, Grinder, crossed the short distance between them and enveloped Morris in a bear hug before slapping him on the back. "I thought you bit it, man!" he said, visibly choking back emotion. "You crazy son of a bitch, I can't believe you made it back. God, it's good to see you again."

"I got lucky," Morris said, thinking of Lancelot's F-15 exploding midair from a Soviet heatseeker. "Real lucky. And I had some help."

"Help?"

"Swedish Home Guard. Resistance fighters I guess. They found me when I went down out there and they made sure I got back over the lines."

Grinder raised a curious eyebrow. "Resistance, huh?" He

whistled. "That's crazy. I want to hear all about it! Come on, let's get under cover." Grinder motioned and Morris followed toward a thick stand of trees on the opposite side of the landing area. Behind them, the Norwegian army chopper revved up and took off, angling away toward the cloudless horizon.

"I can't tell you how glad I am to see you, Voodoo. We seriously thought you were a goner."

"You and me both," Morris said. "Like I said, it's dumb luck that I made it out and Lancelot didn't. Could have just as easily been the other way around...."

Grinder looked at him. "Sure. Could have been him down there, or me, or any of us. That's the rub, isn't it?"

"I guess," Morris said.

"No need to guess," Grinder said, fixing Morris with a stern look. "You're here. He isn't. It sucks. It's sad for him, but that's how it is. We miss him like we missed you, but we're not out here trading lives or playing 'woulda coulda shoulda.'"

Grinder's tone caught Morris off guard. "That's cold, man."

"Cold?" Grinder said. He looked almost surprised, like he hadn't considered it. That uncertainty only lasted a moment and then was gone. "Maybe. But when and if I'm the one smeared across the ground somewhere, then know that it was just my time to go. Life rolls the dice, the chips fall where they do." He shrugged.

Morris couldn't buy in as easily as Grinder did to such a fatalistic view, but he had to admit that there was a certain poetry to it. It would certainly make it easier to sleep at night. Still, he wasn't interested in engaging in a philosophical debate right now. After days of being shuttled across Norway and undergoing extensive debriefing to wring out every drop of intelligence he could provide, he was just glad to finally be back with his squadron. "So they moved us out here?" Morris asked.

Grinder nodded absently. "Right after you got shot down the squadron transferred from Farsund to here. Soviet missile attack from Denmark jacked the fuel tanks on site, so we had to move. Runways are in short supply, you know." He gestured broadly toward the airport. "So they stuck us out here with a few more spare birds. Right now we're sharing Gardermoen with civilian air traffic. The squadron's in reserve until we can get caught up with aircraft readiness. We pushed too hard for too long and now we've got to pay the price."

Maintenance was a dirty word in war time, but something which couldn't be ignored. A faulty or overworked component could be just as deadly as an enemy missile.

"How's that going?" Morris asked.

"Mixed bag," Grinder said with a shrug. "Feels like we're sitting with a nice big bullseye on our backs. Russians have been plastering airfields like there's no tomorrow, pounding every strip of pavement that can fit a fighter. Just a matter of time before they come after this one too, I think."

Morris knew from personal experience that no air defense network was foolproof. It was just a matter of finding the right gap in the defenses, the right weak spot, or just a willingness to swallow the losses a concerted attack would suffer.

Nearing the woods, Morris saw that they were in fact parking spaces for the squadron's F-15 Eagles and a handful of EF-111 "Sparkvark" electronic warfare craft. Ad hoc earthen shelters had been bulldozed and taxiways established to get the fighters onto the main runways of the airport. Not far from the sheltered hangars, Morris saw an air defense missile battery, as well as a couple prefabricated structures, makeshift barracks, and storage facilities.

"So, tell me about this 'help' you had," Grinder said. "Resistance fighters?"

Morris nodded. "I ran into a platoon of Swedish stay-behind troops operating in the rear areas. Good guys. They took me in, kept me fed, and made sure I got out of there."

"Lucky break!" Grinder said. "I bet they *loved* lugging you around."

Morris's thoughts wandered back to the Swedes, in particular he thought about Astrid and the slip of paper she gave him with her name and address.

So you can find me after the war. After this is all over.

Morris had promised her he would, and he'd meant it, but now he wondered where she was. Still living in the cold, dark woods? Still fighting? Maybe she was dead. He couldn't worry about Astrid and the others right now, he had his own family to worry about. He'd confirmed during his debrief after being recovered that his family had been notified that he was missing. That status was in the process of being updated, but knowing what he did of military efficiency, he figured that news hadn't reached his family yet. Beyond that, he wanted them to hear his voice; he knew damn sure if the situation were reversed he'd want to hear theirs.

He thought about Stefan and his kids back in Arvika. They were counting on more than just a phone call for their family to be safe.

"You good?"

Morris looked up to find Grinder staring at him. "Just thinking about the people I left behind."

His wingman nodded sympathetically. "We lost a lot of good people. It's—." He stopped, apparently unable to continue. He shook his head. "It's a lot. I'll sort it out when this thing is over."

Morris shared the sentiment. "Yeah." It was too much too soon and he just didn't have the time or energy to unpack everything. Not right now.

Grinder opened the door to the small barracks and waved Morris in who was startled to see the pilots of the squadron assembled. The second he noticed them they cheered. It was a classic ambush. Morris was hugged, slapped on the back, passed a beer or two, and welcomed with all the enthusiasm the squadron could muster. After all, it wasn't every day that one of their own came back from the dead. Survival in a war was reason enough for celebration.

Everyone wanted to shake his hand and everyone had a smartass remark.

"Any excuse for some fresh air, huh?"

"Hey Major, anyone tell you that you smell piney fresh now?"

"Glad you're back from vacation, Major."

"Voodoo, back from the dead!"

Morris endured this gauntlet with as much dignity as he could until someone in the squadron shook a beer can and cracked it open. Foamy beer showered the collected pilots in place of more traditional celebratory champagne.

"Jesus guys!" Morris protested, laughing in spite of himself.

"Speech!" Grinder called, a cry soon echoed by the other pilots.

The commotion died down, the pilots and ground crew here stood back enough to let him take a moment to look them over. Everyone was beaming, everyone was ecstatic to have him back, even the people he didn't know well, which—looking over their faces—was most of them.

Of the pilots, Grinder was one of the few "old hands" remaining. Less than half of the squadron were men who he'd flown with before the war. Everyone else was dead. Time and attrition had worn the squadron down bit by bit.

The others here were new, "Rooks", fresh pilots from Stateside sent to replace the losses of the early war. He had to remind himself that even the newest of these pilots had been fighting the war for weeks—almost as long as he had. They weren't inexperienced, but they also weren't the same men he'd flown with over Kaliningrad.

In that moment, with all of them looking at him, he felt like they weren't just glad to see a comrade back, but that they saw him as something else. A mentor, a leader. Sure. he'd held the rank before all this started, but now he started to feel like he'd earned it.

Morris held up the can of beer someone had shoved into his hand a moment ago. "We've got a lot of people counting on us back home," Morris said. "We've got a job to do, and we're gonna see it done. No matter what it takes. We're gonna make it count for the people who aren't coming back." Callsigns came unbidden to his mind. "Lancelot. Joker. Mint. Daisy." Morris listed the names of those who'd they lost, a list that got longer with each passing week.

The other pilots with drinks held them aloft, the mirth on their faces now sombered to seriousness as he listed off each of the men Wyvern had lost, men who he'd led into death and failed to bring back out.

Morris cracked open the beer and drank. It was warm but he savored it all the same. "Let's do what we have to do and make sure the rest of us get home."

The pilots sounded agreement and those with booze drank and slowly began to disperse, breaking into small groups of conversation or retiring to try to grab some shut eye before the next sortie.

Grinder found his way back to Morris. "Some speech."

Morris shrugged, "I'm not much for words. I'm just ready to get back in the saddle."

Grinder laid a hand on his back and steered him away from the others. "Relax, man. I've got a ride lined up for you. Viper's out. Caught some shrapnel in the attack on Farsund, so he's passing his Eagle to you while he's getting sent back."

"Are we that short on planes?" Morris asked.

Grinder nodded somberly. "We have more drivers than birds right now. They're going to start putting us in Phantoms if we're not careful."

Morris wasn't keen on the idea of flying a thirty-year-old fighter into battle. Although he'd seen the Soviets do it, he'd also seen how easy they were to send down in flames. "Let's hope it doesn't come to that."

"For sure. Goddamn. Just glad to have you back, Voodoo."

"You and me both. Hey, does this place have phones?"

Grinder nodded. "Yeah, the airport has international lines open."

Morris ran some timezone math in his head. "It's what, about eight AM in Dayton?"

Grinder shrugged. "Probably? Yeah I think so. Gonna call home?"

Morris nodded again. "I need to let my family know I'm okay. Last they heard I was missing in action."

Grinder winced. "Yeah, I was afraid of that. That's gonna be a tough call. They'll be glad to hear you though. Glad as hell, I bet."

"Hope so," Morris said. He wondered how Mike would cope with the knowledge that his father was safe after all, but that he was going right back into danger. It almost didn't seem fair to give them that hope and then threaten to take it away again. "I'm ready for this to be over," Morris said.

"Sooner the better," Grinder agreed. "Come on," he added, "I'll drive you there."

A Humvee waited just outside the barracks. Grinder climbed into the driver's seat and put the behemoth in gear. It was baking hot from sitting in the sun, but Morris didn't bother trying to mess with the climate control. He'd never once seen a Humvee with working AC and saw no reason for his luck to change now.

The nearer they drew to the terminal, the more crowded Morris realized it was. Busses stopped periodically to unload flocks of wide-eyed civilian families who were herded by military police through steadily winding lines into the terminal and then guided to the correct gates.

Norwegian soldiers worked in shifts unloading planes, hauling off supplies and equipment before packing the holds with civilian evacuees. The whole operation was like a revolving door: war material came off and evacuees went on.

It was organized chaos and it made Morris sick to see it. Any one of the children he saw could easily be his son or Stefan's kids in Sweden. These people were walking through a waking nightmare. Morris only hoped things would look better for them when they got to wherever these flights were taking them.

Grinder had already been desensitized to the sight and parked the Humvee in a designated spot before leading Morris into the main building. They ascended an exterior metal staircase by a loading gate and came into the terminal itself. The interior design was sleek, clean, and modern with gracefully arched ceilings and shining metal accents. Banks of windows which normally allowed waiting passengers to watch air traffic now showed only scenes of the frantic activity outside. This particular section of the terminal was barred to civilians and so was almost completely deserted.

"This way," Grinder said. Their footsteps echoed in the empty terminal.

"Where are those people going?" Morris asked.

"Planes to the UK," Grinder replied. "From there? Who knows. France, Spain, probably Ireland. I don't know. Wherever will take them. Danes, Swedes, Norwegians, you name it, everyone wants out while they can."

"Hard to blame them," Morris said.

The defense line that stalled the Soviet attack was tenuous. It was only through extreme, bloody effort that NATO held back the Soviet onslaught. Everyone knew that line could be broken at any time and the Russians would steamroll what was left of free Scandinavia. Morris and his men were almost guaranteed a flight out of here if that happened. The same couldn't be said for the civilians outside.

Grinder brought Morris to a bank of payphones lining the wall. "International calls are free, just dial zero and give them the number."

Morris exhaled, trying to shed the tension he felt. "Got it."

"I'll be waiting in the Humvee. Just come get me whenever you're done. No rush."

Morris waited for Grinder to get out of earshot before he picked up the receiver and dialed zero. After a brief exchange with an operator, the call connected across the ocean with an audible click. The line began to ring.

"Hello." The voice was Luke, Mike's stepdad. It felt like hearing someone from another lifetime.

Morris had no idea what to say. How did you even start this conversation? 'Oh, by the way, I'm not dead'?

"Hey, Luke," he said instead, "It's me. It's Ken. I'm okay."

"Ken?" Luke sounded stunned. "My God, it's good to hear from you! I thought...we heard...."

"Yeah," Morris said. In that instant he couldn't face the truth anymore. He couldn't bear to have his family know what actually happened to him and how bad things had been. Not yet anyway. "I think there was some kind of mistake. Some huge mixup. Listen, is Samantha around?"

"Yeah," Luke said, "yeah of course. Let me grab her."

After a few moments of muffled rustling Samantha picked up. "Ken?!"

"Hey," Morris said. He felt embarrassed about this whole thing but couldn't really say why. He supposed he didn't like the attention, he wasn't the kind who wanted people to worry about him. "Yeah. I'm okay. Look, there was a mistake and—."

"Ken, they told us you were missing! We thought—."

"No, no, no," Morris said quickly, trying to cut off any emotional reaction. The last thing he needed was to make his ex start crying on the phone. He didn't know what he would do if Samantha started to cry. Despite how things had turned out between them, they were still close. They'd been a high school power couple. A football player and a cheerleader, it had made sense for them to be together. Until it didn't. There were no hard feelings. He was lucky enough that they'd both been able to recognize their mutual incompatibility. "I'm fine," Morris said. "Really. Totally fine. Here, alive and well."

"You're a shitty liar, Ken," Samantha said.

Ken winced as she sniffled back tears, but he didn't correct her.

"Where's 'here'? Where are you?"

"Oslo," Morris said. "Norway."

"I know where Oslo is," she retorted, sniffling again. "They keep talking about it on the news. The war and the election. That's all it is. We've been really worried, Ken. Are you sure you're okay? What happened?"

Morris hesitated, he hated lying but, "Nothing. Just a mixup.

Stupid screwup with the paperwork or something."

"Ken, it's been two weeks, don't bullshit me."

He couldn't deny it, but he also couldn't come clean. Maybe it was childish to deny he was ever in any danger, but it was all he could bring himself to do.

"Look, I'm okay. I wanted you to know. I want you to know that I'm safe here." Another lie.

"Safe, right," Samantha didn't hide her skepticism.

"How's Mike? Does he know?"

"No," she blurted. "No. We…we didn't tell him anything yet. I didn't know how to."

Morris breathed a silent sigh of relief. "That's good. Listen, keep it that way. Information is going to be pretty spotty coming out of here. Things are kind of crazy on the ground."

"How bad is it?" Samantha asked, her voice lowered.

Again Morris hesitated. Even if he wanted to, he couldn't tell her everything. "It's safer for me than the army guys. That's all I can really say."

"Alright."

"I have to call my folks," Morris said. "I just wanted to make sure that you and Mike knew and everyone was okay."

"We're fine." she said. "Ken?"

"Yeah?

"You made a promise to come back."

"I didn't forget it," Morris said. It was all he could say. "Give Mike my love."

"I will."

There was nothing else for him to add. "Bye for now."

"Bye, Ken."

***

4

Captain Roy "Venom" Metcalf lay on his bunk and stared at the mail in his hands. He'd opened it the day before, but right now he left the letter tucked away safely in its envelope, as if it would shield him from the contents within. Reading the return address—Dearborn, Michigan—was as close to home as he'd been in years. Had it been years? As Metcalf counted back dates and holidays he wondered if maybe it was closer to a decade. One constant he'd discovered in life was the longer you lived, the faster it went and there was no slowing down. Months could pass in the blink of an eye, years lost in the headlong race into old age.

The letter felt heavy in his hands despite only containing a thin sheet of paper, as if the ink forming the words held the weight of their meaning. But still he didn't put it down. He couldn't put it down and even if he did, it would make no difference. The letter weighed on his mind even when it wasn't in his hand. There was no escaping and no avoiding it.

The shipwide PA system—the 1 Main Circuit or 1MC—heralded the chiming of bells, marking time onboard *Shiloh*, though Metcalf didn't react. The bells were followed with a muster announcement—more damage control drills. A regular occurrence in peacetime, combat deployment had made such drills a constant feature of life on the ship. War or not, life on the ship went on, even as Metcalf felt like his own life was coming apart.

Metcalf lost track of the minutes until the door to his stateroom opened and his bunkmate came in with his typical boyish swagger, a youthful cockiness that seemed incompatible with his age.

"Howdy, Rabbit." Metcalf didn't take his eyes from the letter.

"Shit," Lieutenant David "Rabbit" Barlow said, startled. "Didn't realize you were still here. Scared the hell out of me, Roy." The other pilot laughed nervously, tossing a handful of dirty workout clothes into a nearby duffel bag.

"No mean feat," Metcalf said, lip twisting in a half grin.

Rabbit shook his head and sat on the bed across from Metcalf, pulling off his shoes. "They pay me to fly planes," Rabbit said, "not for my rocksteady nerves, man."

Metcalf grinned wide enough to show teeth. "Right. Easier to be brave when you're packing Phoenix missiles."

Rabbit snorted. "Some of us have more brains than balls, I guess. No one's making you fly around unarmed."

"Keep it up," Metcalf teased. "Just remember that next time you're counting on some jamming."

Rabbit chuckled. "If you think I'm about to risk brig time by insulting a superior officer, then you're dumber than you look." Before he could twist the knife more, Rabbit's smile faltered, "You got mail? I thought that was all on hold."

Being on combat maneuvers had interrupted a lot of the facilities that Metcalf, Rabbit, and the others had taken for granted in peacetime. Even during his stint in Vietnam, Metcalf could rely on regular mail service. Vietnam felt like a lifetime ago, a different war, a different part of the world.

"It is," Metcalf said. "Old letter." Metcalf tucked the envelope into his breast pocket. "Old news."

"God, I hope it's good," Rabbit said. "Gomez just got the 'Dear John' treatment. Man, dude's bitching up a storm. He's talking off ears about it. I mean, don't get me wrong, dumping a guy in the middle of a war is ice cold, but I think he should have seen it coming. She was a real piece of work. Total ballbreaker. Probably should have cut her loose first."

Metcalf turned his head slightly to regard Rabbit. "Can't get your heart broken if you don't ever sit still. Isn't that right, *Rabbit*?"

Rabbit grinned sheepishly. "Not like it's hard for a Tomcat driver to get tail pretty much anywhere. I don't know how it is for you Prowler guys. I feel like you're the kind that prefers to sit back and watch."

"Never had trouble in my day," Metcalf said. "Had to beat them off with a stick."

"Yeah, I bet. Probably that Magnum P.I. soup filter on your face," Rabbit said. "Maybe I should grow my own 'stache," he rubbed his upper lip and studied himself in the mirror. "Like what Gomez has, huh?"

Metcalf smirked but said nothing. As much as he wanted to settle in and live in the moment, he kept getting pulled back out by the letter. He couldn't stop his expression from darkening, no matter how he tried.

Rabbit frowned. "What's up, Roy?"

"My daughter's getting married."

Rabbit was taken aback. The words were positive, but the tone wasn't. Metcalf hadn't expected to say it outloud. He hadn't told anyone yet. It was a secret he had intended on keeping that way. He didn't have any use for a bunch of sympathy, not right now. But now that he said it, there was no reason to stop.

"We don't–I haven't–" the right words wouldn't come. "It's been a long time since I've seen her. Things between us...aren't great."

Rabbit gaped silently.

"The letter is about her." Metcalf took it back out, holding it up for Rabbit to see, as if to prove its existence. "She's getting married to a guy I've never even met."

Silence.

Metcalf sighed to himself. "I hadn't seen her in a long time. Years. She didn't even tell me herself. This is from my wife. No way in hell I can get back home for it either, even if I was invited."

"Shit," Rabbit said, sitting back on his bed heavily. "I didn't... Roy, I'm real sorry to hear that, man."

"Me too," Metcalf said. "Just bad timing." The worst.

"Can I ask—?"

"Why we don't talk?"

Rabbit nodded.

"Stupid stuff," Metcalf said. "Little things. Disagreements. Politics. Life. She's so much different from how I was when I was her age. We don't see eye to eye. Don't agree on anything. And with the Navy it feels like I hardly see her."

"I know how that is."

"I told myself I was going to get out last year," Metcalf said. "But I feel like everyone says that every year."

"Just about," Rabbit agreed.

"You close with your parents, Rabbit?"

"I try to see them every year," Rabbit said.

"Not enough," Metcalf said, taking out the letter and looking at it again. "When this thing is over, go and see 'em. Don't let time get away from you. Time doesn't stop for nothing."

"I'll do that. And look, you never know." Rabbit said, trying to appear confident. "Things can change. I mean, it's not too late to reach out to her. Maybe she'll warm up to you."

Metcalf knew just how likely that was. "Maybe."

Rabbit crossed the narrow stateroom to lay an awkward hand on Metcalf's shoulder. "I was going to drag Gomez out for some chow. I figure it's better than letting him stew in rejection. You should tag along. Assuming you can stomach his moping."

Metcalf fired back a placid smile. "I'll let the young guns have their fun," he said. "Better I stay here, I think."

"Sure," Rabbit agreed. "Listen, if you need someone to talk to —."

"You're first in line."

Rabbit nodded and turned to go. He stopped in the doorway and looked back. "Free advice? I'd write a letter. Mail isn't running right now, but it could be soon. You never know."

"You never do."

Rabbit hesitated like he wanted to say more, but it remained unsaid. He left without another word.

After the door clicked closed, Metcalf took the letter back out and read it again.

***

5

"When this is over," Karlsdotter said, "I swear to never go hiking again."

Beside her, Bergman laughed.

The two of them followed along with the rest of their platoon, marching along the side of the road moving west, toward the defensive line waiting ahead. It was cold and overcast.This morning it had felt like hell frozen over when Karlsdotter had to get out of her warm sleeping roll, but now she was grateful for the cool weather. Better to march in the cold than in the heat, she figured.

"Never ever," Bergman agreed.

"You hiked before the war?" Karlsdotter asked.

"No," Bergman said, "and now I never will."

Karlsdotter allowed herself a small, tired smile.

"Forget never hiking, I just want to eat a cheeseburger," Fjellner said from ahead of her. As the platoon's sapper, he was laden with a series of circular landmines, but the weight didn't seem to trouble him. He was younger than her, only nineteen, and he'd taken to the business of soldiering faster than she thought possible. Fjellner did his job without complaint and always had a kernel of optimism to share with the others.

Karlsdotter's stomach rumbled sympathetically at the thought of greasy fast food.

"Chocolate milkshake," Bucht said. He adjusted the machine gun perched on his shoulder. The belts of ammunition looped around his neck swayed as he moved. "With whipped cream."

"I miss Nintendo the most," Sundquist, the platoon's radioman said mournfully. "I just got Street Fighter Two. God, it's probably still sitting in my apartment waiting for me if some Russian wolf hasn't swiped it."

Bergman and the others in the platoon laughed.

"When we get back home, I'll play you," Fjellner said. "One on one. So long as I get Ryu."

"I'll take you on that," Sundquist said.

As they marched, the platoon laughed and chatted, reminiscing about the idle creature comforts lost to them. It almost seemed funny now, how idyllic their lives had been. Going to school, going to work, eating what they wanted when they wanted, staying warm, staying dry, staying alive. It seemed like a fantasy now—like a dream.

As her thoughts turned to home, Karlsdotter found herself wondering about her boyfriend again. She'd told herself several times that she would just have to accept his fate as a mystery until later. "Later," of course, was a nebulous goal. In actuality, it ate her up with worry. In a perverse way, she felt like she'd rather know he was dead. If he was dead then she could stop worrying about him at least.

It was a selfish thing to think.

She wanted more than anything for him to be alive, but what if he was in pain? Maimed? Blind? Damaged beyond any hope of recovery? What if he languished in a Soviet prisoner camp, subject to whatever sadistic punishment his captors felt like meting out?

The platoon moved off the road as one, almost without thought, allowing a company of Leopard tanks to roar by on the wet asphalt.

Karlsdotter and the others stood and watched them as they passed. The crew of the tanks were unbuttoned, visible as they drove by. Probably Norwegians, Karlsdotter thought. The Swedes used the turretless S-tank, not the Leopard. It still felt strange to be working with the Norwegians this closely, but of course they were fighting on Norwegian territory now.

The road started to gradually incline, the way getting harder ahead. It meant they were nearing the line.

Within minutes they were at the muster point they'd left for their raid on the scattered Soviet forces. Here they traded in their POWs with a waiting platoon of Norwegian infantry to move them to the rear. Swedish and NATO vehicles lined the edge of the road, covered with camo netting to conceal them from the roving flights of Soviet attack craft that sometimes passed overhead.

Their platoon's APCs were here as well, left behind to allow for a stealthier approach on foot to hunt the enemy. The air was thick with exhaust and dozens of conversations.

"Karlsdotter," Hellström said, startling her. "Have everyone get some rest. We're going to be moving out again after the company briefing."

The responsibility that came with her field promotion wasn't exactly unwelcome, she appreciated that Hellström and their lieutenant trusted her. She also liked that she had more to do, keeping her thoughts occupied. Despite that, she couldn't get used to the idea of ordering anyone around. She simply couldn't accept that she was the best choice for the job. What right did she have to order the others around?

"Yes, Sergeant."

"Once they're settled, I want you at the briefing with me. It'll be good for you to have an idea of the big picture here."

She nodded. "Yes, Sergeant. I'll be there."

Getting the platoon settled didn't take much. At the first hint of a chance to take a break, soldiers dropped their packs and sat in the cover of the evergreens. Men and women lit cigarettes and sipped water from canteens as Karlsdotter hurried off to catch up with Hellström.

A passing platoon of recon vehicles forced her to wait at the edge of the road a moment before crossing and following a well-trodden path to a small clearing just off the main road. A circle of officers and NCOs stood surrounding a captain with graying, close-cropped hair as he detailed the deployment plans.

Karlsdotter found Hellström and came to stand beside him.

"Our hit and fade attacks have put the Russians on their back foot," the captain was saying. "We've left them guessing about our next move and forced them to spend valuable time and effort digging in instead of advancing. We've also managed to capture quite a few prisoners—."

"Wolves," someone in the group interjected, eliciting a wry grin from the captain.

"Vultures," he said. "Pirates. Bandits. Thieves. Whatever you want to call them. We'll be getting valuable intelligence from them on how to bury the rest of their kind in all the Swedish and Norwegian soil they could ever want."

A few soldiers laughed, others just looked grimly determined.

Karlsdotter found herself studying the captain's face. Based on his age, she expected that he was a reservist. He looked tired, his eyes baggy. As he spoke, she couldn't help but wonder what he'd done in life before being called back to service.

"I want to address some rumors," he said. "Rumors move faster than anything else in this war. Firstly, Russian paratroopers have *not* landed in Oslo, or Bergen, or anywhere else behind the line, although we'd like it if they tried."

More laughter.

"Secondly, there is *no* intention to evacuate the army from Scandinavia. We will fight to the last if we must, but we won't surrender. Not ever."

At this, no one laughed.

The captain's expression grew grimmer still. "Thirdly, supplies are short, it's true. Pre-war stockpiles are already nearing exhaustion."

This news was met with stony silence.

"That's the bad news," the captain said, "The good news is that fresh supply is on its way now from Canada, Britain, and America. The battle isn't over, and neither is the war."

The captain allowed a few beats of silence for everyone to absorb this news.

"A fresh defensive line has been prepared not far from here.

Strong ground for holding out. We will redeploy there and gather our strength, allow the Russians to bleed themselves on it."

Another retreat, Karlsdotter mused. Less humiliating than the bounding leaps they'd fallen back by, but a step back was still a step back. She frowned but said nothing. Weren't things supposed to change once the Americans arrived here? She'd seen neither hide nor hair of them, but had heard rumors of a mountain brigade deployed somewhere in the country. Where was the might of the American military? Stealth fighters and cruise missiles should be raining down on the Russian invaders. She supposed that it just meant they would have to liberate their homes on their own.

The rest of the meeting proceeded by the numbers, the captain detailing marching orders and deployments on the new defensive line. He tasked a couple platoons with acting as a rear guard to prevent the Soviets from tailing them too closely.

When the meeting broke up, Karlsdotter followed Hellström back toward their unit. Day to day it was hard to think about anything besides staying alive. But from time to time, especially now during downtime, her thoughts returned to Stockholm, to home.

"Do you think any of our families made it out?" she asked.

Hellström looked back at her. "Maybe. Hopefully. Maybe it's lucky that any of us made it out at all."

Karlsdotter said nothing, stewing in uncertainty.

The sergeant stopped and faced her. "Ingrid, you wish we'd stayed and fought. I know. It isn't an easy thing to live with, leaving our families. But we have more important things to worry about. If we cared so much about our families, then we should never have even signed up for this damn army. We're not here for them, understand? We're here for the whole nation, for everyone's families."

Karlsdotter was taken aback and wasn't sure how to reply.

"We have to worry about each other, about the platoon and

about this war. We won't be able to do a damn thing for our families if we lose."

"I know that," she said. "I do. I just—."

"I know," Hellström said, his tone soft. "I hate it too. Every day I wonder. But we can't afford it. We have enough to worry about right in front of us."

Karlsdotter nodded.

"Our team is counting on us. On you."

"Right."

Hellström slapped her shoulder affectionately. "Let's get them ready to move out. We have a date with the Russians."

***

6

Every sound Foreign Minister Andrei Gradenko made in the cavernous concrete halls of the D-6 complex echoed back tenfold. He'd spent more than enough time in this grim underground facility to get used to its quirks, yet he had stubbornly resisted any acclimation to this necropolis. He could never shake the impression that this place was nothing more than a gigantic morgue. Everything about it felt that way, from the bone-chilling cold to the cloying scent of industrial cleaners and disinfectant used to combat the spread of mold through the humidity-choked ventilation system, and of course the ever present echoing.

This section of Moscow's secretive, underground command facility was given over to the Stavka—the Soviet High Command. It was an administrative body not seen since the Second World War. Given the depredations of the Tsar and his aristocratic cronies in the Imperial Russian Army, the Communist party was traditionally distrustful of the military, doubly so of officers, triply of the upper echelons of command. The realities of military structure, obedience to authority, and the need to think critically ran contrary to much of the collectivist preachings of the Communist Party. Beyond that, the military was seen as a potential "fifth column" against the state and party. Marxist orthodoxy called for vigilance against "Bonapartism"—counter-revolutionary movements among the officer corps seeking to undermine the power of the proletariat in favor of an oligarchy.

The reasons the Soviet Union had traditionally neglected its officer corps—treating them as pariahs rather than a welcome or preferred class—were legion, but just as it had before, the realities of war made such lofty idealism counterproductive.

A pair of stiff, well-uniformed sentries saluted Gradenko as he passed through an armored hatchway.

Nothing about his appearance suggested the power he wielded. He wore a plain, ill-fitting suit and walked with his head bowed as if by a tremendous weight. His eyes were ringed with shadow and he felt like a shell of what he was before all of this began—before the intervention in Yugoslavia, before the war, before his son was taken.

A junior officer stood outside the door Gradenko approached. The soldier snapped to attention once the foreign minister came within sight. "Comrade Minister, the Stavka are expecting you."

Gradenko only nodded in reply and the sentry pulled open the door to admit him inside.

A long, unadorned table marked the center of the room, running perpendicular to the doorway Gradenko entered through. On the opposite wall, a granite carving of a hammer and sickle loomed above a phalanx of generals, admirals, and field marshals, each of them bedecked in stiff-collared dress uniforms, their chests heavy with medals, their faces lined with worry, appearing as brutal as the stone socialist icon behind them.

Gradenko overcame an absurd, almost compulsive desire to come to attention or salute these men. He assumed it was some kind of primal, residual impulse dating back to the dark days of serfdom. He held no more respect for the high command than was strictly necessary. Gradenko was many things, and in many ways he was far from the ideal communist, but he was a believer. At best the military was a necessary evil, but it *was* an evil all the same. In peacetime the military had been a bottomless well, draining the wealth from the Soviet people with no tangible benefit in return. Impressive May Day parades of missiles and tanks on television didn't put bread on the table. Now, even in the midst of a war, Gradenko could only reflect on the course that led them here. Wasn't it that same ravenous military system which gave men like Karamazov a false sense of invincibility that started this debacle? No, the military was a parasite, a leech. It was not to be respected, only disdained.

Gradenko kept all of this from his face as he returned the cool gazes of the officers here. He noted the absence of its most prominent member, General Tarasov, who was out touring the front and doing what little he could to instill order there.

"You requested my presence?" Gradenko said at last. He put particular emphasis on "requested." The military didn't pull his leash, he refused to allow the tail to wag the dog.

There was no preamble. A balding man with thick eyebrows spoke. He wore the dark uniform of the Navy—an admiral. His chest held enough medals and ribbons to stop a low-caliber bullet. "We have, Comrade. Our latest plans have been drawn up given our successes in Scandinavia. We hope that we may coordinate our efforts with the political front for maximum effectiveness against the West."

"You're speaking of the American presidential election." Gradenko was almost surprised that these fossils would give a care for anything beyond pushing flags around on a map.

The admiral nodded. "To be frank, given logistical realities, it is unlikely that we will achieve supreme victory purely by force of arms. Some aspects of diplomacy will be required."

That much was obvious to Gradenko and had been from the beginning. Even if they achieved all their most optimistic military goals, then they would secure the Rhine and possibly the remaining land between that river and the English channel. That decisive hammer blow failed to materialize, but it was a moot point anyway. Even if it *had*, then the next step for victory relied on NATO's willingness to admit to defeat and resolve the conflict diplomatically. Given the distances involved and the raw numbers, anything like total military victory was vanishingly unlikely. The English Channel and, beyond that, the Atlantic Ocean meant their main political adversaries might as well have been on the moon for all their ability to reach them. Rather than explain this, Gradenko said, "I share that assessment."

"What do you rate our chances of holding successful negotiations with Bayern, assuming military success?"

"Low," Gradenko said without hesitation. "Bayern is a military man. He was a naval officer. He isn't likely to surrender, even if pressured to do so by his allies."

It was clear from the lack of any reaction that the old men were expecting this answer. "What can you tell us of his opponent?"

It was a personality that Gradenko had spent some time studying lately. "Harry Nelson, born Hercules Nelson. He is the child of Haitian refugees. A member of America's watered down leftist party. His background is primarily with local politics. City management."

"Someone more likely to negotiate then?" It was impossible to miss the hint of hope in his voice.

"More likely than Bayern, yes. Bayern bears responsibility for this war. It was he who ordered the strike on our port facilities and his administration under President Simmons which contested our intervention in Yugoslavia. Call them warhawks. They can't back down on the point of war without admitting that it was a mistake in the first place."

The officers shared looks which Gradenko found impossible to read.

"And you've kept abreast of the election?"

"So far their polls have it as a close race, but Bayern holds a healthy lead in enough states that his re-election seems a safe bet."

"But it is not too late to undermine confidence in his leadership and this war."

"It won't be too late until the final ballot is cast," Gradenko said. "This is an uncertain time in America."

"If this Nelson wins the election, then we may hold the key to victory." It was more a statement than a question, so

Gradenko didn't reply directly. "You have something in mind?"

The admiral blinked and adjusted his glasses, reluctant to speak.

"I'll remind you that the politburo has top level clearance," Gradenko said, mustering all the authority he could. "Any schemes you cook up will ultimately require our acquiescence. With Comrade Tarasov no longer on the council, it would do well to have at least one friendly voice, no?" Gradenko was a diplomat by trade, but part of diplomacy was knowing when to throw weight around.

The admiral hesitated and then seemed to crumple, yielding to civilian power. "Plans have been drawn up for a two pronged attack. An opening of offensive operations in the Black Sea Region—Turkey and Greece—to draw Western attention south before we deal our true blow."

"Which is?"

The admiral hesitated and another of his comrades spoke up, this one wore the green of an Army general. "With NATO air power in Norway heavily reduced, the Norwegian Sea is open to our fleet. With a swift strike, we can threaten the United Kingdom and Iceland, perhaps with enough strength to shake Western confidence in victory. If we can secure a foothold in Iceland then we will have an unsinkable battleship to strike at Scotland and open a path to the North Atlantic for a renewed submarine campaign."

Gradenko took in this information and processed it with his limited understanding of strategy. He knew enough to know that the Soviet Navy was a shadow of what the West could muster, even with the heavy Andropov-era investments and the 1980s development and production campaign. Any victory there would have to rely on cunning and intellect rather than brute force. It was a longshot at best, but it was perhaps the only shot. "Has any thought been given to the inclusion of our Warsaw Pact allies in the plans for the south?"

"It has been considered, but Germany and Scandinavia are our top priorities. We can spare little for this operation. The

Bulgarian and Romanian militaries are yet uncommitted, but both are extremely underdeveloped, and the political situation there is tenuous."

Gradenko sensed an opportunity. "Leave the politics to me," he said. "I will ensure their cooperation." Those nations—especially the Romanians—were fair-weather allies even in the best of times, but commitment to serious combat would be a tough pill to swallow for both. However, if there was one thing both governments were more adverse to than war, it was economic depression. Threatening to withhold participation in the Soviet Union's ever-growing guest worker program, or the promise to greatly expand the numbers of workers brought from those nations for lucrative jobs in the Soviet Union, would serve as carrot and stick to those countries. Beyond that, it would also necessitate increasing the foreign ministry's relative power within the USSR as it managed the legions of fresh guest workers imported to replace the increasing numbers of Soviet men drafted and recalled to military service.

While a war raged for the survival of the Soviet Union outside its borders, a similar one was preparing to break out within the halls of government, a war for the heart and soul of the nation, one which could see Gradenko victorious or undone. There was surely no harm in bolstering his ministry's power beforehand.

"It may also be possible to secure cooperation from our Arab allies as well," Gradenko said. "The use of air bases, for example. I will arrange it."

Something akin to relief crossed the features of the men here. Their world view was pitiably limited, Gradenko mused. They truly were only concerned with moving flags across a map. They didn't yet realize that they were simply pawns in another game being played within the Kremlin.

"See to your preparations, comrades. Have your final requisitions of our allies sent to my ministry and I will do whatever I can in my power to assist."

"Thank you, Comrade Minister. You are a true asset to the people."

Gradenko smiled back blandly and hoped that was true.

***

7

Admiral Fyodor Zharkov walked the passages of *Tashkent* before stopping outside of the hatchway to the conference room. He took a steadying breath, running a hand through his thick, graying hair. He had been in the Soviet Navy all his adult life; it was more home to him than anywhere else. As his superiors had retired or been promoted, he'd clawed steadily upward. Equal parts officer and politician, the climb to the top had not been an easy one. The Soviet surface fleet was considered by many to be subordinate to the submarine forces which in turn were subordinate to the USSR's vast army.

This secondary status had made Zharkov's crusade all the more difficult, but it hadn't deterred him. Through wit, determination, and sheer bloody-mindedness, Zharkov had made his dream a reality.

Before Leonid Brezhnev's assassination, the Soviet surface navy had been defensive in character, possessing virtually no fixed-wing capability, intended only to defend the small White Sea bastion. That had all changed under his longer reigning successor Yuri Andropov. Andropov had been more interested in projecting Soviet power abroad, something that a submarine fleet couldn't do, but a surface navy could.

Zharkov had become a crucial element of this plan. He had made allies—vital connections within the navy and the ship design bureaus, willing participants in his naval expansion scheme. His dream of a carrier fleet had been made policy and brought to life. True, blue water naval aviation had come to be seen as a necessary stepping stone for protecting Soviet global interests and supporting worldwide communism. How else, beside a powerful navy, could the Soviet Union truly make itself felt on a global stage?

Within thirty years, the Soviet Union had forced its way into the world of top-tier surface fleets. It went from having no history of naval aviation to sailing a total of seven aircraft carriers of all sizes from the miniscule *Kiev* to modern supercarriers—the *Ulyanovsk*-class.

Despite these incredible strides forward, the Red Navy was still utterly shadowed by what the West could wield. America alone operated a dozen aircraft carriers, each more than a match for the capabilities of any of the Soviet's three best.

Zharkov set his jaw, mentally reminding himself of how far they'd come. It had taken decades of hard work, a lifetime, but they were nearly there. They were so very close to their place in the sun. He stood aboard living proof of that.

This vessel—*Tashkent*—was the pride of the Soviet Navy. He was an *Ulyanovsk*-class carrier on par with the latest American designs. Its development hadn't come without troubles. Earlier iterations like the *Riga* and *Kiev* had stumbled into problems that Western designs had conquered decades ago. Even the *Ulyanovsk*—the first of the class—suffered from a long list of embarrassing failures: problems with the steam catapult system, arrestor wire failures, electrical faults, onboard fires, not to mention more fundamental problems like faulty, unreliable engine designs. *Tashkent* benefitted from the missteps of its predecessors, virtually free of the problems that plagued *Ulyanovsk*.

Unwilling to delay any longer, Zharkov pushed open the hatch to the conference room and entered the cabin, his face betraying none of the nervousness that he felt.

The eyes of every man in the room went to him at once and, although the assembled fleet officers stood respectfully at attention, there was a hunger in their eyes.

Zharkov was going to play the role of politician as much as tactician today, and he was going to be doing so in shark-infested waters. The only difference between this meeting and the countless others of his career is that this one stood on the precipice of the Soviet Navy's crowning achievement, a victory over the West.

The cramped room was taken up almost entirely by a square table which itself was overrun with maps, charts, surveillance photographs, and dossiers. The rear wall was blocked off by a large white board filled with the details of the deployments of the force he led, the Red Banner Northern Fleet.

Seated around the table were the "sharks"—Zharkov's subordinate commanders in this expedition. Each one of them was a rival for his position. Though this fleet was a product of Zharkov's dream and hard work, it was no sure thing that someone else wouldn't attempt to claim it from him. Each one of them had ambition to spare and was almost as invested in Zharkov's own personal failure as they were in collective success.

"Comrades, thank you for joining me." Zharkov circled the table, keeping his pace swift, his eyes ahead. "I have at last received our orders from the Stavka via coded transmission. The order is simple. 'Attack.'" Zharkov stopped before the whiteboard and turned to face the others. Framed by a broad map of the Norwegian Sea, he allowed them a moment to digest this information.

The men gathered here were all flag officers of the combined Red Banner Northern Fleet, chiefly among them were the two rear admirals who each commanded one of the fleet's divisions centered around an aircraft carrier as its flagship. In total, the Soviets mustered seven carriers, and two of those were *Kiev*-class—not really a true aircraft carrier in the Western sense of the word as they were suitable only for launching light VTOL aircraft and helicopters. By some measures they were glorified missile cruisers which also happened to carry a large complement of helicopters. A further two were *Riga*-class—superior to the *Kiev*, but still limited by lack of a steam catapult, instead requiring the use of a ski-jump to launch aircraft. Only three were roughly the equivalent to

45

America's latest class, the *Antietam*-class. Each of these three was the core of its own combat group, attended to by one or two "lesser" carriers and an assortment of other surface combatants, most notable among them were the titanic *Kirov*-class ships, what the West enviously referred to as "battlecruisers." They were the largest surface ships built since the great battleships of the Second World War. Zharkov knew that if he turned his head to look out one of the portholes that dotted the wall behind him he would be able to see his own group's battlecruiser, *Kalinin*.

"An attack order, Comrade?" The question came from the rear admiral of *Ulyanovsk*'s division. *Ulyanovsk* was the oldest of the new supercarriers, and by far the least mechanically reliable and the ship's commander was little better. He was an outlier among high ranking Soviet officers in that he was an ethnic Estonian.

"That is correct, Comrade Olesk," Zharkov said.

"Forgive me, Comrade," Olesk said, rubbing his nose absently, "but has the tactical situation changed significantly? Last report was of heavy losses among our submarine forces and overwhelming numerical superiority among NATO's surface combatants. We can muster only three modern carriers; the West has at least three times that many at hand." Olsek's tone was conversational despite the grim nature of his report, he might as well have been discussing rising prices in a fish market for all the concern he showed.

"Warfare is more than math, Comrade," Rear Admiral Yevdokimov, the commander of the *Novosibirsk* combat group, replied sharply. Zharkov would have preferred someone a bit more creative in charge of *Novosibirsk*, but Yevdokimov would have to do. Whatever Zharkov's criticisms about Olesk's attitudes and political reliability, he was a capable commander or he would not have reached this lofty position. Yevdokimov had none of these advantages and had achieved this position largely through a combination of connections within the Party and through an uncanny ability to be agreeable to his superiors. He'd certainly gone out of his way to avoid upsetting Zharkov.

Olesk shrugged, not deigning to meet Yevdokimov's passionate stare.

"The tactical situation *has* changed," Zharkov replied coolly. He gave a cursory glance to the remaining officers present before continuing. "Our comrades in the ground forces have successfully secured much of Norway's northern coastline as well as its air facilities and the final push to crush the remaining pockets of resistance has begun. Once the last air bases are secured we will secure total air supremacy in the region. The enemy's use of improvised road bases is prolonging things, but they are temporary at best, unable to maintain high tempo operations. Because of this, we have greatly reduced NATO's air coverage." Zharkov continued, "We've finished gathering and re-arming our remaining submarine forces after their successful sortie in the North Atlantic, and we've finished embarking a regiment of naval infantry from Murmansk aboard our amphibious landing group." Zharkov laid his palms on the table and leaned forward imperiously. "These elements will make up the building blocks of our battle plan. We have laid the groundwork for this operation already. As Comrade Yevdokimov has indicated, this will not be a battle of raw numbers or attrition. I aim to defeat the West through a combination of misdirection, speed, and local superiority. *Maskirovka* holds the key to our victory."

It was the same principle that the Soviet Army had relied on for victory—successfully in Yugoslavia and with mixed results in Germany. *Maskirovka* was the military principle of deception pulled straight from Sun Tzu's writings. No amount of sheer force could match the destructive power of deception, misdirection, and subterfuge.

"I'm eager to hear how you intend to gain surprise over our Western adversaries," Olesk said, his tone betraying none of the challenge that Zharkov imagined he detected behind those words.

Zharkov didn't let his mask slip and only projected calm. He mentally counted to three before speaking. "Comrades, I fear that you have forgotten a crucial truth about our existence. The capabilities of the West are well known. The American Navy—and by extension, all the navies of the West—are tools without rival. They are escorts, submarine hunters, aircraft detection and missile platforms. They serve humanitarian missions around the globe, maintaining 'freedom of navigation' and aid deliveries." Zharkov let the words sink in. "Yes, the American Navy is a tool to which we cannot compare. This, comrades, is because our navy is *not* a tool. It is a weapon. We were designed, constructed, and trained for one purpose, and one purpose only: to sink the West."

Zharkov clasped his hands behind his back and continued. "We exist to strike the West, destroy their carriers, and sever the artery that runs from America to Europe. Never forget that we are the blade to their neck, the gun to their head. We may only have one shot, but one shot is all we will need."

Olesk looked unimpressed with Zharkov's speech, but the admiral refused to acknowledge that. "Comrades, tonight we will sail south, following the Norwegian coast, staying within the protective umbrella of friendly SAM coverage and land-based aircraft. Our comrades in the army and air force, as well as those in the submarine branch will begin the final step in our preparations: the destruction of the remaining NATO air combat capabilities in Norway. Attack orders have been prepared to be distributed to your air wings and missile batteries." Zharkov indicated the folders waiting before the commanders. "Once they believe they know our goal, the West will re-double their defense of the corridor between Norway and the UK." He allowed himself a smile. "A vital artery that they cannot afford to let us sever."

"The enemy aren't stupid, Comrade Admiral," Olesk said. "They will welcome a chance to face us. They will wait until we stick our necks just far enough out so they can chop off our heads. If it comes down to a head-to-head battle, we will lose."

Another man might have exploded at Olesk's insubordination. Telling a superior his plan was fatally flawed was an easy way to gain a one-way ticket to Siberia or worse. Instead Zharkov let the remarks wash over him like a gentle breeze. It wouldn't matter once everything was said and done. Rather than shout, or shoot back, Zharkov nodded. "Yes, Admiral. Your thinking is tactically correct. In a direct engagement the West holds all the advantages: numbers, technology, experience even. They would win and the West will know this too." He allowed himself a half-smile. "What is the phrase? 'Tilting at windmills'? Yes. Let them think this is a joust. The West loves a joust. A showdown. They can't refuse it. We act as if we are playing into their hands. They will doubtlessly expect us to press our attack with aircraft and submarines."

"But we won't," Yevdokimov guessed, straining the limits of his tactical imagination.

"While NATO concentrates for a battle," Zharkov said, "they will see from us what they want and Iceland will be that much more vulnerable."

"Our plan?" Olesk asked.

"We follow the coastline south as if we aim to move our carriers into a better position to attack. We make full steam and allow the West's spy satellites to make a pass over us and confirm our heading."

"And then?" Olesk asked.

"Then we break west for Iceland while they maneuver to the south, leaving them out of position long enough for us to slip by their concentrated defenses." Zharkov paused here, looking over the gathered officers, savoring the surprise and awe on their features. It gave him a measure of joy to know that no one else could have anticipated the boldness of his scheme. If his own subordinates were surprised, he could only imagine how the enemy would react. "This will be the first blow we land," he said, "but far from the last. Return to your ships and ready your pilots." Zharkov smiled. "Victory awaits."

***

"'Victory awaits,'" Rear admiral Olesk muttered under his breath as he descended a narrow, metal ladderway. "What suicidal nonsense."

"Comrade Admiral?" his aide spared a glance over their shoulder from ahead of him before ducking through a tight hatchway.

"Nothing," Olesk replied. Rank had its privileges, but he had to remind himself that he also wasn't irreplaceable. He'd heard the rumors about purges of the officer corps in the army— men who had failed to live up to expectations or who had simply made enemies of the wrong people. Complacency and cronyism had been a benign cancer in peacetime, but now with the war it threatened to turn malignant unless it was excised. Olesk had not reached this position by being careless, and he wasn't about to start now. As an Estonian, he'd had a steeper slope than most to climb, and—agree with his commanding officer or not—he wasn't going to throw that away on a careless remark.

Olesk and his aide reached a landing and stood aside to let a small team of flight crew move past, talking loudly and excitedly, eager for the future. More fools. The more time wore on the more Olesk felt like he was the only one in the Soviet Navy without a death wish, the only one with any real perspective. Could they really not see the danger of this plan? The folly? Or were they so blinded by desperation and a lust for glory that they would ignore the obvious risks? Everything about their force was inadequate for the task at hand—inferior numbers, inferior weapons, inferior training. What chance did they have?

His aide opened a final hatch for him and Olesk emerged into the cold, open air of the carrier's flight deck. While the basic layout was shamelessly ripped from American designs, it was still a marvel of engineering. It was one thing to simply

copy the form of a thing, it was something else to make it
actually work. From the carefully developed nighttime landing
system to the steam catapult and the detection and air defense
suites he carried, *Tashkent* was a marvel. Olesk couldn't help
but wryly think that it had taken the Soviet Union decades to
reach this level of naval sophistication. He wondered how long
it would take to throw it all away.

A stub-tailed helicopter idled nearby, waiting to return him
to *Ulyanovsk*. Not far off sat a sleek, jet fighter—the naval
variant of the Su-27—its wing pylons laden with missiles,
more technological wonders ready to be carelessly thrown
away against the West.

Ducking under the wash from the overhead rotors, Olesk
climbed awkwardly into the helicopter which throttled up and
took off, banking north toward the horizon and his task force.

Tashkent and his escorts grew tiny beneath him, looking for
all the world like a game piece on a vast blue board. He hoped
Zharkov's self-confidence wasn't misplaced. The admiral was
right, the Soviet Navy was a weapon with only a single use. It
still remained to be seen if it was up to the task.

***

51

8

The single, narrow porthole that graced Seymour's cabin showed the golden light of dawn outside. Seymour wasn't required to man the bridge quite yet, so he spent his morning catching up on some of the duller aspects of his job—administration—as he ate breakfast.

Seymour ran his eyes down the report and noted key figures: tonnage of fuel remaining, approximate range of operation, time till next rendezvous with a supply ship, number of remaining Sea Dart missiles. He sipped his orange juice and tried to internalize all these minute details and commit them to memory. What seemed trivial at a glance may turn out to be crucial when making an important decision.

His breakfast still lay mostly untouched. He'd forced himself to eat the dry, rubbery scrambled eggs first. They tasted better than they looked, but Seymour suspected that was more of a product of his hunger than the skills of his ship's cooks or the quality of the food. Even so, it was more exercise than indulgence. Each bite was a calculation of calories, the acknowledgement that just like *Somerset* needed fuel for her engines, he needed food to function. The muffin and sausage patties lay uneaten on the side of his plate, now room temperature. Despite his hunger, Seymour simply had no appetite. While he was grateful to at last be underway, he couldn't shake the nervous tension that lurked in every moment.

It was more than just the fact that there was a war on. He'd mostly grown accustomed to the dangers involved. While it was true that there could be a Soviet torpedo or missile with his ship's name on it closing even now from out of sight, there was little he could do that he hadn't already done. All precautions were taken, his men were as trained as they could be. There was nothing left but random chance, and Seymour was damn sure not going to let something as fickle as luck keep him awake.

He also found himself worrying about his family. His son was as much in harm's way as he was, maybe more so, but he was a sailor and knew what he was signing up for. Seymour wouldn't allow himself to dwell on it. His parents and his wife were back in York, safe he hoped. Fighting hadn't yet reached the UK, but it wasn't as if the Soviets couldn't reach it, especially now that they controlled Denmark.

Seymour set his stack of paperwork down and rubbed his eyes in an effort to chase away his lingering tiredness and finished dressing.

"Action stations! Action stations! This is not a drill. All hands to action stations."

The blaring announcement made Seymour nearly jump out of his skin, fatigue forgotten in an instant.

He stood quickly and hurried for the bridge, dodging sailors likewise rushing through the crowded passageways to their combat positions, readying the ship for battle as weapons systems came online. During drills, it took only minutes to prepare for battle. Seymour saw no reason it would be different this time.

Seymour reached the bridge only moments later.

"Captain on the bridge!"

Seymour and the others were too busy to pay much heed to formality.

"Status?" Seymour demanded.

A junior officer stopped beside Seymour to deliver his findings. "Sir, *Gloucester* reported a sonar contact north of our position but they're unable to get a fix. Might have been a false positive return, sir."

"We're not going to take a chance that it's a false positive,"

Seymour said.

Smith arrived on the bridge a moment later, hurriedly buttoning his jacket.

"Possible sonar contact from *Gloucester*," Seymour explained.

"Submarine making a pass at the convoy?" Smith asked.

"Cheeky if they are," Seymour replied. "This close to the coast? We're well within aircraft coverage."

"Cheeky or desperate to sink tonnage," Smith suggested.

Seymour half-shrugged. "We'll be relying more on the helicopters and *Gloucester* to defend against that sort of thing," Seymour said, handing the note back. A jack of all trades but master of none, *Somerset* wasn't defenseless, but she wasn't made for hunting subs the way *Gloucester* was. Armed with an array of Sea-Dart anti-air missiles as well as a 4.5 inch naval gun, *Somerset* excelled primarily in air defense.

Both *Somerset* and *Gloucester* were a part of the broad ring of defense ships encircling the convoys strung out in the middle of the formation. It fell to them to keep the merchants safe. With no onboard detection or combat capabilities, the transports were wholly reliant on their escorts to handle incoming threats.

The Soviets had been trickling submarines back through the GIUK gap recently. They were "spent" boats returning to Polyarny for fresh torpedoes and missiles mostly. NATO had collectively sunk dozens of them so far already. If the Russians kept this up, their submarines would be in danger of extinction.

It wasn't impossible that one enterprising—or desperate—captain had deviated south with intent to sow chaos.

"Check in with *Nauls* and see that we're not being led by the nose. A decoy would be a hell of a thing to chase right now."

"Aye, sir." The XO left Seymour to relay the message and Seymour remained to observe the graceful dance of order on his bridge as attention was given to anti-submarine warfare and sonar sweeps increased. Seymour looked out the forward-

BLACK SEAS

facing window banks at the choppy azure surface of the sea beneath the twilight sky. What deadly secrets did those waves hide?

They weren't kept waiting long before they received another return.

"Captain, possible sonar contact, bearing 320."

Seymour's skin crawled. "Range?"

"Can't tell, sir. The return is faint."

The XO returned to Seymour's side a moment later. The two of them shared a glance, their faces steeled against fear. A surface ship engaging a submarine was both the hunter and hunted. Seymour looked to Smith. "Get to operations and standby there." He didn't have to say "just in case." It went without saying that having both commanding officers in one place during combat posed a risk of losing all command from a lucky hit.

"Aye, sir."

As Smith left, Seymour issued another order. "Get the Lynx airborne."

As her primary offensive weapon against submarines, *Somerset* carried one Westland Lynx, a multi-purpose naval warfare helicopter. Armed with a quartet of anti-ship missiles, a pair of torpedos, and a powerful dipping sonar, the Lynx was a capable oceanic hunter.

"Blackjack is in the air."

The Lynx thundered over *Somerset*'s bow, flying north, toward the anomalous sonar contact.

"Full stop," Seymour said. The ship's screws slowed and stopped, going as silent as possible to give the passive sonar the best chance of detecting any underwater activity. It also made *Somerset* a less obvious target if they were being hunted. So much of it was a waiting game. Impatience could be fatal. If there was an enemy submarine out there, they would be listening, probing for a gap in the NATO fleet's defenses, just as Seymour and his men were listening for them.

Seymour kept up his slow pacing of the bridge as the

minutes ticked by. He had to maintain an illusion of control. After all, hadn't he been pining for action just a short while ago?

"Captain, *Gloucester* reports sonar contact. Bearing matches our earlier detection."

That sealed it. Two independent contacts were more than operator or equipment error. There was something out there in the water with them. "Any news from Blackjack?" Seymour asked.

The officer who addressed him shook his head. "Nothing yet, sir."

Seymour stepped over to the nearest window and lifted a pair of binoculars to his face, scanning the horizon until he spotted Blackjack conducting its search pattern. The helicopter zipped to a location and then descended until its sonar array dipped into the water. There the helicopter hovered for a moment, its rotors sending concentric ripples across the surface of the ocean, until it suddenly rose into the air to repeat this process nearby, forming a circle around the ship, listening for activity beneath the waves. If they could get a return from Blackjack, then they had a much better chance of honing in on the enemy's exact position. The helicopter's speed and maneuverability made it far better suited for detection than either *Gloucester* or *Somerset*.

"Possible contact at 300," a bridge officer said, relaying information from the detection officers.

"From us or Blackjack?"

"Us, sir. Approximately twenty kilometers out."

Torpedo range. It was a long shot, but not impossible. Seymour hid a grimace. "Relay that to Blackjack and *Gloucester*."

"Sir."

"Isn't *Gloucester* supposed to be the bloody ASW ship?" Seymour grumbled, low enough that no one else could hear. It occurred to him that maybe the Soviet submarine knew that as well and that's exactly why it was coming straight for them.

Another officer spoke, interrupting Seymour's thoughts. "*Gloucester* is pinging."

Either *Gloucester* had high confidence on the target or they were trying to flush it out. Seymour looked at the map plot. *Gloucester* was accelerating toward *Somerset* and pinging.

"Do we have a fix on that contact?" Seymour asked, suddenly concerned that his ship was now standing in the way of a frightened and desperate submarine as it was being driven by *Gloucester*.

"No, sir."

Seymour wanted to swear. "Helm, take us up to flank speed. Begin active pinging and come about to 290."

The ship accelerated and banked, swinging toward the strange sonar detection. It would give their bow-mounted sonar a better picture of the area and would likewise make *Somerset* present a smaller profile to target. Moving at speed like this would leave them deaf for undersea sounds, but the active sonar would ideally detect any lurking threats first.

There was also the matter of wakes. All NATO naval officers knew the Soviet Type 53 torpedo didn't use conventional automatic guidance. Most torpedoes homed in on sonar returns and noise. The Type 53 was special in that it detected the turbulent water left in a ship's wake, and followed that right to the source: the ship itself. As such, Type 53s were immune to all countermeasures. The surest defense was simply not to let them shoot first.

"Contact! Sonar contact at 310. Captain, we have high confidence on target. Seems to be a *Victor*-class. We make cavitation sounds."

A submarine running at high speed, straight at them.

"Where the hell is Blackjack?" Seymour demanded.

The officer didn't answer him, speaking quickly into his headset. "Blackjack, we need bloodhounds in the water immediately."

The helicopter was out of position, and a *Victor*-class submarine would be on top of them in only a minute at flank speed.

"Helm to starboard," Seymour said. "Port side torpedo battery, fire one."

The ship banked, presenting her torpedo tubes toward the oncoming enemy. A moment later, an anti-submarine torpedo lept from the tube and splashed into the water.

Seymour chewed his lip and watched the map plot as their position was updated, closing in on the enemy submarine. Each sprinted toward the other like jousters.

"Torpedo is pinging."

"Helm, hard to port. Full stop."

"Aye, sir."

Somerset swung left with enough momentum to send unsecured pens and pencils skittering off console tops and onto the floor. A second later the propellers shut down, leaving the ship to coast along silently. They could only hope and pray that the enemy hadn't fired a torpedo of their own.

"Torpedo closing on target." The seaman fell silent as he listened to his headset. "Impact."

"A hit?" Seymour asked.

The sailor hesitated, then nodded, a boyish grin breaking out across his face, the sudden release of tension. "Yes, sir. We make transients. She's hit, sir."

Seymour stared blankly at the map for a moment before nodding. "Have Blackjack confirm."

"Aye, sir."

Seymour wasn't going to be satisfied so easily. He counted the seconds as Blackjack flew to the spot they'd last detected the Soviet submarine and dipped its array below the waves.

"Blackjack confirms, sir. They make clear transients. One stricken submarine."

There was no cheer, no celebration on the bridge, just a sort of muted satisfaction. Whatever joy the men took in their work, it was tempered with the knowledge that they'd just killed dozens of other sailors.

Seymour nodded grimly. "Mark it down in our logs," he said.

"One Victor."

"Aye, sir."

The kill was logged, ordinary activity resumed. Smith returned to the bridge moments later as if nothing had happened.

"*Gloucester* sends their compliments, sir," the communications officer said, glancing back from his station.

"They bloody well ought to," Smith said under his breath. "We did their job for them, didn't we?"

"A victory I'll take," Seymour said, knowing it easily could have gone the other way. With the immediate threat of the Victor dealt with, broader problems returned to Seymour's mind. The war was far from over. The Soviets had dozens of *Victor*-class submarines alone; losing one hardly made a difference. Beyond that, the Soviet surface fleet remained intact. All the same, they weren't going anywhere.

Seymour took solace in this as his ship stood down from action stations and resumed its sweep.

***

9

Commander Nathan Grier lifted his glasses to rub his eyes, dry from spending so much time staring at computer screens. Currently they were fixed on a monochrome green display flashing with blips and lines like some kind of anemic video game. As dull as it all was, it was important all the same. As the commander of the USS *Raleigh*—a *Los Angeles*-class fast attack submarine—Grier had to be on alert at all times. It was up to boats like his to sniff out the enemy before they stumbled into the rest of the fleet.

"Keep an eye on it," Grier said at last to his XO, flashing a warm smile. "Probably nothing but—."

"—but no sense slacking off," the XO finished the commander's well-used adage.

Grier grinned a bit wider. "Right."

"Will do, sir."

Grier straightened up from leaning over the sonar plot and made his way back through the cramped bridge of the submarine. For all of its cutting edge technology, it was just as crowded and industrial as submarines were in his father's time in the service. Pipes, tubes, cabling, wires, and gauges studded every available surface. The only indication of *Raleigh*'s high tech guts were the handful of television monitors mounted at sailor's stations which displayed data about every detail of the sub.

Grier longed for a coffee, ached for it really. It was a bad habit he'd not ever been able to fully kick. A low-grade caffeine headache was knocking at the back of his brain already. Given another hour or so and it would be rattling through his entire head. He told himself weekly that he was going to quit—that it wasn't worth this kind of suffering–but then he ran headlong into a caffeine-free morning which knocked him right back off the wagon.

He rubbed his eyes again and re-seated his glasses. In his bleary exhaustion, he almost ran directly into another sailor making his way forward. "Whoops! Excuse me, Versetti."

"Sorry, sir," the young seaman replied, looking exhausted.

"Good sleep?"

Versetti grinned sheepishly. "Not really, to be honest, sir."

Grier waved it off. "Ah, don't sweat it. You'll be sleeping like a baby in no time. This is a hell of a first cruise, but ask any of the old hands: get tired enough and you can sleep in the seventh circle of hell."

Versetti smiled a little more naturally, "Yes, sir."

The crew of any ship—but especially a submarine—was a family. In a space this small there just wasn't room for big egos. Grier didn't see the need in trying to distance himself or build some sham of mystique around himself. His men would trust him better if they liked him, and trust was a currency without comparison on a vessel like this.

Grier's thoughts were interrupted by a raised voice. "Commander?" His XO beckoned him back over with a nod of his head.

"What's up, Briggs?" Grier asked, standing by his XO at the sonar station. "Got something?"

"We picked up transients. High confidence," the sonar operator said. "Ten kilometers north."

"Transients?" Grier asked, peaking an eyebrow. They'd been chasing a ghost out here for a while now. Maybe this breadcrumb was the clue they needed.

"Yes, sir. Metal for sure. Maybe a hatch opening."

The sonar capabilities of the *Los Angeles*-class were nothing short of astounding, virtually unrivaled in the seas, certainly leagues ahead of their Soviet counterparts. While the Soviets were well ahead in the numbers game, the West made up for it with superior listening capabilities. In this battlefield, being detected was the first step before being dead.

Grier looked at Lieutenant Commander Briggs, his eyebrow still raised quizzically. The XO gave a slight shrug, acquiescence. "I think that's worth investigating." He looked at the sonar operator. "Don't you?"

"Hell yes, sir."

"Right. Helm, new course." Grier moved from the sonar station to the map plot and studied the chart there with a well-practiced eye, taking in factors like relative depth and natural rock formations. "Take us heading zero. Ahead one third."

"Aye, sir, one third."

The XO came to stand by Grier. "Not supposed to be any Russians this close to the coast." He kept his voice low, his words only meant for Grier's ears. *Raleigh* was posted almost exactly between the Shetland islands and the Norwegian coast, theoretically these were safe waters, heavily patrolled by NATO air and naval forces.

The commander nodded. "Exactly why one of them might try to slip in here. You don't expect to find a fox in the hen house."

Briggs opened his mouth to reply but was interrupted by a commotion from the sonar station. "Commander, new contacts! Missile launches, sir."

Grier's heart skipped a beat. There weren't many reasons for a submarine to launch missiles, but the first one to spring to Grier's mind was nuclear payload delivery. He pushed that aside. Any Boomer launching nuclear missiles would do so from much further out. Instead, Grier forced himself to remain calm as he answered. "Missiles? Any idea what they're targeting?"

"Not sure, sir. But I count six distinct launches."

Grier felt the focus of the bridge crew's attention honed in on him, sharp as a razor's edge. This was the decision moment. He didn't hesitate. "Helm, give me three-quarters speed and take us down another hundred feet."

"Aye, sir."

"And get our tubes flooded."

"More contacts, sir," Sonar said. "I've got screws going to flank."

"Any ID?" Grier asked.

"Sounds like an *Oscar*-class, sir."

The Oscar, one of the largest submarines in the sea, a cruise-missile platform, had range enough to strike from afar. It was just dumb luck that *Raleigh* was nearby when the Oscar had fired.

"Oscar," Grier said. "Big girl."

"What could she be shooting at?" Briggs asked. "Those are carrier-killers and there's nothing like that out here."

"Probably ground targets," Grier replied. "My guess would be the runways in Norway. Maybe the airport at Bergen." In the wake of American success with cruise missiles during Operation Crescent Storm, there had been rumors of the Soviets adding ground-attack capabilities to their anti-ship Granit missiles. It seemed to Grier like those rumors were true after all.

"There are no bases there." Briggs looked disgusted. "That's a civilian airport."

Grier tightened his jaw grimly. "They were. Given how the Russians have been pounding the Norwegians I don't doubt that they're using any runway they can. Civilian or not, they're a legitimate target."

Briggs didn't look happy about this, but accepted his commander's logic.

"Do we still have a bearing on that Oscar?" Grier asked. A glance at the plotting table answered his question. An ensign with a grease pencil marked the Soviet submarine's position periodically on the chart.

"Aye, sir. She's maintaining speed and heading."

"Running," Grier mused. "Must be scared out of her mind."

"Fox in the hen house," Briggs reminded him.

"No change in heading means she probably doesn't know

we're here and she's going too fast to pick us up."

"At that speed it'll take time for our torpedoes to catch her," Briggs said.

Grier nodded, eyes not leaving the map plot, running math in his head. "No choice. I'm not going to let her get away. Weapons, fire tubes one and two. We'll guide the fish in by wire, no sonar."

"Aye, sir!"

Leaving the torpedoes in passive sonar mode would hopefully delay detection long enough for them to enter lethal range. An Oscar couldn't outrun them, but moving at flank away from them would greatly increase travel time. It would take several minutes for the torpedoes to cross that distance.

Both tubes were fired a few seconds apart, with fresh torpedoes quickly being reloaded. The torpedoes' progress was added to the chart with the stroke of a grease pencil.

Grier kept a close eye on a stopwatch hanging at his station as the numbers raced toward the time when the two points would meet.

"Sir, change in behavior. The Oscar deployed a noisemaker."

The decoy wouldn't make a difference to wire-guided torpedoes. It was a desperation move, but it also signaled to Grier that the Soviets had heard his torpedoes. He ground his teeth together with nothing else to do but wait.

"Hull pops," sonar said. "Oscar is diving sir, going low."

"What's her depth?" Grier asked.

"Five hundred meters and descending."

"Take us to flank," Grier said, clenching his jaw tighter.

The previously silent hum of the engine became a powerful thrumming as the screws cavitated and formed air bubbles. Right now Grier was more concerned with closing distance than being detected. It would do nothing to help the already launched torpedoes reach their target, but it would get them closer for any followup action.

Grier looked back to the map chart and ran the numbers in his head again. Three minutes to weapon impact.

"Oscar is at six hundred, sir."

The Mark 48 torpedoes in hot pursuit had a crush depth of about eight hundred meters.

Briggs read his commander's mind, "What's the crush depth on an Oscar?"

"Deep," Grier replied bitterly.

"Six hundred fifty meters. Seven hundred."

"Two minutes to impact."

Grier watched the second hand of the stopwatch sweep across the minute mark like an executioner's blade.

"Oscar depth is eight hundred meters and continuing to descend." The sonar operator's expression flashed with worry. "She's cut speed, sir. Silent running."

"Helm, drop us to one quarter speed," Grier said. He wasn't foolish enough to run headlong into a trap if that's what the Soviets were laying.

"We've lost contact with torpedo one," weapons said, scowling.

"Set two to active sonar," Grier said.

"Aye sir."

It was no use. Grier watched the sonar blips put off by the hunting torpedo vanish a moment later as it dove too far. The irresistible oceanic pressure fractured the weapon's metal skin like an egg, crushing the delicate electronics within.

"Lost contact with torpedo two."

Grier wanted to swear. If the Oscar could dive out of weapons range, then he couldn't touch her. Even if he was willing to take his own boat down that far it wouldn't do any good if they couldn't fire torpedoes. "New heading," he said, "Two nine zero, one-half speed." If he could no longer hear the Oscar, then he wanted to ensure that they couldn't hear him either. He had no doubts that unless they were also adjusting their heading to prevent easy tracking.

There would be no retribution for whatever unlucky people had fallen under the Oscar's deadly missile attack.

***

10

Pencil scratched on paper in the relative quiet of the barracks. Morris sat at the long folding table that served as a makeshift mess for the pilots. Already his fingers were starting to cramp up. He hadn't written a letter since middle school, and he was paying the price. His awkward, block letters filled half the page. Morris dropped the pencil and flexed his hand, trying to work the cramps out as he re-read his progress.

Mike,

I'm sorry in advance if you can't read my handwriting. If you have trouble with it, I'm sure your mom can make sense of it. I'm not much of a writer, but I thought that you might like something like this for when you're older, or if I'm not around to tell you about it. You're just a kid right now, and I'm sure everything that's happening is confusing, and maybe a little scary. I never imagined that anything like this could ever happen in your lifetime. I was younger than you are now when the Vietnam War was going on. I don't remember it much, but I know that it was pretty scary for a lot of people. You're growing up in uncertain times. It's comforting to think that everything is under control and everything will always be the same forever. It's scary when you realize that there are things in the world that you just can't control.

I joined the Air Force right out of college because I wanted to give you and your mom a comfortable life. I wanted to serve my country and I wanted to do something good. I thought the military was the way to do that. I thought that somehow, everything would just work out. Of course, life got in the way. Things didn't turn out the way I had planned, but I want you to know that you're very lucky to have a mom and stepdad who love you very much. And

I love you very much too. You mean the world to me. Right now I don't know how things are going to turn out and I don't know when I'll see you again. Someday, when you're ready, I hope you and I will read this letter together and have a laugh. If I'm not there, I want you to know that I'm proud of you, and I always will be.

Morris wrinkled his nose, trying to find a way to put into words how he felt about everything, how to tell his son he was scared himself, that he wanted to go home. He wanted to write that he was tired of being a pilot, that he didn't want to fight anymore. He wanted to write about seeing Lancelot's fighter explode, or how it felt to watch cannon fire shred Daisy's cockpit. Morris had been at Daisy's wedding. He knew his wife, he had shaken hands with his dad. He wanted to write about meeting Astrid and the others, about knowing each day could be his last.

How could you put any of that into words?

Morris put pencil to paper again.

It's 1992. You just turned ten years old. I'm in Oslo, and the war hasn't ended yet.

I love you.

Daddy.

It would have to do.

Morris creased the paper carefully into thirds and folded it delicately into an envelope which he licked and sealed.

He'd already written similar letters to his ex-wife and to his parents. He wasn't sure he'd ever deliver them, but if something happened to him, he would have some last words.

Morris stared at the newest blank sheet on the pile, his hand aching. He felt like he still had another letter he wanted to write. Morris started with the greeting.

Astrid.

Morris stopped. This was stupid. He hardly knew the woman. What the hell did he have to say to her? He thought about the coffee they'd shared at Stefan's house. He thought about trying to describe Ohio to her and listening to her describe her favorite movies. He thought about all the questions he still wanted to ask her. He thought about the feel of her hand on his.

He continued writing.

I'm writing letters to everyone right now because I'm afraid I'm going to die. I know I don't really know you, but I'm writing to you too because I think I wish that I knew you.

The frankness of the words surprised him. Morris hadn't known what he was going to write until he did it. He felt a mixture of relief and embarrassment.

"How could a bunch of illiterate farmers in the Civil War write poetry and I write this crap?" Morris asked no one in particular. He thought about crumpling the page, but instead found himself writing on.

I met you on one of the worst days of my life. Maybe that's part of what made meeting you so good. I'd just watched a friend die. He died because I failed him. I lead us right into a trap. I didn't know it at the time, but that weight was crushing me. You told me that I was lucky. I was lucky to be alive at all.

You were right. I was lucky. I am lucky.

We didn't get much time to know each other but I have your name and your address still. To be honest I have it memorized. I keep it with me. I know, it's stupid. Some dumb good luck charm or something. But I made you a promise to find you after this war is over. I'm going to do that. If I survive this, I'm going to find you and by God I'm going to have another cup of coffee with you. This time not just Folgers, but something good. I haven't—

The piercing roar of an air raid siren made Morris jerk with surprise.

For a moment he, and the other resting pilots in the barracks shared blank-faced looks of disbelief before they scrambled to cover. Morris crouched down and ducked under the folding table as if it offered any shelter at all. Others threw themselves flat or slid under bunk bed frames.

His heart hammered inside his chest and his eyes darted wildly around the room. Was this it? Was this where he was going to die?

He could just barely see through a low window set in the wall of the barracks. Morris watched a pair of F-15s scream into the air—the alert fighters launching. Further off, he saw the white streaks of missile launches from the Patriot air-defense batteries outside of the airport, targeting whatever was closing to attack the airport.

A moment later, the ground crew fled from the earthen aircraft shelters in the nearby woods, sprinting toward the air raid trench dug a short distance away. Morris could only watch helplessly as they desperately tried to put distance between themselves and the most likely target of the attack.

They ran with everything they had, but it wasn't fast enough.

There was no warning as the first missile exploded. Coming in faster than the speed of sound it erupted in the midst of the aircraft shelters, stripping leaves from the surrounding trees and igniting foliage around the blast.

At least one of the parked F-15s exploded in a rolling fireball as its fuel tank ruptured. The others were apparently protected by the thick walls of the earthen shelters, though the nearby ground crew were not nearly as lucky. Men caught in the open were simply obliterated, the blastwave blew their clothes from their bodies before erasing any trace of their existence.

Morris flinched away from the sight of people being shredded as the window exploded inward with a hail of glass shards. His ears rang so intensely that he couldn't even hear himself screaming. He only marked additional missile impacts as bass thuds that he felt in his chest rather than heard. Morris counted six of them in total. The impacts seemed to be moving farther away rather than closer.

Morris counted to ten after he felt the last impact and lifted his head enough to peer through the shattered window.

One of the aircraft shelters was burning and many trees were cut to splinters. Worse than that, Morris saw a dozen bodies of Air Force ground crew laying in the open, some whole, others in pieces like they'd been passed through a wood chipper.

Gradually his hearing returned, enough that he recognized the distant wail of a civilian fire engine approaching.

Morris climbed to his feet, willing his legs not to shake and looked at the others in the barracks who looked equally shaken.

"Get to the trench!" Morris said. There was no telling when another salvo would come in, and there was no guarantee it wouldn't hit the barracks this time.

The pilots and personnel in the barracks scrambled out on the double, wasting no time in hurrying for the perceived safety of the air raid trench.

Morris paused only to grab his letters and followed them out.

Thick, black smoke rose from the distant airport terminal, drawing him to a stunned halt. The building was visibly burning, flames licking skyward. It had taken a direct hit from one of those Soviet missiles.

Morris thought about the packed crowds he'd seen inside and around it. Women, children, families. He tried to suppress the nausea that washed over him. All those people....

Grinder grabbed his arm. "What are you doing?"

Morris turned away from the burning airport and followed the others toward the trenches. They passed near the aircraft shelters where the ground crew had been. The tarmac was slick with dark blood. Scattered meat and scraps of cloth littered the ground. It was so horrific, so grotesque, that Morris's mind couldn't mentally connect these inanimate objects to the men they had once been.

A crewman in sergeant's coveralls lay face down just ahead. Unlike the others who had been dismembered, he seemed uninjured.

Without thinking Morris knelt beside him and rolled him onto his back before freezing.

The airman was dead, his tongue—thick and purple—protruded from his mouth like a bloated slug. His eyes bulged sickeningly in their sockets. It wasn't shrapnel or fire that had killed him, but a titanic wave of air pressure that ruptured organs and burst blood vessels.

Morris turned away, his breath becoming rapid, his skin suddenly clammy. The image of the dead crewman filled his mind, overwhelming all his senses. With only a moment of warning, Morris doubled over and threw up. He dry heaved a second time before he felt strong enough to get back to his feet. There was no helping the crewman now. He had to go on.

Feeling strangely detached from the carnage around him, Morris saw that the aircraft shelters were mostly intact. The squadron was operational. If they still had aircraft, it meant they could still fight.

Forcing himself to run again, Morris put physical and mental distance between himself and the dead men on the runway. Almost to the air raid trenches, he finally realized that the runway was pocked with dozens of craters, the pavement cracked and shattered by scattered bomblets. The Soviets hadn't destroyed the squadron, but they had ruined the runway. Even with working jets, no one would be getting into the air. An airbase without a working runway was little more than a garrison.

Still, they were prepared for things like this. Engineers could patch and fill the craters with relative quickness and get the runways back up and running in short order. The base's engineering vehicles had just begun to trundle out when the sound of emergency sirens was overtaken by the roaring of the air raid siren again. More volleys of missiles climbed skyward from the Patriot launchers.

Morris ran for all he was worth toward the air raid trench, ran until his legs felt like rubber. He was scared out of his mind, but the more he ran, the more he realized that he was also furious. Without a functional runway, he couldn't do anything. After all that work to get him back to his squadron, he was just as useless as before. All those men who had died would have died for nothing if the squadron couldn't fight.

Morris finally reached the trenches, dropping and rolling into the nearest one just before the second salvo of missiles walked across the airport runways a second time, dropping in with a mix of shrapnel and high-explosive payloads which slaughtered men in the open and destroyed exposed machines.

Morris kept his eyes squeezed shut and his letters clasped to his chest as he thought of his son and his family. He was going to make it through this. Somehow he would. For them.

***

11

A light, cool drizzle fell steadily from the thick gray clouds overhead, pattering down on the leaves above Karlsdotter to bead and drip onto her shoulders and tap on her helmet. Her shoulders ached and her feet were sore, so she was glad to finally be sitting. She sat on the edge of a foxhole, her legs dangling inside as she sipped cool water from her canteen.

The sounds of nature—birds and chirping insects—competed with the far away rumble of artillery fire, like distant thunder. When the barrages stopped, it was easy enough for Karlsdotter to close her eyes and imagine she was just out for a hike back home or maybe in her family's cabin in the mountains.

She brushed a loose strand of hair out of her face, trailing a fingertip across the half-healed scar above her right eyebrow. It was the product of hot Russian steel, a mortar splinter that grazed her. If it had been a little lower she would have lost the eye. A little faster and it might have punched into her brain and killed her. She'd gotten it from the same shell that killed Larsson, a macabre reminder of his death that day.

She closed her eyes and let the memory wash over her. She saw Larsson turning to run for safety. She saw him thrown like a discarded toy, his body broken. She felt pain lance through her face. She felt the dread certainty that she'd been blinded.

She pressed a hand to the wound.

"Cigarette?"

She blinked and looked up to see Bergman standing over her, offering a half-crumpled pack of cigarettes.

"No," she said. "That's a nasty habit. Cigarettes are

disgusting."

Bergman shrugged and lit his own. "Suit yourself." He sat down beside her on the edge of the foxhole.

While she and the others had done enough digging to last a lifetime already, this particular fighting position hadn't been made by them. Their Home Guard platoon had rotated into this spot, replacing some other unit—maybe Swedish army, maybe Norwegian, or maybe the American mountain infantry she'd heard rumors of. Her platoon held a wooded ridgeline that sat between the Soviet army to the east and Oslo to the west. They held a hinge between a Swedish army company and a Norwegian one to their north.

This rugged, undeveloped stretch of natural park was one of the last barriers between the Soviets and the Norwegian capital. Defense of Oslo was vital for more than just the obvious reasons. Oslo was one of the two anchors of the NATO enclave in Scandinavia, the other being the city of Bergen. These two port cities enabled the survival of the enclave here even as other Norwegian and Swedish holdouts dotting the coast were isolated and crushed or evacuated. If either of those cities fell, it would probably undo the whole line and thus doom the last remaining foothold NATO had in Scandinavia.

"I only just got Johan to quit," Karlsdotter said, staring out at the forest.

"Hm? Your boyfriend, right?"

She nodded. "He smoked when we met. I think he thought it made him look cool or something, but they stunk. I made him quit. Mostly." Karlsdotter fiddled with a wrinkle on her pants. "He only smokes when he gets really angry or stressed." She frowned. "I bet he's smoking a lot right now."

"Maybe not," Bergman said. "Maybe he's more afraid of upsetting you than he is of the Russians." He smiled hopefully.

Karlsdotter didn't smile. "Maybe."

"Have you asked anyone? Maybe someone knows where his unit is."

"Who would I ask?" she retorted. "We're here in the

goddamned woods." She sighed. "His unit was on the coast and I haven't heard any rumor of them since the invasion. There is a good chance that they were all destroyed." She clenched a fist and thought of the fear in that Russian's eyes as she stuck the muzzle of her rifle into his stomach.

Bergman shifted uncomfortably. "I'm sorry. I don't know what happened to Johan. But I am certain that...if he is alive, he's fighting like hell to be with you again."

Karlsdotter at last looked at Bergman and saw the genuine worry in his eyes. She allowed herself a tight, tired smile and felt something within her threaten to give way. The emotional dam she'd been building since her first night in combat weakened ever so slightly, promising an unstoppable deluge of feelings if she didn't keep it in check. The smile died on her face and she furrowed her brow. "Alive or not, we're going to have to make the invaders pay for coming here. We're going to make this place their grave."

Silence lapsed and they both listened to the idle chatter of the platoon in nearby fighting positions and the grumbling of heavy guns farther off.

"Were you close to Larsson?" Bergman asked at last.

"Close? No. I liked him though."

"Me too," Bergman said. "He was a good man."

"Yes."

"Karlsdotter, can I ask you something?"

She looked at Bergman, surprised by his tone of voice. He was a few years older than her, university was behind him, but in this moment he looked strangely weak, vulnerable. "What?"

"If I...you know if I don't...." Bergman's voice hitched and he swallowed. "Can you tell my mother that I did good? That I fought well?"

Karlsdotter stared dumbfounded.

"I was always a screw up. Never could keep jobs or anything," Bergman continued, the words coming in a rush. "This Home Guard thing was to prove to myself I could do something. I want my family to know that...that I did all this. You know?"

Again, her emotional dam shifted. Karlsdotter swallowed her feelings and nodded. "Yes. I can do that. Of course." She felt she had to say more. This was her comrade in arms. He had his quirks, but he wasn't a hopeless screw up. "Bergman—."

They both reacted on instinct to the sound of whistling, jumping into the narrow foxhole. Their knees knocked together. It was a tight fit–they were shoulder to shoulder with each other, wedged in the rifle pit.

Karlsdotter clapped her hands over her ears, closed her eyes, and opened her mouth. She'd heard it was supposed to help with overpressure from shelling. but she didn't know for sure.

The first artillery shells exploded in the treetops, raining branches and leaves down on the fighting positions below. Frantic, shouted commands were lost as the barrage increased in tempo and severity. Soon there was no sound but a steady concussive thumping of shells and the occasional shriek and whine of shrapnel whizzing by overhead.

Karlsdotter and Bergman remained like this, huddled together in mutual mortal fear, waiting for the barrage to end. After what seemed like an eternity, it finally began to taper off. A heavy chemical fog lingered in the air—a smokescreen to blind their position, denying them clear fields of fire.

As Karlsdotter's hearing returned, she became aware that Bergman was praying fervently, hands wrapped tightly around his rifle.

"On your feet!" she said, following her own advice to straighten up and take aim with her rifle into the haze. Her nerves were frayed, every shift in the fog appeared to be a figure looming forward.

Movement behind her made her whirl in surprise.

Sergeant Hellström, keeping as low to the ground as possible, approached from the rear. "Be ready," he said. "The Russians will probably drop another volley and then launch infantry assaults on our position."

"Should I get back to my position, Sergeant?" Bergman asked, as if afraid of the answer.

"No time. Stay here with Karlsdotter. Keep low, stay calm, don't panic. Got it?"

"Yes, Sergeant," Karlsdotter said.

And then Hellström was off, moving to the next firing position to check the rest of the platoon. Karlsdotter was momentarily in awe of the sergeant's bravery when she heard the howl of more rounds incoming and ducked back into the foxhole.

A nearby explosion showered her and Bergman with dirt. Bergman checked his magazine and primed his rifle before looking up at her. There was fear in his eyes, but also determination. It was a feeling she shared.

A nearby burst of gunfire was the only warning of Soviet infantry. The Soviets had gotten quite good at closely following behind their rolling barrages so they could pounce the moment they let up. It was impressive, but Karlsdotter wasn't going to let it cow her. She pulled the priming handle on her own rifle, feeding a shell into the breech and stood again. She leaned against the earthen edge of the foxhole to brace her elbow.

She squeezed her off eye shut and peered into the shifting smoke cloud. The second she saw movement, she opened fire. With visibility so low, it would be suicide to let the enemy get any closer than absolutely necessary.

Bergman joined his fire to hers. Shell casings spun past Karlsdotter's head but she didn't flinch. The two of them hammered away at faint movement in the fog. It was impossible to know if they hit anything, but they added to the hail of gunfire their platoon was putting up. From somewhere nearby, Bucht's machine gun stitched out a belt of rounds, firing in long, chattering bursts as it swept the woods before them. Rifle and machine gun fire was soon joined by mortar rounds dropping among the Soviets.

Just beneath the roar of gunfire, Karlsdotter could faintly hear the wailing of wounded. So long as those sounds came from downhill, she was happy.

Another volley of mortars burst among the Soviets and their fire slackened off substantially. They were falling back. The Swedes had held. For now.

"How's that for a taste of Sweden!?" Bergman shouted after the retreating enemy.

Karlsdotter let out a breath she hadn't realized she was holding.

Berman continued to scan downhill, his eyes as wide as dinner plates.

Pitiful moaning sounded from close by.

"Someone's hurt," Karlsdotter said. "Wait here."

"They might come back!" Bergman protested, but she didn't wait.

With every ounce of courage she had, she crawled from the foxhole and moved along the ground on her belly. The sound of battle to their north was intensifying. The Soviets were pressing the Norwegians there for all they were worth and Bergman was right, there was no guarantee the Soviets wouldn't renew their attack or their shelling here.

Karlsdotter found the wounded Swede lying behind a splintered stump, holding his thigh, trying to stem a steadily spreading purple stain. As she drew nearer, she recognized him.

"Sergeant?"

Hellström looked over at her, his teeth clenched against the pain.

Karlsdotter crawled over beside him. "Let me see it."

He shook his head. His face was ghostly white. "Bastards hit the femoral artery. Tourniquet. Tie it off." He spoke through clenched teeth.

Karlsdotter didn't argue. The lessons of first aid returned quickly. She tied the tourniquet in place above his wound, twisting again and again until the loop was so tight against his leg that it wouldn't turn anymore. Then she tied it in place. Her fingertips were slick with his blood.

"Get back to Sundquist," he said, his voice tight. "Radio for medevac."

With the intensity of the fighting to their north, Karlsdotter knew as well as he did that any evac wasn't likely to be swift in coming,

"I'll get you back to cover," she said instead.

He shook his head again, sucking in a breath against the pain, still holding his leg. "No way you can move me. Get back to cover in case they come back."

Karlsdotter felt a swelling of anger. "Don't be stupid. Give me your arm. We're not leaving you here."

After a moment of hesitation, Hellström held out his arm.

Karlsdotter took it, turned and pulled Hellström's stomach against her shoulder before heaving up, lifting with her legs. She momentarily struggled against his weight, her muscles protesting. She wasn't going to be able to lift him, technique or no, he was too heavy.

Karlsdotter grit her teeth and pushed with all her might, struggling fully upright.

Once she was certain she wasn't going to collapse, she started back toward the rear, one step at a time, knowing that she wouldn't have to go far before finding help.

"You're stubborn as hell, Karlsdotter," Hellström said.

She didn't answer.

"People are going to look to you now," he said. "Make sure we get through this alive. Take care of everyone." Hellström's weight for a moment was more than physical. The weight of responsibility bore down on her. She had to do more than kill invaders, she had to make sure her people survived.

"You're not going to die," she said finally. "Save your breath."

They came into sight of another fighting position, emerging out of the smoke.

"God!" Fjellner exclaimed. "Sergeant?"

"Come help me," Karlsdotter blurted, pleased to see the young man scramble out and hurry over to help carry Hellström.

"Take care of them, Ingrid," Hellström said. "Don't forget

why we're out here. We can't avenge the dead, but we can protect the living."

Karlsdotter didn't answer. She couldn't.

***

12

From twenty thousand feet in the air, the ocean below looked like a blue silk sheet rippling under an unfelt breeze. Sunlight flashed and glittered from the endless expanse of wavetops below. From the driver's seat of an F-14 Tomcat, Rabbit was the king of all he surveyed. Between the fighter's powerful radar and long range television camera, there was nowhere to hide, and with the array of missiles including the lethal and huge Phoenix, anything they could see they could reach out and touch.

Cruising just off their wingtip was a second F-14 in identical configuration—Lancer 108. The two of them were a sliver of the air defenses swirling around USS *Shiloh* and its escorts. They were far out, over three hundred miles south east of *Shiloh*, covering the North Sea south of where the *Bastogne* and *Belleau Wood* groups sailed. With both of those carriers' air wings pre-occupied with combat patrols and ground attack missions over Norway, it fell to the pilots of *Shiloh* to watch the seas.

Despite the fearsome array of military hardware, war was far from Rabbit's mind right now. Their scope was clear, the skies were blue, and he was dreaming of The Course.

"The Grand Old Lady," Rabbit said.

"Oh, God," Gomez groaned from the seat behind him. "Not this shit again." Robert "Gomez" Adams was Rabbit's RIO, Radar Intercept Officer, sometimes derisively known as the GIB—guy-in-back. He sat behind Rabbit and operated their Tomcat's weapons and radar systems to leave Rabbit free to focus on flying. If Rabbit really wanted to aggravate a RIO, he would just refer to him as a "Goose," not that he particularly enjoyed any comparisons to Maverick.

"The oldest golf course on planet earth, man," Rabbit continued, smiling to himself. "Scotland."

"Scotland. Right. Ask real nice and maybe they'll drop us off to play a round."

"Oh ye of little faith," Rabbit said. "That course is calling my name. I had a chance to play it last summer and I passed it up. What a fool I was."

"No surprise there," Gomez replied. "So why didn't you go? What was her name?"

"Caroline." Rabbit smiled to himself.

"Caroline," Gomez repeated mournfully.

"Stunning girl," Rabbit said. "Long hair, longer legs, beautiful accent."

"Jesus, rub it in, why don't you?"

Rabbit bit off the rest of his reminiscing. "Ah, sorry man."

"Sorry," Gomez repeats. "God, I'm the one who's sorry. What the hell am I doing out here? Why the hell did I even sign the papers? I should be back home knocking back brews with Alison."

Rabbit didn't feel it was tactful to remind Gomez that his girlfriend would probably be awful in or out of the military. It was his professional opinion that some people just didn't have a loyal bone in their bodies, and Gomez's ex was one of them.

While his RIO continued to bemoan his unceremonious dumping, Rabbit mentally berated himself for bringing up the topic of women. "Look dude, we can hit the green when we get back. Tee off at dawn, grab a pint afterwards. I'm telling you, it's going to be great."

"Yeah? When the hell is that going to be? Gonna ask the Russians for a timeout or something? Cause from where I'm sitting we're stuck here until we can kick in Kavinsky's teeth, or Karamazov's, whatever old fart they have running that shitshow. Sound about right?"

Rabbit frowned to himself. "Yeah. I guess that's right. Look, it's a promise, okay?"

"Right," Gomez said bitterly.

Uncomfortable silence lapsed in the cockpit, broken a moment later by Rabbit.

"You hear about Venom's daughter?"

"Who?"

"Metcalf," Rabbit explained. "Prowler driver."

"Oh right. You bunk with him, right?"

"Yeah. Just found out his daughter's getting hitched and she didn't clear it with him apparently. They're not on speaking terms, sounds like."

"Shit," Gomez said. "That's a tough break."

"No kidding."

"How's he taking it?"

Rabbit shrugged to himself. "Hard to say. Venom keeps this stuff close to his chest, but how would you be taking it?"

Gomez's reply was interrupted by the radio.

"Stagecoach to Lancer 103."

Rabbit responded automatically. "Lancer 103 reads you. Go ahead, Stagecoach." On the surface he was calm and cool as always, but inside he felt his heartbeat start hammering his ribs.

Stagecoach—one of the ACWAS Hawkeyes from *Shiloh*—was off their nine o'clock, so far out that it was invisible. It was this aircraft which fed them tactical data from their redar returns. If it wasn't for Stagecoach, Rabbit wouldn't know about the dozen or so surface contacts dead ahead of them— NATO escorts and convoy craft crawling their way north east toward Norway. If Stagecoach were reaching out to them, it was because something important had changed. In war, that meant trouble.

Stagecoach proceed without preamble. "We've got bogeys on scope. Flight of ten at 350, seventy miles out, angels ten bearing 190. They're emitting on the Fencer radar band."

Fencers. Sukhoi-24s, Soviet attack craft, probably loaded for anti-ship work.

Now Rabbit's heart was really pounding but he echoed the words. "Copy, ten Fencers. Angels ten at 350." He toggled the radio off to speak to Gomez directly. "You seeing that?"

"Wait one," Gomez replied. "Yep, got it. Ten bandits." Gomez continued tracking the enemy contacts on his radar as they moved south. "They're making for that convoy."

"Lancer 103, you're clear to engage contacts as hostile. Copy?"

"Solid copy, Stagecoach," Rabbit said. "103 out." Then, to Gomez—"Let 108 know."

Gomez was already doing it. He toggled on the radio, checking that the frequency was set to the band they shared with their wingmate.

"Lancer 108 this is Lancer 103. Ducky, you copy?"

"Copy, 103. Go ahead."

"Stagecoach has bogeys on scope. Flight of ten Fencers at 350, seventy miles out. Orders to intercept and knock 'em down before they tangle with that convoy."

Ducky's voice came back strong and clear, his excitement impossible to miss in his voice. "Copy. We'll follow you in. Good hunting, 103."

"Copy." Gomez killed the channel. "Let's get 'em."

Rabbit angled their aircraft in on an intercept course, Ducky automatically following his lead. He took a deep breath and let it back out, unhappy to feel how shaky it was. This was the real deal.

***

The only warning of the enemy missiles was the cataclysmic ripping sound of the close-in weapons system firing off *Somerset*'s starboard flank as it warded off the attack.

Seymour turned his eyes to the left just in time to catch the flash of a missile exploding a few hundred meters off. The wasted projectile boiled into a ball of flame which, in turn, tumbled into the ocean with a splash and gout of steam.

Shrapnel scattered across the sea in a ring of splashes.

The bridge erupted into commotion, orders and information were called out back and forth. Seymour had just long enough to be shocked that the automated defenses reacted before his crew could to the surprise attack. The Soviets had launched without being detected, likely from low altitude, evading detection by radar.

Seymour mentally berated himself for his delay. He turned to Smith. "Get damage control teams on standby. Take us to action stations."

"Aye, sir!"

"Where the hell did that shot come from?" Seymour demanded, turning to the radar station.

"Scope is clear, sir!" the officer protested. "No tracks."

Seymour ground his teeth. There wasn't much he could do against a target he couldn't see.

"Find them," he said. "Find me something to shoot for God's sake. They're going to be after us again."

"Message from the *Fuchs*, sir: multiple Soviet craft detected on approach. Identified as Su-24 Fencers. Confirmed by AWACS from *Shiloh*."

USS *Joel Fuchs* was an *Oliver Hazard Perry*-class, American, like *Nauls*.

"Get Blackjack up," Seymour said. If more missiles were inbound, he wanted to try to spare the Lynx from getting caught, while allowing it to act as a missile decoy by flying low and close to the ship, potentially drawing fire away. "And where is our air cover? Anything from *Shiloh*?"

There was no time for an answer.

"Targets tracking, sir. I make four Fencers coming for a run from the West. Designate Raid One."

"Get our missiles in the air. Check targets with the other escorts. Make sure we're not doubling up." Seymour hesitated before adding, "and make *damn* sure we're not targeting our own planes!"

"Aye, sir!"

Radar waves swept the air, returning signals to *Somerset*'s targeting array where two Sea Dart missiles were primed and waiting on their launch mount. *Somerset* opened fire, launching both available missiles.

The Sea Darts streaked away from the launcher arm, one after the other, climbing for invisible targets. The second salvo was loaded swiftly. So much was automated now, there was little Seymour could to but listen impotently to the battle unfolding around him

"Captain, *Callenburgh* is issuing a general distress signal. Sounds like she's hit."

Seymour lifted his eyes from the plotter chart and saw dark smoke climbing from further up the convoy off *Somerset*'s bow. He gritted his teeth. It seemed everyone hadn't been as lucky. "They're going to have to wait." First neutralize the threat, then deal with the aftermath.

The first pair of Sea Dart missiles found their target.

"Hit. I mark one hit. Splash one."

"Tracking another group of targets coming in. Designate Raid Two."

"Defensive countermeasures are active."

Muffled bangs sounded from both sides and canisters of metallic chaff were launched a few hundred meters to either side of the ship where they burst, forming phantom targets for radar-seeking missiles.

"Vampire! Vampire!"

Seymour's blood froze. Enemy anti-ship missiles had been detected on radar.

The bridge exploded to life, orders going back and forth. Sailors hunched over their control consoles and spoke quickly into their headsets.

In the bowels of *Somerset*, nervous damage control teams stood by with oxygen hoods and fire suppression gear. If death came for *Somerset*, it would come quickly. There would be no warning.

"Do they have us?" Seymour asked, voice edged with alarm.

"Negative, sir. No radar returns."

Unless the missile closing on them hadn't yet activated its radar.

Four hundred meters. Three hundred. Two.

The missile streaked by *Somerset*'s port side scarcely two hundred meters out. It sailed clear through the fading chaff cloud they'd deployed. If it had been a ship, it would have been a bullseye.

The silence that came next was sweet.

"*Nauls* has marked another splash, sir."

"Any damage?"

"None for us, sir."

For all the high tech firepower around him, Seymour couldn't help but feel like a mouse caught in a mousetrap. "Where is our bloody air support?"

***

The Tomcats closed on the enemy at the speed of sound, but it was still too slow for Rabbit's taste. Each second was an eternity. His gut churned with nervous fear and he felt the lessons he'd endlessly drilled into his mind become fleeting and intangible. His mouth was dry, his palms sweaty.

"Nails!" Gomez called.

Rabbit's blood went cold. The Fencers were painting him with radar waves just as he was them.

"Lancer 108, take it up to Angels twenty."

If they went high enough, they could fly in above the Soviet radar cone and have a height advantage when it came to throwing missiles at one another. Superior altitude would allow for more options in either attack or defense.

Rabbit kept nose on the Fencers as they closed distance.

The Soviet aircraft were flying erratically, breaking and circling, probably engaged in a missile duel with the convoy. It would make them easier pickings once he got in range.

"Two targets breaking from the flight," Gomez said. "They're

88

accelerating. Looks like Foxhounds."

Fast, long-range interceptors, but no match for the Tomcat.

"Ducky, take the left one, we'll take right."

"108 copies."

Ducky peeled away, banking out of visual range as they moved into combat spacing.

They had closed to within thirty miles of the bandits and were now racing toward one another, the Foxhounds climbing from low altitude.

Rabbit's heart beat faster still, he almost felt nauseous from equal parts fear and anticipation. He gulped deep breaths of oxygen-rich air in a vain attempt to settle himself. "Gomez, lock him up."

Gomez fired without warning. "Fox one!"

The sparrow raced off the shoulder pylon toward the Foxhound, startling Rabbit. Gomez hadn't told him he was going to do that.

The Fencers turned as if on cue and accelerated away from Rabbit and Ducky.

"Bandits going cold," Rabbit said, trying to keep his voice level.

Gomez's sparrow closed on the Foxhound's radar blip before sailing harmlessly past. A miss.

Gomez swore. "Sparrow went wide! Fox one!" He hastily launched a second radar-seeker.

Rabbit glanced to his left as if he could see Ducky's F-14 shadowing them. At combat spacing, his wingman was so far away as to be almost invisible.

"108, take the shot!" Rabbit said.

"No tone!" Ducky replied. "Goddammit. We don't have lock!"

"Shoot him, man!" Rabbit insisted. There was no reason why 108 shouldn't have a lock at this range.

Ducky didn't reply and he didn't shoot, apparently preoccupied with whatever technical glitch was fouling his weapons systems.

"Splash!" Gomez cried triumphantly. "We got him!"

"Nice kill," Rabbit said automatically.

He saw the other Foxhound going defensive on his radar, turning away and diving for cover. Had he fired? Rabbit couldn't discount it. They were now within twenty miles of the enemy, well within range of a heatseeker and if one were closing on them, he wouldn't know until it was too late. He acted. "Lancer 103 defending!" Rabbit hauled his stick over and worked the foot pedals, turning the F-14 over on its head and diving down for the ocean. He felt his stomach drop out as G-forces worked over his body.

"Lancer 108, fox two!" Ducky said at last.

Rabbit felt a small degree of relief to know that his wingman wasn't dead weight anymore. Leveling out above the ocean, Rabbit pulled the F-14 into an airframe-shaking bank turn, recommitting to bring his nose back on target.

"Splash!" Ducky said.

"Good kill, 108," Rabbit said.

"Fencers are hightailing it," Gomez said. "We're going to lose them."

"How about a parting gift?" Rabbit asked, feeling the invincible high of having been shot at without result. "Put a Phoenix up their ass."

"Lancer 103," Gomez said, "fox three."

"108, fox three," Ducky's RIO echoed a moment later.

Given their weight, size, and the sheer power of the rocket motor, it wasn't possible to launch a Phoenix off the railing like you would a Sparrow. Instead it decoupled and dropped straight down like an old dumb bomb. Wobbling like a football, it fell for a heartbeat until its rocket ignited. The Phoenix sprinted off on a trail of white smoke, climbing for thinner air as it raced toward the enemy.

The Phoenixes had their own terminal guidance radars, but those would only come into play once the range was below twenty kilometers. Until then, they would either fly on in a straight line or rely on data fed to them by the parent craft.

Rabbit waited a painful minute before the missiles

crossed the intervening miles and finally reached the Soviet formation. Here in the open ocean, they had nowhere to hide.

"Splash! Two splashes. Nice kills."

Rabbit saw black smoke on the horizon in the direction of the convoy. For all the elation he felt, he soured at the realization that the Soviets had probably come out ahead in this little exchange. Whatever damage they'd done to the convoy overshadowed a handful of aircraft losses.

It was further soured by the realization that these were just Fencers and a pair of Foxhounds. Fencers were no challenge–old, fat, relatively slow. They were easy prey for a machine like the Tomcat. The Soviet naval air force's pride and joy, the Backfire, was the real test. Like yin and yang, the Backfire and Tomcat were opponents made for one another.

And it was only a matter of time until that fated nemesis made its appearance, Rabbit thought.

***

The radio on *Somerset*'s bridge buzzed with traffic as the NATO vessels in the area coordinated their movement with each other and the civilian shipping they were here to protect. The chaos resulting from the initial shock of the Soviet missile attack still hadn't worn off. The merchant marines were mercifully untouched by the attack, but they'd all seen one of their escorts get struck. If their protectors were vulnerable then, they thought, what chance did they have?

Somerset's course naturally carried her past *Callenburgh*'s smoldering hulk.

As they drew gradually nearer to the macabre site of the attack, Seymour took a coat from a metal hook by the wall and stepped out of the heated bridge and into the frosty air outside. Here on a freezing metal walkway jutting from the flank of the bridge, he could get a better view of what was going on, ignoring the wind whipping around him.

The wave-tossed, frigid waters of the North Sea played host

to a haunting scene of carnage. *Callenburgh* floundered in the choppy seas, her once-proud gray flank marked with black burn patterns where a pair of missiles had struck. All around her, like spawned offspring, were orange life rafts, tossing in the waves. A spreading oil slick covered everything, turning the ocean into a shimmering, dark thing.

Captain Seymour pulled his parka tighter against the chill air, but it couldn't keep out the chill in his heart.

Somerset forged ahead slowly, desperate not to plow through any possible survivors.

Seymour knew that only those who had made it to the life rafts had any real chance at survival and given the speed and ferocity of the attack there would be many who never had a chance to get to a raft. The water was scarcely over freezing, hypothermia would have set in long ago for anyone treading water without an insulated wetsuit. Evidence of this bobbed lifelessly in the oil-slick waves all around them.

There was no chance *Somerset* could stop to mount a proper rescue. As they passed they threw down inflatable rafts and a radio beacon to mark the site. Stopping here would only leave the convoy that much more vulnerable.

Callenburgh's bow steadily tilted skyward as the hull filled with seawater. In another minute it would sink beneath the waves forever.

A moment later they were past, their wake churning the oily waters and sending the dead bobbing around.

Seymour remained until he could no longer make out the bodies before he turned away. Storm clouds rumbled on the horizon ahead of them. Leaving the windswept gantry, he re-entered the bridge.

Smith met Seymour by the end of the bridge. "We've confirmed that *Oslo* is still en route. She has a fix on the radio beacon."

"How long?" Seymour asked.

"She's two hours out," Smith said grimly.

How many men would still be alive out there after two

hours? "Very well."

"It wasn't meant to go like this, sir," Smith said. "This war."

Seymour tensed his jaw. "No," he agreed. "It wasn't.

Seven more hours to Bergen.

***

13

Major Fedorovich frowned behind his oxygen mask as he studied the laminated map square fixed to his thigh. He had been in the cockpit for nearly two hours now, including the idle and taxi time at Arkhangelsk Air Base. It was a drop in the bucket compared to his total flight time but anticipation was making him anxious. The brilliant, turquoise backing of the instrument panel before him contrasted sharply to the dull, gray clouds his craft currently passed through. Although Fedorovich was nominally the pilot of this craft, as the squadron commander he had a broader responsibility that meant his co-pilot, Babayev, handled the actual flying.

Turbulence vibrated the cockpit and Fedorovich sent Babayev a hooded look. His co-pilot remained stony-faced and pretended not to notice his commander's displeasure.

"Are you hitting every pocket of rough air between here and Arkhangelsk on purpose?

Babayev remained stoic, but Fedorovich caught the glimmer of amusement in his co-pilot's eye.

"My apologies, Comrade Major. I assure you it isn't intentional. This old boy simply likes to dance."

Fedorovich sighed.

The "old boy" in question was a Tu-22M long range naval bomber, one of sixty in Fedorovich's regiment. As a variable-wing, supersonic bomber, it was purpose built to swiftly cross huge distances and deliver a spread of equally-long range anti-ship missiles. Known as the "Backfire" in the West, the Tu-22M was a purpose-built carrier-killer. One Backfire was a threat, a full regiment of sixty were a death sentence.

"Just keep it smooth and level," Fedorovich said.

Almost reading his thoughts, Pavlov—the weapons system officer—spoke up over the craft's intercom system. "Babayev, you pirate. I think I still have some of my breakfast in my stomach. You're losing your touch." The fuzz of Fedorovich's headset robbed Pavlov's voice of some of its cutting tone.

Babayev smirked. "Give me time. We are not there yet."

Fedorovich toggled on his own microphone so his voice could be heard by the two airmen in the rear compartment of the Tu-22M. "Alekseev, how far until the landing site?"

"We are fifteen minutes out at current estimate, Comrade Major!" The navigator, Alekseev's response was fast and stiff, betraying his nervousness. He was the newest of the crew and clearly uncomfortable with his posting aboard the regiment's lead aircraft.

Alekseev's estimate matched Fedorovich's own calculations, and fit with Babayev's expectations as he began to gradually give altitude, bringing their craft below the cloud cover.

Feodorvich toggled his radio on, connecting to the regimental command frequency. "Osprey One this Osprey Three. We're approaching landing site Fyodor. No incident. Beginning final landing approach."

The regiment was landing at several sites around Trondheim since no single airfield would be able to handle all sixty of the immense bombers. The twelve Tu-22M's Fedorovich led were en route to a point on his map labeled as "Orlond Air Station," a small airfield outside of Trondheim, Norway. The rest of the regiment was likewise traveling to other captured airfields, including Trondheim Airport itself, as well as the Alesund and Molde airports.

An aircraft the size of a Tu-22M required a dedicated airfield to launch from. Operating from primitive road bases was possible for something rugged like the MiG-21, but the Tu-22M was a precision machine. Requiring purpose-built airfields limited their deployment options and left them somewhat vulnerable on the ground. It was a consequence of its impressive flight performance, but one that couldn't be avoided.

The colonel responded a moment later, broadcasting from the specialized Tu-16 command plane following the regiment. The colonel himself was slated to land at Trondheim airport according to Fedorovich's notes.

"Affirmative, Major," Osprey One replied a moment later. "Continue approach and contact us when you've landed."

"Acknowledged." Satisfied, Fedorovich flipped his mic off and rolled his neck in a vain effort to relieve tension growing there. Contrary to his initial expectations, his squadron had seen no action since the war started. In fact, in the months since the Yugoslavian intervention, the regiment had been hastily brought up to strength. If the Soviet military could be categorized under a single cardinal sin, it was sloth. Inefficiency and corruption plagued everything and the Andropov-era reforms could only go so far toward resolving that. Fedorovich had seen complacency and corruption rot away their on-paper strength in peacetime. Only at the last minute did they attempt to correct this grievous damage.

As fighting kicked off in Yugoslavia, the pace of training and maintenance had increased threefold. Missing personnel and pilots were brought in and hurriedly trained, inoperable aircraft swiftly brought back to readiness. Fedorovich had heard on good authority that another half-strength Tu-22M regiment had been cannibalized to bring their's up to full operability. Men like Alekseev were green, untried, but the new recruits were dispersed as evenly as possible among his veteran crews. A lot of Fedorovich's veteran crews had been unhappy about this, tight teams were being broken up after all, but Fedorovich knew the new people would learn faster and perform better when paired with more experienced hands. Military service wasn't widely seen as desirable in the Soviet Union, and so they were constantly hemorrhaging trained crew as men cycled out of the service. This was the best way to retain as much professionalism as he could.

Fedorovich was an administrator, of course, but he was a fighter first and foremost. He did not join the air force so he could scribble his signature on requisition forms. He joined to fight the enemy and protect his homeland. So when they came below the clouds and into the late afternoon light, he smiled at the sight of Trondheim ahead through the Tu-22M's rain-streaked windscreen. He was eager to get to work.

As they passed over the dark waters of the Trondheim fjord, Fedorovich craned his neck to look down on the city itself which smoldered with a score of fires across its face. "This was all supposed to be cleared," he muttered.

"Let us just be glad that the Norwegians down there don't have advanced SAM missiles to hit us with or this would be a very short assignment, Comrade," Babayev said.

Fedorovich didn't like imagining dropping from the sky like a stone; the thought turned his stomach more than Babayev's flying. "No argument."

Beyond the fjord lay the airfield Lit against the dying daylight by banks of high-powered lights and burning flares along the runway strip, it was unmissable.

"We'll go down last," Fedorovich told Babayev. "We will make sure the others touch down correctly. Put us into orbit."

"As you wish, Comrade."

The Tu–22M banked to lazily circle the airfield below as Fedorovich watched and counted as his bombers landed in pairs. He was pleased to note that the airfield's facilities were more than adequate. He noted circular aircraft shelters, covered hangars, refueling areas, and repair sheds. While it was small, this had been a NATO military airfield before its capture, and so would serve this role nicely.

After the last of his planes touched down, Babayev likewise brought them in for a landing approach while Fedorovich established radio contact with the tower.

"Orlond tower, this is Osprey Three. I saw some damage from the air. Do we have refueling capabilities?"

"Yes, Comrade Major. We have established air defense

around the airfield to deter more NATO raids."

Fedorovich noted that he said "deter" and not "prevent." The painful truth was that no one could truly *stop* NATO's tremendous air power with air defense alone. He shuddered to imagine the damage the enemy could wreak on his regiment if the enemy struck while they were on the ground. "Excellent. Begin refueling straight away. My orders are to be ready at a moment's notice."

"We will do our best, Major. Orlond out."

Fedorovich noted that again they promised nothing.

The Tu-22M shuddered as its landing gear punched the pavement. Fedorovich and the others were pressed into the straps of their seat harnesses as the plane decelerated rapidly and taxied toward the earthen shelters on the edge of the runway.

Fedorovich finished relaying their arrival to regimental command and looked out his window at the damage to the air base. The main terminal was charred from high explosive impacts across its face, and a collection of dead bodies in the uniform of Soviet paratroopers were lined up in rows near the control tower.

A bit further on, Soviet infantry patrolled the perimeter of the base, watchful for renewed resistance. A high price had been paid for this base and had been paid recently. It was up to Fedorovich to make sure it was worth it, and that largely depended on the men higher up than him.

"And now we wait again," Babayev said, taxiing the massive bomber at the direction of ground personnel.

"For now," Fedorovich agreed. "Until the right time."

"Don't tell me you're excited," Babayev said.

"Aren't you?"

The co-pilot shrugged.

Fedorovich chuckled. "We're here for a purpose, Babayev. We're pointed at the heart of the enemy and just waiting for someone to pull the trigger."

"Fuel isn't cheap," Babayev said. "They've paid a hefty price

just flying us out here. Probably not long now."
"No," Fedorovich agreed. "Not long at all."

***

14

"More news," Admiral Ernest Alderman said to himself as he looked over the print out he'd been handed. "None of it good."

Standing beside him, Captain McNamee, the commander of the USS *Anzio*, agreed. "No, sir. Looks like things are heating up."

Alderman laid the printout down by the telex and ran a hand through his close-cut hair. Heavy was the burden that rested on his shoulders. All NATO naval forces operating in the Norwegian and North Seas fell under his purview. His normal youthful vigor was bowed somewhat because of this. Those who knew him before the war would have said his energy had no bounds. How he wished that were true.

Alderman crossed the bridge in a few steps and looked out over the flight deck of the carrier. The USS *Anzio* wasn't the newest of America's *Antietam*-class carriers—that honor would go to *Khe Sahn* once she was completed—but she wasn't far off.

Support crew clad in bright fluorescent colors flitted about the deck, checking aircraft, refueling, rearming, and launching them. *Anzio* sat in the center of a storm of activity, controlling not just her own squadrons and escorts, but by extension of the admiral, controlling *all* of the combined naval assets of NATO in the North Sea.

"Trondheim," Alderman said, repeating the name from the telex. "Gone already. What a disaster." The small enclave around that city hadn't had good prospects for holding out, being so isolated from the main NATO lines as it was. Really, Alderman knew he shouldn't have been surprised to hear that Soviet forces finished securing the city. There had been talk of re-deploying some of the Norwegian army units from the far north by sea to bolster the city's defenses but it was a pipe dream and it always had been. Even discounting the interference they were sure to encounter from Soviet submarines and aircraft, there was just no time to arrange an effective defense. The city was a death trap, or it had been. Now it was gone.

McNamee didn't argue, didn't say anything. What could be said?

Through the windows of the bridge, Alderman watched an F-14 Tomcat swoop in low, engines roaring, tires touching the deck of the carrier. It flashed by and a moment later snagged the arrestor cable with its tailhook, jerking the fighter to a shuddering halt.

Alderman was no stranger to command. He'd commanded the Red Sea strike group that conducted the bombing campaign in occupied Somalia during Operation Crescent Storm. Before that he'd commanded the old *Constellation*-class carrier USS *Independence* during Vietnam. But this was different.

No matter how sideways things went, there was never any real risk to his carriers then. Nothing the Ethiopians or Vietnamese or anyone else had could really touch them. The Soviets, however, were in a different league.

Defeat still wasn't really a possibility. No matter how successful the Soviets were at sea, no matter what they did, no matter how lucky they got, they would still lose out, even if through weight of numbers alone. Alderman had seen enough war games to know that. When it came to an all-out fight between East and West, the winner was obvious—at least at sea.

Gettysburg was still in drydock in Taranto, Italy, undergoing repairs from the torpedo hits she'd taken in the Adriatic, and *Khe Sahn* hadn't taken to the seas yet. But even discounting them, the Soviets just couldn't match the numbers the West could bring to bear.

No, there was no possibility of a Soviet victory. Alderman wouldn't entertain the notion. But that wasn't what concerned him. It wasn't defeat, but loss.

In all his time in command, Alderman had never had a ship lost. Now he'd seen dozens sent to the bottom by missiles and torpedoes. NATO had a formidable naval arsenal poised to shield Western Europe and the rest of the Atlantic from Soviet attack, but it only took one. One slip up, one missile, one torpedo slipping through, and people would die. Stopping them all was impossible, but he couldn't help trying to stop as many as he could.

Alderman paced the rows of desks and consoles where sailors worked, plotting navigation, checking flight paths, coordinating with other vessels, scanning the air and water with radar and sonar, ever vigilant for attack.

"Admiral," a young officer said, snapping to attention. "High priority call for you from Washington. Admiral Gideon, sir."

"Gideon," Alderman repeated. He knew the name well, but wasn't sure he'd heard correctly at first. It was unusual for the chief of naval operations to call a fleet commander directly like this. But these were unusual times and Alderman and Gideon went way back. "I'll take the call in my quarters."

As Alderman left the confines of the bridge for the even more confining passageways twisting into the guts of the ship, he mused on the past. Gideon had been his superior officer when he'd commanded *Independence.* After that war they'd become golf buddies when their schedules allowed it. As both men advanced through the ranks, they had less and less free time for drinks and golf, but somehow their friendship had survived.

Alderman entered his quarters and closed the door behind himself. Modestly sized relative to an equivalent space in a shore-side facility, they were palatial compared to the otherwise cramped living space aboard a carrier. Ships like this were built for a primary mission, centered around basing aircraft. Housing a human crew comfortably was an afterthought.

The office was dominated by a desk and every open space was decorated with mementos of a long and celebrated naval career. On the desk sat a small die-cast model of a Grumman F6F Hellcat marked with the roundels of the United States. On another wall, a black Jolly Rogers flag hung, a parting gift from some friends of his when he was given command of *Independence*. There were maps, flags, patches, and photographs on the walls as well. He was pictured shaking hands with everyone from foreign officers to presidents. The photograph of him alongside President Slater was especially dear to him.

Alderman ignored all of this and took a seat behind his desk beneath a solitary porthole which let in a modicum of natural light. He picked up the phone receiver that sat on his desk, allowing a moment for the line to connect.

"I'm here. Patch him through."

After a series of clicks, the call connected by satellite, causing a slight delay on the line.

"Admiral Gideon, sir," Alderman said.

"Ernest," Gideon replied. "Did you hear about Trondheim?"

"Damn shame," Alderman said, matching Gideon's informality, "but we knew it was coming."

"Doesn't make it hurt any less. I just got out of a meeting of the Joint Chiefs about the whole Scandinavian front. What's your take?"

Alderman thought before speaking. He knew Gideon well enough to know that he was testing him. "We're going to lose the remaining minor enclaves no matter what we do. Soviets are holding all the cards there since they cut through Sweden. Logistics are slowing them down, but it's a matter of time. I would personally advocate evacuating the holdouts north of Bergen and using them to reinforce the Bergen-Oslo line."

"I'm sensing a 'but.'"

"But," Alderman allowed, "that's a hell of a tall order. We'd be sailing into a shooting gallery, under Soviet air cover and within range of land-based anti-ship missiles. We'd take a pounding without a hell of a lot more backup. We'd be stretched thin to provide air cover for a sea evacuation and also hold the gap."

"We can't be everywhere at once," Gideon said. "I agree with your assessment, and I don't think we can risk an evacuation in these circumstances. The prize is Bergen-Oslo. Orville wants a win; losing Norway is a non-option."

Orville—General Orville, the Chairman of the Joint Chiefs —had been forced to swallow a lot of defeats, starting with Yugoslavia. Norway falling could be the final straw for NATO. If the country fell, it would spell disaster, not just militarily but politically as other NATO member states would see their own necks next on the chopping block. Losing their foothold in Scandinavia would also greatly reduce their ability to conduct air operations in Europe and would provide the Soviets incalculable benefits, not the least of which was providing more air bases to stage attacks on NATO shipping from.

"What about the Air Force?" Alderman asked.

"The Soviets have knocked out just about every airfield we have left in Norway," Gideon said. "They're driving like hell on the rest of our forces there. They have us on the ropes and they know it."

It wasn't good news. Fixed airfields made inviting targets for Soviet aviation and artillery. His carriers, by virtue of their mobility, avoided a lot of those problems. Unfortunately, ground attack would mean diverting more attention from his air patrols hunting Soviet subs and aircraft in the North Sea, not to mention exposing them to greater risk from Soviet SAM sites. Like Gideon said, they couldn't be everywhere at once, sacrifices were going to have to be made.

"We can provide air cover," Alderman said. "If we move closer to the coast, then we can step up aerial interdiction and ground attack missions inland. With a little extra air power maybe we can stop those assaults."

"It would certainly help," Gideon said. "And there's something else," Gideon said, his voice dropping conspiratorially. "Something I wanted to tell you ahead of official channels...."

Having friends in high places had its benefits. "I'm listening."

"Brace yourself. Satellite imagery shows that the Soviet Northern Fleet has assembled and is sailing south, following the coast."

Alderman was so stunned that he was certain he'd misheard his friend. "The *surface* fleet?"

"The whole damn thing," Gideon said.

"Coming out for a fight?" Alderman was incredulous. "After blowing all that time and money on that boondoggle they're going to throw it all away? What are they playing at?"

"It hasn't been made official yet, but safe money is that they're gunning for the sea lane between Norway and the UK, trying to cut the flow of supplies and reinforcements and strangle the beachhead."

"That's a hell of a big risk. They have to know we'll kick their teeth in if they try."

"That may be, but Ivan's likely under a lot of pressure to win this thing and fast. We can't discount that this is a political order rather than a practical one. It wouldn't be the first time in history the Russians threw a fleet away. Plus, you said it yourself: they blew all this money on a fancy fleet, how can they not use it?"

Alderman was still stunned. It was suicidal. He just couldn't believe the Soviets would throw their fleet away on a fool's crusade. There was a part of him that was worried they knew something he didn't. He dismissed the thought as quickly as it surfaced. There was nothing the Soviets could surprise him with. He had enough forces to cover the whole Norwegian Sea and then some. If the Soviets wanted a fight, he was happy to give it to them.

"Then we'll sail out to meet them," Alderman said. He

could have the *Belleau Wood* and *Anzio* groups take up a close position to the coast. It would allow them to more efficiently conduct air support missions and also oppose anything the Soviets might send that way, yet still leave enough forces to screen the GIUK gap. Two birds with one stone. He wasn't quite ready to play his full hand yet. He'd wait to see what the Soviets had up their sleeve before committing. But if the opportunity were to arise then he could concentrate the fleet and smash them.

"If we can take the Northern Fleet off the board, it will be a huge win. We need one," Gideon said.

"Yes, sir."

"Well, you know what you're doing. Let's make sure we get a USS *Norwegian Sea* on the lists, eh Ernest?"

Alderman smiled grimly. He certainly hoped there would be no need to commemorate a battle, but if there was going to be one, he would make damn sure they won it. "Yes, sir."

***

15

The destruction scattered across the tarmac wasn't total, but it was extensive enough to leave Morris feeling anxious. Grinder steered the humvee around the craters that pocked the runway. Tires rumbled over loose chunks of asphalt and scattered missile and bomb casings. A civilian Boeing 747 sat burning on the edge of the runway, nose down in a ditch, its fuselage peppered with shrapnel holes.

Worse than the mechanical carnage were the bodies. Casualties had been heavy among the ground crew of Wyvern squadron. Their bodies—what was left of them—had been painstakingly lined up and tagged for burial. Morris watched a team of NCOs travel the lines of corpses trying to identify men whose faces and bodies were mangled beyond recognition. Sometimes all they had to go on were wedding bands or tattoos.

It turned Morris's stomach just thinking about it, and what he saw next was worse.

The area around the main airport terminal was lit a strobing blue and red courtesy of the flock of fire trucks and ambulances surrounding the building. Its modern exterior was marred with burns and entire sections of the roof had collapsed.

A mixture of military and civilian rescue personnel filed in and out of the building, sometimes hustling quickly out with someone on a stretcher, other times carrying out a limp body.

Grinder parked the Humvee in an open spot and swore under his breath. "Those bastards."

Morris assumed he meant the Russians, and couldn't

disagree. Both pilots got out of the vehicle and moved closer to the rescue operation, pushing gracefully through a milling crowd of civilian onlookers. Many of them were wide-eyed, shocked. Plenty others were covered in ash and soot. Some wept, others were furious. Morris thought of his own family and imagined them being in this sort of danger. The thought boiled his blood but, unlike the people here, he had the power to *do* something if they could just get the runway repaired.

Evidence of calm pre-war life was intermixed with the chaos of the present day. A bulletin board by the doorway held a poster for Gardermoen Raceway with a picture of a drag racer alongside notices looking for missing people. People sat dejectedly on the pavement of the taxiway amidst medical debris, bandage packaging, and wrappers.

A loud American voice carried to them through the din of the crowd. "Not good enough. Round up whoever you can. Cooks, clerks, I don't care. We're gonna need more boots on the ground before the day is up."

Following the sound, they found the eye of the storm. A cluster of NATO officers—a mixture of American, British, Danish, Norwegian, and Swedish military—were coordinating the rescue effort with intensity. At the middle of this flock of uniforms was a tall man in the mottled green/brown camo pattern of Norway. His hair was a shock of white, his face craggy and severe. His orders were being relayed through the noisy American—a major—that Morris and Grinder had heard.

Morris pushed forward to approach them, snapping to attention and saluting them once they'd noticed him. A glance at the nametag and rank of the Norwegian gave Morris everything he needed to address him. "General Dahlsen, sir. Major Morris, Wyvern Squadron."

Dahlsen fixed Morris with his cool gaze. "Wyvern?" He asked through the interpreter. "The fighter unit here?"

"Yes, sir."

"You can see we have a lot on our plate, Major," the interpreter said, speaking for Dahlsen. "What is it?"

"Sir, I'm looking to get my people airborne. We can't do any good on the ground. But we need the runway repaired."

"You have engineers for that, Major."

"Yes, sir," Morris agreed, "But they took a beating in the missile attack. A lot of their heavy equipment was destroyed. A lot of people are dead."

"We've got over two hundred dead here," Dahlsen returned coldly.

"I understand, sir. But to get this runway clear, we're going to need civilian assistance. If we can get in the air then we can hit back, or at least run air patrols to stop follow on attacks."

Dahlsen glanced at his aide, the American major, wordlessly leaving the answer to him.

"We've got every backhoe and bulldozer in Oslo tied up digging trenches and clearing streets right now," the major said. "There's nothing to spare, Major. You're going to have to make do."

"Sir," Morris pressed, "with respect, once we're in the air you can have the bulldozers return to other tasks."

Again, the general didn't need to answer, he let his aide do the talking. "Morris, do you know how long it will take to move a half dozen bulldozers across the city to clear the runway? That's assuming we can even round up what you're looking for."

Morris's heart sank further. There was no help coming. He was stranded.

"If you can't fly, grab a shovel. We need all the hands we can get." With that, Dahlsen and his flock of officers moved on, bringing a semblance of order and control to the chaos where they passed.

Once they were out of earshot, Morris swore loudly.

"You said it," Grinder said.

"'Grab a shovel'? Give me a break. Every minute we're sitting down here, people are dying out there. We can do more than move dirt around!"

"We knew it was a slim chance," Grinder said.

Morris sighed and sat on a cement parking barrier, staring at the flashing lights of a nearby fire truck.

"Listen, maybe the general is right. We're grounded. Unless you have a spare runway we might as well start digging. At least it's something."

Morris looked at Grinder like he'd said something insightful. "Oh my God."

"What?"

Morris stood up and hurried back the way they came, weaving around civilians.

"What? Voodoo?" Grinder called, following along behind him.

Morris reached the bulletin board they'd passed and snatched a flier off of it, showing it to Grinder.

Grinder looked awestruck. "You think we're gonna be that lucky?"

"Let's find out," Morris replied.

A minute later they stood at the southern edge of the Gardermoen Raceway, a stretch of pristine pavement just over a kilometer long and just wide enough to admit an Eagle.

"Think it'll work?" Morris asked.

Grinder surveyed the drag strip. "For takeoff? Sure. Landing will be…impossible. Too short."

"We'd have to switch fields," Morris said, nodding. "Again. One way trip."

Grinder thought it over. "I guess that's not our call. That's for higher up the chain."

"Right," Morris agreed. "Let's round up who we can and see what it will take to taxi our Eagles over here on short notice. I want to be ready if they want us to go."

Grinder shook his head, amazed. "Crazy. Using a dragstrip to launch an F-15."

Morris thought of the Swedish soldiers who'd gotten him to safety, and Astrid. "We do whatever we must."

***

16

White-hot shrapnel whistled through the foliage over Karlsdotter's head, sending her ducking lower in her fighting position. A heartbeat later another shell burst nearby, momentarily deafening her. Karlsdotter felt more impacts from shells in the hollow of her chest as the blasts walked over the Swedish positions. Short of a direct hit or an overhead airburst, they were relatively safe in these dugouts. The Soviet barrage was all fire and fury with little to show for it save for acres of craters and splintered trees.

It was an agonizing minute before enough of Karlsdotter's hearing had returned that she could speak again. She heard a final dull "thump" not far away. It was a sound they'd heard more of lately, the sound of a dud round striking the ground and failing to detonate.

"Fire support?" she said again, her voice hoarse from shouting over the ringing of her ears.

Sundquist, the platoon's radioman, shook his head, pressing his headset to his ears. "The same message, Corporal, all assets tasked."

"Bullshit!" Karlsdotter returned. "Where are our mortars? Artillery? Where is the God damned Air Force?"

Sundquist could only shake his head apologetically.

The Soviets were pushing everywhere at once, it was the only explanation, and a lone platoon of Home Guard infantry in a rural stretch of woods was low priority.

The barrage was tapering off which likely meant another infantry assault wasn't far behind. This one would have to be repelled without Sergeant Hellström's leadership. The others in the unit would be looking to her. It had only been with the help of mortar fire that they'd thrown off the last Soviet assault. She wasn't sure they could do it alone, but what choice was there?

Karlsdotter turned to Sundquist, about to speak when a flash of movement and a spray of dirt in her face cut her short. She fell back on instinct, away from the threat, looking down to see what caused it.

An artillery shell stuck from the ground directly between her and Sundquist, buried in the damp clay in the trench floor.

She stared at the shell lodged in the dirt scarcely a meter from her, knowing that she was going to die. She couldn't move. There was no chance she could get away from the blast in time anyway, there was nowhere to go. One heartbeat became two, and then became many, the shell remained inert.

The certainty that she was going to die was gradually replaced with a certainty that she *could* have died.

Karlsdotter looked up at Sundquist who stared back, eyes wide with the same revelation.

There was no guarantee the shell couldn't still find its deadly voice, but Karlsdotter found hers first. "Get the mortar section on the radio. Get me *anything*," she said, voice level. "If they take this hill, they'll unravel kilometers of line."

Sundquist stared back blankly.

"Sundquist!"

He blinked. "Y-yes. Right!"

Karlsdotter began to climb from the dugout, stopped, and looked back at him. "And find a new position! Move toward Bucht's position on the left, I'll meet back there." When Sundquist hesitated, she added a firm "Go!"

They both scrambled out of the muddy hole, away from the danger posed by the dud shell and into the open air. Out of the frying pan, into the fire. Karlsdotter stayed on her belly, worming across the leaf litter of the forest floor.

Shells howled banshee-like overhead, mercifully crashing down on other parts on the line instead of on top of her.

Groping her way across the ground, she didn't dare lift her head more than a few inches from the ground. She kept thinking of Sergeant Hellström's severed artery and Larsson, limp and still, facedown in the dirt. It only took one shell splinter to forever alter the trajectory of her life and end her story before it even started.

Reaching out, her hand found a void, a foxhole.

Karlsdotter pulled herself in, rolling on top of its current occupant awkwardly. After a moment of struggle she disentangled herself. An apology died half-formed on her lips when she saw that the man she shared the narrow fighting position with was dead.

He was curled in a fetal ball, knees to his chest, head leaned against the earthen wall, eyes blank. The ground beneath him was pooled with sticky red from an unseen wound. He looked so young, like a child, his face drained of all color. She didn't recognize him at first until she saw the panoply of explosives worn on a bandolier looped around his body.

"Fjellner," she said the name aloud, a one word eulogy for the platoon's sapper.

It was then that Karlsdotter realized she could hear herself again. The barrage had stopped, replaced with a terrible silence met by the keening in her ears.

Springing to her feet, she primed her rifle and took aim from the fighting position east, downhill, into the shattered woods.

At other fighting positions, the men of her platoon were readying for the assault that inevitably followed the shells. Seconds ticked by, a minute. She was just beginning to think there would be no attack when she heard the throaty growl of a diesel engine struggling uphill.

This was new and "new" wasn't good.

Machine gun fire ripped through the remains of the undergrowth, cutting up the hill, probing for the Swedish positions.

Karlsdotter ducked reflexively, uncertain of the origin of the gunfire.

Return fire came from a friendly machine gun position. Rounds belted into the forest with wild abandon before being silenced with a deafening boom.

The foxhole—scarcely visible off to her right—volcanoed up in a shower of dirt. Karlsdotter thought maybe it was a lucky hit with artillery until she caught sight of the tank working its way up the hill.

T-62. The identification swam to the front of her mind from some half-forgotten training session, enemy recognition lessons. It was a main battle tank, but an old one. Capped with a circular turret and wreathed with smoke pouring from its gun barrel, it accelerated, fighting through the undergrowth.

"Tank!" Karlsdotter cried out, unsure if anyone could even hear her. "Tank!" her voice cracked from the strain.

The tank fired a staccato series of bursts from its coaxial machine gun, sweeping the fire over her head.

Every nerve in her body screamed at her to flee, to throw down her rifle and run from the metal monster. It would have arguably been the smart thing to do. But she didn't do it, something kept her anchored here in this hole. She couldn't say for sure what it was, just that she wasn't allowed to run. Not anymore.

More rifle fire cracked out from Swedish positions at the tank. Maybe they were targeting weak points like vision blocks, but Karlsdotter couldn't imagine they'd have any luck.

The tank fired its main gun again, felling a towering pine tree which crashed over the scarred battlefield in a shower of branches and needles.

A rocket from a Carl Gustav roared out and hit the tank dead center, square in its heavily armored glacis plate. The anti-tank munition burst harmlessly in a flurry of smoke and flames. Karlsdotter was painfully aware that her platoon was too short of those rounds to keep up that game.

Although the tank was apparently without any close infantry support, it was also untouchable.

She wasn't willing to start throwing away the lives of her

men in a losing battle. The line was undone.

There was nothing she could do but watch as the vehicle continued on, firing idiotically, blindly.

Blindly.

Another dim memory of combat training. Visibility from a tank was poor at the best of times. Now, advancing through a hazy forest, it was a miracle the crew could even navigate around the trees. If it couldn't see, and with no escorting infantry, they had a chance.

Karlsdotter risked lifting her head and looked around for someone, anyone, who may have an unfired rocket.

The only Swede in sight was poor Fjellner.

Karlsdotter looked with sudden realization at the sapper's body and the landmines he carried.

She crouched down and lifted one up, reading labels until she found what she was looking for: **FFV**. An anti-tank mine. She picked up two of the dinner plate-sized mines and set the delay timers with shaking hands. Sixty seconds to arm. It was enough, it would have to be.

She stood and peered over the lip of the foxhole at the steel monster rattling steadily closer. There was only one chance to do this before the Soviets followed up this attack with infantry.

Standing, she scrambled from the hole and onto unsteady feet. She held a mine in each hand as she ran forward, all too aware that she was carrying ten kilograms of explosives straight at a vehicle which could crush her flat in an instant.

Dodging stumps and leaping fallen logs, she found herself directly in the tank's path. She watched the treads crush a toppled tree with a crack of dead wood. She had only a second to eyeball the tank's intended path. Because the trees forced it onto a narrow path, the press of the woods made it easier to see where the tank would be in moments.

How much time did she have left? Were the mines armed now?

She couldn't worry about it. With her heart in her throat, Karlsdotter crouched and set her mines up a few feet apart, hopeful that at least one of them would find the vehicle. When she looked up the tank loomed huge, roaring and crashing toward her.

She turned away from her approaching mortality and ran.

Over the sound of the diesel and clatter of treads she heard the whine of electric motors as the turret turned to take in a new target. Her.

The foxhole was impossibly far away. Her breath burned like acid in her lungs, her legs felt like lead. She wasn't going to reach it.

Another body crashed into her, knocking her flat a moment before a pair of tremendous explosions snuffed out her hearing again. Hot air washed over her, the blastwave scattering her with leaves and bark.

Sitting up, she looked back and saw the T-62 had thrown a track, smoke and flames licked at its sides. The hatches came open and the crew emerged like men crawling from the belly of a beast.

Rifle fire cut the gunner down, dropping him back into the tank.

The second man out of the turret was likewise struck, but he managed to get free, rolling down the side of the vehicle to land on the ground. No one else emerged.

"Are you alright?" Bergman asked, out of breath.

Karlsdotter looked at him, momentarily puzzled before realizing he'd tackled her. "Stupid to leave your hole," she retorted.

Bergman snorted and broke into a boyish grin. "That's what I was coming to tell you."

A new sound interrupted any reply: the low, rising whine of jet engines.

They each looked up just before a pair of American F-18s tore through the sky above them, trailing a deafening cone of noise in their wake. After the fighters passed they could speak again.

"God bless Sundquist," Karlsdotter said, adrenaline making

her hands shake. "Come on, back to cover."

"Yes, Corporal."

***

17

Bergen. Bergen at last.

Seymour breathed in the sharp Norwegian air. He'd come out onto the deck to smoke but instead found himself transfixed by this place's natural beauty.

Pink and blue streaks colored the horizon to the west of Bergen. Rays from the sinking sun streamed through clouds as it dipped slowly below the horizon. The light chop of the waves around *Somerset* flashed the colors of this pastel display back to the men on deck.

The city of Bergen was picturesque. Red-roofed houses scaled the green-gray mountainside behind them. Just above them the crest of the mountain stood out against the gauzy gray of low clouds beyond. Nestled in one of Norway's fjords, the city was a tourist haven and commercial hub, a fact that now made it a critical port on the Scandinavian front.

From out here, the city looked postcard perfect, but Seymour knew it was an illusion. Every day Bergen's city streets became more and more congested with refugees fleeing the fighting further north and east. Bergen carried the hope of escape or safety and, while it was slim to be sure, it was a better chance than zero.

The escorts of the convoy held back in the broad bay, joining with the other NATO warships here to form a loose cordon around the city. Even without binoculars, Seymour could faintly see the fruits of their labor—the merchant ships of the convoy—anchored just outside of the city or moored at the docks, loading and unloading.

Given its proximity to British airfields in Scotland, Bergen was in a good position for holding out against any concerted Soviet attack to take it, provided the Scandinavians could stem the Soviet tide. It was also full of hungry mouths and short of the infrastructure needed to house the mobs of refugees that fled from the encroaching Soviet war machine. As soldiers shuttled in, non-combatants shuttled out, filling the holds of vessels like the cruise ship *Million* to be evacuated back across the sea to relative safety in Britain, France, and Spain.

Back.

The notion sent a chill down Seymour's spine.

The sight of *Callenburgh* burning and sinking still haunted his mind. He could see the pale oval faces of both the living and the dead as they bobbed in the surf.

It could have been his ship—his boys dying in the frigid ocean. Him.

In a matter of days, they would take that trip again, bringing the convoy back again through hostile seas.

Really, it was just a numbers game. How many trips could he make back and forth unmolested? How many Russian submarines were still lurking in the deep? How many bombers and missiles were free to strike out at them?

Dwelling on it would do no good. Seymour scowled at having spent his entire short break out here pondering instead of smoking. Reluctantly, he turned back and ducked in through the hatchway, back into the ship. Within a minute he'd reached the bridge.

While free from the threats of the open ocean, the bridge crew were no less active now, monitoring sensors and checking weapon readiness.

By the fjord's nature they were ringed with high mountains with the open mouth of the bay at one end and the city at the other. This meant any attack would have to come in high, but it also meant it could drop below the horizon of the mountains if it felt threatened.

Seymour turned his gaze out to sea again, this time to the small knot of American combat vessels they'd met in Bergen.

He raised his binoculars to take in the flagship, the *Virginia*-class cruiser USS *Arkansas*. It was in the process of firing a salvo of Tomahawk missiles, sending up periodic pillars of smoke. Each rocketed up and out of the vertical launch tube before leveling off and burning north east. The missiles were directed at Soviet command and control centers further inland, part of NATO's combined effort to shake the Soviet's dogged grip on the peninsula. Seymour didn't know if it made a significant difference, but he had to believe it did.

The other warships were, like *Sommerset*, here to provide air support to the city and ward off Soviet air attacks on a juicy target like the port facilities of Bergen. On the opposite end of the harbor, far from the warships and clearly marked, was the American hospital ship *Mercy*. Her wards were full of the sick and wounded, with more coming every day.

"It's just a matter of time before we're loaded up and ready to shuttle back," Seymour said, more for his own benefit than for Smith's. "By the way, did we ever confirm if *Oslo* found survivors from *Callenburgh*?"

Smith opened his mouth to reply but never got a chance.

As before, there was next to no warning before the enemy came.

"Contacts on radar! Numerous contacts!"

Seymour startled to action. "Take us to action stations. Damage control teams to their posts." And once again the dice of fate were rolling, the lives of his crew at stake.

The PA warbled to life. "*Action stations, action stations.*"

Seymour found his way to the radar station, moving among sailors bent over their stations.

The escort ships in Bergen harbor collected data individually, each representing its own keyhole image of the battlefield. This data was parsed and relayed to the USS *Arkansas*, the centerpoint of the task force. Collectively, this intelligence collecting network swiftly painted a clear picture of the Soviet attack.

"Three separate groups with different axes of advance," the

radar officer explained to Seymour who looked over his plot. "Designated Raid One, Raid Two, Raid Three. I make about thirty aircraft total. Fencers."

The number left Seymour staggered. He resisted the urge to repeat it for confirmation, knowing it would only further shake his already rattled bridge crew. At times like this a captain had to be a pillar of stability. Thirty craft was a tough pill to swallow. A few missiles had gotten in when they had only been faced with a dozen attack craft. How would they stop all thirty from getting through?

Seymour ran his eyes over the impressive display of offensive power. "Right," he said at last. "Identify only the ones we have a hope of hitting. Clear targets with Bergen air defense first to make sure we're not targeting our own." Seymour paused. "If we have any birds up there. I don't want to risk taking them out."

"Aye, sir!"

Outside, the Sea Dart system swung into action, loading and firing. Missiles streaked away, racing for the clouds and the invisible radar returns they followed.

Somerset joined with *Fuchs*, *Nauls*, and *Gloucester* in unleashing a swarm of missiles at the approaching targets. The Fencers flew high enough for their radar returns to be visible even above the tall peaks of the mountains lining the bay. At this distance, neither side could see the other without the aid or radar, engaging well out of visual range. It was more a contest of computers than men at this point. Guidance systems struggled to identify and hone in on targets as defense systems warmed up to deploy. All the men of the task force kept their attention anxiously on their work, mindful that each passing moment could be their last.

Friendly air patrols were scrambled from Bergen and moved to engage the incoming aerial attack, though it remained to be seen if they had enough numbers to do any good. Ordinarily an orbiting AWACS craft would provide early warning of large air attacks like this, but the Soviets had recently gotten into the habit of targeting them and shooting them down with long range air-to-air missiles. It meant AWACS patrols were fewer and better protected.

Seymour was only vaguely aware of the larger aspect of the battle, being more worried about his slice of it. The Sea Dart was re-loaded as quickly as men and machines could move the missiles and a second salvo was launched.

The monochromatic radar display revealed clumps of dots moving to and fro as NATO aircraft dueled with the Soviet attack groups. Every few moments, one or two blips would vanish.

"Splash, sir. First hit confirmed. A kill."

Seymour felt no joy. All he could think was that if his missiles were hitting the enemy, then theirs would soon find him as well.

"Raid Three is breaking up and turning back," the radar officer said, triumph in his voice.

Seymour frowned, returning to the radar plot. They hadn't lost enough to be deterred. Soviet air tactics were infamous for their high tolerance of losses. The truth was bitter but couldn't remain unsaid. "It's likely they've already fired and turned back."

The color drained from the radar operator's face.

"Fire port and starboard chaff decoys," Seymour said. "Maximum range. And transmit a warning to the task force."

"Aye, sir."

Seymour felt a dull vibration as the decoy launchers activated, filling the air with false targets to tempt the Soviet missiles astray. They didn't have to wait long.

"*Missile sighted to port,*" the warning came over the intercom, "*All hands brace for impact.*"

Seymour clumsily wedged himself beside his radar operator, between two computer terminals. All the high tech gear in the world and they still had to rely on human eyes to spot incoming threats.

A minute passed in tense silence.

"Enemy missile diverted. Repeat, missile threat is clear."

The tension in Seymour's chest relaxed, but only for a moment before the CIWS activated and fired on their starboard side, firing a glowing stream of gunfire at an unseen missile which exploded with enough force to rock the ship.

Someone swore loudly with fright.

Given how low and fast these missiles were, spotting was inconsistent. There were no guarantees that a killing shot wasn't closing on them now.

"Damage report," Seymour said. It seemed they'd been lucky, but that missile had gone off close enough to leave a lingering doubt.

"Just rang our doorbell, sir. No hit. No shrapnel."

Seymour crossed to the front of the bridge and lifted his binoculars to his face, scanning the horizon and until he found *Arkansas*. Mercifully, she was still floating, apparently unharmed. Seymour's relief was short lived as he sighted smoke.

"Who is that?" he asked. "Who got hit?" He didn't need to wait for an answer, he could see it plainly himself. His heart sank. "My God."

"*Million*, sir. She reports hit badly, fires throughout and heavy casualties."

Million, the civilian cruise ship they'd escorted into the harbor was in flames. Her pristine white flank marred with plumes of smoke and charred, blackened paint.

With such a large radar profile, it was no surprise the cruise ship had drawn fire. Seymour could only imagine men, women, and children fighting for their lives as the interior burned up. As was often the case in war, there wasn't time to dwell on the tragedy.

"New missile spread launched, sir," Radar said. "I caught a blip then lost them."

"They're diving to wave-height," Seymour said. That meant they were already close. "Helm, take us to flank speed, put us between *Arkansas* and those launches."

"Aye, sir!"

Somerset accelerated, the bridge listing slightly and the thrum of her engines increasing.

Seymour listened to the chatter and flow of combat as they cruised into a defensive position. Fresh Sea Dart launches, downed enemy craft. The numbers were cold, unyielding, and they weren't on their side.

A voice came over the intercom again. "Enemy missile, port side! Brace for impact!"

Seymour gripped the console so hard that his knuckles turned white and listened to the buzzsaw sound of the CIWS guns firing, a last effort to down the enemy missile as it raced for the kill. He saw only a flash of movement off the bow before the missile closed the distance and struck.

The ship vibrated with the impact. The sensation was subtle, but it took a lot to move a 5,000 ton warship. Seymour knew it could have been worse and really felt like it *should* have been worse. He straightened up, still gripping the edge of the plotter table. The question this time wasn't *if* they had been hit. "Damage report."

A response came back from one of the external lookouts, relayed by an officer. "Looks like it failed to detonate. Glanced off our bow."

Lucky. *Damn* lucky.

"Any penetration?" Seymour asked.

"Damage control teams are checking now, sir. No word yet."

Seymour looked to his XO. "Go forward and link up with damage control. I want you to find out exactly how bad it is." If the hit was more serious than anyone realized, they could already be dead. Seymour needed someone he could trust to take command.

"Aye, sir!" Smith said, ducking out of the bridge at a jog.

Seymour turned his attention back to the task force. He saw heavy black smoke rising to their left, he didn't need to ask to know that it was *Gloucester*.

"God help them," he said.

Ahead, off their bow a fireball blossomed on the waves, billowing skyward before subsiding into roiling smoke. Debris rained down from the hit, splashing across the bay.

"That was *Arkansas*," a sailor said in awe. "God, she's burning."

The attack wasn't over yet. Seymour opened his mouth to say as much when *Somerset*'s bridge exploded with such violence and speed that Seymour was momentarily bewildered at how he'd ended up on the floor. It took another moment to realize that he wasn't breathing. He sucked in a shaky breath and tasted smoke and blood. Sight, sound, and smell came back to him in a terrible wave of burning plastic, the groaning of the wounded, and the ceaseless warbling warning klaxon.

They'd been hit again and this time it wasn't a dud.

The smoke on the bridge was whisked out by a cold dry air which raced in through the blown open forward viewports.

Seymour tried to call out but his voice failed him and he instead let out a violent wet hacking cough. Trying to sit up, he found he was pinned by a weight across his chest. The body of the radar operator lay over him, his uniform stained with blood, his dead eyes staring at the ceiling.

Seymour tried to shift the body off of him and found that his right arm wouldn't respond. His whole body was weak. The pain came a second after the shock, lancing through his right arm and shoulder. Seymour groaned involuntarily.

"Help," Seymour said. He meant to call out, but his voice came as a whisper. He needed a medic, he needed to get off the bridge. He sucked in another painful breath, becoming alarmed at the wet wheezing sound his chest made. "Help!"

If anyone on the bridge was in condition to help him, no one could hear him.

Seymour lay on the cold decking and felt his life ebbing away. His vision grayed at the edges and his hearing faded to a hum. The pain in his right side faded with it, leaving him less agonized and more contemplative. He thought about his son, his wife, his parents, his men still fighting for their lives on this ship. Some part of him was aware that he should be frightened, but he only felt tired.

"Over here!" Smith's muffled voice broke through Seymour's dimming consciousness.

A pair of figures in smoke hoods knelt over Seymour, pulling the body of the radar operator free. He couldn't make out their faces, but he recognized Smith's voice. "He's bleeding, get a doctor."

The second figure moved away at a run.

Seymour's mouth moved but at first no sound came. He tried again. "How bad?"

"Punched through the bow, portside. Hit the forward gun magazine."

"Hydraulics," Seymour croaked.

Smith nodded. "We've got a damage team trying to keep the flames back from the launcher hydraulics."

The gun magazine was bad enough, but if the Sea Dart hydraulics caught fire that would certainly doom the ship.

"Can we save her?" Seymour asked.

"We're getting a doc for you, Captain," Smith replied.

Seymour found that he couldn't see anymore. He licked his lips and tasted blood. "Beach her. Beach her if you have to. Save the boys. Save the boys, abandon the ship."

"Try not to move, sir," Smith said, voice wavering.

Seymour tried to shake his head but failed. "Tell my son. Tell him." He didn't know what to say and there was no time.

"You've got to hold on, sir. Medical teams are on the way. Just hold on."

But Seymour couldn't hold on. He slipped away only a moment later.

**

18

The map of the Norwegian coast pinned to the wall in *Tashkent's* command and control center was increasingly filled with pleasing red marks. Both civilian airports and NATO air bases were marked out or appended with notes detailing their fates.

Seized by VDV landing forces.

Neutralized by runway cratering.

Fuel silos destroyed.

Aircraft storage eliminated.

The pressure being placed on the NATO enclave by his comrades in the army was necessitating a heightened pace of air operations, which was burning out what little stocks the enemy had available. When coupled with intense air and missile attacks, NATO's air capabilities were crumbling. Of course, the Soviets had paid a fearsome toll to exact this victory, but it was a vital part of his plan all the same.

These successes were coupled with the ongoing predation of NATO convoys by his air forces. Heavy losses among convoy ships and their escorts was sapping enemy ground opposition of its strength. Without shells, missiles, and bullets, all of the fighting spirit in the world was useless. The balance of power in Scandinavia was rapidly tilting into favor of the Soviet Union.

A slow, predatory grin crept across Admiral Zharkov's face. He couldn't help but feel a certain amount of giddiness at their success. He should have been tired, all things considered. It was past midnight and he'd been awake for twenty-four hours now, but his master plan required careful oversight. The distant ache for sleep was buried beneath a driving desire for victory.

The hum and chatter of computer consoles and their operators around him reminded Zharkov to retain some decorum and he wiped the smirk from his face, stilling his nerves. His body felt electric, like a live wire, the thrill of the game running through him.

Taking his attention from NATO's airfields, he concentrated instead on the marks across the laminated sea—NATO naval assets, or at least their best estimated positions.

Zharkov was outnumbered, severely so. Any standup fight would be a massacre. He had to rely on the oldest military adages to ensure success, beginning with deception.

"What is the latest word from our AWACS craft?" Zharkov asked. He phrased the question aloud to the air in front of him, feeling no need to address the officer in particular who responded.

"Reports indicate heightened naval-air activity across Norway. We are seeing regular sorties inland. These have been cross-referenced with reports from our comrades on the ground in Scandinavia who verify sightings of naval aircraft, primarily F-18s and A-6s."

Zharkov nodded, satisfied. The American carriers were taking up the slack of the reduced airfields. The Swedish air force was mostly destroyed after prolonged attritional combat with the Soviet air force and air defenses. This would be hell for Soviet forces on the ground, but it meant that many fewer factors for him to worry about.

"We also have indications of aircraft concentration east of Bergen."

Zharkov looked to the marked spot on his map and peaked an eyebrow. "The fleet moving closer." In peacetime the West let their carriers operate solo at the head of small groups of escorts and support craft. With the increased risk against those floating airfields from missiles, aircraft, and submarines, NATO had concentrated them into strike groups.

Carriers operated as teams and redoubled their escorts. It would make it that much harder for "lone wolf" tactics to catch a carrier off guard as had happened in the Adriatic with *Gettsburg*, but it also meant it was easier to keep track of all of them.

"To protect the convoys between England and Norway," Zharkov said. It wasn't a question, but his subordinate answered anyway.

"Yes, Comrade Admiral."

Zharkov nodded once, firmly. NATO was dancing to his tune but still thought they were calling the shots. This fleet concentration could only be in anticipation of a great carrier battle, the likes of which hadn't been seen since the Second World War. NATO was certain to win in such a confrontation fought on its terms. Then the convoys would be safe from Soviet depredation, and Norway would hold out for a while longer.

Once again, a sharp smile slipped past Zharkov's guard. They hadn't yet realized that it wasn't the convoys that he was after.

"I believe that we've put the enemy into an ideal strike range for our comrades in the naval air arm," Zharkov said. "Inform our naval strike regiments that they may begin their first attack."

"Yes, Comrade Admiral!"

Zharkov narrowed his eyes at the mark representing the NATO fleet gathered south of him. Decades of theory were about to be put into practice, the first true blow against NATO naval supremacy. It would be interesting to see how they weathered this storm.

***

Fedorovich's squadron took off just as they had landed, screaming down the runway in pairs before pulling up and climbing dramatically skyward. For all of Babayev's sadistic tendency to put the bomber through rough air, he'd climbed quickly and competently, joining the others as they filled the sky.

The sky was a dull purple slowly burning toward red as the sun threatened to crest the horizon. Fedorovich was tired, a condition he was sure he shared with the men under his command, but just like them, he was excited. Not giddy, but eager. A plan was coming together, a sword was being drawn, and he and his bombers and their crews were on the razor's edge.

As Babayev focused on guiding their aircraft to the assembly point, Fedorovich toggled through radio channels, checking in with his pilots as they linked up in the skies over the Norwegian coast. Satisfied that his men were in good order, he relayed this to Osprey One, the regiment commander, who trailed the attack group dozens of kilometers behind the forward squadrons in a command plane.

One by one, the other squadron leaders also signaled readiness. The tenseness of their voices carried even over the fuzz of the radio. Everyone was poised and ready. Their first combat operation was finally here.

While they would never see with their own eyes the men they were about to kill, they knew that they were as real as they were. More troublingly, they knew there was a good likelihood that they would be killed in turn by enemies they never laid eyes on.

The only reason anyone ever willingly put themselves in danger like this, Fedorovich mused, was that they each expected that it would be someone else who died. No one going into combat for the first time ever imagined it could be him.

As the last of his squadron leaders reported in, Fedorovich checked their position on his map. Assembly point reached, they were to turn southwest, following the coastline and seeking contact with the enemy.

Each Tu-22M carried three, brand new Kh-32 missiles, which had enough range to be launched outside of the engagement range of the feared American Tomcat, an aircraft that was designed to kill their bombers as surely as they were designed to sink carriers. With a vertical attack profile, the Kh-32 was a difficult thing to stop once it had a target. They key would be getting there.

"Take us toward the next point," Fedorovich told Babayev.

"Yes, Comrade Major."

"Intact, please."

Babayev's mouth curled in a wry grin. "As you say, Comrade."

The bombers were traveling fast and light. No escorts, no spotters. Ideally, they would detect the radar emissions of the NATO picket ships before they themselves were spotted. From there, it would be a simple matter of determining the center of the NATO defense formation, which would surely be where the carriers were stationed. The Kh-32s were smart enough to find their own targets if they could get them in the right area.

Fedorovich toggled on the intercom to the aircraft's rear compartment. "Alekseev, distance to estimated firing area?"

"Approximately two hundred kilometers, Comrade Major!" The young aviator had been anticipating the question. Good. He was on his toes.

Fedorovich snapped the intercom back off. "Thirty minutes," he murmured to himself. Without external targeting data, they only had to get within two hundred kilometers of their prey in order for the missiles to do their deadly work. "Thirty minutes."

***

The last of the Soviet bombers finished climbing skyward, afterburners flaring, before Sergeant Landvik dared to move. Slinking back from the lip of the ridge, he stayed low, ducking through the tall grass on the hills outside of Trondheim, followed closely by a second Norwegian soldier, Kristiansen. A cool breeze from the fjord chilled him to the bone but did nothing for his hammering heart. He could faintly smell the smoke wafting from the city, the lingering after effects of the

Soviet attack.

Landvik's blood thundered in his ears, driven by nervous fear loud enough to drown out the early morning chirping of birds. He was exposed out here, vulnerable. He didn't dare relax until he reached the darkness of the woods at the base of the hill.

"Those were Backfires," Kristiansen said.

"You're positive?" Landvik asked.

The air traffic controller nodded and awkwardly slung his rifle. Unlike Landvik, his normal day job didn't require him to carry one. As a part of base security Landvik was better adapted to this sort of physical activity, but only slightly.

Kristiansen nodded. "No doubt. Easy to recognize."

Landvik was relying on the controller's technical knowledge here. He grunted acknowledgement. "Let's get back to the others, we'll want to call it in."

Both of them ducked into the woods, pushing through leafy undergrowth that ringed the edge of the forest before entering the clearer woods beyond. The forest was shaded from the thick canopy of overhead vegetation. While it meant the woods were marginally colder than the open field they'd come from, it also meant they were safer from being spotted by patrolling Soviet aircraft.

After a minute of walking, they were confronted by a voice. "Hold it!"

The man who stepped into view wore the uniform of a civilian police officer. His highly visible baby blue dress shirt was half-covered with a surplus camouflage jacket. He kept a captured Kalashnikov rifle close at hand.

The policeman, Erlend, grinned. "Any luck?"

"Don't jump out at us like that," Landvik growled.

Erlend only grinned wider. When the Soviets captured Trondheim, he had been one of the brave souls to join Landvik's small partisan band.

"Backfires," Kristiansen said. "Soviet naval bombers."

"Is that useful to us?" Erlend asked, the technicalities

meaningless to him.

"Not to us," Landvik said, moving past Erlend so the policeman followed behind. "But to someone."

Beyond another thick press of undergrowth was the main camp. The others here were a ragged mix of air base security troops, home guard, local police, and bold and enterprising civilian partisans.

They were dirty and exhausted, some of them wounded from the fighting in the city, armed with an eclectic mix of NATO, civilian, and captured Soviet weapons. It was a ragtag force which had fought hard before slipping away, avoiding the same fate as the rest of the overwhelmed defenders of the city. The night after Trondheim finally fell had been full of the sporadic crack of rifles and grenades as splinters of the trapped NATO defenders fought on, but those had since gone silent as small bands like Landvik's went to ground.

They didn't have enough ammunition to conduct any significant resistance anymore, and their food supply was equally bad. They were problems for the near future. Landvik wasn't worrying more than a single day in advance, but he knew he would likely have to disperse his force or surrender at some point.

He crossed the small camp, moving past the handful of wounded being treated at the base of a poplar tree by a volunteer medic. "Where is the phone?"

Another soldier pointed him toward the heavy case holding the satellite phone, their lifeline to the rest of the free world.

"Kristiansen, call it in. I counted at least twenty bombers taking off."

The other soldier picked up the phone case by its strap. "That's bad news for anything at sea. Maybe we can save some lives."

"Or maybe pay them back for Trondheim," the policeman added hopefully.

"Yes," Landvik said, "that too."

They didn't yet know it, but the info would come in time to

do only one of those things.

***

19

The airspace north of NATO's fleet was thick with radar waves as forward-deployed picket ships and patrolling aircraft prowled, searching for any would-be threats to the fleet. Major Fedorovich didn't have to see it with his own eyes to know it was there. What his aircraft's instruments couldn't detect he could imagine well enough, not to mention the data which was fed to him from the regimental command plane which collated information from sources across the sea including patrols of Soviet AWACs aircraft.

Even with Norway's airbases all knocked out or captured, there were plenty of threats. The British Royal Air Force, operating from Scotland, would be able to put out patrols of Tornados to scour the North Sea. Fleet-based aircraft posed their own threats. Harriers from the British, Mirages from the French and, most dangerous of all, the American F-14 Tomcats. That was not to mention the possibility of scattered road-based aircraft mounting patrols. With no escorting fighters, his Tupolevs moved fast enough to strike with little warning, but it also meant if they were intercepted, then they were virtually defenseless.

Fedorovich snapped the intercom toggle with a gloved finger. "Alekseev, position?"

"In the vicinity of the launch point, Comrade Major."

"Pavlov," Fedorovich continued, "Contacts?"

"Lots of radar returns, Major," Pavlov said. "None of them are from carrier-based transmitters."

"No surprise there. The Americans are smart enough to keep those switched off. They know we're looking for them after all." Fedorovich spared a glance out of the forward cockpit. He could faintly see a half dozen other bombers in combat spread. Their variable-geometry wings were swept back for maximum cruising speed. Even at Mach 2 they were still vulnerable. The safety speed provided was mostly illusory.

"Squadron leaders, Osprey One. Report positive contact with enemy fleet, over," the radio buzzed. A transmission over the regiment-wide band was risky. Command was antsy.

A steady chorus of negatives came in, which Fedorovich joined a moment later. "Osprey Three, negative contact." He had hoped to have a clear target at this point and was frustrated that their returns were minimal so far.

"Regiment hold course and maintain combat formation," Osprey One returned a moment later.

Fedorovich chewed his lip for a moment before swearing under his breath.

Every minute meant they were a minute closer to the NATO screen and certain detection. The longer they held this course the more likely it was that they would be detected and intercepted before they had a chance to deliver their weapons.

Babayev gave him a quick glance but said nothing.

Fedorovich answered his co-pilot's wordless question with a cold, silent look.

So they cruised on in tense silence. Fedorovich checked his map regularly and conferred with Alekseev, verifying they were on the heading command had fed them, the one they'd promised him would bear fruit.

"Contacts! Comrade Major, contacts!" Pavlov said, voice electric with excitement.

Fedorovich straightened up in his seat. "What do you have?"

"A glimmer southwest. Just a faint return, but I think it is a carrier group. It looks like the search radar of an *Arleigh Burke*-class."

An *Arleigh Burke* was an American anti-aircraft destroyer which was likely to be part of the outer picket line of any carrier group. That was almost certainly a hit, but Fedorovich needed to know for certain.

"Acknowledged. Babayev, change course to bear on it. Pavlov, ready the missiles. I want to make sure we have a positive lock before we fire." As the lead plane, once Fedorovich fired, the others in his regiment would fire as well. It would be beyond embarrassing to waste such a titanic volley on a mere escort. To be certain they had the right firing solution, they would need to fly at the enemy until they could triangulate the center of their fleet based on the dispersion of their escorts.

When Babayev turned their craft, the rest of the squadron aped them.

Fedorovich flipped on his radio back to the command plane at the rear. "Osprey One, this is Three. I think I have something."

***

"*Battle stations, all hands battle stations. This is not a drill. Repeat, not a drill.*" The 1MC boomed through the USS *Anzio* like the voice of God, startling Alderman so much that he nearly dropped his pen. He looked up from his desk where he'd been signing off on a work order and blinked a few times.

"Shit."

He was up from his desk before he realized he'd moved, pressing through the cramped passageways of the ship as sailors scrambled to get to battle stations. He passed a section of men donning firefighting hoods and distributing extinguishers and cutting gear. Similar damage control teams were assembling all over the ship and across the fleet. An insurance plans in case of the worst.

Heavy steel doors squealed closed and crewman locked the watertight hatches, sealing off non-vital compartments.

Somehow, Alderman made it through this turmoil without running into any trouble. It helped that his rank tended to clear a path for him. In less than a minute he'd reached the combat information center—the brain of the vessel. It was dark and hummed with dozens of computer terminals.

"Status report?" Alderman asked. "What are we looking at?"

The watch officer didn't hesitate. "Backfire raid. Reports are coming in from AWACS and our forward pickets. Looks like at least fifty. A full regiment on attack."

Alderman resisted the urge to swear in front of the men and instead nodded stoically. "Make sure fire control for all ships are interlinked and the alert fighters are scrambled."

"Captain McNamee just launched them, sir," the officer said.

Alderman took a moment to remind himself that he was admiral here, he didn't need to worry himself with tactical details. He glanced around the CIC, seeing that there was little more he could do. "Any contact yet?"

"Combat air patrol has a handful of Tomcats on intercept course. We're routing all available fighter squadrons."

Now it was a race to see who would fire first.

***

Pavlov swore loudly over the intercom.

"Comrade Major, fresh returns. I make aircraft closing at high speed. Probably F-14s."

"How far out?" Fedorovich asked, knowing that they had minutes at best.

"Maximum detection range," Pavlov said, panic rising in his voice. The incredible and deadly range of the AIM-54 Phoenix missile was no secret to them. "Major, I advise we fire now."

Fedorovich's pulse pounded like a drum in his ear. There was no second chance at this, but he also wasn't going to risk his squadron hoping for a guaranteed hit on a carrier that may not even be there. "Do you have a fix on the center of the formation?"

"We have contact with two surface radars," Pavelov said.

Fedorovich swore. Two wasn't enough to be certain. Those F-14s were going to reach him well before they had a solid position for the carriers.

A realization dawned on Fedorovich. F-14s meant carriers. "How many? How many F-14s?" he blurted over the intercom.

"Three flights. Six aircraft."

"The closest ones will be ready air patrols," Feodorvich said. "The farthest is likely the alert fighters launching. Use that data to calculate the position of the carriers. Prime the weapons. Relay targeting data. Center fire on that furthest F-14 contact. We'll let the missiles find their own targets."

"Acknowledged."

It was a guess, but at least it was an educated one. Fedorovich switched to the regiment frequency. "Osprey One, enemy carrier fleet sighted. We're firing. Confirm." He only half-heard the response from command. He was operating on training at this point. A half minute later, the craft lurched three times as each of the heavy missiles decoupled and dropped from the bay before igniting their rockets and quickly outpacing the bombers. Following the inertial guidance fed into them by Pavlov, they closed at supersonic speed toward what he hoped were the carriers.

Just as they launched, so did the other sixty aircraft in the regiment. Each one loosed a trio of anti-ship missiles. Not all of these activated properly. Some failed to decouple from the weapons pylons, others dropped dead into the ocean below as their motors failed to ignite. Others still suffered internal guidance failures and were doomed to race off toward the horizon until they exhausted their fuel. Accounting for the duds, all told over one hundred and sixty "carrier-killers" raced southwest.

The Tomcats would no doubt intercept some of them, as would the plethora of defensive weapons at NATO's disposal, including their vaunted Aegis missile system. Most of the Kh-32s would be destroyed well out of sight of the ships they were targeting.

Most. But not all. Fedorovich had seen the math, he'd seen the studies, the simulations, the exercises. They all showed the same thing. Through sheer volume of fire, some would get through and they would be enough.

"It only takes one," he reminded himself.

The missiles were already climbing, racing to gain altitude and fly out of the range of NATO's air defense missiles before conducting a terminal diving attack at supersonic speeds.

The moment they'd fired, the regiment's role delivering weapons was finished and now it became a race for safety. Babayev leaned into a hard turn, mimicking the other bombers as they pirouetted as one, a well-rehearsed ballet in the air.

There was no doubt that at least some of the American fighters had already fired, their missiles racing toward his regiment. Some of his men were going to die. Fedorovich just hoped he wouldn't be among them.

Fedorovich nudged the throttle forward, but it was already at maximum, afterburners engaged. He glanced at Babayev. Now it was just a matter of luck for them.

***

The Kh-32 was a deadly and sophisticated weapons system, purpose-built for the job of sinking the reportedly unsinkable. It was among the newest missiles in the Soviet arsenal, only having just superseded the aging Kh-22 the year prior. Fast-tracked development spurred on by heavy investment into Soviet naval forces had allowed the weapon to be deployed ahead of schedule with select naval air regiments.

The lead most Kh-32 streaked along at the head of a wave of over one hundred and sixty others targeted at the American ships ahead. Each one traveled at several times the speed of sound, carrying with it five hundred kilograms of high explosive and a dedicated radar guidance system.

They cruised at around forty kilometers above sea level, well above the flight ceiling of NATO's Aegis air defense system, and effectively untouchable until they began their final dive. For now they flew blind, trusting in their inertial navigation systems, waiting until they would finally come within range of their targets when they would activate their onboard radars and dive on the enemy.

Now it was just a matter of time. Inside their cold electronic minds, software waited with inhuman patience to execute their terminal, fatal dive. Soon.

Soon.

***

Aboard *USS Anzio*, things were far from patient and calm. The operators and maintainers of all the uncaring electronic devices onboard waited in sweating, silent fear which was only occasionally interrupted by buzzing announcements over the 1MC. Death had them all in his sights and the survival of any one person was out of their hands. An electronic roll of the dice was their only shield. They relied on circuit, semiconductor, and software to safeguard them.

Battle stations had been called as soon as the Backfires were picked up on radar minutes ago, and things had only grown more tense since then.

"No sign of follow on attacks," the radar operator reported to Admiral Alderman. "The last of the Backfires have gone off scope." They'd fired and fled as per their doctrine, no surprise there. It seemed the attack was coming on only a single axis. The only way this could possibly be worse was if they were caught in a crossfire.

Despite the chill of the air conditioned combat information center, Alderman felt a thin sheen of sweat on his upper lip. "Thank God for small favors. What's the latest tally?"

"The Tomcats splashed fifteen missiles," the sailor said.

"That puts us at what? A hundred forty five?"

The sailor nodded mutely, eyes on his screen, tracking the incoming missiles as they ticked closer with each sweep of the radar array.

"Did we get any bombers?" Alderman asked.

"CAP splashed four."

Only four out of sixty. It was a bitter pill, but with the immediate threat the missiles represented, they'd had to prioritize.

It was up to the Aegis system now.

***

Far overhead, the surviving missiles reached their pre-programmed attack point and activated their targeting radars. In moments, their electronic minds were flooded with radar returns from the surface. Enemy ships. After orienting themselves with their targets and closing the remaining distance, they executed a new set of instructions: dive.

Each one nosed down and accelerated, quickly climbing past four times the speed of sound. Their radars pinged continuously, checking and rechecking targets and verifying they were aligned properly. Far beneath them, the Aegis system opened fire.

***

The air defense batteries of the carrier group released their missiles as one. Vertical launch cells studding destroyers and cruisers snapped open and spewed flames and smoke as SAMs streaked into the sky. Aegis was an advanced computer-controlled, missile-based, anti-air system which paired a high volume of fire with pinpoint accurate missiles. Engagement time would be short since the Kh-32s were diving straight down onto them, but they still had a few dozen kilometers to cross.

For the lead waves, it was like running into a brick wall. Aegis missiles zeroed in and destroyed carrier-killers with clockwork precision. The skies over the fleet were full of blossoming fireballs and puffs of black smoke as missile fought missile in an electronic duel.

Vessels equipped with the Aegis system seemed to unleash a continuous stream of missile fire as cells launched in succession. So long as the Aegis missiles kept launching and hitting, there was no chance of anything getting through.

Unfortunately for the men in the American fleet, however, even computers make mistakes.

The first Aegis missile to miss its target was swiftly rectified by a second missile following behind it, swatting the targeted Kh-32 down.

Soon enough though, errors began to compound, misses mounted, and the anti-ship missiles were getting through, first in singles, then pairs, then nearly a dozen all told.

***

Alderman listened with growing concern to the chatter of the battle.

"Sixty targets left. Fifty. Forty."

Soviet missiles were dropping, but not fast enough. Some were getting through. Worse still, some ships were already exhausting their anti-air missile supplies.

"*Guilford Courthouse* is winchester for SAMs."

"*Wilford Blair* reports winchester SAMs."

The 1MC blazed to life. "*All hands brace for impact. Brace for impact.*"

Alderman hunched in place and gripped the desk, eyes fixed on the radar monitor as deadly blips closed in.

***

Eleven of the Kh-32s made it through the maelstrom overhead though one of them had a dead guidance system and was destined to dive into empty water. The other ten fell with godlike speed on their prey.

The last line of defense engaged. Decoy launchers fired, filling the air with radar-reflective chaff clouds. Close-in weapons systems angled vertically and spooled up their ammo belts.

The lead most Kh-32 found its targeting system enchanted

by a seductively large metallic cloud and missed USS *Bastogne* by a mere fifty meters, screaming demonically overhead.

Others were fired on by the fast-firing CIWS guns which chewed through another half dozen missiles before one finally slipped through the fusillade.

The target, USS *Guilford Courthouse,* wasn't an aircraft carrier, but it found itself locked in the pitiless sights of a swarm of anti-ship missiles.

The lead missile slipped through *Guilford*'s defenses and punched down through the cruiser's deck just behind its forward gun turret and exploded with white hot intensity. Even a single missile hit was often enough to spell doom for a ship, but through dumb luck this one found the primary magazine for the *Ticonderoga*-class's five inch bow gun. The blast ripped off the nose the vessel and sprayed deadly metallic fragments back through the bridge and superstructure, slaughtering the crew. No sooner had the last of *Guilford*'s debris finished raining down than secondary explosions tore her guts out. In seconds, the entire warship was nosing down into the waves, a final, fatal bow.

Another Kh-32 nearly reached the deck of *Anzio* before it was hit by CIWS fire. The missile exploded mid-air over the flight deck with a puff of smoke and flame, peppering it with shrapnel and burning debris. Exposed men and aircraft were raked with that deadly rain. Those who could scattered for cover while the wounded writhed and the dead moved no more. A parked F-18 Hornet caught fire, adding to the chaos. Sailors had to step over the dead to fight the flames with extinguishers as others dragged the wounded to the relative safety of *Anzio*'s interior.

USS Inchon wasn't as lucky as her sister ship. Two Kh-32s struck her deck one after the other, each blast scattering debris and chunks of hull. The first detonated on the flight deck itself, outright killing everyone unlucky enough to be nearby. The second missile punched through the deck and into a hangar below before it exploded.

The hangar became a death trap. Parked aircraft, stored fuel, spare ammunition, and the men who worked in that compartment were almost instantly incinerated by the conflagration which erupted as a vivid red-orange fireball that spewed from the deck. Choking smoke and fumes filled the passages of the ships, flowing like poison through veins to smother and strangle sailors. The second impact severed water lines which prevented automatic fire suppression systems from activating to contain the blaze and intense heat fried circuits and melted wiring, plunging men into smoke-filled darkness.

At the tail end of this parade of carnage, a final Soviet missile passed through the American defensive fire. Its radar fixed on the relatively untouched USS *Anzio* and it dove in for the kill. Unlike the first Kh-32, this one managed to hit its target, striking the deck but failing to detonate. Instead, the missile glanced off, scattering burning rocket fuel across the flight deck. The deck— already littered with dead and wounded crewmen— was thrown further into chaos as would-be rescuers themselves became victims. *Anzio's* deck was thick with flame and bodies in fluorescent vests, stained with blood and soot.

***

Alderman felt the ship shudder with that last hit, her hull ringing like a dull bell. For a second, there was silence before an eruption of activity ended it. Damage control teams from across the ship reported clear or responded to the hits. Alderman left the status of the ship to Captain McNamee.

"What's the condition of the fleet? Any more vampires?'

"We have reports of hits across the fleet," a lieutenant said, keeping his headphones pressed to one ear. "*Guilford Courthouse* is abandoning ship. She's going under."

Alderman knew her captain personally. He hoped to God he got all his people off, but he knew that would likely be impossible. "Carriers?"

"*Inchon* took two hits. They're reporting serious damage and a major fire below decks. We took a hit to our flight deck, but no apparent penetration."

"Casualties?"

The lieutenant could only swallow and nod.

Whatever hits they'd taken, they survived. But survival was a poor consolation when there was no target to hit back at. The Soviet surface fleet would take a concerted effort to crack, one that NATO wasn't ready to make so long as the Russians remained in range of their land-based air bases.

Alderman crossed the CIC to the main tactical plot. "Any attacks on the other groups?"

"No, sir. Not yet."

Alderman was starting to think that maybe they'd gotten lucky. This attack had been poorly coordinated. Conventional wisdom held that the Soviets would strike with aircraft and submarines simultaneously. He doubted their submarine forces were in condition to do much at the moment though.

"Admiral, message for you, sir." The ensign who offered the printout looked terrified, and Alderman suspected it wasn't just from the attack.

He took the printout and skimmed it.

Norwegian ground sources report Backfire regiment taking off from vicinity of Trondheim. 63°25'47"N 10°23'36"E.

Alderman read the timestamp. This was sent fifteen minutes ago.

He swore out loud, making the sailor who'd delivered the message flinch. How many lives could have been saved if they'd received this fifteen minutes earlier? Instead of ruminating on it more, Alderman turned to the tactical plot, examining the map of Norway. His eyes traced along the jagged coastline from Trondheim to where his fleet was marked.

"Safe bet those Backfires are racing for home. Do we have anything in the air that can catch them?"

"I don't think so, sir," an officer replied. "Anything we

launched would get intercepted by the fighters they have stationed along the coast."

"They've got to be low on fuel," Alderman mused. "It's a straight shot for them. They're sitting ducks if only we can get to them." Norway's air bases would be perfect for this sort of operation. "Do we have any update on land-based aircraft?"

"Last report was all airfields in Norway were out of action, sir."

Alderman nodded grimly. "Double check that. If we've got anyone who can fly, let's get them airborne. We won't get a better chance to clobber those Backfires."

The officer he spoke to was dubious, but knew better than to say so to an admiral. "We'll check again, sir."

"Someone has got to be able to take off," Alderman repeated. "Anyone."

Less than five minutes later, he had his answer. "An F-15 squadron out of Oslo Airport reports limited readiness, sir. They can be airborne in five minutes."

Alderman looked at the map and eyeballed the distances involved. An intercept would be difficult, but possible. It was a longshot, but one he was going to take. "Get them in the air. It's time to hit back."

***

20

Morris had never taken off from anything other than a purpose-built runway. The dragstrip his Eagle currently pointed down would do the job, but it was novel enough to elevate his heart rate. In theory there was no reason why this couldn't be done. Hell, the Swedes had been doing this basically since the war started. But Morris was all too aware of the frequent—sometimes lethal—gaps between theory and practice.

"First time for everything," he said, securing his oxygen mask in place.

Bleachers lined the strip to either side of him. They were all empty of course, but he couldn't shake the feeling that he was performing for an audience.

When he'd cooked up this harebrained plan, he hadn't expected to be called upon to use it so soon. They'd only just finished taxiing over their remaining F-15s when the order had come through for an intercept. Urgent.

"Wyvern One, cleared for take off," his radio said. "Good hunting and good luck."

Morris didn't give himself time to doubt. Using this dragstrip was a one way trip. It was too short to land on, so unless they somehow cleared the airport runways before he came back then he would have to divert his squadron for Aberdeen, Scotland. That also meant there was no way to test the strip. They'd walked it, swept it for debris, and measured it. In theory, it would work.

In theory.

Morris throttled up and felt the surging power of his

fighter's thrusters press him back into the seat. The end of the strip came racing toward him alarmingly fast, bleachers blurring by. It occurred to Morris that he was probably setting a new speed record for this track.

Morris started pulling back on the stick the second he hit the correct speed and felt his craft's tires leave the ground. He let out a held breath and felt himself relax slightly. He was airborne.

One by one the other aircraft of Wyvern Squadron joined him, their final sortie from the Oslo Airport. The fighters formed up and set off north. Their flight path was convoluted. They would have to travel low and stick to Norway's numerous valleys in order to cross over the occupied country undetected and unbothered. It would be hell on their fuel supply and it would take a toll on them, but it was the only way.

He repeated his new mantra. "We do whatever we must."

As they left Oslo Airport behind, Morris realized there was a good chance he wouldn't return to Norway until the war was over. Now, more than ever he felt like he was abandoning Astrid and the others. If all went according to plan, he would end up safe in Scotland while they were still stuck behind the lines.

Morris shook his head. He had a role to play and he was going to do it the best he could.

***

For what felt like the first time since launching, Major Fedorovich let out a shaky breath. He'd made it. The noon sun hovered over the horizon off their port wing, shooting golden rays through the spiderweb of micro-scratches on the Tu-22M's cockpit viewscreen. He'd made it. The regiment had made it. He flipped on the intercom. "Lieutenant Pavlov, do we have any contacts in pursuit?"

"None, Comrade Major."

Fedorovich's lips split in a broad grin. He cut the PA system and turned to beam at Babayev. The pilot's eyes were hidden behind the mirrored lenses of his helmet. Looking at Babayev, Fedorovich could only see the reflection of the sun.

Without a word, the major held up a hand, palm parallel with the floor. It trembled visibly.

"Why do you think I have not let go of the controls, Comrade?" Babayev asked.

"Nothing like your first time," Fedorovich replied.

"I just want to get back and have a smoke," Babayev said.

Fedorovich laughed. He allowed himself to relax a bit more. He'd heard it said that any mission you could walk away from afterward was a good one. While some of the bomber crews wouldn't walk away from this one, it was a small price to pay for the success they had undoubtedly secured. He would have rather they all came back, but everything considered, they had gotten off easy. This had been a good mission. He toggled the intercom. "When we get back, drinks are on me. Excellent work, all of you."

"Nothing to it," Pavlov replied.

"That's it then? We did it?" Alekseev asked.

Fedorovich snorted. "For now, yes. There will be a next time for us. Many of our enemies can't say the same thing."

"We'll learn how we did when we get back," Pavlov said, "but I know our missiles did not miss."

"So certain are you?" Fedorovich teased.

"I stake my honor on it," Pavlov replied.

Even Alekseev laughed, flushed with victory. They were less than thirty minutes from base, and a true celebration.

***

"Tally!" Grinder called over the radio. "I count just over fifty bandits bearing 046, Angels fourteen. That's got to be them." They'd encountered the returning Backfire raid twenty minutes after take off. The F-15s of Wyvern Squadron had flown low and fast, weaving through the valleys and fjords of southern Norway until they emerged over open sea out of Sognefjord. The enemy were less than ten minutes from home, which was a little less time than Morris had to spare for them if his fuel gauges were to be believed. They were going to be cutting this close.

Backfires were capable of intense bursts of speed, but only for short periods given their fuel expenditure. These were currently traveling at subsonic speeds. They would be sitting ducks.

"Pick targets," Morris said. "No one double up. Sparrows first, then we'll switch to heatseekers when we get close."

"Affirmative, lead."

The squadron climbed, rapidly gaining altitude for better firing position, while also putting themselves in detection range of Soviet radar. They lit their targeting radars and painted the flatfooted Soviet bombers.

Morris lined up his own shot. "Locked." He fixed on a target and fed it to the radar-guided missile on his under-wing pylon. "Wyvern One, fox one."

A chorus of voices sounded off as the rest of his pilots fired. Nearly a dozen missiles streaked out, following the electronic returns of the enemy.

"Get as close as you can," Morris instructed,"I want confirmed kills. We won't get a better opportunity."

Morris watched his instrument panel keenly, tracking his missile as it closed on the Backfire force. A minute later, ten of the blips vanished from his radar, winking out one by one. Morris switched targets, locking another one. "Wyvern One, fox one." The Eagle vibrated as the missile decoupled and fired its engine, streaking toward the horizon.

Now the Backfires were accelerating again, going to afterburners in a vain attempt to escape their pursuers. Some dove for sea level while others climbed higher. They were panicking. It was like shooting fish in a barrel.

Morris's target flickered and vanished. "Splash," he said, already lining up the next target. "Wyvern One, fox one."

151

***

"Dive! Dive!" Fedorovich cried, even as Babayev did so. The heavy, old Tupolev nosed down, shuddering as they accelerated for the denser air below.

"Enemy radar lock! Radar lock!" Pavlov shouted, his voice fuzzing out Fedorovich's headphones.

Panic was setting in, clawing at Fedorovich's mind and gut. The enemy had caught them somehow and they were almost totally defenseless."Countermeasures, you bastard! Activate counter measures!"

As a legacy of a much older past, every Tu-22M was equipped with a tailgun, a twenty three millimeter autocannon, once intended to be used for shooting at pursuing interceptors. In the post-missile era it was instead mated to a high tech sensor suite and configured to fire chaff and flares directly at pursuing weapons.

Fedorovich had never before had to fire the gun.

The aircraft juddered as the cannon fired, pumping out a stream of decoys to ward off pursuing missiles.

He looked up in time to see a climbing bomber flash by, close enough to make him yelp. For all the West was doing to kill him, he nearly lost his life in a collision with his own pilots.

"Maintain formation!" he shouted over the regiment radio frequency. Any further chiding was lost as he saw a distant Tu-22M explode into a rolling fireball, its wings wrenching free to tumble away toward the ocean below.

The tail gun continued to hammer away at unseen pursuers and Babayev cursed loudly as he pulled back on the stick, struggling to level the aircraft out while also avoiding similarly evading bombers around them.

Another flaming Backfire fell from the sky ahead of them. Missing a wing, it left a spiral of smoke as it corkscrewed toward its grave. The radio was full of the panicked cries of his pilots, shouting, cursing, pleading.

"Lock broken!" Pavlov said.

Fedorovich's pulse hammered in his veins. How had the enemy caught up with them? Where were they coming from? He regained enough of his composure to remember that he was supposed to be in charge here.

"Osprey One, emergency! Emergency!" he blurted into his radio. "Contact with NATO interceptors!"

The delay before an answer dragged on for painful seconds.

"Osprey One, come in!"

At last, command answered, the radio operator flustered. "I-I'm sorry Comrade Major, I don't have the frequencies for the interceptor squadron."

"Useless bastard!" After a brief struggle with a laminated chart of radio frequencies he found the one for a squadron of Su-27s stationed nearby and dialed it in. "Basilisk Six, this is Osprey Three, emergency! Respond!"

***

Morris fired a heat seeking Sidewinder missile and faintly saw it burst against the arrow shape of a Backfire, breaking the bomber's spine.

"Splash another!"

"Voodoo, fresh contacts coming from the east. Looks like interceptors," Grinder said.

The party was over. A glance at his displays showed him his fuel was nearly at the point of no-return and his missiles were all expended. He didn't have anything left to engage the fighters.

"Copy. Wyverns, come about 255 and make a run for it." He saw that his pilots had downed about half of the Backfires within ten minutes. "We call this one a win."

***

"Enemy contacts disengaging," Pavlov said, his voice still shaking.

Fedorovich felt rage, fear, and shame coursing through him in equal parts. He felt sick. He'd listened as his pilots were sent down in flames one by one. Many of them had died begging for help.

Assuming the enemy didn't spring up from the earth again, Fedorovich would likely walk away from this mission. It was little comfort given the horror he'd just been forced to witness. Fedorovich pounded a fist into his armrest and swore.

***

21

The sun was past its highest point in the sky for this latitude by the time Admiral Zharkov received the after action reports of the naval bomber regiment strike.

"Fifty percent?" he repeated.

The officer who provided him the papers nodded solemnly. "Nearly, Comrade Admiral. Our Tupolev regiment was ambushed by American fighters on the return trip from the attack. The most recent report is twenty-five bombers lost and another six seriously damaged.

"Which leaves what? Thirty left?"

Again, the officer nodded.

Zharkov furrowed his brow in irritation. This was an unexpected setback. He'd hoped the Tupolevs would be able to make a clean strike run; after all, he was going to need them again. This meant he would need to change his plans. His lack of sleep was starting to tell on him. He felt the first stirrings of a headache at his temples, moving behind his eyes. Unfortunate, but there was nothing to be done about it; he had much longer to go before he could sleep. Right now, more than sleep, Zharkov longed for a cigarette.

"Very well. Dismissed."

He turned his back and paced across *Tashkent*'s CIC. He passed rows of men and boys hunched over glowing terminals, each of them pretending not to feel the admiral's presence over their shoulder.

As he walked, he leafed through a thick stack of reconnaissance photographs. It was obvious that they'd been taken through the periscope of a submarine based on the crosshairs and the low waves breaking along the bottom edge of the grainy, black and white image. It showed smoke rising from the horizon, but nothing more.

The Western media had been uncharacteristically tight-lipped about the attack. Ordinarily, the Soviet intelligence arm could rely on the gabby journalists of the West to break stories they were unable to. An unpleasant consequence of a free press was that they were free for good and for ill.

Of course, Zharkov knew they wouldn't provide detailed intelligence like losses and disposition, but they could typically count on video or photographs to provide eyes-on data.

In this case, they had none of that. Nothing beyond the most vague "missile attack" headlines. This led Zharkov to believe that the attack had stung the West, but not devastated them. It was bad enough that they didn't want to discuss it publicly, but not so bad that there was no hiding it.

He laid the blurry photographs down by his station which took up the middle of the room and pursed his lips in thought. The Soviet Union had always lagged far behind the West in reconnaissance and intelligence gathering. With no Soviet recon satellites left to speak of, he had no way to know for sure what the West was doing. He would have to make some guesses.

Zharkov crossed the CIC again, this time ending up at the communications station.

"Get me direct communication with rear admirals Olesk and Yevdokimov. Priority."

"Right away, Comrade Admiral!"

Zharkov paced anxiously as his subordinate commanders were summoned. They would need to be of one mind about this if his plan was to have any hope of succeeding. As he paced he rubbed his temples absently.

Within minutes, Zharkov was handed a headset and patched into the multi-ship conversation.

"This frequency is encoded, Comrade," the radio officer said, "but—."

"I will keep it brief," Zharkov promised, perhaps snappier than he intended. He gave the nervous young man an empty smile to try to soothe his nerves. There was no guarantee that NATO could not crack their encryption, if they hadn't already. He seated the headset and adjusted the microphone. "Comrades?"

"Olesk here."

"Go ahead, Comrade Admiral," Yevdokimov said.

"I have heard back from our comrades in the naval air forces. The bomber attack was a success."

"Do we have confirmed losses?" Olesk asked.

Always looking for chinks, Zharkov thought with a scowl. "NATO's losses remain unconfirmed but are thought to be serious. I would expect at least two carriers crippled."

"Two is a start," Olesk said. "If we follow up with attacks from our air wings, I think we stand a chance of dealing them a serious defeat here."

"Your courage is admirable, Comrade," Zharkov said. *But foolish*, he mentally added. There was no chance the untested pilots of their carrier air wings would be able to do much to NATO's superior aircraft and pilots. Even with ground-based support it was a losing game, one NATO was counting on them to play. "However, our bombers have suffered serious losses and will need time to regroup. A direct attack isn't our plan."

"Admiral," Olesk protested, "we have them where we want them, do we not? We should follow through and exploit this success."

Zharkov violently drummed his fingers on the metal console of the communication station, eyes firmly fixed on the ceiling. His headache threatened to grow worse still. Patience, he told himself. "Any victory here would be strategically insignificant. Recall, Comrade, that we are greatly outnumbered."

"What will you have of us?" The stalwart Yevdokimov asked, steering the conversation back on track.

"We have hurt the enemy today," Zharkov said, "but we must do more than hurt them to win. The time has come to execute the second phase of the operation. Prepare your divisions."

"Yes, Comrade Admiral."

"As you say."

"We execute on codeword 'unity,'" Zharkov said. "Understood?"

"Understood."

"Understood, Comrade Admiral."

Zharkov handed the headset back, taking a moment to relax his mind. This was it, the point of no return.

"Comrade Admiral, your orders?"

Zharkov looked to his communications officer. "Contact our comrades in the interior. It's time to blind the Americans."

"Yes, Comrade Admiral."

Zharkov checked his watch. In fourteen hours they would be within striking range of Iceland.

***

Four hours later, a veritable constellation of Western satellites passed through the sky overhead like a celestial parade. Each one had scanned the ocean, their electronic eyes fixed unblinkingly on the miniscule Soviet fleet as it cruised south following Norway's jagged coastline, just as all predictions assumed it would. The white feather wake of disturbed water that spread behind the ships was easy enough to read for their advanced optics, even from low Earth orbit. Just as the West had hoped, the Soviets were riding into the jaws of death. The joust was on.

As each satellite passed beyond the horizon, it moved into range of Russia's central Asian missile ranges. The Soviet Union had a very limited stock of anti-satellite missiles and so could only use them sparingly. This salvo would be one of their last. The initial devastation wreaked by the secret Sky Sweeper hidden in Mir II had since worn off as the West boosted fresh spy birds into orbit one by one, rebuilding their eyes in space. It was an engineering feat that the Soviets couldn't hope to replicate; instead they would have to satisfy themselves by tearing it out of the sky.

As each satellite passed by, it was struck in turn by a missile that had laboriously climbed the gravity well before obliterating it in a hail of metal shards.

The last satellite in this string would be no different.

It was meticulously tracked by ground crews in Omsk, relaying data to waiting missile batteries which oriented themselves and fired on signal. The booster stage burned yellow-hot until separating and releasing a final kill-vehicle. Coasting into the blue-black void above, this smaller warhead matched orbits with the satellite. Once the two were on an convergent trajectory the missile accelerated, launching itself at the satellite. A radar-tripped proximity fuse triggered the moment it came within killing range.

The signal pulsed from processor to warhead. Detonate.

And nothing happened.

The warhead carried on another ten meters, another twenty another thirty before finally detonating.

Shrapnel whirled through the airless vacuum, deadly and silent, perforating the million dollar satellite with coin-sized holes. One of its solar panels crumpled from the hit, but the other was unscathed. Short on power, but otherwise very much alive, the satellite went silent as it passed into the Earth's shadow.

On the ground in Omsk, the missile specialists there confirmed detonation and a spread of debris. Another kill. They relayed mission success to the fleet. The operation could proceed safely knowing that NATO would be none the wiser.

An hour and a half later, the stricken satellite had nearly completed a rotation of the earth. As it passed back into the sunlight, its intact panel fed enough power into its banks by this point to re-activate it. It lived long enough to snap and transmit another series of photographs before dying, this time for good.

Two hours after the Soviets had begun their maneuver, the West realized they were turning toward Iceland.

***

22

"Gentlemen." Alderman entered the small briefing room aboard *Bastogne* well after the various senior officers of the fleet had gathered here, as was the privilege of his rank. The truth was that, rather than some dramatic display of power or primadonna behavior, he'd spent every possible moment gathering and interpreting all the data he could on their situation. "Thank you for your time."

The men of the command group that had assembled here had done so at great expense, both in terms of time and money. Each had been flown by helicopter from their various commands out here to be a part of this assembly. It was a risky endeavor, but war was full of risk, and if Alderman was right, they had less than twelve hours to get this right.

Alderman himself had only just managed to get his command transferred from the damaged *Anzio* onto *Bastogne*.

He came to a halt at the far end of the room and looked up at the gently tiered rows of seats now occupied by some of the finest officers in the navies of the West. The crowd was primarily American, but he also recognized the uniforms of France and Britain which each had their own carriers on deployment.

"I'll start with the bad news," Alderman said, avoiding any preamble. He'd become intimately familiar with bad news since the Backfire attack on his carrier group. *Anzio* and *Inchon* had both suffered grievously. *Inchon* in particular was at risk. As far as he knew, fires were still smoldering away within her and she was no longer under her own power, being towed back to the UK. *Anzio* fared better, but with the damage to her deck it made carrier operations difficult to say the least. Worst of all, *Guilford Courthouse* had sank nearly an hour ago as a result of the catastrophic damage she'd suffered dragging down over three hundred souls with her.

Alderman looked back at the map board behind him, the major battle groups marked with labels in the Norwegian Sea.

"Until about an hour ago, we were under the impression that the Russians were sailing south," he traced a hand along their anticipated path. "A rendezvous with destiny. A death ride. But we've just received satellite intelligence that suggests otherwise." He quickly sketched out the sudden Soviet course change. "They've turned west, something they think we don't know yet."

Alderman's audience had enough self-control not to titter among themselves, but he saw surprise roll through them like a wave.

"Ivan has done his damnedest to take out all of our spy satellites capable of tracking his fleet, but I'm told he missed one. At this point in time, it seems like their most recent attacks were intended to maneuver us into place for them to put their navy between us and their objective." Alderman grimaced. "And it's worked damn well so far."

"And what do you suppose their objective is, Admiral?" A British officer asked.

"At this point? It's hard to say," Alderman said. "It might be to punch a hole through the GIUK gap, clear a corridor to get their subs back in the Atlantic."

The men here had seen full-well what Soviet submarines on the loose in the Atlantic had done. The proposition of another round of high intensity submarine warfare was unsettling.

"We outnumber them," Alderman continued. "Ships, planes, everything but subs. The problem then is intelligence. With Soviet control of Norwegian airfields, we can't risk dispersing our planes all over the sea. Not to mention the risk of further land-based attacks on the fleet. And, like it or not, we still need to hold the supply corridor open between Norway and the rest of NATO. That means our carrier air groups are going to be relatively fixed unless we can get a strong hit on the enemy. The Russians *have* done a good job of pinning us between a rock and a hard place. If we chase their fleet, they can go after our convoys. If we guard the convoys, their fleet has a fighting chance." Alderman mused silently on this a moment before continuing. "We have a heading and can extrapolate from that, but exact positioning is going to require close reconnaissance. Eyes on, at least until we get more satellites put in orbit."

Alderman took a breath, looking over the map as if it were a cipher to be unscrambled or a puzzle to be solved. "The Soviets are traveling in three divisions, each one centered on one of their *Ulyanovsk* class supercarriers. If we can catch one alone, it should be simple enough to kill it."

"Our approach is going to be multifaceted. Land-based aircraft from the UK and mainland Europe are going to maintain air patrols looking for submarines and further Backfire attacks. Our naval assets will be concentrated in three groups. *Bastogne* and the *Belleau Wood* group are going to remain on station here, defending the Norwegian convoy route. To the far north—," Alderman indicated the gap north of Iceland, "*Iowa* will move south to screen the direct approach to Iceland supported by aircraft from Kleflavik AFB. Lastly— Dunner, where are you?"

"Here, Admiral," Rear Admiral Dunner said with a half-raised hand.

"Dunner, you're going to have *Antietam* and *Shiloh*'s air groups scouring the sea, running sweeps to the north looking for the Soviets. Keep enough aircraft in reserve that we can respond to any more Soviet missile attacks and so we can pounce if we find them."

"Yes, sir."

"We can't assume this isn't all part of some feint to draw us out of position for more Backfire strikes." Alderman clasped his hands behind his back, surveying the gathered officers. The easiest part of the job was making a plan. The hard part was making it work. "Now, all that we have to do is find them."

***

23

Second chances didn't come often in war, yet that was exactly what Commander Grier was hoping for as *Raleigh* plied the ocean depths.

"Still nothing on sonar, sir."

Grier grimaced, only partly from his lingering headache. "Keep up the sweep," he said. "Keep speed below one half. She's still out there somewhere."

"Yes, sir."

Grier turned from the sonar station and rubbed his temples. He was itching for another shot at that *Oscar*-class. The one that got away.

An Oscar was a big target and not known for her stealth. Still, her captain and crew were professionals. They had to be, to still be alive after this long in NATO-controlled waters. The chaff had blown away, the weak weeded out. On this Darwinian battlefield, only the strong survived.

Grier sighed. "Where is—Oh."

A yeoman offered him a steaming mug of coffee. "Here, sir," he said with a wry grin.

"Thank you." Grier sipped, savoring the warmth and even the bitterness. He was operating without much sleep and even more stress. The fact that they'd let that Oscar "shoot and scoot" only added fuel to the fire burning in his chest. If that wasn't bad enough, there was the lingering threat of her ability to cause yet *more* damage. Unlike most submarines, the Oscar didn't hunt her prey with torpedoes. She was a missile boat first and foremost. Carrying two dozen long-range missiles which could apparently be used for anti-ship or ground-attack roles. They could only account for the six she'd fired at Bergen Airport, which left plenty more for the target rich Norwegian Sea.

Between the carriers, transports, escorts, harbors, airports, and cities of the coast, there was no telling what she would do next.

Ever since their run-in with the Oscar, they'd been doing patrol sweeps of this area, a broad figure-8 search pattern which grew wider with every sweep. With the power of their passive sonar, they should ideally hear the Oscar before she heard them, although there was no guarantee of that.

"Commander, sir," Briggs said. "We're scheduled for a ULF check in in ten minutes."

The ULF or ultra-low frequency was a special radio wavelength which allowed submerged submarines to receive instructions from inland control centers. It was valuable in peacetime and irreplaceable in war. It meant that boats like *Raleigh* could receive changes of instruction without having to return to shore or surface and expose themselves.

Right now though, it was an unwelcome distraction from Grier's relentless hunt for the Oscar. Well, maybe not so relentless since relenting is exactly what he had to do.

"Right. Okay, break off the search," Grier said, trying not to sound exasperated. "Helm, take us up. Set depth to thirty meters." It was shallow, but these waters were patrolled by NATO aircraft so the risk was minimal.

"Aye sir, setting depth to thirty meters."

The ascent was slow and controlled. A rapid ascent would lead to creaks and groans from the hull adjusting to the pressure change, telltale audio cues for enemy submarines to zero in on. Ascending slowly would mitigate some of that risk.

As they ascended, Grier moved from the sonar room back to the control room and attack center, sipping his coffee. The war could still reasonably be measured in weeks, but it felt ancient all the same. Despite all that time, *Raleigh*, her commander and crew, had seen relatively little action. Grier wasn't stupid.

He wasn't keen to go looking for trouble, but he also hadn't expected to spend the war cruising around chasing shadows.

Grier saw his XO coming from the comms station, printout in hand. From the expression on his XO's face, Grier knew their circumstances had just changed.

"What do we got?" Grier asked, sipping his coffee.

"Change of orders," Briggs said.

"Good or bad?" Grier asked, holding out a hand for the sheet.

Briggs was undecided for a moment. Finally he answered, "Interesting."

Grier read it over.

A heading and coordinates. "Orders to move north," Grier summarized as he read. "And—," he stopped and looked up at Briggs. Each of them looked apprehensive. "Locate the Soviet surface fleet."

"Yes, sir," Briggs said.

"Heavy stuff," Grier added.

"Yes, sir."

Grier set his coffee down and read over the orders again. They were moving away from defending NATO's shipping lanes and moving to intercept the enemy. Reconnaissance. Locate the enemy surface fleet—specifically the aircraft carriers—and report back. It was the same type of cat-and-mouse game they'd played a hundred times before in peacetime, only this time the stakes were literally life and death.

"Hmm."

Orders were orders, and not suggestions, so Grier had no say in the matter, regardless of his feelings about it.

"Right." Grier said. "Okay. No sense slacking off. Briggs, get this to the helm. Let's set a course and get out there."

"Yes, sir."

As *Raleigh* changed direction and accelerated to three-quarters speed, Grier took a moment to gather his thoughts. This was the first he'd heard of active Soviet surface assets in the area. It wasn't their normal MO. The Soviet surface fleet was a pale attempt to compete with the West in every available arena. They weren't expected to sally out like this in a shooting war. But plans change. Grier's job wasn't to ask why.

Grier found the public-address system and dialed in the shipwide code before picking up the receiver. Across the boat, speakers hissed to life.

"All hands, now hear this," Grier said, his voice echoing through the boat. "This is the captain speaking. We've got new orders. It seems like the Soviets have come out of their naval bastions in the North Sea and are sailing west. We've been tasked with tracking them down and informing the navy. We'll be out on our own, but that's just how we've always operated. Stay alert. We'll be swimming right down their throats and they're not even gonna know it. You know your jobs. Let's get this done so we can all go home." He refrained from adding an "amen" at the end and returned the handset to its cradle.

**

It took nearly three hours of cruising for *Raleigh* to make the first contact with the Soviet fleet. When they finally did, Grier was called to the bridge, rubbing sleep from his eyes. Passing through the control center, he made his way to the forward sonar room.

"What do we have?"

"I think it's a *Kashin*-class, sir."

Grier's addled brain took a moment to tie capabilities to the name. "Kashin, anti-air destroyer."

"Yes, sir."

It meant she wasn't built to hunt a submarine like them, but it didn't mean she couldn't hear them.

"Where?"

"Twenty degrees off our bow, bearing 275." She was headed west.

Grier stood over the computerized sonar plot and watched the contact flicker with life as the sound of her propellers propagated through the ocean.

Beyond her there were other blips of light, intermittent contacts, all labeled as "Unknown" without enough data to positively identify them. He was feeling confident, however, that he'd found his mark.

This Kashin looked like a picket ship, away from the central core of the force, intended to ward off threats and guard against subs and missiles. Slipping past her for positive identification of the fleet would be tricky but—.

Grier frowned at the plot. "They're going awfully fast."

"We make her speed at thirty knots, sir."

"Thirty?" Grier repeated, racking his mind. "That's damn near flank for her, isn't it?"

"Yes, sir."

The Kashin was in a rush, that was for sure, and ships in a rush made a lot of noise.

"She's deaf," Grier said, surprised. He looked to the sonar officer who met his gaze with a predatory grin.

"Yes, sir."

A deaf escort just made their job easier. They still had active sonar to worry about, but at that speed the Soviet's passive detection gear was next to worthless.

"Alright. Very good. Keep monitoring; inform me of any changes in her speed or heading."

"Sir."

Grier left the sonar room, returning to the main control center where he found Briggs. "Russians are rushing."

"Say that again, sir," Briggs said, smirking.

Grier gave his XO an nonplussed look. "They're in a hurry," he said instead. He led Briggs to the navigational chart and watched an ensign update it with the Soviet course. "We're coming up just behind them. We'll jump into this gap here —," he indicated the separation between the Kashin and the next escort in the ring. "And fall in behind them. Maybe get visual on what we're following. Maybe do a little more." Grier surveyed the map, mentally double checking his logic.

Staying behind the Kashin's own noisy screws would leave them effectively invisible. Satisfied, he tapped the chart with a finger. "If anyone picks us up at all, they'll assume we're just an echo from the Kashin."

"Sounds like a plan," Briggs said before relaying the orders to the helm.

Confident that the Soviets wouldn't hear them, *Raleigh* was free to accelerate to close to her own max speed, sticking to the turbulent wake behind the destroyer.

The maneuver was carried out with delicate precision, but no complications. They'd fallen into step with the Soviet ships. Now came the tricky part.

"Take us up," Grier said. "Slowly. Periscope depth."

"Aye, sir."

He needed to see for certain what he was tailing. The only way to be 100% positive was visual acquisition.

Gradually, the ship came up, inching closer and closer toward the surface. If they were spotted, they were as good as dead. There would be no time to dive away and nowhere to run at this close range. Grier's only consolation was that he could take a lot of them with him if that happened.

"Put the radar mast up first. Let's see what it's like up there."

The radar mast tasted the air and filtered out radar waves. They flowed as thick as water but, being this close to the Kashin, they fell into its shadow, protecting them from most of its detection capabilities. The concentration was still dangerously high. Grier was going to have make this quick.

He put the optical periscope up next, standing at the video station and pivoting the aperture in a circle to gather all the data he could. As the periscope made its sweep, a VCR and TV beside him recorded everything for playback. The Kashin's stern loomed large in the monitor, swelled by the magnification of the lens. As the camera swiveled clockwise, he made out other specks on the horizon, a distant ring of escorts.

Not far off, Grier saw them. "Stop, hold there."

The periscope stopped, locked onto the cluster of vessels at the center of the formation. Two of them had the characteristic flat top deck of an aircraft carrier. One was clearly a diminutive *Riga*-class by its sloped "ski-launch" bow, while the other was the much larger *Ulyanovsk*-class. Ahead of both of them was a *Kirov*-class battlecruiser, a giant of surface warfare, only exceeded in size by the *Iowa*-class battleships the United States still floated. That was the deadly core of this group, that was their target.

"Snap that," Grier said.

A telephoto lens on the periscope flashed off a rapid series of photographs of the main combatants.

Grier's heart raced. He had hard evidence of the positions of a significant chunk of the Soviet Navy.

"What now, sir?" Briggs asked. His question was neutral, but his tone wasn't. He was asking if they should attack.

It was undeniable that they had a clear shot at the heart of the task force. A full spread of torpedoes could cripple all three capital ships before they'd had a chance to react. Grier could end this now. Except the price would be his own life, and the lives of his crew.

He wouldn't escape Soviet retribution. Beyond that, there was no guarantee the torpedoes would actually hit and kill their targets. High likelihood, but no promise of anything.

"Discretion is the better part of valor," Grier said reluctantly. "We've got to get this information to the fleet first and foremost. If they want us to come back...well we did it once, we can do it again." Grier keyed the periscope to finish its sweep. He might as well collect data on the whole fleet before their next move.

Another escort ship came into view, this one closer than the Kashin. *Much* closer.

It was a *Kresta*-class cruiser, a formidable anti-submarine warfare ship which was also capable of taking on surface targets, and it was extremely close, just a kilometer or so off their port.

How had they not heard it this close? How had it snuck up on them?

Grier opened his mouth to call for an emergency dive or to retract the periscope and froze. He keyed a command and the periscope stopped its rotation. The *Kresta* was falling behind them as they cruised steadily by. She was stationary, no wonder they hadn't heard her.

Before he had time to puzzle over this, he realized that while the speeding ships of the task carrier group couldn't likely hear him, an immobile one at close range probably could.

"All stop," Grier said. "All stop now. Silent running."

The submarine was silent a moment later as the screws stopped turning.

"Take us down another hundred meters," Grier said, willing himself to appear calm and collected. That would put them below the thermal layer of the ocean and protect them further from sonar.

"You think she heard us?" Briggs asked, voice just above a whisper.

Grier could only shake his head, not an answer, an admission he was just as uncertain as his XO.

Raleigh dove deep into the dark waters, leaving the sounds of the racing Soviet fleet behind until they were alone in the depths.

"Any movement on that *Kresta*?" Grier asked.

"Nothing sir," sonar reported. "She's stationary as far as we can tell. Screws aren't turning."

A stationary ship made a good listening platform since it wouldn't show up on passive sonar if her engines were totally down; however, it also made her vulnerable if she were detected. Shutting down the engines of a ship like that was a huge undertaking, not something to do on a whim, firing them back up even more so.

"Take us to one quarter speed, heading 080. Let's move away from her nice and slow."

"Aye, sir."

As the minutes ticked by, Grier pondered the situation. Why had the Soviets left a cruiser with her engines shut down here? A deadman switch to detect tails like him? If that were the case then she had done a poor job. He couldn't think of any reason for her to be here unless—.

Grier blinked as the pieces fit in his mind. "She's broken down," he said.

"Sir?" Briggs asked

"The *Kresta*," Grier said. "She's broken down. The fleet was moving just below flank, right?"

"That's what it looked like, sir."

"Maybe," Grier said thinking aloud, "maybe they're pushing their ships too hard." He nodded to himself. "Maybe the *Kresta* broke down. Maybe she's not the only one."

"Why isn't she on backup power?" Briggs asked. "Enough for sonar and weapons at least."

Grier could only shrug. "Total systems failure? Too much time tied up in Polyarny rusting away and not enough time at sea. Shoddy inspections, shoddier maintenance. I don't know, but if there's a way to screw it up, leave it to the Russians to find it."

Briggs let amusement show on his face. "Yes, sir."

"Let's get clear of the *Kresta* and we can relay our findings," Grier said. "Soviets are running hard."

***

24

Rabbit took a seat in the tiered seating of the pilot briefing room aboard USS *Shiloh* with more apprehension than normal. He wasn't just nervous because they were in wartime deployment, but also because of the sheer volume of pilots and crew gathering there. He'd heard rumors about a big operation on the horizon, but damn near the entire carrier wing was present in this briefing room.

Beside him, Gomez gave a low whistle. "Looks like a county fair."

Rabbit nodded absently. "Tell me about it." He looked around the room and identified everyone. Some of them were F-14 drivers like him. But there were also crews from A-6 Intruders, F-18 Hornets, even the crew of the carrier's E-C2 Hawkeye AWACS craft. Toward the back of the room, Rabbit saw Metcalf and some of the other Prowler pilots seated together chatting quietly amongst themselves.

Gomez elbowed him lightly in the ribs. "Think we've got a bead on the Russians?"

Rabbit shrugged. "I don't know why else Hendricks would drag us all out here. Whatever it is, it's big."

"Officer on deck!"

Rabbit, Gomez, and the other pilots shot to their feet as one.

"At ease, sit down." Captain Hendricks said as he strode down the center aisle to take his place at the podium at the far end. Hendricks was something of a legend among the pilots of *Shiloh*'s air wing. He had flown an F-4 Phantom over Vietnam in more combat sorties than anyone cared to recount before moving up the chain and becoming the commander of *Shiloh*'s air wing. In Rabbit's own words, Hendricks was "a certified badass." The wing commander gripped the sides of the small wooden lectern and looked over the assembled aviators. His expression was set and hard, but his eyes twinkled with a glimmer of excitement. "Gentlemen, I'm pleased as punch to tell you that the rumors are true. We found 'em."

"Holy shit," Gomez whispered. "I knew it."

"That's just step one," Rabbit returned, trying to sound cool, but feeling a mixture of excitement and anxiety all the same.

Hendricks let a grim smile split his features. "A whole Soviet carrier group in the open and driving west." He picked up a remote and keyed on a projector, calling up a grainy image of a cluster of Soviet ships plying the waves. From the low angle, it was clear this was a photograph taken through a submarine's periscope.

Captain Hendricks waited for the chatter to die down before continuing. "No small nut to crack. One *Ulyanovsk*-class supercarrier, a *Riga*, a *Kiev*, a *Kirov*, and numerous escorts. Even without their air wing, that's a lot of anti-air firepower concentrated in one area." Hendricks paused. "And we're going to send it all to the bottom."

Someone hooted and others clapped.

Hendricks waited for the men to settle down a bit before he continued. "The plan is simple," he said, turning off the projector and trading it out for a dry erase board and marker. "Two strike packages—*Shiloh* group, *Antietam* group." Hendricks marked each in turn on the board. "*Shiloh* group will come in from the west and *Antietam* will follow on later from the south. Our AWACS element—Stagecoach—will follow behind *Shiloh* group. Lastly, our ECM element, callsign, Nightcall—Venom? Metcalf, where are you?"

"Here, sir," Metcalf said, raising a hand.

"You guys will be flying in with *Antietam*'s strike package instead of ours. I figure someone there should know what they're doing."

Metcalf and the other pilots chuckled, but Rabbit knew

electronic countermeasures was dangerous work. Rabbit didn't envy the older pilot, but he also knew he had his own trouble ahead of him.

"After staging, we'll conduct a staggered attack pattern. Western prong first followed by the southern prong fifteen minutes afterwards. Next we'll go over exact dispositions, organization, routes, loadouts, and timetables. Questions?"

No one spoke. They were ready to get this done.

Hendricks nodded, satisfied. "Then let's get to it."

***

"Lancer 108, you're drifting," Rabbit said, his eyes on the instrument panel of his Tomcat.

"Copy 103," Ducky said.

An entire carrier wing—five full fighter squadrons—cut a dramatic sight through the warming, morning skies. Above them the sky was streaked with red and gold clouds catching the sun's rays. Beneath them the waves glittered as they rolled with four-foot swells. A beautiful morning in the fickle and harsh Norwegian Sea.

Fifty American fighter aircraft flew north in four parallel waves, loosely spaced. The Tomcats led the attack, their variable wings swept back in cruise configuration. Just behind them were two squadrons of the newer, multi-role F-18 Hornets, with the venerable A-6 Intruders behind them. The entire wing was armed to the teeth.

Each of the F-14s carried two active radar AIM-54 Phoenixes on their belly hardpoints. These missiles were enormous at four meters long and weighing over 1,000 pounds each. Rabbit and the other pilots could feel them weighing their craft down, making them sluggish alongside the heavy drop tanks they carried. They would lighten up substantially once both of those had been released. They also carried AIM-7 Sparrow semi-active radar missiles, as well as AIM-9 Sidewinders, a heatseeker for short range engagements. Lastly, each Tomcat held a twenty millimeter rotary autocannon in its nose for close range dogfights should it come down to that. Their weapons loadout centered entirely around air-to-air engagements, leaving any anti-ship activity to other aircraft in the wing.

Trailing miles behind the Tomcats, well out of sight, was a single Boeing E-2 Hawkeye AWACS craft running with its powerful search radar currently powered off. Driven only by turboprops, it couldn't hope to keep up with the powerful jet engines of the fighters when they accelerated for the attack, not that it needed to. The Hawkeye would do better spotting radar targets while it was safely away from the fighting.

Rabbit held formation with a minimum of effort, checking his instruments from time to time. Gomez handled all the navigational duties, so right now Rabbit's only job was to fly straight and level, something he was capable of doing in his sleep.

In order to mask their origin point and prevent the enemy from being able to easily strike back, they'd traveled north for three hundred kilometers before turning starboard and approaching the Soviets head on, flying into the rising sun. So far Rabbit and the others had remained at the edge of Soviet radar detection capability, following the careful direction of Stagecoach's radar intercept officer who ensured the fighters didn't blunder into detection range beforehand. With all of their own radar equipment powered down, the Soviets wouldn't see them until they were ready to attack.

The Soviets relied on carrier-based Yak-44s, known to NATO as the "Merit." It was effectively the Soviet counterpart to the American E-2 Hawkeye. The Merit sported a powerful Vega radar dome with a tracking radius of about 200 kilometers. It wouldn't be possible to stay invisible from that once they began their attack run.

"Just about there," Gomez said from behind Rabbit. "This is it."

Rabbit felt his stomach tighten though he forced his body to remain relaxed. He took slow breaths of the cold, dry oxygen his mask fed to him. He'd had a taste of combat chasing off the Fencers from that convoy, but this was going to be different. Worse. The enemy didn't have the option of running away here.

"*Shiloh* group," the Hawkeye's radar intercept officer said. "This is Stagecoach 01. Come about to 090."

Rabbit obeyed without hesitation, gracefully banking his aircraft to maintain formation as the squadrons wheeled their line like a troop of twentieth century cavalry. The sun filled Rabbit's canopy. Once arrayed, they advanced east.

"Stagecoach. All craft, fangs out."

The Hawkeye activated its powerful radar array, a moment later imitated by the fighter squadrons screening it. As their radars snapped on, three hundred kilometers away the Soviets registered them like spotlights in the dark.

***

These fresh radar sources instantly alerted the radar officer of the Merit hovering over the Soviet fleet. The information was gathered and transmitted to the division flagship.

Aboard *Novosibirsk,* Rear Admiral Yevdokimov read the report with a growing pit in his stomach. Not only had the enemy appeared, but they'd done so directly in front of his group.

"Enemy attack group plotted," an officer in the CIC said. "Attack Group One closing at Mach one. Altitude 6,000 meters. Mark fifty aircraft. Radar emissions indicate at least twenty of them are F-14s. Estimate ten minutes till arrival."

Yevdokimov listened to the information as it was called out, handing the print out report back to the junior officer who'd given it to him without a word. *Fifty* aircraft? An entire carrier wing. This wasn't some picket force he'd stumbled into—this was an orchestrated attack. The enemy had somehow known he was here. He'd known there would be combat, it was unavoidable, but he didn't want to be the first to face this threat. His division held the southern edge of the advancing fleet. Zharkov and Olesk's divisions were farther still to the north, well out of visual range. For now at least, he was on his own. Yevdokimov felt sick.

"Admiral?" the captain of *Novosibirsk* said. The eyes of his staff were all on him. This was it, the moment of combat. He had worked his whole career for this. So why couldn't he speak?

Silence seemed to come over the CIC as more sailors turned to look at their commander, waiting for orders. Damn them all. Damn the Americans and damn Zharkov for putting him out in the open on the left of their formation.

Yevdokimov turned to him and blinked a few times. He felt himself beginning to sweat. He only had ten minutes. It should have been an eternity, why was it going by so damn quickly!?

"Launch fighters," Yevdokimov said, forcing the words out. "Launch all fighters. Have the Su-27K squadrons from *Riga* and *Novosibirsk* form and intercept the enemy attack wave. The farther out the better." The Su-27Ks—the naval variant of what the West called the Flanker—would be a match for whatever aircraft the enemy put forward. By engaging the Americans farther out, he could keep his precious ships safe. Though nowhere near as sophisticated as the American Aegis system, the anti-air weapons his escorts carried were still capable enough in their own right—or they would be under ideal circumstances.

The actual facts were quite different.

The Soviet naval expansion program of the 1970s and 80s had been hugely successful, granting them blue water capabilities beyond anything they had before, but it came at a cost. So much of this equipment—especially the more high tech systems—was poorly understood by its operators and poorly maintained. It was just as likely as not that these weapons systems would fail. Not only that, the fact was that Yevdokimov didn't trust his air defense to properly identify friend from foe.

Yevdokimov knew full well about the dismal quality of his crews. How could he not? After all, he'd been the one to sign off on so many forged readiness reports. He'd done what he could to cover his ship's shortcomings in peacetime because it was his ass on the line. But now the appearance of readiness wasn't enough anymore. It was time to perform.

Yevdokimiov swallowed a lump in his throat.

His task force also held a third carrier, *Baku*. A *Kiev*-class, *Baku* was small enough that it was incapable of carrying or launching conventional fixed-wing aircraft. He had aboard only helicopters and a squadron of twelve Yak-41M fighters, known to NATO as "Freestyles." Like the more famous British Harrier, these were vertical takeoff and landing craft able to operate off of *Baku*'s small deck. They were also woefully outmatched by just about every other fighter the West operated.

If the Americans got through his Su-27Ks, then it would be up to his ship's anti-air defenses; otherwise there were going to be serious losses across his force. Yedokimov wiped sweat from his brow and felt an instant rush of fear and embarrassment. He had to maintain his veneer of control. He had to keep his subordinates in line. If they saw how scared he was....

"The Yaks will form up and provide defense against a second-wave attack." The Yak-41M was a technical marvel, but it was also no match for an American F-14 or F-18. He outnumbered the American fighters here, but he couldn't discount the idea that there was a second force waiting to pounce on him. It would be better to keep the Yaks in reserve.

Sweat beaded down his temple and this time he resisted the urge to wipe it away. It was up to his untested fighter crews now.

He noted that no one was carrying out his orders. "Quickly!" he barked.

His KAG—*komandir aviatsionnoy gruppy*—or aviation group

commander scurried off to scramble the fighters, giving Yedokimov a moment to collect himself as he crossed the bridge to the communications officer.

"Flash a message to Admiral Zharkov," Yevdokimov said, trying to sound confident. "Inform him that we have encountered an American air wing on attack." He glanced back at the tactical plot marking the American craft. "He can zero in on their AWACS and kill off whatever we miss. They've underestimated us to their own detriment."

"Yes, Comrade Admiral!"

Yevdokimov kept his face implacable, but he felt his cheek twitching. If his fighters let anything through...he shook his head. It wouldn't come to that. If he could hold the Americans here, Zharkov could close and finish them off from behind. The more he thought about it, the more optimistic he felt about his chances. It was just fifty aircraft. Americans or not, his pilots could handle them. They had to.

On *Novosibirsk*'s deck, steam catapults launched fighter after fighter into the air, their blue and white camouflage configuration momentarily a blur as they fired their engines full tilt and shot off into the sky. *Riga* nearby was likewise launching, only with no catapults his fighters shot off the sloped edge of a ski ramp, afterburners engaged, to achieve the necessary speed and altitude to avoid crashing back down into the waves.

Trailing at the rear of the formation, the Yak-41Ms lifted vertically from *Baku*'s deck with a scream of jet engines. Once airborne they spread out and took up station in a loose orbit of the carrier group.

In the middle of the fleet, between the three carriers, the massive battlecruiser *Kirov* warmed up his radar and air defense suite. A thin ring of escort vessels just over the horizon likewise provided additional SAM and gun batteries in the case of an American missile attack. Ready or not, it was time for battle.

***

25

Sixty Su-27Ks made up five squadrons of fighters arrayed in tiered lines formed for battle against twenty Tomcats and twenty Hornets. Each was fully laden with a selection of air-to-air missiles. Their pilots were the best of the best of the Soviet air forces. Only the most gifted were selected for the intensive training program which acclimatized them to the unique challenges and dangers of carrier-based operations. Despite their obvious qualifications, they were nervous. They knew better than anyone their own abilities—and more importantly—their limitations. The Su-27K was a fine aircraft, just as maneuverable as its land-based variant, but with engagement ranges that measured in the hundreds of kilometers the performance of an aircraft often mattered less than its weapons.

The Flankers carried the R-77, an active-radar homing missile built to take down high altitude, long range targets. The R-77 had an effective range out to eighty kilometers. The R-77s were joined by R-27 and R-73s—rough equivalent to the American radar-guided Sparrow and heat seeking Sidewinder respectively.

That said, the pilots of these craft were nervous because they knew about the one weapon to which they had no equivalent, the Phoenix.

The American AIM-54 Phoenix—unique to the F-14—had a killing range over nearly two hundred kilometers, more than twice that of the R-77. The Phoenix also carried a sixty kilogram high explosive warhead—three times the explosive power of the R-77—enough to blow an aircraft into ribbons rather than simply killing it with shrapnel.

The longest range weapon available to the Soviet pilots fell short by almost a hundred kilometers. It would be almost a full minute before the R-77 would enter firing range. At max closing speed that meant the Phoenix would be twenty seconds from hitting them before the Soviets could even fire back. It would be a very long sixty seconds.

It was all the Soviet pilots could think about as they closed distance, following the radar data fed to them by the Yak-44 AWACS craft flying in a holding pattern over the fleet. They hardly needed any input from the command craft though; the Americans' own AWACS plane was clear as day on their search radars, as were the oncoming Tomcat squadrons.

With a word, the Soviet pilots readied their missiles and acquired missile locks on their opponents. Now they had to count the seconds until they could fire.

**

"Nails," Gomez said. "Twelve O'Clock."

There was no surprise there. They'd been watching the Flankers closing on them through the data link Stagecoach provided. It looked like sixty in total.

"Let's drop tanks."

Rabbit decoupled the detachable fuel tanks and felt the Tomcat shed the dead weight, lightening his craft and limbering it up for combat.

"Jesus, that's a lot of them," Gomez said, reading his radar.

Rabbit didn't need his RIO's opinion to realize that. Forty fighters against sixty Flankers weren't good odds. They needed to even the score. "Just keep them pinned." He would need to keep the enemy in sight until the Phoenix could get close enough to find them with its own radar.

Gomez worked his magic in the back, keeping the enemy formation lit with the Tomcat's targeting radar.

Rabbit flexed his hands anxiously where he gripped the

controls. He rolled his head in a circle, trying in vain to work some of the tension out of his neck. He could feel his pulse pounding. This was it.

The radar ticked off the distance as they closed at mach one. Two hundred kilometers. One ninety. One eighty.

"All fighters, this is Stagecoach. Weapons free."

"Fox three," Gomez said from the back.

"Lancer 103, fox three," Rabbit echoed.

With a squeeze of the trigger, Gomez launched one of the Phoenixes.

Rabbit felt the heavy missile fall away, his Tomcat wiggling slightly. A half second later it ignited boosters, closing quickly on the enemy fighters.

On cue, Lancer squadron fired their volley of missiles a moment before the other F-14s in Javelin squadron did the same from behind them.

Rabbit's Phoenix was one of twenty launched. Out of this salvo, one failed to ignite its motor and fell dead toward the ocean. Another launched correctly but reported an onboard radar guidance failure, racing idiotically for the horizon.

The Tomcats cruised on, closing range for another thirty seconds before they fired their second volley. Freed of the heavy drop tanks and Phoenixes, the pilots were ready for a dogfight.

Now it was up to the missiles, at least until they could get closer.

***

Death was coming for the Soviet Flanker pilots. It was a mathematical certainty that most of them would be dead in less than two minutes if they didn't do anything to protect themselves and they wouldn't even be able to fire back for sixty seconds. Before they could worry about that, they had to juke the Phoenixes.

Since the Phoenix did not require a radar lock to launch,

the Soviet Flanker pilots couldn't know for sure when the Americans had launched. There would be no lock tones until the Phoenixes began their terminal attack run. All they knew for sure was every passing kilometer was another step further into the engagement envelope of the enemy. Without knowing when the enemy launched, they wouldn't be able to run until they were already in the zone of no escape, too close to the missiles to feasibly outrun them. So they had to act as if they were already under attack

The Soviet formation split, half cranking to the left, the other half to the right.

Alone it wouldn't be enough to stop the encroaching American missiles, but every drop of energy they could bleed from the Phoenix was another half-chance that some of them would survive. The only hope they had to survive this onslaught was to either trick the onboard radars on the Phoenix when they activated or get lucky and evade them. The Soviet pilots still had to keep nose-on to the Tomcats, enough to keep them painted with gimbal-mounted radars. With the gimbals in their nosecones, they could paint targets at an angle from their flight path. They needed to hold on them just long enough to fire off their R-77s.

Seconds passed like years as the range for their missiles crept nearer and nearer. The Flanker pilots anxiously scanned the horizon, desperate for any glimpse of incoming missiles. Sixty seconds later, the Flankers' radar lock warning bleated in their ears, a reminder of their mortality. The Phoenixes were activating their onboard radars. The Soviets had about thirty seconds before the missiles reached them.

The order was given, but it wasn't necessary; the Flankers fired, volleying one after another. The R-77s leaped from their pylons like demons, roaring forward. By the time their missiles closed the distance to the enemy, some of them would already be dead at the hands of the Americans. With no time left, they broke, turning cold and dropping countermeasures or flying perpendicular to the missile to 'notch' it and disappear on the pulse-doppler radar, becoming effectively invisible against the ocean backdrop for a short time.

Waves of missiles thundered through the skies toward one another seconds before they crossed paths, closing with murderous intent on their targets.

***

Rabbit took slow, controlled breaths which rasped behind his oxygen mask. He kept his Tomcat cranked to the right, paralleling half of the Flanker formation two hundred kilometers off his starboard wing. With careful piloting, Rabbit kept the enemy forces at the limit of his radar's gimbal as each dragged the others' missiles while keeping radar lock. His radar warning receiver was silent for now. It wouldn't start trilling until a Soviet R-77 activated its terminal guidance radar.

Rabbit kept checking his RWR, gripping his controls tighter than he should. "How long?" he asked.

"Almost," Gomez said, too focused on his displays to sound worried.

The Phoenix closed on the enemy at nearly two kilometers per second, inching closer to terminal range. Once it was within twenty kilometers of the Flankers, its own onboard radar would take over and the missile would go "pitbull"— relentlessly pursuing its target until it either struck or missed.

"Gomez, how long?" Rabbit asked, more insistently.

"Almost...ha, got it! Missiles are pitbull," Gomez said.

By its nature as an active-radar homing missile, Rabbit didn't have to babysit it on the final leg of its journey into the enemy formation. He was free to start worrying solely about the enemy return volley.

"Lancer 103 defending!" Rabbit said.

As the Phoenixes opened their electronic eyes and started hunting their prey, the Tomcats of Lancer and Javelin teams turned hard, going defensive to evade the return salvo, followed by the Hornets and Intruders behind them. By refusing a head-on shot, they'd rob the missiles of much of their relative velocity and force them to expend more limited fuel to close the range. They had only seconds of lead time on the R-77s, but they made it count.

***

The Soviets tried to notch or dupe the Phoenixes with chaff as their radar warning receivers twittered and wailed radar lock warnings. They faced a tough balancing act between evading and keeping their own missiles on course to the enemy, something for which they would pay a heavy price.

The Phoenix was built to ensure kills on bombers, which outmassed the Flankers by several times. They were not ideal for tracking small, nimble targets, and as such, many of them missed, either losing the Flankers to background clutter or being suckered away by chaff clouds.

Many of the Phoenixes cut harmlessly through the Soviet formation, sailing dumbly on, but some found their marks, and when they struck it was with catastrophic force.

Handfuls of Su27Ks were wiped out in as many seconds. Phoenixes burst with frightening power, tearing planes in half and hurling lethal clouds of shrapnel through the air. Aircraft were obliterated by direct hits, and sometimes crippled by debris thrown from hits on comrades' aircraft.

Still, the Flankers persisted, juking missiles as they continued to push on the Americans, losing a second volley of R-77s when they lost their pursuers.

Now it was the Americans' turn to dance.

***

"Spike!" Gomez called—an enemy radar lock. "Missile, R-77 pitbull on us!"

Rabbit deployed countermeasures right away as he rolled over and dove. The rear-mounted chaff dispenser dumped dense clouds of metallic ribbons to sucker in radar-seeking warheads. Blue ocean flashed up at him as the Tomcat's nose swung down, sending Rabbit's heart into his throat. G-forces sent blood surging from his head to his legs and blackness edged his vision. He gritted his teeth and breathed hard as the radar lock warning chirped and chirped and chirped.

"Oh, Jesus," Gomez said as his own stomach dropped out.

All around him, the others in the wing were defending too, scattering, diving, and notching missiles where they could.

Pulling back on the stick, Rabbit leveled a few kilometers from the ocean waves. The chirping stopped. They'd lost the radar lock and they were alive. It had missed. He forced himself to exhale and start climbing again.

Any elation he felt was short-lived. Not everyone was so lucky. Half a dozen American fighters were killed or damaged in the onslaught. The Soviet missile barrage had been heavier than the Phoenix salvo, but since the Russians had launched closer to their maximum range, the R-77s had less fuel for intercept maneuvers.

Rabbit internalized all of this subconsciously, working through the relative math like it was second nature even as he committed, turning back into the fight. He saw a distant trail of black smoke—one of Javelin's Tomcats turning back with heavy damage. Rabbit sent a quick positive thought their way for all the good it would do.

"How many did we splash?" Rabbit asked.

After consulting his instruments Gomez said, "twelve I think. Lost four. No, we lost five."

Rabbit swore under his breath, feeling his heart racing. He had a moment to collect himself before they closed into range with their other weapons. Squadrons, both East and West, wheeled and formed back up. With every instinct telling him to run, Rabbit did the only thing he could.

"Get another one locked."

"Lancers break by pairs," the squadron leader said over the radio. "Tear 'em up."

The distance to the enemy blinked by until they were thirty kilometers out, well within Sparrow range.

"Spike, twelve o'clock!" Gomez said.

"Get us a lock, dude!"

"Locked! Fox one," Gomez said.

"Lancer 103, fox one!"

It would take only seconds to reach their target—a Flanker—which was now closing in on them. The RWR continued frantically trilling, drilling into Rabbit's mind as they jousted with the enemy fighter. Rabbit gritted his teeth. Who had fired first, him or the enemy? Who would blink first?

"Rabbit...," Gomez said tensely.

Rabbit swore. He wasn't going to gamble with his life. "103 defending!" He broke the lock and dove, popping flares and chaff. Rabbit's blood rushed to his legs as he corkscrewed down and away. The sound of his breath rasped in his flight mask and he fought against the graying of his vision. The RWR kept up its incessant chirping.

"C'mon!" Rabbit growled, pulling the stick back tighter still.

A missile flashed over their wing, cutting across their nose, suckered away by the decoys.

"Holy shit," Gomez breathed a moment before Rabbit pulled the stick back, recommitting them.

"Where is he?" Rabbit asked, craning his neck.

The sky was cut by contrails of both missiles and fighters as they swirled and chased one another in the skies.

"Got 'em! Dead ahead!" Gomez said. "Fox two!"

"Lancer 103, fox two!"

The Sidewinder launched, racing away toward the faint heat signature of the Flanker which was likewise turning to track them.

"Flares!" Rabbit called, already turning defensive again. He rolled upside down, passing back through the smoke left by the falling flares.

"Shit!" Gomez said, " I lost him."

"Did we get him?" Rabbit asked.

"No splash. There! Ten o'clock!"

Rabbit caught the metallic glint of the enemy fighter a moment before a stream of tracer rounds flashed past his craft. They'd closed to gun range in the blink of an eye. Again he hauled over, diving for the ocean surface and turning tight.

"Still on us!" Gomez said, looking over his shoulder to keep an eye on the Flanker racing after them.

"Come on. Shake off, you bastard." Rabbit knew the math, he knew how unlikely he was to get a Flanker off his tail at short range. For all the Tomcat's many virtues, it fell behind the Flanker in terms of raw maneuverability.

The RWR blared its near-continuous warning in his ear as they fell in and out of the Flanker's radar cone. At present, Rabbit didn't need to worry about it; they were too close for fox ones, but heat seekers were another matter. As long as Rabbit could stay away from the Flanker's nose, he could keep out of gun range until—"Ducky! Dammit. 108, where are you?"

Ducky's voice came through the rest of the chatter on the radio clear enough. "Above you, 103. I'm on him. Take him to the deck."

"Don't miss," Rabbit said, saying a quick prayer before banking and diving. Once again inertia crushed him, his vision dimming, blood thundering in his ears. He had no idea where Ducky was or what he had planned, but whatever it was, he needed it. Rabbit continued his downward spiral, circling around with the pursuing Flanker in a lethal ballet, desperate to stay out of the Soviet's field of fire.

"108, fox one!"

Rabbit prayed that Ducky's RIO locked onto the right target. He caught the briefest glimpse of Ducky's aircraft as it flashed overhead. A moment later he saw the white trail of the Sparrow fly by, unable to turn tight enough to catch the diving Flanker.

Rabbit looked up and back, catching sight of the menacing, sky-blue fighter as it pirouetted around them. It had cranked hard to dodge Ducky's shot, killing a lot of its velocity and shaking free of Rabbit's tail. An opening. Rabbit floored a rudder pedal and hauled the stick back again, ignoring Gomez's sounds of discomfort from behind as they were buffeted by G-forces.

"Sidewinder, him," Gomez said.

Rabbit clenched his jaw as they came around, pulling the Flanker into their sights as it came around. "Fox two!"

It was close enough that Rabbit saw the hit. The missile struck the Flanker just behind its cockpit, tearing off a canard and flaring out one of its engines.

"Splash! Splash!" Rabbit called, juking around the stricken enemy fighter as it fell into a flat spiral, circling down toward the ocean below. When he leveled out and came around again, he saw the smoldering debris of the Flanker rolling down into the ocean below.

"Nice shot, Rabbit," Ducky said.

"Thanks for the assist." Rabbit was already looking for his next target as he climbed back into the dogfight.

**

26

Captain Ostrovsky walked the cramped bridge of *Krasny Krym*. The vessel was old, a *Kashin*-class destroyer. Designed to ward off or destroy NATO aircraft, the purpose of this vessel was the same as the others in the outer ring of defense ships: protect the carrier.

Krasny Krym's anti-submarine helicopter was on patrol, making vast circles around the ship with its dipping sonar, listening intently for nearly silent Western submarines.

Truth be told, Captain Ostrovsky wasn't worried about submarines. At the speed they were traveling, any pursuing submarine would only have a brief window to take a shot at them and would have to be lucky enough to be directly in their path to really get a good shot. The entire carrier group had been undertaking erratic, unpredictable course alterations to prevent just such an ambush from taking place. No, submarines were far from his mind. A much more pressing threat was the ever-present risk of breakdown. With how Zharkov and the rest of the command staff were pushing them, it was a miracle they had ships afloat at all. The Soviet Navy was an impressive thing on paper, but the truth was that was exactly where most of that strength remained—on paper.

"Update on the boilers?" Ostrovsky asked a subordinate.

"Pressure holding steady, Comrade Captain."

Ostrovsky grunted and continued his patrol. Outside the forward windows of the bridge, beyond the men at their stations, the waves were gray against the bright blue of the sky. He passed by the communications station and glanced at the ensign there, diligently transcribing radio traffic with pencil and paper. Given the size of this formation, none of the picket ships were within sight of the main body, and so required constant updates via tightband, encrypted radio to ensure they were keeping course and speed with *Novosibirsk* and his escorts. *Krasny Krym* was stationed on the southern edge of the *Novosibirsk* group and as such were well out of range from the American air attack.

"Any change in course?"

"No, Comrade Captain."

Ostrovsky scowled to himself. Besides his concerns over the reliability of the ship's boilers, there was also the matter of the targeting radar array.

Krasny Krym was an anti-aircraft destroyer and, as such, he needed to be able to see targets in order to take them down. The problem was *Krasny Krym* couldn't do that. The eyes of the ship—his multiple target acquisition radars—were all powered down. For reasons which were beyond Ostrovsky's understanding of electronics, the radar array was interfering with *Krasny Krym*'s radio equipment. When the radar was online, *Krasny Krym* was deaf and mute, and when the radios were working, *Krasny Krym* was blind.

The solution was as simple as it was crude: they alternated between the two states. Five minute increments of radio listening to ensure they were following the movements of the fleet properly, and five minute increments of radar sweeps to ensure they weren't under attack.

Ostrovsky glanced at his watch, tapping at the crystal face. "That is long enough I think. Lieutenant, power on the acquisition radar again. Full sweep."

"Yes, Captain."

Ostrovsky tried to hide it, but he was excited to see the results of the air battle developing a hundred kilometers north west of them. With about two hundred kilometers of electronic visibility, they should be able to at least make out if their own fighters were returning to the carriers or not.

The radar scope flashed with green backlight as it warmed

up. The familiar sweep line appeared and began its revolutions. It made one quarter rotation before the circular display suddenly filled with white haze as if from a thousand returns at once.

A look of shock and horror crossed over the radar operator's face.

Ostrovsky blinked at the radar, dumbfounded. "What is that?"

The operator looked at him, horror becoming panic. "We are being jammed, Captain!"

***

Eighty kilometers south of *Krasny Krym*, Metcalf flew on the cutting edge of a wing of American attack aircraft. While he led them in, he carried no weapons of his own, not that he needed missiles to destroy an enemy's ability to wage war.

The EA-6B Prowler he flew was one of a quartet of electronic warfare craft screening dozens of other conventionally armed fighter aircraft with a haze of electronic noise.

Seated side-by-side behind Metcalf, two electronic countermeasures officers kept the Prowler's powerful jammers focused on the Soviet ship, blinding her radars with a flood of false return waves, refusing the enemy vessel a peek at exactly what was closing on her.

"Boom! Targeting arrays just went active," Lieutenant Coleman said. "She's lit up like a Christmas tree." With the flip of a switch, he engaged the Prowler's jamming equipment. "And now she's blind again."

"Knock knock," Bradshaw added from beside him.

Metcalf allowed himself a tight grin. "Copy. How long till the game is up?"

"We'll be in burn-through range in seven minutes," Coleman said. "Any closer and we could pop popcorn off the rays she's putting out."

Metcalf toggled a switch with a gloved hand and connected

to the attack squadron tailing him. "Gunslinger, this is Nightcall 100. Target is hot. Repeat. Target is hot. We've got her jammed but estimate burn through in seven minutes."

Gunslinger's reply was quick in coming. They'd been waiting long enough. "Copy, Nightcall. Keep her blind, we'll take care of the rest."

Metcalf tightened his grip on the stick and focused all his attention ahead.

Behind him and the other Prowlers flew a panoply of fighter craft. F-14s, F-18 Hornets, and A-6 Intruders—the attack variant of the Prowler—came on as a deadly wedge.

"Gunslinger to all elements, master arm. Let 'er rip!"

The lead elements—Intruders from *Antietam*—started things off with a staccato launch of AGM-88 HARM anti-radiation missiles.

Metcalf watched one streak by to his right, following *Krasny Krym*'s radar waves straight for the kill.

***

"Comrade Captain, we're blind on all arrays. No contacts."

Ostrovsky tried not to panic. If they were blind, it meant he had no idea what was coming for them. Was it a lone electronic warfare craft probing for the carriers? Or was this the herald of their destruction—a second wave? He had to warn the flagship of course, but to do that meant powering his radars off again, right before they possibly came under attack.

"Can you pinpoint the source?" Ostrovsky asked.

The operator shook his head, fiddling with his controls. "It is targeted at us. At least two sources of jamming. Maybe more."

Whatever was coming, if it got too close, it would show up on their radar despite the jamming. He just had to hope that other ships in the screen were detecting this jamming as well. He wasn't about to power off the arrays and leave the ship completely helpless at such a critical moment.

He didn't have to worry about this dilemma for long.

"Captain, fresh tracks! I make two—no—six missiles incoming."

"Bring countermeasures online!" Ostrovsky snapped.

The HARM missiles sailed in, diving on their target as it prepared to receive them. Chaff mortars flung enticing metallic clouds into the air around the ship. An anti-ship missile might have been successfully seduced by this defense, but the HARMs weren't keying in on radar returns, they were following the waves from transmitter itself, and those burned just as brightly as before.

Krasny Krym's portside CIWS guns spotted the missiles scant seconds before impact and opened fire. Streams of bullets scythed the first two missiles out of the air effortlessly, but the second wave of four was too many to handle at once.

A trio of missiles struck along the ship's superstructure, detonating and obliterating her radar arrays with a scattering of metal. Just like that, *Krasny Krym* was blinded for good.

Captain Ostrovsky picked himself up off the floor of the bridge and looked around in shock. The concussion of the blast had blown out some of the forward viewports, leaving a sailor with lacerations across his face. There wasn't time to worry about the wounded. He whirled to the radar array to see it dead, the operator frantically flipping through a manual to troubleshoot this problem. Ostrovsky didn't need the manual to know their radar was gone.

"Get me radio!" he demanded, feeling perspiration beading down his face. "Get me Admiral Yevdokimov!"

***

Rear Admiral Yevdokimov hovered just over the shoulder of his KAG as the tactical plot was updated with the latest radar data fed in from the nearby Yak-44 AWACS craft. His teeth were clenched so tight it was starting to hurt. The air wing commander updated the unit roster, striking off aircraft as they were confirmed downed. He kept track of approximate locations of points where craft were lost. If things played out in their favor, they could try to recover pilots after the battle, assuming hypothermia didn't claim them first.

Yevdokimov watched the changing tactical plot like a gambler watching a roulette wheel. Somehow, against all odds, his pilots were holding their own. They were taking losses faster than the Americans, but they stood at least a fair chance of coming out on top. Yevdokimov calmed his nerves knowing that even if the Americans did somehow fight through, they would still have to face his ship's anti-air defenses. No matter the outcome of this fight, he would win this battle.

Thin strains of the pilots' radio chatter bled from the headphones of the air controllers manning the stations here. Yevdokimov heard frantic shouts, curses, commands, and pleading seeming to all come at once. The criss-cross pattern of missile fire and evading planes were too complex to accurately track on the tactical plot, so he had to rely on his imagination.

"Have we heard anything from *Ulyanovsk* or *Tashkent*?" Yevdokimov asked.

"No, Comrade Admiral. The attack group is likely maintaining radio silence."

Yevdokimov grimaced. Where the hell were the reinforcements he asked for? Three squadrons of Flankers had been dispatched and were zeroing in on the enemy AWACS. They couldn't arrive soon enough, but once they did it would be all over for the Americans. Caught between his own fighters and this fresh wave, the Americans would suddenly find themselves in a shooting gallery with no escape.

He'd rather not have to worry about this particular American wing making trouble in the future, especially not with so many of his fighters gone.

Yevdokimov found himself daydreaming again, though this time instead of imagining defeat, he saw victory. The first victory for the Soviet carrier-arm in its—admittedly short—history. No doubt there would be a promotion in his future.

Maybe a ship named for him.

"Admiral Yevdokimov?"

The lieutenant who called his attention was ghastly white, his eyes wide. Bad news. Yevdokimov felt his stomach drop out alongside his visions of glory. "What?"

The young man held out a printout with a shaking hand and the admiral snatched it from him, eyes flying across the short message.

"*Krasny Krym* is under attack," Yevdokimov repeated the message, feeling numb. Air attack on a different axis could only mean one thing: a second wave. This attack he was facing down was just a diversion.

"Scramble the Yaks to intercept. Recall the Sukhois," he said to the air wing commander. "Now!"

Twelve inferior Yak-41Ms wouldn't be much of an obstacle if this raid was as substantial as the first. He had to brace for the worst.

"All ships prepare for air defense. Have *Kirov* move between us and the attack vector!"

* * *

The battlecruiser *Kirov* was the lead ship of his class. Over two hundred and fifty meters in length, he displaced nearly 30,000 tons when loaded for combat. A behemoth of the waves, he cut a menacing figure through the water. Nuclear powered and packing the most advanced radar arrays and targeting suites the Soviet Union could supply. Like most ships in the Soviet Navy, he was built around a sole purpose: delivering salvos of long range missiles on the enemy. In this case, the ship's twelve SA-N-6 launchers were readied. The launchers—vertically oriented rotary clusters like the cylinder of a revolver—powered up, their hatch covers pistoning open, missiles ready to fly.

Kirov throttled up, weaving delicately through the trio of carriers in the center of the formation, moving to screen them from attack.

All across the division, warships accelerated and fanned out, maneuvering carefully so as not to collide. It was a delicately orchestrated deployment, one that put the skills of the inexperienced sailors of the Soviet Union to the test, though they managed without collision. Their true test was only just beginning.

***

With the main target acquisition radar array offline, the only warning Ostrovsky had before *Krasny Krym* was hit again was the rip-tear of his CIWS guns. With their own fire control radar, the defensive batteries operated independently from the rest of the destroyer's targeting systems and were, in fact, fully automated. Of the spread of Harpoon anti-ship missiles targeted at the destroyer, the CIWS guns managed to cut down three before another three slammed into his hull at multiple points along the waterline. Every missile detonated a moment after it struck, blowing fiery chunks out of the doomed destroyer.

Each blast shook the whole vessel which bucked like a dying animal, throwing Ostrovsky into the control panels in front of him. A moment later the lights on the bridge flickered and died. The darkness was accompanied by an unnatural silence as the ship's engines failed.

"Emergency power?" the captain asked, knowing it was hopeless.

The sailors on the bridge were stunned into inaction, looking at one another with dinner plate eyes.

"Power!" Ostrovsky barked, setting them to motion.

Crew checked their stations, attempting in vain to power them on.

Ostrovsky smelled a faint whiff of smoke. His ship was burning. Through the forward viewport he saw the first curls of black smoke rising from the gouges in the vessel's side.

Mortal wounds. No damage control team could save him, least of all the poorly-drilled and worse-equipped teams on his ship.

"It's hopeless," Ostrovsky said, not waiting for an answer from his men.

A mislaid pencil started rolling left across the apparently flat top of the radar console. The ship was starting to list.

"Abandon ship," Ostrovsky said through gritted teeth. "Relay to all stations, abandon ship."

***

27

Metcalf craned his neck to look down on the dying destroyer as he crossed over its bow. The stricken warship was smoking like a chimney, dead in the water.

With *Krasny Krym*'s demise, they'd punched a hole in the Soviet picket ring.

Metcalf led Nightcall directly into that gaping wound, their onboard radar jammers masking the makeup of the raid and preventing long range radar lock.

The other A-6s—just over twenty in all—carried four Harpoon anti-ship missiles each under their wings and a HARM anti-radar missile hanging from the fuselage. The much newer F-18s were even more heavily armed, equipped with a potent mixture of anti-ship, anti-radar, and anti-air missiles. Forty of these aircraft followed Metcalf and the other Prowlers of Nightcall in, their own targeting radars hot and ready, sweeping for targets.

As they passed through the hole in the picket ring, Metcalf had to fight a profound sense of agoraphobia. Every second of flight time carried them deeper into the belly of the beast– into the open jaws of the Soviet fleet. It only took one mistake to turn a bold maneuver into a slaughter.

He tried not to dwell on it. He was here to do a job: the sooner they got Gunslinger into firing range the better.

With the Prowlers howling electronic noise straight into the faces of the enemy, the Soviets were temporarily blind.

Most of them were anyway.

The radar warning receiver squawked an insistent warning.

"Gunslinger, Nightcall," Metcalf said. "Bandits twelve

o'clock. Looks like a squadron of Freestyles."

The Yaks were outnumbered by more than three to one, but were apparently undeterred.

"Copy Nightcall, we'll handle this. Gunslinger out."

"Coleman, can you put the whammy on them?" Metcalf asked.

"If I told you how many different targeting radars are trying to fix on us right now you'd shit a brick," Coleman said. "Let Gunslinger handle it."

Metcalf felt that agoraphobic sensation rising. It was a hell of a thing to trust something as intangible as radio waves to keep him safe. He could only watch as the Freestyles unleashed a volley of R-77 radar-guided missiles which was met right afterward by a salvo of AAMRAMs from the Hornets. The sluggish Soviet VTOLs stood no chance and fell in droves as AAMRAMs swatted them down like insects.

It was little consolation to Metcalf as his RWR suddenly blared warnings for radar locks.

"Nightcall 100 defending!" He shoved the control stick forward, sending the Prowler pitching down toward the waves. "Coleman! Whammy it!"

"Trying!" The ECM officer fought with his own console, cycling through frequencies and channels to scramble the lock without unblinding the naval radars fixed on them.

The Prowler's airframe dated back to the early years of Vietnam. High tech guts aside, it was an old bird and had poor odds in a duel with a Soviet missile.

Metcalf held the swooping dive, hoping to find relative safety in the denser air below.

"Got it!" Coleman called.

The warning tone stopped, the pursuing missile sent blind.

Not all of the attack group was so lucky. A handful of missiles from the Freestyles had found their marks, sending Tomcats and Hornets down in flames.

Metcalf was relieved to see that return fire from the American planes had cleared the sky of Yaks, but that feeling didn't last long.

"New returns," Bradshaw said. "Missile fire from the surface fleet."

"Too far out for infrared," Coleman said. With their jammer still sweeping missile frequencies, that really only left one option.

"Got to be home-on-jam," Metcalf said, gritting his teeth.

"Most likely," Coleman agreed.

These missiles didn't need radar or heat signatures since they were designed simply to follow the radar waves of the jammer itself, next to impossible to evade, at least when you were strapped to a radar jammer like Metcalf was.

Metcalf watched the salvo on radar as it crossed the distance, drawing steadily nearer to his Prowler. So long as the jammers were active, there would be no way to guarantee a miss.

"Coleman?"

"Ready when you are," the ECM officer said.

Metcalf flipped on the radio again. "Gunslinger, Nightcall 100. We're going quiet. You're going to have a lot of attention in a minute."

"Copy Nightcall. Don't leave us in the cold for long."

"Roger." Metcalf flipped off the radio. "Coleman, do it."

"Going off air."

Coleman powered down the Prowler's powerful jamming equipment and at once they found themselves lit up with dozens of target acquisition radars pinging them, feeding targeting data back to waiting missile batteries. With no more jammers to home on, the incoming missiles went stupid, sailing harmlessly through Gunslinger group without finding any targets.

"They're going ham now," Coleman said.

Kirov and a half dozen other Soviet vessels pumped streams of anti-aircraft missiles skyward, wreathing the vessels with columns of smoke, targeting the now visible American attack craft. Gunslinger's planes were perfect targets, flying directly at the primary launch platform—the range was close and the missiles were traveling at multiples the speed of sound. Evasion would be impossible so long as the Hornets and Intruders were painted in vivid shades by the targeting radars.

Metcalf watched the missiles closing for a handful of moments. "Nightcall, going live."

Behind him, Coleman switched the radar jammers back on, instantly fogging out the enemy radar and sending the SAMs careening away wildly after ghost returns and shadows. The jammers aboard the four Prowlers of Nightcall cycled through frequencies, pumping out electronic noise to prevent any proper locks or target tracking. By working in concert they were able to blind the enemy once again, at least for now.

Metcalf smiled to himself.

A well-trained anti-aircraft crew would intermix home-on-jam and traditional radar-guided missiles in order to overwhelm the ability of the electronic warfare aircraft to blot out their vision. With patience and skill, they could saturate the group and take out the pesky jammers before whittling away at the attack craft behind.

The men of the *Kirov*—despite the magnitude of high tech weaponry and detection equipment at their disposal—were not a well-trained crew.

More good news followed.

"Gunslinger 207, I have targets on radar, looks like the carriers!"

"Copy 207," Gunslinger 100 said. "Weapons free."

Gunslinger sighted their weapons on the radar returns of the four capital ships that were clustered in the center of the formation and fired. The radio came alive with pilots and weapons officers calling bruisers—anti-ship missile launches—as they filled the sky with Harpoon missiles. Over one hundred anti-ship and anti-radiation missiles launched squadron by squadron. As they decoupled from wing pylons and boosted away, the Harpoons dove down to fly only meters above the waves while the HARMs stayed high. Each

Harpoon—packed with a two hundred kilogram warhead of high explosive—followed inertial guidance toward the programmed target locations where active radar would guide the missiles in on their targets without the need for any outside interference whereas the HARMs simply had to follow the Soviet radar waves back to their source.

Each Harpoon carried a two hundred kilogram warhead of high explosive.

"Gunslinger, all squadrons break and gate for rendezvous point."

The attack craft came about by squadrons, turning cold to the Soviet fleet and racing away.

Metcalf ruddered left, banking around to follow in the wake of the withdrawing attack wing.

The cyclical jamming sweep was coming apart at the seams. Being so close to so many targeting radars made it impossible to suppress all of them all of the time. The Soviet radars were burning through.

An A-6 Intruder caught a Soviet missile and rolled over into the ocean below a moment before a Hornet ahead of them exploded in a shower of flames and debris.

Metcalf throttled to full and felt the airframe shudder as they accelerated, chased by a haphazard spread of missiles burning through the jamming.

Coleman and Bradshaw kept up their work, struggling to ensure that nothing got a good enough whiff of them to lock on. Radar-seekers couldn't touch them.

But heatseekers weren't fooled by fancy electronics or phantom radio waves and one struck their tail with no warning.

With a cataclysmic bang, the Prowler heaved and rolled. It tumbled end over end as its aerodynamic profile failed catastrophically, metal skin ripping away as the airframe fractured and disintegrated.

Alarms and rushing wind both howled in Metcalf's ears as the world spun around him. Someone in the back was screaming—Coleman or Bradshaw. Metcalf couldn't breathe, he could hardly think, he just knew they had to get out. Animal fear replaced any conscious thought, all he could think of was escape.

He groped for the ejection handle, feeling the seconds bleed away as their tumble became a flat spin, gravity pressing him painfully to the side.

His fingers brushed the handle. Almost. Almost.

He was going to make it home. He was going to see his daughter again.

He gripped it a moment before the craft smashed into the water with enough force to shatter bones. Then nothing.

***

Rabbit felt more like his namesake than he ever had before. He ran. He ran as fast as he could. The low roar of his pulse matched the roar of the Tomcat's thrusters. He didn't like running. Putting his enemy behind him felt wrong no matter how intentional it was.

As this dogfight wore on, Rabbit felt the toll wearing on him. He'd lost any awareness of his squadron and only had the dimmest idea of where Ducky was in this maelstrom.

"Bandit still on our six," Gomez said.

RWR blared with a missile launch alert.

"He's launching!"

"Countermeasures," Rabbit said. He was too focused on keeping the Tomcat defending, undertaking a sweeping turn as he dove further down still.

The Tomcat left a trail of chaff and flares behind it. The Soviets liked to mix heatseekers and radar-guided weapons in an effort to overwhelm their opponents and Rabbit was doing his damndest to make sure that didn't work on him.

Gomez whispered foul curses under his breath as Rabbit took the F-14 through a tight corkscrew down.

The airframe rattled under the strain of buffeting winds

and G-forces. Rabbit sustained the hard maneuvers as he felt his vision begin to gray out, even past the radar lock warning falling silent. There was always the possibility of a heat seeking missile on their tail, and there would be no warning until that hit.

Rabbit brought the fighter all the way to the deck and pulled up just above the waves before throttling to full. He was dimly aware of the high fuel expenditure he faced by going so fast and so low, but right now it was the least of his concerns.

Finally satisfied he'd shaken off any possible missile pursuit, he straightened out, scanning for his pursuer.

"Stagecoach 01 to all groups, Flankers are turning back. Repeat, bandits are going cold."

That meant that Gunslinger was likely in the henhouse, wreaking havoc. Rabbit wasn't sure if any of the strike craft in his own group had gotten shots off at the Soviet fleet, but it didn't matter anymore. It meant they'd been successful in drawing off the carrier group's primary defense.

"All fighters stay on them, don't let them disengage."

Rabbit nosed up to gain altitude before banking around, feathering his control stick, and brought his craft back into pursuit position. A moment later he had a firing solution on the fleeing Flankers.

"Fox two!"

Their last Sidewinder streaked away, chasing after their would-be pursuer.

Coaxing what power he could from the Tomcat, Rabbit and the other F-14 pilots raced after their quarry.

***

As the Harpoons and HARMs emerged from the receding jamming cloud, they were picked up by *Kirov*'s targeting radars and the data fed into the colossal ship's combat information center. The range was short, time was shorter. The order was given and the ship's anti-air missile batteries were re-tasked.

The retreating American aircraft weren't a threat anymore, but the encroaching missiles very much were.

With the Harpoons flying so close to the waves, the full extent of the missile salvo was unclear. Even if *Kirov*'s radar arrays were capable of tracking that many targets at once, they could still only catch glimpses here and there of the radar returns as flickers and pings.

The SAM battery fired missiles as fast as they could be readied. The missiles climbed vertically and then arced away on plumes of smoke. *Kirov* wasn't alone in this either, the other capital ships were hardly defenseless and each added their own SAM fire to the defensive umbrella. The SAM systems onboard *Kirov* and his charges were all automated. Radar vectors were plotted, priorities assigned, and missiles launched without any intervention from a human operator. In fact, a human touch would only slow the process.

Each ship pumped out waves of missiles, easily enough to cover all one hundred approaching missiles. The problem they faced, however, wasn't numbers.

As the missiles flickered in and out of detection, the SAMs gravitated toward targeting the most clearly visible: the higher flying HARMs. Every second they drew nearer to their targets, the number of missiles actually being targeted shrank gradually until less than half of the American missiles were at risk.

The Soviets lacked the West's advanced Aegis system which was so effective in preventing SAMs from doubling up on incoming missiles. With the Aegis—in theory—one hundred SAMs could evenly target one hundred incoming anti-ship missiles with no overlap, leaving the remainder that slipped through to be cleaned up with CIWS guns.

The Soviet SAMs had no such control and so clustered up on targets.

Within a minute, the lead-most missiles were struck with SAMs, blasting them from the sky with puffs of smoke, throwing rings of debris across the ocean waves. The deadly flock was thinned, but it still came on. The Harpoons' ranks were virtually unchanged as they closed to CIWS range.

Kirov fired chaff. Mortar tubes hurled decoys up into the air, directly above the ship. Each round burst with streamers of metallic smoke, increasing the apparent radar signature the Harpoon was fixed on, and thus gradually steering it off course.

Leaving nothing to chance, the close-in weapons systems of the warships snapped to life. Each spooled up its rotary cannons and fixed onto a target.

The CIWS guns opened fire with a mechanical sawing sound. Thousands of rounds spewed out, slashing through the sky to track missiles on terminal approach. Soviet CIWS were roughly on par with their Western counterparts and were excellent at shooting down any missiles they could see. Harpoons exploded left, right, and center with thundering booms.

The problem came from the missiles they couldn't see.

The first Harpoon which struck *Kirov* never even appeared on the CIWS's radar, lost in background clutter and drifting chaff clouds. The missile hit the ship on his portside bow, just below the 152 mm anti-aircraft gun mount, detonating on impact with the hull. The explosion blasted the steel hull to ribbons, leaving a ragged hole several meters in diameter that almost immediately began sucking in ocean water.

More Harpoons were close behind the first. Some were scythed from the air by the CIWS within a hundred meters of the ship, casting a rain of shrapnel and debris rattling off his metal hide. The chaff cloud above and behind *Kirov* lured in more missiles, sending them racing aimlessly onward. Some of these were also tracked and destroyed by CIWS guns, sometimes leaving them out of position to stop the next wave of incoming missiles.

The second and third hits struck *Kirov* amidships, punching into the hull and igniting a roiling inferno that burned through the ship's innards, turning his interior into a noxious hell.

A fourth hit his superstructure and lobotomized him in an instant, obliterating the navigational bridge and much of the ship's radar equipment, taking with it irreplaceable command crew.

A fifth missile lanced his heart, plunging into the engine room before exploding, killing main power and propulsion. *Kirov* was dead even as his crew fought to stay alive, frantic to escape the smoke and flames boiling inside.

Kirov wasn't the only target of the Harpoons. With only two hits, *Baku* was luckier than *Kirov*. One blew a smoking hole in his nose—a dramatic hit but one which held no mortal danger to the ship. The other Harpoon punched into the aircraft hangar below deck, failing to detonate. Burning missile fuel swept across the decking, washing over men and material without distinction. Smoke and fumes filled the bay, suffocating sailors and crew. Damage control teams fought their way into the hangar, trying to smother the flames with water and foam, desperately trying to save what lives and equipment they could. Within five minutes, *Baku's* luck ran out as the flames reached a stack of air-to-air missiles waiting to re-arm the returning Yaks. The missiles and their fuel exploded with fiery fury, erupting from the confined hangar bay via hatches and passageways. The fuel stores for the helicopters and their weapons added to the conflagration which volcanoed through *Baku's* hull, rupturing it along a fatal seam. The ship went down in minutes, dragging just over a thousand souls with him.

In the last moments of the missile attack, all the defense guns of all the ships fired wildly through the air, chasing stray missiles or cutting down active threats. The flagship—*Novosibirsk*—was shielded from all of this by *Kirov's* bulk as the battlecruiser took hit after hit. It likely would have remained safe if not for *Kirov's* chaff clouds.

Two of the Harpoons were seduced by the spreading metallic cloud hanging above the battlecruiser and pulled up, aiming for the center mass of the radar return. They each sailed harmlessly through the cloud without finding anything solid enough to trigger their warheads. For a single half second, the silicon minds of the missiles were at a loss. With their enticing target having apparently vanished and their mission still unfulfilled, they switched back into hunting mode. Almost instantly they were gratified to find a juicy new radar return before them. *Novosibirsk*. The Harpoons quickly dropped back down to wavetop altitude and closed on their new target.

The CIWS guns aboard *Novosibirsk* were no less watchful than any others in the group. They swept the seas with radar waves, searching for incoming missiles. The problem arose from *Kirov* and his drifting chaff clouds directly in their line of sight which kept throwing false returns for the guns, preventing them from seeing the two Harpoons sprinting directly at them.

***

Yevdokimov listened with wordless horror as the ships of his division suffered blow after deadly blow. *Kirov* had stopped responding and *Baku* faced a serious fire burning through his belly. A disaster. A catastrophe. Yevdokimov's dream of naming a ship had transformed into a horrifying nightmare.

"All hands brace for impact! Enemy missile inbound, port side!"

Yevdokimov's head snapped up, his mouth wide with shock. A missile? *His* ship? He'd scarcely turned to find the ship's captain when a Harpoon lanced into the hull, driving itself into the *Novosibirsk*'s heart before exploding, burning out the guts of the carrier including the CIC—and Yevdokimov.

***

Novosibirsk took two hits just above the waterline. One plunged into the ship's flank while the other detonated on impact, wrenching apart tempered steel plates and letting the ocean in. The carrier floated for now, but time would tell on him as a portside list would soon become a desperate flounder as water penetrated his lower decks, rushing through unsecured hatchways and flowing around faulty watertight doors.

Somehow in all of this chaos, only *Riga* was left unscathed. He'd warded off or shot down every one of the Harpoons targeted at him. He floated at the tail end of the *Novosibirsk* group and could only watch as the rest of the division went to hell.

***

28

Tension aboard Stagecoach 01 gradually gave way to post-mission elation. The crew of the American AWACS could only watch and grimly mark the casualties among the fighters as they entered the fray. There was nothing to be done but dutifully feed up to date radar data to the other aircraft of the raid and grimace at each friendly blip that disappeared from the plot. At the height of the dogfight, Stagecoach's escorts had been committed to the melee, leaving them on their own over the cold ocean waves.

But now the death and violence were mostly behind them. Gunslinger had gotten in, delivered its deadly payload, and was in the process of exfiltrating. The Tomcats were chasing down the last of the Flankers. And Gunslinger was free to pick off scattered picket ships as they fled and attempted to regroup. It was as clear a mission success as there ever was.

Stagecoach's radar intercept officer allowed himself an easy smile. He felt the tension in his chest lessen just slightly. They'd pulled it off.

That relief died when he saw fresh tracks appear on his radar.

He leaned in, double checking his signals, and attempted to verify their identity. That became clear enough when they activated their targeting radars.

Flankers, thirty of them, closed from the northeast. They were two hundred kilometers out and moving fast.

For a few seconds there was only numb shock. The RIO couldn't believe what he was seeing. Three enemy squadrons closing on him with not a single escort anywhere nearby, nothing between him and them. He ran the numbers. The Flankers were less than five minutes from firing range.

The E-2 Hawkeye was too big to evade missiles and too slow to run. A little more simple arithmetic showed that even if they turned around now, the Tomcats wouldn't be able to reach them in time. No matter what else happened in the next few minutes, they would all find themselves in the frigid waters of the Norwegian Sea.

As the radar intercept officer began to dutifully feed this new data to the Tomcats, the crew of Stagecoach checked their water survival gear. If they were lucky enough to survive the initial attack, then they would be needing it soon.

***

G-forces pressed Rabbit and Gomez mercilessly as they banked hard into a sharp turn, slotting themselves behind a juking Flanker desperate to stay out of their sights.

"Guns! Guns! Guns!" Rabbit triggered the autocannon and walked a spray of shells across the Flanker.

The enemy aircraft caught the rounds and shuddered like a sick animal, its engines burning out, leaving only a trail of black smoke as it went ballistic, arcing down toward the ocean.

Rabbit was only faintly aware of the enemy pilot punching out as he sailed by.

The Soviets were outnumbered and floundering against their American adversaries. As long as nothing changed, then this was to be an unquestioned American victory. Rabbit and the others had turned the tables on their Soviet opponents and were now just mopping up the remains.

Rabbit's radio crackled. "Stagecoach to all wings. Be advised we have a new threat vector. 330, one hundred and fifty kilometers, Angels twenty. We mark at least thirty Flankers closing on afterburners." Despite the professional demeanor, the radar intercept officer who spoke sounded afraid, as scared as anyone Rabbit had ever heard. "We're going offline," he said.

"We'll come back if we can." A pause. "Stagecoach out."

Fresh arrivals of enemy fighters from the north was going to be a problem for the fighters of the wing.

"Oh, shit," Gomez said quietly.

"Lancers, this is lead." Lancer 100's voice carried over the radio loud and clear. "We're winchester for foxes. All craft break off and go to afterburner. 103, 108, hold back and bring up the rear, confirm."

"103 confirms," Rabbit said, followed a moment later by Ducky's own confirmation.

When the Tomcats began to peel off, *Novosibirsk*'s Flankers took their chance to flee, going low and fast back the way they'd come.

"We're down to our last two Sparrows ," Gomez said. "Better pray we don't have to use them."

Rabbit said nothing, holding wide of the rest of the wing as they fell back, ensuring none of the Flankers took a chance to take a potshot at the fleeing Americans. Once he was satisfied they were clear, Rabbit and Ducky fell in behind the others, racing back for safety.

Rabbit felt some of the tension he felt released once he put the enemy behind him. His second engagement and he'd come out in one piece. He let out a shaky breath and focused his attention on flying. All he wanted right now was to make it back to *Shiloh*. His thoughts were straying to the pilots who'd punched out and were now adrift in the open ocean. He didn't envy their chances.

"Uhh," Gomez said. "Rabbit, we've got nails."

"What?" Rabbit asked.

"Nails six o'clock," Gomez answered. "A hundred twenty five miles out. Flanker band. It's— shit. Lost it."

"You're sure?"

Gomez was silent for a moment. "Positive."

Rabbit gritted his teeth. Maybe it was a fluke, one of the fleeing Flankers checking to ensure they weren't being followed.

Five minutes later they caught the flash of the radar again. There was no mistaking it.

Rabbit flipped his radio on. "Lancer 100, this is 103. Looks like we're being shadowed. I think the new arrivals are tracking us in."

***

"We're sure they're being followed back?" Rear Admiral Dunner asked.

"Rear elements of Lancer are reporting intermittent radar lock from their six o'clock. Looks like Flanker-Ds."

Dunner grimaced. Bad news on top of good news. This was supposed to be a clean sweep. The last anyone had seen of the carrier group they'd attacked—now positively identified as *Novosibirisk*—it was burning and sinking, its fighter squadrons decimated, escorts scattered. With one group scratched, it was just a matter of zeroing the last two. Unfortunately it seemed like they'd found him first.

The men of *Antietam*'s CIC were professionals and remained about their work. Even as the Hornets and Intruders savaged the Soviet ships there had been no cheering, no celebration, just a faint, grim satisfaction. Now was no different, they were about their work.

"How long?" Dunner asked.

"The Tomcats are thirteen minutes out, the Flankers will be just a couple minutes behind them," the officer replied.

It wasn't a good situation. With all of *Shiloh* and *Antietam*'s fighters low on ammo and fuel from their operation, they didn't have anything to intercept the air attack that could be following behind them. It would be up to the air defenses of their picket ships. The saving grace would be that Flankers weren't capable of carrying as deadly an array of anti-ship missiles as Backfires could. "How long till they enter radar range of our picket?"

"We'll have hard force numbers in five minutes. *Richard*

Clark should pick them up first."

***

Ulyanovsk's Flanker squadrons flew in staggered lines, following in the wake of *Shiloh*'s fighters. Heavily loaded with anti-air missiles, they were more than a match for whatever token resistance the American fighter craft could mount without reloading their depleted missile stocks. Toggling radars intermittently, they kept the Americans in their sights, tracking them straight back to the carrier group.

The forward-most squadron leader grinned at his radar display as he watched the enemy fighters circling and losing altitude, beginning their landing approach on what had to be their carrier.

A moment later his RWR trilled a warning about a surface radar lock.

They were hitting the edge of the American SAM umbrella, yet more confirmation that they'd found their quarry. The downside to their air-to-air loadout was that they had no means of engaging American ships at range.

"Break and go low," the squadron leader said. His pilots followed his lead to defend against the approaching missiles. At this range, with the missiles coming tail on, their velocity would be low enough that dodging or fooling them should prove no challenge.

The Flanker pilot togged his radio on. "*Ulyanovsk*, this is Minotaur One. We've found them."

***

29

Four hundred kilometers north of *Shiloh*, the Soviet *Ulyanovsk* battle group eagerly awaited the return of their air wing. Rear Admiral Olesk frowned to himself and tapped his foot with nervous regularity. He knew full well how vulnerable they were out here. NATO was holding every advantage and, unlike Admiral Zharkov, he didn't believe that misdirection was enough to win the day. The grim fate of Yevdokimov's carrier group was all the reminder he needed of the risks here. It was a small miracle that *Riga* had survived to recover what was left of *Novosibirsk*'s air wing. Last Olesk had checked, Yevdokimov himself hadn't been located by damage control teams aboard the stricken *Novosibirsk*. No great loss as far as Olesk was concerned. Maybe it was better for that sycophantic fool to stay wherever he was. In his opinion, Yevdokimov's survival would really only be a win for NATO.

"There," Olesk's operations officer said, indicating a point on the map. It was unremarkable save for the fact that it sat at the convergence of a number of detected Western radar systems.

Olesk leaned over the table and stared at the empty blue spot. "The American carriers?"

"They must be there, Comrade," the operations officer said. "Their radar coverage rings it, their escorts defend it. I would estimate they are within a twenty kilometer radius of this spot."

It was a broad net to cast, but that was the only kind of net they could cast given the overwhelming superiority of NATO air defense.

Olesk nodded. "Good. Recall the Sukhois then. Ensure they

are ready for air defense." It was only a matter of time before the West located his group, and he was determined not to meet the same fate as Yevdokimov. "Flash this data to Zharkov," he said. The Soviets couldn't hope to match American anti-ship carrier aviation and their Backfires were occupied keeping the rest of the NATO fleet busy. It was time for them to deploy their primary offensive weapon, the Granit missile.

In sharp contrast to the Western model, Soviet aircraft carriers were more than simply floating airfields. Each one was armed with a dozen P-700 Granit cruise missiles, each of these carrying nearly four times the explosive force of a Harpoon missile. When combined with the missiles aboard the *Kirov*-class battlecruiser they were able to fire nearly fifty of them. "If we launch simultaneously we have a good chance to overwhelm them," Olesk said. "And check with submarine command. If any of our missile subs are still alive, now is their chance."

***

Across the *Ulyanovsk* group and what was left of the *Novosibirsk* group, missile tubes disgorged their lethal contents. The heavy cruise missiles momentarily blanketed their launch vessel with billows of gray smoke, before streaking out and banking to the south, following pre-plotted inertial guidance fed to them by the returning Flankers.

No matter how closely together the weapons were fired, they could never truly be simultaneous and so they swept forward in waves of a half-dozen each, skimming low to the ocean, like the Harpoons did, to baffle detection and deterrence.

Further to the east of the formation, the *Oscar*-class missile submarine *K-186* joined this salvo, firing its own tubes using targeting data fed to it via ULF.

***

To the advanced passive sonar systems of the USS *Raleigh*, the firing of *K-186*'s missiles may as well have been the ringing of a dinner bell.

Raleigh's control room erupted with activity as the launches were picked up.

"Where is she?" Grier demanded, moving forward to the sonar room. "Is that the same one we heard earlier?" He wasn't about to miss the same target twice.

The sonar operators were deep into triangulating the source of the sound, watching waveforms on screens and listening intently on their headphones.

"Either an Oscar or an Echo, sir!" an officer replied at last.

"Oscar," Grier said. "Gotta be. No Echo could hide out here this long. What's the range?"

"Estimate about 30 kilometers, sir."

She was practically right on top of them all this time. That put their torpedoes over fifteen minutes out. Plenty of time to evade again. Grier didn't answer but moved back from sonar to attack and control. "Helm, set heading straight for that acoustic signature and take us to three quarters speed."

"Aye, sir. Three quarters."

With the racket of firing so many missiles, hopefully the Oscar wouldn't hear them for a minute or two. He had to buy all the time he could to close range. The Oscar was a missile boat, but that didn't mean she was defenseless. "Set depth at one hundred fifty meters."

The helmsman repeated the depth and *Raleigh* began to descend. Deeper, denser water would help to prevent their propellers from cavitating, buying them a bit more time to close range. Less than a minute later, sonar reported that the Oscar had stopped firing—likely exhausting its limited missile supplies.

They didn't have time to fool around. Grier wasn't going to lose them again.

"Fire tubes one and two," Grier said. "Helm, take us down to half speed."

The tubes unloaded as *Raleigh* decelerated. Both torpedoes thrummed through the water, trailing guide cables behind them linking them to *Raleigh*'s control room.

It was not a quick process. Even at max speed, the torpedoes would take time to cross the kilometers of distance between submarines. All Grier could do was wait patiently.

The Oscar had gone silent, likely dropping slowly down into the depths as her ballast tanks filled with seawater. With no sounds to track, she had effectively vanished. But Grier knew she was still there.

The torpedoes were approaching terminal range where their active sonar would switch on when *Raleigh* detected a fresh contact. The operators in the sonar room didn't need to reference an audio database or waterfall display to identify it.

"Torpedos! Hostile torpedoes closing bearing 045. Distance twenty kilometers and closing."

Grier felt his blood run cold. "From the Oscar?"

"No, sir, I don't think so. The bearing is wrong."

He'd discounted the idea that there could be more than one Russian sub lurking in these waters, a mistake that might prove to be his last.

"Helm, depth two hundred meters, take us to flank. Weapons, deploy a noisemaker and get me a reciprocal heading on shooter two."

They had just about ten minutes before those torpedoes reached them, and less than two before theirs reached the Oscar.

"We have a bearing sir, but no range," Weapons returned.

Without a range they had no way of knowing where to program the torpedo to go active to hunt for its prey. Too early or too late and they risked a miss altogether.

"They already know we're here," Grier mused. "Helm, come to 045. Sonar, start active pinging."

"Aye, sir!"

Raleigh turned toward the approaching torpedoes and let

out a titanic pulse of her active sonar.

"Returns! We've got a target."

"Give 'em two more. Fire three and four," Grier said.

"Firing!"

Raleigh fired again.

"Torpedoes one and two are going active. They've got a fix on a target."

Either the Oscar, an eddy in the water, or a decoy. They would only know once they hit or didn't.

"We've got a make on the second target, sir. *Victor*-class. She's accelerating."

Unlike the Oscar, which was a big, fat missile boat, the Victor was an attack sub, sleek and deadly. The difference between the Victor and *Raleigh* was that the Victor was old and her sonar gear was subpar.

"Drop another noisemaker," Grier said.

The decoy produced sound and a reflective sonar contact by producing high volumes of bubbles. It would just be dumb luck if the enemy torpedo chose the decoy over the real thing, so Grier decided to make their own luck. "Full reverse, fill the tanks, take us down another hundred meters." He had to hope the Soviets would cut their guide wire to maneuver away from his shot, otherwise this ploy wouldn't work.

"Aye, sir!"

Raleigh reversed, slowing and ponderously stopping before beginning to move backwards.

"Impact! Torpedo one has struck the target. I make transients."

Torpedo two hit the Oscar again a moment later, finishing it off. The groans of metal and expulsions of air sounded fatal.

"How long till the enemy fish get here?" Grier asked.

"Six minutes until enemy torpedo impact."

It was going to be close.

The Victor continuously pulsed its sonar as it closed on them, doggedly tracking their quarry as they continued to drop a trail of noisemakers hoping to evade Grier's torpedoes.

Raleigh's own reverse course moved it backward through the cloud of bubbles produced by their noisemaker, putting a reflective sheet of turbulence between them and the enemy. With their ballast tanks filling they descended, dropping lower in the ocean between the noisemaker ahead of them and the one behind them.

"Four minutes to impact."

The Soviet torpedoes would get here first. Grier just prayed his feint worked. If the Soviets turned away and severed the cable then he stood a chance. Otherwise....

"Two minutes."

"Engines full stop," Grier said.

"Aye, full stop."

The submarine went silent except for the constant pinging of the torpedoes.

"Keep squawking, you bastard," Briggs said, forehead sheened with nervous sweat.

"Depth is three hundred."

They could hear the sounds of undersea combat through the steel hull of the submarine; the whir of the approaching torpedoes, the churning of the noisemakers in the water, the sharp pings of the Soviet sonar searching for them.

"Sixty seconds."

"All hands brace for impact," Grier said. It was a precautionary command-any impact at this depth would be the end of them. By now the Soviets had to be turning hard, trying to evade his torpedo. They had to be.

Everyone on the bridge heard the torpedoes as they passed through the bubble cloud overhead, losing their target. A moment later, the onboard sonars of the torpedoes picked their prey up again, closing distance for another thirty seconds where they struck with explosive force.

"Torpedoes have hit our first noisemaker," weapons said, breathing a sigh of relief.

A moment later, they heard the sound of Victor dying as one of their mark 48s found it.

The boom reverberated through the ocean.

"Victor hit," Sonar said. "She's breaking up. I heard an implosion."

Grier looked at his XO with a nervous smile. "That's two."

***

30

The surface pickets of *Shiloh* and *Antietam* saw the oncoming Granit missiles only as flickering, intermittent radar contacts. Flying at wavetop height and closing fast, they were difficult to pick out from the normal background clutter of the waves. There was still time left to intercept them though.

The Phoenix missile was just as capable of intercepting cruise missiles as it was aircraft, a job the Tomcat was perfect for. Weapons and fuel depleted from their sortie against *Novosibirsk,* the Tomcats of the carriers took off again as fast as they could be re-armed. They hardly had time to strap a fresh brace of missiles onto each craft and top off their internal tanks before they were screaming off the deck. It was a desperate, well-coordinated waltz of technicians, planes, and equipment.

While deck crew rushed into position to decouple refueling hoses and finish mounting a fresh batch of Phoenix missiles on the Tomcat's undercarriage, Rabbit and Gomez tried to recuperate themselves. Rabbit drank a few mouthfuls of lukewarm Gatorade from a squirt bottle before passing it back to Gomez who did the same. They'd been in the cockpit for hours now without respite. There wasn't even time for a bathroom break, something Rabbit tried not to think about.

When Gomez finished with the bottle, he handed it through the open cockpit to a waiting crew chief.

"All set, sir?"

Rabbit flashed him an OK with his thumb and forefinger and the cockpit was lowered back into place. Truthfully his legs and back were aching from sitting for so long. He rolled his head and shoulders trying to relieve some of the tension.

"How you doing, Rabbit?" Gomez asked.

"Ready for a shower," Rabbit said. "Ready to get home again."

Gomez chuckled. "I hear that. No rest for the wicked though."

"None."

They were nervous. They'd just been through hell, and they knew that hell was back, bearing down on the fleet at one and a half times the speed of sound.

From *Shiloh*'s deck they had a clear view of the sparkling waves of the Norwegian Sea. The tranquility of the scene belied their deadly purpose here.

Rabbit watched as Ducky's F-14—just reloaded—launched with a burst of energy as the steam catapult propelled the heavy aircraft off the deck and into the air. It dropped toward the waves for a moment before climbing skyward.

"Lancer 103, you're up next," a voice buzzed in Rabbit's ear. It was paramount to get *Shiloh*'s wing into the air as soon as possible, not just to assist with the intercept of the incoming Granits, but also to empty the hangar in case of a hit. Every plane flying was one less possible piece of collateral damage.

"103 copies," Rabbit said.

Once the deck was clear, Lancer 103 taxied into position and locked onto the catapult rail. Rabbit and Gomez ran through final weapons checks, testing circuits and verifying they were ready for a fight.

"Lancer 103, ready for takeoff," Rabbit said at last. He settled into his seat and kept a firm grip on his controls.

"Standby, 103."

Seconds ticked by into a half minute.

"What's the holdup?" Gomez asked, echoing Rabbit's thoughts.

"Control, what's the problem?" Rabbit asked. "We've got Vampires in the air, don't we?" His heart was racing. They were losing precious time.

"Confirm, 103. We have Vampires inbound, but there's a change of plan. A new spread of Vampires has been detected south."

"South?" Gomez asked off the radio. The Soviet carrier group was north. How had *Shiloh* gotten pincered like this?

"We're redirecting you to intercept."

"Copy, Rabbit said. "How many?"

"Unknown, 103."

That meant at least one but probably more than one. They only carried four phoenixes. This would be tight. "Copy. Just get us in the air."

After running through final takeoff procedure, Rabbit got his wish. Lancer 103 was thrown off the ship where the wind caught her wings seconds before she would have dropped into the surf. Rabbit throttled up and angled the aircraft's nose, gaining altitude before turning south toward the fresh missile contacts.

He and his quarry were closing at multiples of the speed of sound. Time to contact would be short.

"Anything?" Rabbit asked.

"Not yet," Gomez said, monitoring the F-14's radar. "We're still—Wait...there. Got 'em. That's them. One strong return and a couple weaker. I keep losing them against the background."

Most of the missiles were flying too low, but one wasn't. Higher than the others, it fed targeting data back to the rest of the swarm tailing it, acting as a spotter. Lose that one and the others would be blind.

"*Shiloh*, this is Lancer 103. I've got Vampires on scope. Can't make exact numbers. One spotter and a swarm of tailers."

"Copy, 103," the air wing controller replied. "You are clear to engage."

"Lock one up," Rabbit told his RIO. "We'll take it at maximum range."

"Rog," Gomez said. "We're locked."

"Lancer 103, fox three."

The craft juddered a moment as a heavy Phoenix missile

fell from the belly racks. A moment later it ignited and lanced down toward the low-flying missiles.

It was a head-on shot made from high altitude, giving them a huge velocity advantage. It was almost a guaranteed hit.

As Gomez counted down the range to the target, Rabbit kept it fixed in the deadly gaze of the Tomcat's radar cone until the Phoenix was able to engage its own terminal homing.

"It's pitbull," Gomez said.

The Phoenix came on with single minded purpose and struck the Granit midair. The flash of explosion was faintly visible to Rabbit and Gomez.

"Splash one vampire," Rabbit said.

Without a spotter, the swarm was less likely to be able to find the carriers. They were blind.

In response, the computers onboard the Granits registered the loss of their leader and after a millisecond of deliberation, selected a new one. This freshly appointed spotter climbed again, using its own onboard radar to again paint the distant targets of the surface fleet.

"Oh, shit," Gomez said, watching this development unfold on his monitors. "Hey, Rabbit, we've got a new spotter missile."

Rabbit felt a cold sweat break out across his skin. He only had three more Phoenixes. How many more Granits were in that wave? Something told him it was more than three. "Get me another lock," he said. There was nothing else he could do.

"*Shiloh*, this is Lancer 103. We're saturated with vampires here. I expect you're going to have company soon."

Rabbit heard the tension in the controller's voice when he replied. "Roger, 103." After all, it was his ass on the line.

Rabbit gritted his teeth. "103, fox three!"

***

While the Tomcats of *Shiloh* and *Antietam* were busy swatting down the wave of missiles fired from *Ulyanovsk* and his escorts, the missiles from the submarine *K-186* closed from the south, virtually unmolested except for the four Phoenixes Lancer 103 carried, leaving fourteen Grantis still closing on target.

Rabbit and Gomez could only watch impotently as the surviving missiles passed by beneath them on their death ride.

Flying so low to the waves, it would be difficult for the long range SAMs of the task force to target them. Once they had their target fixed, the spotter missiles dropped down to the deck as well, flying as low as the others.

While receiving the occasional weak return on radar, the anti-air operators of the fleet couldn't be wasteful with their precious ammunition. After all, every missile they fired was one less missile to use against possible Backfire attacks from Norway. But they couldn't do nothing either.

A handful of missiles were fired every minute or so across the task force, most targeted north toward the massive wave from the Soviet carriers, but some were aimed south at the submarine-launched missiles.

Of these, a few found their marks, blasting anti-ship missiles to shreds and filling the horizon with fireballs and smoke.

In another few minutes, the surviving missiles passed through the gauntlet, some coming into CIWS range of the escort ships. A dozen were cut from the sky by sprays of twenty millimeter gunfire. One was suckered into a decoy chaff cloud and missed, but a few made it through, closing on the carriers.

USS Long Beach and *Cowpens* were the innermost escorts for the two carriers and focused their undivided attention on the goal of destroying each of the missiles that came up on their scopes. These two cruisers were state-of-the-art, equipped with advanced detection suites and the Aegis system. Well-drilled crews managed their computers as the ships' anti-air systems did their work.

SAMs launched like clockwork, meticulously categorizing and prioritizing incoming threats. One by one the Granits were destroyed, breaking up or crashing down in the waves. One came close enough for *Long Beach* to pin it with her CIWS guns and obliterate it. Finally, their scopes were clear of missiles. There had been no hits.

Though their scopes were clear, one missile still remained, evading detection by nature of its low, swift flight. The Granit struck *Antietam* by its port-side elevator and exploded with the equivalent of seven hundred and fifty kilograms of TNT, incinerating the crew closest to the blast point and throwing countless others around as the ship lurched. Smoke and flame poured into the hangars and passageways of the stricken carrier.

***

At the moment the Granit struck his vessel, Rear Admiral Dunner was safe, nestled deep within *Antietam*'s heart in her combat information center, and that was exactly what he found so frustrating. Through some small mercy the power didn't fail, but there was no telling how long that would last. The shockwave of the blast ran through *Antietam*'s hull like a shiver. Even in the depths of the CIC, Dunner felt the force of the hit.

Dunner began speaking as soon as the tremor of the blast subsided. "Where did we take it?"

"Rear, portside elevator, sir!"

"How bad?" Dunner asked, hoping against hope that the missile hadn't actually detonated.

"We have a Seahawk on scene assessing the damage."

All around the CIC, weapons and systems operators chattered not so quietly into their microphones and to one another, coordinating with the carrier group's air defense, her air wing, damage control teams, and other vessels in the force. They were shaken, it had been a serious hit and there was no guarantee they were out of the woods.

In that moment of chaos, Dunner allowed himself a display of weakness. He swore loudly. It didn't make him feel much better. "Let me know the second we find out."

"Yes, sir!"

Given the low-level attack profile of the Granit, it was likely the hit was at or near the waterline which meant *Antietam* would be taking in seawater.

"Helm, engines full stop until we know how bad things are," Dunner said. The thrum of the engines subsided in a few moments as the ship slowed to a stop. The last thing Dunner needed was the force of their own movement worsening the damage to their hull. But a stationary warship was also a vulnerable warship, especially if the Soviets had attack submarines lurking in the area. The last thing he needed was to suffer *Gettysburg's* fate.

He took a few tense breaths. If things were bad—*truly* bad—then there was a possibility they were going to lose the ship, and if it was bad enough, then their remaining time on the surface could be numbered in minutes. It was up to Dunner to make the call to abandon her though. If he did it too soon, they might lose the ship unnecessarily, too late and he would be wasting lives. The seconds before the Seahawk made its report were painful eternities.

"Twenty meter gash above the water line. Elevator is totally destroyed."

"Are we taking on water?" Dunner asked.

"Some. Not enough to be an immediate concern."

Dunner allowed himself to exhale. If the ship wasn't sinking, they only had to worry about the fires.

"Damage control teams are responding to internal damage," the officer continued. "Fires have been largely contained. So far there's no risk to fuel or ammunition stores."

"Small favors," Dunner said. "Casualties?"

The other officer blanched. "No firm numbers sir."

"Give me an estimate." Dunner found that he was terrified of the answer.

"Estimating at least one hundred, sir."

Dunner swore again. "Goddamit." Men died in war. He

wasn't stupid, he'd always known that. But somehow he had always hoped it wouldn't be *his* men dying. He couldn't go to pieces, not now, not while people were counting on him.

As more information came in from sections across the ship, it became clear that *Antietam*'s damage was severe but survivable, provided they acted quickly, carefully, and didn't allow things to get worse. They could save the ship, but they would have to turn back for land. They were going to have to break off the attack.

***

31

The Su-27K's engines and tires howled as its arrestor hook caught the wire strung across the deck of *Tashkent*. The wire yanked the aircraft to a halt where deck crew assisted with taxiing it out of the way for the next landing plane.

Admiral Zharkov watched from the angled windows of the carrier's flight control tower as the fighter was successfully recovered. The Flanker's mottled baby blue camouflage scheme contrasted sharply with the blood red sky. The crew of the control tower kept at their work, their eyes fixed on displays and monitors. They were focused, perhaps more than they would have been had the admiral not been present. Some of them murmured quiet commands into headset microphones which were relayed to orbiting aircraft still waiting to land.

Each step in this process was a movement in a ballet as elegant and tightly choreographed as any in Leningrad's Kirov theater. Zharkov felt a certain muted pride. These were *his* men, *his* aircraft, *his* systems. They'd drawn blood from the West, though it hadn't been without cost.

The death of Rear Admiral Yevdokimov and the virtual annihilation of his division was troubling—beyond troubling. Just thinking about it made Zharkov's stomach churn.

But, despite the losses, he still commanded a formidable force: two *Ulyanovsk*-class, three *Riga*s and an obsolete but functional *Kiev*-class shepherding the amphibious landing group trailing the fleets, not to mention the multitude of escort craft including two powerful *Kirov*s.

There were also his undersea forces. Soviet attack

submarines were scattered throughout the Norwegian Sea. Ostensibly they were to cooperate directly with his surface and air elements. In practice though this was proving easier said than done. They simply couldn't maintain communication with these submarines and keep them hidden from the enemy at the same time—with some exceptions, like the timely intervention of *K-186*, or the report from *K-432* he held in his hands.

AMERICAN CARRIER 'ANTIETAM' TURNING WEST. HEAVY SMOKE. BELIEVED SERIOUSLY DAMAGED.

Zharkov read the brief report again and tried to force himself to smile, but he couldn't. One American carrier damaged in exchange for Yevdokimov's entire group was far from a fair exchange. The fact was that his ships and aircraft simply couldn't afford to fight the West on even footing. This was the enemy's domain he was intruding in.

Assuming the news from this submarine was to be believed, the carrier group harassing his forces was at least fifty percent reduced, if not more. That left the carriers hugging the coast of Norway still, and not to mention whatever lay ahead. In his audacity, Zharkov had maneuvered his meager fleet directly into the midst of the enemy. It remained to be seen if he could maneuver out of it.

When he re-folded the printout from *K-432*, his hands trembled.

Ideally, he would simply order this submarine to put a torpedo down the throat of the remaining American carrier, and finish off the damaged one. Of course, the world didn't give a damn about ideal circumstances. The submarine was monitoring the American carriers from extreme range and was only still alive because it hadn't done more than shadow them. Even then, its days—or more likely its hours—were numbered.

No matter, their goal was close at hand. They'd swept past most of NATO's naval forces and were ready to deploy their trailing marine complement to Iceland's rocky shores.

"Comrade Admiral," a junior officer said, holding a headset, "Rear Admiral Olesk on the encrypted line."

Zharkov scowled, causing the sailor to flinch. Olesk was precisely the last person he wanted to hear from right now. With Yevdokimov dead, Olesk didn't have any more competition and would likely be gunning for Zharkov's job.

Zharkov took the headset and put it on. He snapped his fingers at the operator who connected the line. "Go ahead, Comrade Olesk."

"We have recovered all attack aircraft," Olesk said, his voice calm and level. "Losses among Yevdokimov's air wing are severe. Fortunately the survivors can all be landed on *Riga*. We're lucky he's still untouched."

Zharkov said nothing. His headache continued boring into his skull, growing only worse, throbbing with his heartbeat.

"Comrade Admiral, what is the plan? Without *Novosibirsk* —."

"There is no change in the plan," Zharkov replied sharply. "We maintain course for the Icelandic coast."

"Comrade, with respect, that's suicide. We've gotten lucky this far. Now the Americans know where we are, more or less. You can bet they'll send everything they have."

"You are a coward, Olesk," Zharkov said, sparing none of the vitriol he felt in that moment. "A coward. You would throw everything away and run back for Polyarny with our tail between our legs? You would return with nothing to show for what we've lost?"

"Admiral, we will lose much more if we do not turn back. We've damaged two carrier groups. Let us swing south and bring everything we have to bear on the nearest group. We can finish them off. We have been lucky twice now. There will not be a third time."

"No," Zharkov agreed. "There will not. *This* is our time. Our *only* time to strike! This plan only works once, you see?" His face was flushed red, sweat beaded down his temples and neck. In that moment he noticed the control staff were focused on him, glances furtively up from their work to stare anxiously at their fuming admiral. Zharkov forced himself to be calm. "The Americans are the ones who are out of time. Our lead AWACS craft indicate there is only a small task force before us. Do not worry about the other carriers. Our comrades in the naval air arm will handle things."

"This is a mistake, Admiral," Olesk warned.

"The only mistake was allowing you command of a division," Zharkov returned sharply. "Our bombers will sortie soon. The Americans know it. They will either stay busy fighting them or they will flee, leaving the convoys to Norway vulnerable. You see? We have them!"

Olesk didn't reply.

Zharkov frowned deeper. "Maintain speed and course. *Riga* will join your division since you are closest. Feint south with your air wing to keep the Americans on the defensive. They will be concerned we intend to finish off *Antietam*. Let them believe that."

"Yes, Admiral."

Zharkov handed the headset back to the radio operator without a backward glance. He wouldn't give the Americans a chance to breathe. The naval bombers would just have to go out again, regardless of the risk to themselves.

He felt himself relaxing marginally. What he was feeling were just jitters. It was understandable given the scale of the operation here. He came to stand by the windows again and watched another Su-27K on final approach.

Casualties and losses were inevitable. Great battles simply weren't won without them. Once the GIUK gap was closed to the West, then the tides of this war would change in the Soviet Union's favor.

The Su-27K pulled back, decelerating as it dropped toward the deck. It came in too steeply, too fast. The plane struck the deck as its port side landing gear collapsed.

Someone nearby swore loudly as the fighter skidded across the deck in a shower of sparks, careening into a nearby parked

Su-27K.

Deck crew scattered for cover as an emergency team raced in, preemptively dousing the crashed aircraft in fire retardant foam.

Zharkov felt the pit in his stomach only growing larger.

***

At Orlond Air Station, there was no celebration for the surviving Tupolev crews. Nearly half of them had been wiped out in the American sneak attack during their return trip. What had started as a wildly successful raid ended in a dismal retreat back to safety.

Fedorovich's hands hadn't stopped trembling since the mission. He leaned against the exterior wall of a vehicle shed and smoked, his eyes staring ahead, unfocused. When he closed his eyes he saw the flaming aircraft of his squadron falling around him. The tobacco smoke he breathed in was the acrid stink of melting plastic that filled their cockpits, the world outside tumbling to oblivion.

Fedorovich exhaled and held out a hand, cigarette between his fingers and watched it shaking almost imperceptibly. He swore.

"You too?" Babayev asked, holding up an unlit cigarette of his own.

Fedorovich offered his co-pilot a lighter, not trusting himself to try to light it.

"The bastards," Fedorovich said.

"The Americans?"

Fedorovich nodded. "Any word on re-arming?"

Babayev leaned beside his commander and puffed on his now lit cigarette for a moment. "Within the hour is what I heard last. I think they will send us out again today."

"Good," Fedorovich said, shoving his shaking hands into his pockets. "So much the better."

"Aren't you afraid?" Babayev asked.

"Afraid? Yes. Of course. But I am also angry."

Across the tarmac, the regiment's remaining bombers were wreathed with light from flood lamps as ground crews worked them over, refueling and rearming.

"We owe the Americans another visit now, I think," Fedorovich said.

"Was the first not enough for you?" Babayev asked.

"No," Fedorovich said. His cigarette had burned down to the butt. He threw it onto the pavement and stomped in flat, crushing it with a twist of his boot. "Not nearly enough."

***

32

Admiral Alderman sat at his desk with what felt like the weight of the world on his shoulders. His stateroom—no different than when he'd last been here almost twenty four hours ago—felt like an alien place. He looked over the various photos decorating the office until his eyes stopped on one. It was a photograph on his desk of him, his wife, and his children in front of their Maryland home. Thanks to him, a lot of families weren't going to get their boys back.

No. Not thanks to him, Alderman reminded himself. Thanks to the enemy.

Alderman wasn't alone in the room. Standing opposite his desk was a solemn group of officers—the command staff of his carrier group. They all looked as tired as he felt. Even in peacetime, war had been the profession of the men gathered here. It haunted their thoughts and occupied their days. But war had been academic before, just numbers. Now it was all too real and personal.

"What's the latest from the Dunner and *Antietam* group?" Alderman asked.

"Heavy damage to the flagship." The officer who spoke didn't bother to consult any notes. "Admiral Dunner believes *Antietam* can be saved, but he's withdrawing the group to safeguard it. There's a risk of air attack or submarines. He feels it's best not to risk splitting the group."

Alderman nodded as he listened. "Stiff price to pay," Alderman said. "But Dunner made the right call. No reason to risk the carrier."

"With respect sir, is that the right call? *Shiloh*'s wing took serious losses, but if we shift aircraft around we could mount another strike on the Soviets."

Alderman considered this for a moment before sighing. Of all the situations to find himself in, re-enacting Midway wasn't the one he expected. "We never did any carrier-fleet engagement drills," Alderman said. "Not like this I mean. Who the hell would have expected the Soviets to sail out for a straight up fight like this?" The question was rhetorical, he waited for no answer. Instead Alderman rubbed his tired eyes. "We're all just going off of our gut and what we remember from fighting the Japanese fifty years ago."

"If that's true sir, then the Russians are probably just as bad off as we are."

Alderman gave a tired smile. "Their last fleet action was in 1905 at Tsushima Strait. I'd say they're doing a bit better this time around." He mentally steered himself back to business. "What about Russian losses? What do we know?"

"We've identified it as *Novosibirsk* group and it's been virtually annihilated. Only *Riga* managed to escape. Air assets from Scotland and submarine forces in the area are hunting them. The whole division is combat ineffective."

Finally, good news, although Alderman didn't feel it. "That leaves two more fleet carriers," he said, "plus those smaller ones. Five fleet carriers total, is that right?"

"Yes, Admiral."

Alderman kept his eyes on the photo of his family as he thought. "And no apparent change in their course?"

"None, sir. They're making for Iceland at best speed."

"So we know where they are and where they're going. And they have to know that we know that too."

"Looks like it, sir."

"The question then is 'why.'" Alderman rocked back in his chair. "There's nothing of strategic value in Iceland except for Keflavik, and that's on the wrong side of the island."

That's a whole lot of effort to reduce one small airbase."

Alderman nodded. "Unless it's the island itself they're after," he mused.

"Admiral?"

Alderman picked up the old satellite recon photos from his desk and shuffled through them, looking at the small wakes of warships turning west. "Maybe we've been so focused on the teeth that we've forgotten about the tail." Coming to the end of the stack he found another photo of a group of ships on maneuver, this one tailing well behind the lead fleets. The only identified vessel was a *Kiev*-class VTOL carrier at the center of the formation, likely focused on anti-submarine protection. Aside from a ring of pickets, all the ships in the interior were labeled as auxiliaries. Oilers and transport craft, the logistical elements needed for long-term fleet operations, except the Soviets couldn't be planning on any long term *naval* operations.

"Easy answer," Alderman said, laying the photo down. "They're going to try to land troops."

"That's insane!"

"Definitely," Alderman agreed. "But once they put boots on that shore, we're going to have a damn hard time getting them out. The British and Dutch Royal Marines there were mostly redeployed to Norway. The island is close to defenseless."

"Even if they get past us, sir, they don't have any way of supplying whatever they land. They'll starve out on that rock," an officer said.

Alderman fixed him with a serious look. "No doubt of that, Commander. Even if each of those ships is packed stem to stern with bloodthirsty Soviet marines and tanks they wouldn't have a hope of fighting for long. Not with no way of being resupplied. But imagine for a second that those freighters carry a few dozen SAMs and anti-ship missiles each. They might be able to put a real thorn in our side, possibly even hold open the GIUK gap for their sub fleet again. They won't have to beat us in some big naval battle if they can make a straight fight too costly for us to attempt. Whether or not their marines starve is immaterial to them so long as they can set up and operate enough missile batteries to make operations in the gap difficult for us."

Alderman's subordinates looked both shocked and horrified, not just by the audacity of the plan, but also by the prospect that it just might work.

"Sure, we can wait them out," Alderman continued. "But that's days—maybe weeks-of time we can't afford to waste. This whole war could turn on a dime and Soviet long range anti-air and anti-ship batteries on Iceland would certainly go a long way toward hampering our operations here. The Soviets are one good breakthrough away from smashing our Scandinavian beachhead. That's tens of thousands of troops and weapons we can't afford to lose, plus the morale factor—." Alderman drew himself short. He was ranting. The admiral closed his mouth and thought again about his family—all the families counting on him to bring their brothers, husbands, and sons home. "The Soviets are likely going to hit us with everything they've got. If we send all our fighters out to take the remaining carrier groups, we'll be vulnerable to attack from shore-based aircraft and missiles. Backfires." The terror and destruction left in the wake of the last Backfire attack was still fresh in his mind. "We haven't had time to completely replenish our SAM magazines, so we're vulnerable to saturation attacks."

"We should pull the fleet back, sir. We can't take the risk of them getting more good hits in."

Alderman shook his head. "The Russians have us in a bear trap here. If we stay, they hit us. If we leave, they can hit the convoys. They've got us where they want us. All that we can do is fight our way out of it."

Expressions were muted all around. No one looked happy with the situation, but Alderman was right. There was nothing else to be done. All they could do was act.

"The Soviets have locked down our air assets pretty well," Alderman said. "But that's not all we have. We'll put out an ULF broadcast to our attack subs. If we can find and hit the landing group, we can moot the primary goal of this operation."

"We'll make it happen, sir."

"Until then," the admiral said at last, "we've got to double down and wait."

"What's left between the Russians and Iceland?" a commander asked.

"*Iowa*," Alderman said.

A small task force with an impossible mission ahead of them. A single refitted battleship facing off against four carriers and two battlecruisers.

"God help them."

Alderman didn't have time for empty platitudes. "The British group—*Illustrious*, *Invincible*, and *Ark Royal*—are north of them holding Denmark Strait and *Chancellorsville* is steaming north to link up with *Shiloh*. Once we get *Antietam* back safe, *Chancey* and *Shiloh* can recommit." He sighed. "Until then, it's up to *Iowa* group."

"What about the Backfires, sir?"

Alderman grimaced. "Still our main concern. With their launch range, engaging them efficiently in the air is nearly impossible unless we know they're coming. They could come after us here or strike further afield. Those British carriers are especially vulnerable so far out. The Soviet surface fleet is between us and them and we can't risk the Soviets ganging up on them. Taking out the British fleet would open a hole in the GIUK gap, not to mention the political damage it would do. We need to deal with the Backfires before we can have a free hand to operate here." Alderman rubbed the bridge of his nose before continuing. "To that end, we're going to hit them on the ground. We're working in coordination with land-based air force assets to finish them off and wreck their air facilities."

"How will we know when they're on the ground? Timing on that is going to be tight. If we attack when they're ready to launch, they can put the Backfires airborne before we get there. If we go too late, then the Backfires will already be gone."

"Yes," Alderman agreed. "The only way it will work is if we

hit them right when they return to base. Before they can refuel and scramble them." Alderman smiled. "We've got a special asset on the ground. Callsign Peepshow. Peepshow is the key to making this work. We've played by the Russians' rules so far," he said. "Let's change the game."

***

33

Raleigh and her crew sailed on in the fading high of sending two Soviet submarines to the bottom of the Norwegian Sea. Grier updated the boat's log personally, feeling a sort of perverse satisfaction in the work. It felt wrong almost as much as it felt right, taking such pride in butcher's work. He took some solace in knowing that he'd probably saved more lives than he'd taken in dealing with those two predators.

Who knew how much damage two Soviet submarines could do in the most hotly contested waters of the war?

They were their first kills of the war. Grier wasn't sure if he hoped they were also their last.

"Commander Grier?"

"Versetti," Grier was pleased to recall the sailors name. "What do you have?"

"Message on the ULF, sir," Versetti said. He handed the printout over to the captain who came to stand behind him at the communications terminal.

Versetti looked like Grier felt: exhausted. Fatigue ate at the edges of his mind, dulling his reaction time and sharpening his emotions, but there was no other choice but to continue on. For all her high-tech equipment and futuristic weaponry, *Raleigh* was entirely dependent on her flesh and blood crew to function. The weapons weren't sophisticated enough to operate themselves quite yet.

The crew had been at this for hours. Combat readiness for more than a day straight now. When they'd been doing nothing but endlessly patrolling, Grier had found himself wishing for some action; now all he wanted was to go back to doing nothing.

He had to read the printout twice, forcing himself to focus the second time.

Grier grunted after he read it.

"Good news, sir?" Versetti asked.

Grier eyed him. "Between you and me? I think so."

The sailor grinned.

Grier left the coms station and found Briggs, handing him the printout.

"Break off pursuit of the main fleet?" the XO asked incredulously.

"Not that we've had any luck finding them again," Grier said. "Keep reading. Targets of opportunity."

Brigg's eyes widened as he found the pertinent section in the orders. "They're moving us behind the Soviets to bag their amphibious group?"

"Sounds like it."

"Juicy target."

"If we can find them," Grier said. "And if we can hit it. Big ifs. They're going to be more cautious than the combat fleet I think. They can't afford not to be. At least we'll get another shot at playing pirate." He was still bitter that they'd let the surface fleet slip by. Engaging them would have been suicidal, but it irked him all the same. How many lives could they have saved if they had acted?

"Sounds like this is a rush order," Briggs said.

"We might have a shot at intercepting them if we move fast, but it's going to be dicey."

"At least we won't be alone."

"Right," Grier said. The orders mentioned that another attack sub, HMS *Sovereign*, was also being given orders to attack the transport element. "It means we'll have to double check targets though."

"Assuming we even hear her," Briggs said.

"A lot of ifs. Too many to worry about." He sighed and rubbed his eyes. "Well, no sense slacking off. Let's get underway. We've got a lot of ground to cover."

***

Rabbit slept. The echoey cacophony of activity throughout *Shiloh*'s guts was a lullaby to him. The carrier steamed south, accompanied by her sister *Antietam*, toward safety, flanked by a host of escort ships undergoing replenishment from a handful of supply ships as they sailed.

Rabbit wasn't alone. The pilot briefing room had more seating than any one compartment in the carrier save for the mess hall. And as an added bonus, the seats here were comfortable enough to sleep in, at least when you were as tired as Rabbit was.

A dozen pilots slept in the cushioned seats, hats pulled over faces, legs propped up. It was the hard sleep of the overworked. With the high intensity of their latest operations combined with the shock of losing friends, it was all some of them could do but sleep.

It was this same deep, rewarding sleep that he was pulled from with a snort. Rabbit swallowed and sat up, bleary eyed.

"Sorry," Gomez whispered, coming to sit beside him.

"Shit," Rabbit croaked, laying his head back on the seat. "Was dreaming."

"About?"

Rabbit remembered being chased through the skies, his radar warning receiver screaming in his ear. He just shook his head. "Don't remember." He eyed Gomez who was sipping from a disposable cup.

"Couldn't sleep," his RIO said. "Grabbed a drink from the mess hall. Grape. Want some?"

Rabbit nodded and took the cup, sipping gratefully, chasing away his dry mouth and nightmares. "Thanks."

"Everyone is pretty shook up," Gomez said. "Honestly, it's lucky we even have a ship to come home to."

Rabbit recalled the struggle to shoot down the wave-skimming Soviet missiles fired at the task force. Maybe things could have turned out differently if they'd reacted quicker or better. Maybe he could have changed the outcome of all this.

"You should grab something to eat," Gomez added.

Rabbit's mind told him he was hungry, but his stomach was a tense lump. He wasn't sure he could even force himself to eat. Instead he just shook his head and sipped the grape juice.

"And uh, I heard about your bunkmate."

Rabbit looked up, his heart sinking at Gomez's tone and dark expression. "Metcalf?"

Gomez nodded. "Someone said he went down in the attack, screening the withdrawal."

"Damn," Rabbit said, the word failing to convey even a fraction of what he felt. He wasn't that close to Metcalf all things considered, but knowing that he'd never see him again was still hard to take. "You sure?"

Gomez nodded soberly. "Sure as I can be, man."

Rabbit couldn't think of anything to say. Dead. Metcalf wanted to reconcile with his daughter. Now he never would.

Rabbit closed his eyes, seeing the inside of his cockpit, knowing that this lull between sorties was temporary. He needed to rest, he needed to be ready. He needed to make sure that he didn't end up the same as Metcalf.

"I'll be glad when this is over," Rabbit said. "I think I've had enough."

"Me too," Gomez said. He made himself comfortable in the seat beside Rabbit and was asleep a moment later.

***

34

Once again Orlond Air Base was lit only by the flood lamps surrounding the hangars and runway. The surviving Tupolevs of Fedorovich's squadron sat lined up along the edge of the runway, each being hastily administered to by ground crew.

Fedorovich and his flight crew crossed the paved expanse toward their aircraft, helmets held under their arms.

Babayev walked beside his commander. His dark, bushy eyebrows were furrowed with worry but his jaw was set.

Pavlov and Alekseev followed behind them. Fedorovich didn't need to turn around to know they were terrified. Their previous sortie had almost been their last, and no amount of praise from the regiment's commissar for "a death blow struck to imperialism" could drive that fear from their minds.

Fedorovich himself was calm, almost eerily so. He couldn't explain it, especially given his post-mission jitters last time. Part of him wondered if he was simply too tired to be worried. He hadn't slept a wink since they'd landed hours ago. Whatever the case, he wasn't afraid. He was determined to see this through. The Americans had butchered his men—good men, men he'd trained and flown with. He wasn't going to let that go unanswered.

The heady stink of jet fuel fumes washed over him as they reached the craft. Technicians in greasy coveralls wheeled a pair of stairwells into place allowing the crew to board. Fedorovich followed Babayev in and settled into his spot in the cockpit.

A technician offered a clipboard through the open cockpit hatch. "Comrade Major, the readiness check."

Taking the report, Fedorovich flipped through it, nodding at each category asserting the readiness of his craft. He paused at the weapons check.

"Kh-22?"

"Yes, Comrade."

"No, this is wrong." Fedorovich felt his heart sink. "We're meant to be armed with the new 32s. Not the 22s."

The technician was unmoved. "We have no more 32s, Comrade Major."

"How can that be?" Fedorovich demanded, voice raised. "How can we be expected to face the enemy with outdated weapons?"

The technician remained stony faced. "We carried the 32s when we flew in. I imagine that we don't yet have rail lines built from here to Moscow, and those on trucks have probably been shot up by partisans between here and there. So we have what we have. 22s are in inventory, 32s are not."

"We have to have those missiles," Fedorovich said. "Don't you understand?"

"And what would you like me to do about that?" The technician asked dourly.

Fedorovich wanted to scream or hurl the clipboard at him. The Kh-22 was cutting edge—thirty years ago. In comparison to the 32 it was faster, but the usable range was just over half of the 32. Beyond that, the guidance radar on the 22 was ancient and easily jammed. Fedorovich swore and initialed the sheet angrily before shoving it back at the technician.

The tech took it and scrambled away as the hatches were closed.

Babayev started the pre-flight check, verifying first that the ejection system was functional before moving on to checking the radio beacon and survival dinghy. "That bad?"

"Yes," Fedorovich said. He toggled on the intercom. "Pavlov, are you strapped in?"

"Snugly, Comrade."

"Good. They've given us Kh-22s."

His bombardier was silent for a moment, perhaps swearing in the rear compartment. "You're joking."

"I am told we have no 32s left. Alekseev, you will have to plan accordingly. Ensure we get close enough for optimal launch."

"Do they want us to sink the Americans or just give them a fireworks show?" Pavlov retorted.

Fedorovich killed the intercom and scowled at the instrument panel as he went through pre-flight checks.

"Old missiles for an old boy," Babayev said, patting the Tupolev's console affectionately. His mirth faded quickly. "We will make do."

"What other choice do we have?" Fedorovich asked. "Still, we have a good enough idea of where the American ships are. We ought to be able to launch outside of their SAM range. Provided they haven't moved much. The missiles will do the rest."

"Then we will just have to worry about their fighters," Babayev replied, souring Fedorovich's mood further.

The Tupolev's engine whined to life, sending a vibration through the air frame.

Fedorovich pulled on his helmet and secured his oxygen mask. "At least we're not going in alone this time." The ground-based fighter escort he'd been promised would be assembling in the air nearby—MiG-31s, high-speed, long-range interceptors which NATO called "Foxhound."

Those jitters Fedorovich thought he'd left behind were back. He felt sick and his hands shook as he secured his oxygen mask.

Babayev looked at his commander but said nothing. Only his eyes were visible above the oxygen mask, but they were concerned.

"We fire at maximum range," Fedorovich said. "Six hundred kilometers. Then we run. No heroics. Understood?"

It wasn't a hard plan to sell. "Understood."

Fedorovich nodded. He wasn't going to die. "Just get us close enough to launch, and then it's 'goodbye, Americans.'" He tried to sound like he meant it, but all he could see were his squadron mates falling from the sky. Fedorovich pushed these concerns aside. He had a squadron to brief.

***

"There they go again," Erlend said, watching the Backfires climbing into the air.

Landvik nodded, tracking the swept-wing bombers through the dark sky with binoculars.

Trapped here in the wilderness outside Trondheim, Landvik and his partisans were isolated from the outside world except for their tenuous link through the satellite phone.

Since the day they'd first relayed information about the Backfire bombers taking off from Orlond Air Base, they'd been ordered specifically by command to linger here. Landvik didn't like it.

Personally, he'd rather be a million miles away from this place. His supplies were low and getting lower all the time. He couldn't shake the feeling that the higher ups were less concerned with keeping him fed and more concerned with getting all the intel they could squeeze out of him.

If being home safe was off the table, then he'd rather be on the front, striking back at the invaders. The Soviet position in Norway was tenuous. They held a lot of highways and some urban centers, but rural areas were uncontrolled. Partisan ambushes of convoys and lone patrols were common, despite Soviet reprisals. If he could move his group away from Trondheim and into the more loosely held countryside, then maybe they could do something to reverse their dwindling food supply.

Instead, he'd been saddled with this dangerous and dull assignment and a silly callsign.

Landvick and Erlend watched the Backfires take off one by one, their engines burning like coals in the dark of early morning.

"The whole squadron," Landvik said. He carefully took the

satellite phone from his jacket and handed the antenna to Erlend who aimed it skyward like he'd been taught. Once he had a signal he connected to the handler he'd been assigned.

"Camelot. Go ahead." The handler's Norwegian was thickly accented, but passable.

"Camelot, this is Peepshow. Targets are moving. The roost is empty. Confirm."

The delay was killer.

"Confirm, Peepshow. Good work. Hold position and report observations at thirty minute increments."

Landvik sighed. More waiting. He didn't like being so close to the airfield. If Soviet patrols did their job, he imagined they'd pick him up with little trouble. "Copy, Camelot. Peepshow holding."

Landvik and Erlend exchanged a look.

"This better be worth it," Erlend said.

Landvik didn't disagree.

***

"It feels like we just left this party," Grinder said, his voice carrying over Morris's headphones. It had only been the day before that they'd been forced to leave Norway and rebased to Scotland. Now they got to make the same flight in reverse but, unlike last time, this wouldn't be a one way flight.

Morris smirked behind his oxygen mask as he made final pre-flight checks on his F-15. "Duty calls, Grinder."

"And we were dumb enough to answer."

Six aircraft of Wyvern squadron sat lined up on the runway of Lossiemouth Air Base in Scotland. Morris watched as Royal Air Force Panavia Tornados took off one by one, their thrusters lighting the darkened runway as they launched. Each one laboriously gained altitude, struggling against the immense weight of not just their missile payload, but also the heavy external fuel tanks they carried. It was a loadout mirrored by the Eagles of Wyvern squadron. They were going to be the armed escort of a long range bomber raid—B-52s from air bases further south in England.

"We're stretched thin," Morris said. "It's all hands on deck. Too many missions—,"

"And not enough birds," Grinder finished. "Yeah, I know this one."

"It'll be a milk run," Morris said. "Hold the Buffs' hands as they reach the target area. There and back. Piece of cake."

"Sure, every mission is a cakewalk except for the one you don't come home from."

Morris knew that all too well.

"We've got a bunch of Russian carriers out there, right? What happens if we run into some while babysitting a bunch of big ugly bombers?"

"Do you have anything positive to add?" Morris retorted.

"Yeah," Grinder said. "I'm positive that this is a stupid fucking idea."

Morris grimaced. He had a hard time arguing with that assessment. "I just hope to God those navy squids keep the Russian carrier wings busy."

"You and me both, brother."

"Wyvern One," a fresh voice interrupted, "you're clear for take off. Taxi to runway ten. Godspeed to you."

"Wyvern One affirm," Morris said, disengaging the brakes on his Eagle and maneuvering into launch position. Once more into the breach.

***

35

Zharkov tapped his foot as he stood in the CIC of *Tashkent*. An unlit cigarette hung from his lip and he kept his arms folded, eyes unfocused. The Su-27K that crashed has been recovered successfully, its pilot shaken but unharmed, but Zharkov kept seeing it in his mind's eye. Why? Why was he fixated on one botched landing? It was no secret that Soviet pilots didn't get as much flight time as they should have. They say practice makes perfect, but practice also costs money —money the Soviet Union could ill afford to waste. With so much money already being spent on all these fancy aircraft and ships, there was precious little to afford for things like training. Most of the crew of these vessels were conscripts provided only the bare minimum of training. Because of that, the lion's share of work had fallen on the navy's junior officers. Men who should have spent their time supervising and thinking ahead were instead busy with on the job training or in some cases, simply doing the work themselves.

Zharkov tapped his foot faster. His headache had become almost unbearable. He couldn't shake the sensation of someone running a hot iron behind his eyes. Zharkov scowled.

How many mistakes had been made already? A half dozen vessels had reported engine trouble or other breakdowns. Targeting radars were down, ammunition loaders jammed, communications offline, not to mention the cataclysmic failures of damage control systems and teams. Mistakes were piling up and compounding existing problems. They were like hairline fractures eroding the very bones of the fleet. They were invisible but their effects weren't.

"Admiral?"

Zharkov realized it was the second time the other officer had spoken. He looked to the captain, his eyes flashing. "Yes?"

"The air wings report ready, Admiral."

Zharkov nodded absently. He wondered how many of them would be able to land correctly in the dark. "Good." He took the cigarette from his mouth and held it between his fingers as he spoke. "Good. Commence deployment. Su-27s will screen our AWACS craft. Have you coordinated the final plan?"

"Three AWACS with three squadrons each, loaded with a mixture of anti-air and anti-ship missiles. The Americans must be close."

Again, Zharkov nodded. They'd known there was a final NATO battle group between them and Iceland. It had been left guarding the northern passes of the GIUK gap. This group would likely be moving to engage them or the trailing landing group. If they had any hope of putting soldiers ashore at Iceland, then it would have to be eliminated.

"Good," Zharkopv said again. "Orders are to locate the Americans and relay targeting positions to the fleet. Strike if possible, but do not risk our fighters unnecessarily." He had little illusions in the capabilities of his fighters to get through the American air defense screen, but they could at least soften it up. "Understand?"

The air wing commander saluted. "Clearly, Admiral."

"Once we have a solution we will fire a missile salvo to finish them off," Zharkov continued. *Tashkent* and *Ulyanovsk's* groups had enough Granit and Bazalt missiles between them to saturate whatever defenses the Americans had left. He put the cigarette back in his mouth and turned to find his communications officer. "Radio the landing group. Tell the naval infantry to prepare for action. They will be ashore in less than six hours."

***

Lieutenant Yakim Vlasov sat in the cockpit of his Su-27K in the predawn darkness of the Norwegian Sea. The only light came from the display panels of his fighter, casting an eerie green glow through the interior.

The deck of *Riga* shifted and pitched almost imperceptibly around him as it was buffeted by ocean swells. It was too dark to see with the naked eye, but Vlasov knew the rest of the fleet lingered on the horizon. Carriers, cruisers, frigates, and destroyers, all sailing west, ready to strike a blow against the West.

The aircraft was idle, its raw power reigned in, waiting to be unleashed, expressed only as a soft whine. It was just as eager as its pilot to get airborne.

Vlasov had already tasted battle. Flying from *Novosibirsk* he'd faced down Tomcats and Hornets, dueling in the open skies. It had been a miracle he'd come through unscathed, and with two kills under his belt. Of course by the time he'd returned, *Novosibirsk* had been left burning. Now, he flew from *Riga*.

The names and faces of those aboard *Novosibirsk* haunted the edges of his mind. He could see them all, he could almost hear them. Had any of his friends made it off the ship? There was no way to tell, not yet. He likely wouldn't know until this was all over and they were safely back in Polyarny. In any case, he had more immediate concerns.

Re-organized into Hydra squadron, the survivors of *Novosibirsk*'s fighter wing had a more personal stake in the coming battle than any others in the fleet did.

Vlasov reached out with a gloved finger and touched the hand-painted icon taped to his fighter's dashboard. The art was crude, amateurish almost, but it was made by his grandmother so it was special to him. He could hardly see it in the dark, only its gold foil background shone like dull brass. The figure of Saint Mary was nothing but a vague shadow in the dark. Vlasov couldn't see her, but he knew her features by heart. He pictured Mary's noble, solemn face, bowed head and halo.

Vlasov double checked that his microphone was switched off before speaking. "Mother of God, bless me, protect me, and watch over me."

This next battle would be no less dangerous than his first. Their orders were to close on the Icelandic coast and locate the rumored surface group between them and their target. Vlasov was tired, but that went without saying for everyone in both fleets, he imagined. He and the others had been on active alert for over twenty four hours, running patrols and sorties. Even before the ill-fated battle of *Novosibirsk*, they'd been well at their limit.

"And now we do it once again," Vlasov said.

"Hydra 1-2, this is *Riga* control. Acknowledge."

Vlasov put aside his worries. "Hydra 1-2 acknowledge."

"You are clear for launch. Remember to use afterburners, Comrade."

Riga, unlike *Novosibirsk*, had no steam catapult. It was up to the thrust power of his aircraft—and the ramp at the end of the deck—to put him into the air.

"1-2 acknowledge. Thank you."

Vlasov gunned his throttle and engaged afterburners. G-forces pressed him back into his seat as the Su-27K raced over the deck, gradually picking up speed. As he reached the launch ramp, Vlasov felt the weight of the mixture of anti-ship and anti-radiation missiles strapped to his plane's belly pulling against him. Cresting the ramp, his craft's nose lifted and the whole aircraft left the deck behind.

For a moment Vlasov's stomach fell out and he had the sickening thought that he wasn't going fast enough. It lasted less than a second before the fighter gained altitude, climbing up and away from *Riga* and the ocean below.

One by one, the Soviet aircraft carriers put their craft into the dark skies, leaving each one briefly silhouetted against the dying light of the sky before passing from view. Vlasov joined this growing host of warbirds as they first formed into squadrons and then wings. Even in the dark, these maneuvers were trivial to Vlasov and the others. His was just one of three spearheads in total, each centered on a prop-driven Yak-44 AWACS aircraft topped with a large radar dome. These wings advanced north as one, skirting the rocky Icelandic coast and sweeping the waves with powerful radar arrays, hunting for the American battlegroup.

Vlasov glanced at the time. In minutes they would be in combat again, this time to avenge his comrades aboard *Novosibirsk*. He wouldn't fail them.

***

36

"Captain, fast movers detected on the horizon, starboard. USS *George Bennings* reports forty fast movers in two groups. Designate Raid Alpha, Raid Bravo. Flankers leading Merits. Estimated ten minutes to engagement range."

Captain Stewart "Buzz" Fischer felt his stomach knot itself at the announcement.

Fischer had known this moment was coming, though that didn't make it any more palatable. His heart was in his throat. For all his years in the service, this would be his first ship-to-ship engagement. Incidentally, this would also be *Iowa*'s first ship-to-ship engagement since 1944. Somehow, everything had come down to him, his men, and their ships. It was strange to reflect on all the events that fell into place to put him in this ship at this time, facing down the enemy. *Iowa* stood almost alone against the combined might of the Soviet Navy like David facing Goliath, and now there was no more delaying. His rendezvous with destiny was here.

"Relay this data to all ships." Fischer picked up the wall-mounted telephone from its cradle "Get me Keflavik," he said.

Iowa was a battleship from the Second World War. She was a window into another time, but hardly a relic. 1980s modernizations had brought her to the cusp of the twenty-first century. The installation of modern radar, command and control, and weapons systems extended her hitting range from beyond the paltry forty kilometers her 16-inch guns offered. Now armed with numerous Tomahawk cruise missiles, in addition to defensive SAM batteries, she was a force to be reckoned with. But one thing she didn't have were aircraft.

"Keflavik. Go ahead, *Iowa*."

"Soviet strike group spotted on radar six minutes out and closing. I'll relay tactical data."

After a pause, "Keflavik confirms. Squadrons are scrambled. Good luck, *Iowa*."

Fischer returned the phone to its cradle. Through the forward viewports of *Iowa*'s bridge he could only see the matte-black of night. While it was more than possible to run this ship—and the rest of the surface action group—from the CIC nestled in *Iowa*'s armored heart, Fischer preferred to do so from the bridge when possible Normally he preferred the view, though in this case there was none. Keflavik's fighters wouldn't be enough. The base's squadrons had been depleted as aircraft were transferred to the Continent—Norway and Germany—to replace mounting fighter losses there. Now all that was left was scarcely a third of the Soviet strike group racing toward them.

It was funny, Fischer thought. Iowa had been recommissioned and modernized in direct response to the hulking *Kirov*-class Soviet battlecruisers and now these giants faced one another down on the open waves.

The battle was largely out of his hands now. All Fischer could do was wait as aircraft on both sides closed to range.

***

Just over a kilometer above the waves, Vlasov hurtled into the dark, throttled to max. At such a low altitude, his Su-27K burned through fuel reserves with alarming speed, but it was a small price to pay for the relative shelter of the horizon. Heavy with the payload he carried, his fighter was sluggish, lacking the sort of nimble grace it was normally capable of.

Vlasov would be glad to be rid of that weight as soon as possible.

With his radar powered down, he had no clear view of the battlefield, but he knew enough to know that the lead elements of the attack—Python and Minotaur groups—would no doubt be visible to the American ships ahead since they flew at a much higher altitude. All he could do was hope that his own wave was yet invisible since there was no way to evade or defend against enemy attack at this low level.

His radio hummed as the plan was executed. "Python group, fire. Fire."

The lead squadrons volleyed, firing a spread of Kh-41 anti-ship missiles—roughly equivalent to the American Harpoon—toward the horizon.

Vlasov faintly saw the light of rockets above and ahead of him as they boosted away.

"Hostile aircraft spotted!" one of Python's pilots called.

"Turn back for the ships. Go to afterburners," Python leader replied.

While the Americans were worrying about the first salvo of missiles, Hydra group would move in closer, undetected.

Vlasov glanced down at the half-visible icon on his dashboard again, mouthing a silent prayer. God willing.

***

"Tactical to bridge. Raids Alpha and Bravo engaged by friendly fighters and are now turning back. We mark forty vampires inbound."

Fischer kept his hands behind his back, one gripping the other. Forty inbound missiles was significant, especially for his small group, but it shouldn't prove insurmountable. If that was the best the Soviets could do, then there was a chance of pulling through this.

"Have *Bennings* shift fire to those vampires," Fischer said. "Let Keflavik take care of the fast movers. They're just feeling us out."

It wasn't long after these orders were issued that the situation changed.

"New contacts on scope. Third attack wave closing. Same

vector, low altitude, designated Raid Charlie."

They'd managed to get in close, maybe too close. The Soviets were trying to saturate and overwhelm his air defense systems —and they just might succeed. Call them what you want, the Soviets were no fools, Fischer thought. "I'm moving to the CEC," Fischer told the duty officer.

"Aye, sir."

The trip wasn't long, but Fischer felt the minutes burn away as he moved from bridge to the combat engagement center. When he reached it he found it humming with activity. Radar scopes pulsed with electric life and crew keyed queries and commands into their terminals. The CEC was a feature unique to the battleships of the *Iowa*-class. When they were refit in the 1980s, new equipment needed to be added—modernized radar and missile control primarily—equipment which wouldn't fit in the existing CIC. The solution was a separate, modern control facility.

The tactical action officer didn't waste time before filling Fischer in. "It looks like twenty more Flankers advancing in behind that wave of Sunburns." He used the NATO designation for the Soviet Kh-41. "Good odds this raid is armed similarly."

Fischer nodded. "They're in firing range?"

"Forty miles out," Tactical said. "Just barely. Permission to engage, sir?"

Maximum range meant poor chances of a hit, but each passing moment brought the enemy further into their own optimum engagement range.

"Granted," Fischer said.

The CEC sprang into action straight away.

"SAM battery, firing RIM-67 missiles. Booster armed. Standby."

"Missile control, commence firing," Tactical said.

"Execute plan."

Iowa launched a spread of surface to air missiles targeting this low-flying raid. Each missile launch lit the night sea before streaking away toward the horizon.

***

Vlasov's radar warning receiver lit up, warbling an alarm.

"Hydra 1-2, I have enemy missile lock!" Vlasov said.

"Acknowledged, 1-2," Hydra leader said.

Vlasov felt a cold sweat cover over his body. His breathing increased. This low to the ground there was nowhere to evade. With a head-on flight path, the enemy missiles were almost certain to hit.

"1-2 requests permission to fire," Vlasov said.

"Hold fire, 1-2," Lead said. "Not yet."

Vlasov killed the channel and swore to himself. He checked his instruments. They were within engagement range for the Kh-41 anti-ship missiles they carried, but the Kh-31P anti-radiation missiles were still too far out. Without the 31Ps, the American radars would be able to continue operating safely.

Another pilot spoke up. "Hydra 2-6, firing missiles!"

"Not yet, you bastard!" Hydra lead blurted.

Off to his starboard, Vlasov saw the orange flash of a rocket booster engaging followed shortly by another.

"2-7, firing!"

"Lead, 1-2 requests permission to fire!" Vlasov said.

Seeing that he couldn't force his pilots to fly into death, Hydra Leader at last relented. "All planes, fire weapons and break."

Vlasov armed and fired his missiles, savoring his fighter's restored dexterity. "1-2 breaking!" He worked rudder pedals and stick to bank his Su-27K around and went to afterburners, hoping to outpace the enemy's own return missiles.

***

"Vampire. Vampire. Fresh contacts, Sixty missiles on scope and closing."

Fischer's stomach tightened further still. All he could do was watch the radar displays as *Iowa*'s escorts picked off the first wave of Sunburn missiles. They'd only just managed to clear this volley successfully when the second wave came racing in.

"Raid Charlie turning cold," Radar said.

They'd already fired their payload, there was no more reason for them to stick around.

As the missiles came closer, twenty of them activated terminal radar guidance while the others remained silent.

"Looks like anti-radiation missiles," Fischer mused.

Whatever they were, most of them began dropping from the scope about a mile out, losing altitude until they disappeared. The same couldn't be said of the Sunburns. The anti-ship missiles spread out as their radars picked up on separate contacts. Fischer listened to the chatter of the CEC as one by one the Sunburns were struck down with SAMs or CIWS fire from the picket ships.

"*David Palmer* reports she's been struck, starboard side. Serious damage."

"No more vampires. Scope is clear."

Palmer would have to turn back if she could, likely headed south toward Scotland. Iceland lacked any naval repair facilities on its eastern coast. But sending *Palmer* south would also mean sending a stricken ship off on her own.

"Find out if she can be kept afloat," Fischer responded. "We don't have anyone to spare to escort them back to shore." As that was carried out, he addressed Tactical. "How are we for SAMs?"

As the numbers came in, Fischer's spirits sank lower. *Bennings* was virtually empty, and most of his other escorts were low. The next time the Soviets came at them, they could practically walk right up and not. But there could be no retreat. *Iowa* was the end of the line. The buck stops here.

"No choice," Fischer said to himself.

***

37

Admiral Zharkov watched the glowing blips on *Tashkent*'s tactical display as they closed and broke with enemy contacts on the radar plot. An attending officer kept the radar returns labeled using a grease pencil to bring a little clarity to the confusion. American F-16 squadrons pursued his initial attack waves which were involved in a fighting withdrawal, each side reluctant to commit to the fight but also not quite willing to break off.

His follow on wave, Hydra, was still invisible on radar due to their low altitude, he only knew they were still alive from their radio traffic.

"Hydra leader to *Tashkent*. Have engaged enemy surface group. Missiles fired and withdrawing. Estimate ten surface combatants." His voice failed to project the cool demeanor he was likely hoping for. He sounded rattled even over the fuzzy speakers in *Tashkent*'s CIC.

"Confirm that with AWACS," Zharkov said, waving toward his tactical officer.

As he waited, Zharkov's stomach twisted in his guts. This operation increasingly hinged on this engagement. If he'd miscalculated, if the force in front of him were a ruse of some kind, if the Americans had conjured one of the carrier groups in front of him—.

"AWACS confirms. Radar emissions are consistent with an *Iowa*-class battlegroup."

"*Iowa*," Zharkov tried the strange word. He wiggled the cigarette between his teeth and stared down at the tactical plot. *Iowa* had survived the Second World War. A single, ancient battleship and her attending ships were no obstacle at all. She'd crossed oceans of time just to die here.

"Do we have confirmed damage from the air wings?" Zharkov asked his KAG.

"No, Comrade Admiral," the KAG said, reluctant. "Heavy SAM fire forced them back before we could gauge the effect."

"Estimate."

The KAG hesitated. His silence lasted longer than it would have to come up with a natural answer. He was weighing if he should tell Zharkov the truth or couch it in lies.

"Fire was conducted at maximum range. I expect there will be some minor damage to the picket ships, but the surface fleet is most likely still combat capable."

"But they will be low on ammunition," Zharkov said. He'd seen the expenditure rates from *Novosibirsk*'s battle and knew how catastrophically high missile use had been during that brief fight.

"Yes, Comrade Admiral."

"My pilots could get close," the KAG said, "close enough to attack again. But losses would be significant."

The time for limited gains had come and gone. Olesk's plan of savaging the American Navy and withdrawing to safety was no longer possible, not after losing *Novosibirsk*. With almost a third of his navy sunk or burning, the only possible course of action left to him was to achieve a victory. Only total victory would make that cost worth swallowing.

"Your pilots have done their job. No reason to throw their lives away," Zharkov said, longing to light his cigarette. He dared to feel a sliver of hope. They were almost there.

"We have a firing solution now. Fire a weapons salvo. Granits and Bazalts. The range should be short enough. Fire half of our stockpile. That should be sufficient to overwhelm their defenses. Send the *Iowa* to the bottom."

Within minutes, *Tashkent*, *Ulyanovsk*, and their associated missile cruisers fired a fresh salvo of wave-skimming anti-ship missiles to finish off the troublesome battlegroup.

***

"Admiral Alderman, sir? *Iowa* is reporting inbound missile tracks. Soviets must have got a solid solution on her."

Alderman winced. He knew there was a good chance this would happen. It wasn't realistic to hope that *Iowa* could hold on until after the Backfires were dealt with. Sometimes lives had to be risked in war. Alderman knew this was one of those times, but that didn't make him like it.

The command staff of the CIC were tense. If *Iowa* went down, then there was nothing left between the Soviets and Iceland.

Alderman wrung his hands together uselessly. There was nothing he could do, not until the Backfires were neutralized. *Iowa* was just going to have to take it on the nose and hope they pulled through.

"All I have to offer them are prayers," Alderman said reluctantly. Until the Backfires were neutralized—.

"Fresh contacts! Designate Raid Alpha. Bearing 010."

Alderman looked up in surprise as the radar contact was called out. "Speak of the devil and he shall appear," he said.

A heartbeat later, a second batch of radar contacts was picked up. "Designate Raid Bravo, bearing 110."

"We've got problems of our own," Alderman finished, replying to the officer who gave him the news about *Iowa*. He turned to the tactical plot and watched as the counts were finalized.

"Raid Alpha has about sixty aircraft and Raid Bravo has half that."

"Ninety Backfires?" Alderman said. They'd gotten hammered by a single regiment, what would thirty more planes mean?

"Looks that way sir. One from Norway and the other probably from Denmark or the Baltic."

"Coordinate with air wings. We'll have to split our attention.

Get all aircraft up and moving."

"Yes sir!"

"And relay this to NATO command in Germany. Get them to divert some aircraft to intercept those Baltic bombers on return!"

Klaxons blared throughout the ship. *"Battle stations, battle stations."*

***

38

The Tu-22M was a supersonic aircraft. It crossed the sound barrier as easily as a person might step through a doorway. It was fast enough to outrun many threats, or at least make interception problematic. The real trouble was not a lack of speed, it was a lack of fuel. Going to afterburners and thus going supersonic ate up fuel at a tremendous rate. It simply wasn't possible to remain at supersonic speeds for the duration of the flight. So a fundamental choice was left to the regiment commander. They could either race in to attack and walk out, or walk in and race out. Osprey One had chosen the latter. God help him, he had chosen to walk his men into the jaws of death.

"Enemy radar lock!" Pavlov warned.

The Tomcats were going to come into range well before the Tupolevs had a chance to fire their own missiles and flee for safety. It was a mathematical certainty that Fedorovich didn't want to acknowledge. They'd gotten the drop on the Americans once, but not this time. Advanced Tomcat pickets were already moving into range.

Fedorovich looked up, staring ahead into the inky blackness through the bomber's forward viewports. He couldn't see them with his eyes, but radar returns showed the squadron of MiG-31s leading the attack. They were hopefully going to ward off some of the fire meant for him and his helpless bombers, but it was no guarantee of anything.

"All planes, stay on target," Fedorovich said, struggling to keep his voice level. "The fighter escort will keep us safe." He heard the half-hearted and shaky acknowledgements from his pilots come in one by one. He shared their skepticism. Fedorovich knew there was no guarantee the fighters would keep them safe. And he knew his men likely knew that as well, but there was no point drawing attention to it, especially not when the truth became obvious a minute later when one of the Tupolevs exploded off their port wing.

Babayev swore.

"Was that one of ours?" Pavlov asked over the intercom.

"Focus on your duties!" Fedorovich returned. "Alekseev, time to firing range?"

"Three minutes."

Ahead of them, Fedorovich watched the struggle of the MiGs on his radar display as their returns winked out or fell away into the ocean. Here and there an American fighter would vanish as well, but it wasn't nearly enough.

A second Tupolev took a hit off to their right. Its engines flamed out and the craft lost power, nosing down toward the black ocean like a fiery comet.

"Alekseev!?"

"Sixty seconds!"

"Nearly there," Pavlov said, voice shaky.

Fedorovich kept a white-knuckle grip on the controls. Until that predestined moment, they could do nothing but fly dead ahead and pray none of the American missiles found them.

In that minute, three more Tupolevs exploded midair and a fourth suffered a fatal hit from shrapnel. The bomber's crew shouted frantic maydays over the radio as the pilot struggled to bring the aircraft about and return to safety, mission forgotten.

"Firing range!" Alekseev shouted.

Pavlov didn't wait for Fedorovich to give the clear. He launched, joined by the rest of the surviving regiment. Each Tupolev unleashed three Kh-22s, a pitiful volley of just over forty missiles blazed toward the distant American fleet.

Fedorovich flipped on the squadron radio. "Break starboard and go to afterburners." He wasn't sure how many of his planes were still in the air or how many crews were still alive, but he could worry about that when they got back home.

It was a blessing, the moment they'd all waited for, the moment they could run.

The Tupolevs turned as one, banking hard enough to judder the frame of the craft. Fedorovich gritted his teeth against the G-forces and felt a certain relief when Babayev engaged afterburners. Now they were supersonic and headed away from danger, leaving the surviving MiGs to cover their retreat. Fedorovich didn't even know if any of them were still alive, and right now he didn't care.

The radar warning receiver blared on Fedorovich's console. Radar lock, this one from a Phoenix missile.

It was a dance Fedorovich didn't want to repeat.

"Engaging countermeasures!" Pavlov said as the tail gun began to hammer away, firing a stream of flares and chaff to draw away the Phoenix and save their aircraft again.

This time it failed.

A catastrophic bang shook the bomber and threw Fedorovich in his restraints. Alarms wailed in the cockpit and the instrument panel burned an ominous amber.

"Babayev!?"

"We have engines," the co-pilot replied, wrestling with the control stick. "Fuel gauge is falling." He swore. "He's fighting me. Something is badly damaged."

Fedorovich realized that as he was trying to assess the damage to their aircraft, Alekseev was babbling over the intercom, his words running together, a mixture of curses and prayers.

"Shut up, you fool!" Fedorovich shouted, "*Shut up!*" He couldn't hear himself think. "Pavlov, how bad is it? Do we still have the gun?"

"He's dead!" Alekseev wailed. "God in heaven, it took his head clean off! There's so much blood!"

Fedorovich felt nauseous. Shrapnel had pierced the rear compartment. The hit was bad, worse than he had feared.

"We are losing altitude," Babayev said. "I think we are going to lose control."

"We have to eject!" Alekseev continued over the intercom. "We're going to die in here!"

The vibration was getting worse. Outside the viewport was nothing but blackness, but the major could tell the aircraft was shuddering like a sick dog, its nose swaying as drag played over the shrapnel-riddled hull.

Fedorovich felt himself acting without conscious thought. "Osprey One, this is Osprey Three. We're hit and losing altitude. Acknowledge?"

The radio hummed mindlessly back. No reply.

"Osprey One, come in. Answer me, dammit!"

"I can't keep him together," Babayev said, glancing at Fedorovich.

Fedorovich considered trying to raise the other planes in his squadron, but what would it matter? No one could help them. He looked at the ejection handle that would fire all four seats of the bomber, including the one holding Pavlov's bloody remains. It would save them from dying in the bomber, but it would doom them to dying in the dark on the waves below.

"We will die out there too," Fedorovich said, his voice weak.

He looked at Babayev. Even in the dim light he saw the look of fear in his co-pilot's face.

"Ocean water temperatures here are so low that exposure will kill us in minutes."

The Tupolev lurched hard.

"We have the dinghy," Babayev argued.

"We will have to find it in the dark," Fedorovich said.

"For the love of God, Major! Eject!" Alekseev continued to plead over the intercom.

Die for certain in here, or likely die out there in the cold.

"We have to try," Babayev said.

Fedorovich nodded. It was no choice at all. He gripped the handle and pulled and the world became roaring darkness.

***

39

Admiral Alderman watched the fighting as a dispassionate dance of lights and numbers on the consoles of *Bastogne*'s CIC. Two waves of Soviet Backfire bombers closed in from two different directions. With the forewarning that Peepshow provided, his entire carrier wing had been able to put to the air and were savaging the oncoming bombers.

Both waves had suffered heavy losses. In particular the smaller northern wave—Raid One—was down to a quarter of the thirty aircraft that had begun the attack. Alderman took a small amount of satisfaction knowing that the home airfields of both raids were targeted for long-range missile strikes the moment they touched down. Hopefully. That wasn't Alderman's ballgame though. He had his own match to worry about.

A hundred missile tracks screamed in from two different directions, pincering in toward the fleet. The missiles had activated onboard radar guidance and were single mindedly barreling in toward the carriers in a semi-ballistic trajectory. It was a small favor that these were older models without the high-altitude, top-attack profile of the last raid. They weren't able to fly above the SAM's flight ceiling and so were in firing range for much longer. They would have to cross over the outer picket line before they could get to the carriers.

But despite their age, each single missile packed enough explosive power to destroy a smaller ship or cripple something the size of a carrier. If only one got through, hundreds of people could die.

"How many total?" Alderman asked, afraid of the answer.

"We count one hundred and seventy vampires in the air."

The news was like a gut punch. The Backfires had been decimated by the waiting Tomcats, but it wasn't enough to stop them. They still had enough numbers to unleash a fearsome spread of anti-ship missiles.

It was once again up to the integrated air defense network to make sure that nothing got through. Tomcats picked off as many bombers as they could before they even had a chance to fire. Once the missiles were in the air, the Tomcats switched targets to take out the missiles, plinking them down in ones and twos. When they ran out of missiles, they switched to guns, thinning the numbers still further.

Once past the Tomcat screen, the remaining Soviet missiles ran a gauntlet of high-volume SAM fire, put up first by the outlying escorts and then by the inner defenses of the carrier group.

The fleet's SAM magazines weren't bottomless, they relied heavily on the machine intelligence of the Aegis system which prioritized targets and prevented wasteful double-targeting.

Numbers of missiles dropped precipitously, both friendly and enemy.

American radar jamming fouled the primitive sensors on the older 22s and blinded whole flocks of them. Unable to see, they carried on aimlessly groping through the night for their targets, ignorant that they had no chance of ever reaching them.

Despite all of this, despite the SAM barrage and electronic warfare, some missiles made it through. This small handful fixed their hungry gaze on the largest radar returns in the center of the fleet. Tearing over the seas at supersonic speeds, the Kh-22s counted time to impact in seconds.

CIWS gunfire lashed out, chopping missiles from the sky, peppering the ocean waves with shrapnel and debris.

Of this titanic salvo, only one reached its target. The missile struck the *Virginia*-class anti-air cruiser USS *Texas* amidships, punching in its starboard flank and blowing explosively out the portside, ripping open the cruiser's steel belly. *Texas* rolled onto her side like a dying creature, back broken. Sailors leapt into the freezing ocean waters and blaze orange liferafts deployed, collecting those who they could save.

As *Texas* died, the rest of the fleet was safe. The Soviet Backfire regiments were decimated beyond repair while *Bastogne* and *Belleau Wood* were untouched and out of danger.

The same couldn't be said though for *Iowa.*

***

Captain Fischer watched the radar tracks of the Soviet missiles as they closed with absolute certainty on his ships. The lights flashed benignly, far removed from the deadly intent they represented. The radar returns were inconsistent, some blips vanishing and not reappearing, others seeming to show up out of nowhere. Until they closed range, these low-altitude missiles would be difficult to track.

"Tracking vampires. Five minutes," Radar said.

"Let them get closer before engaging," Fischer said. They didn't have the SAM reserves to waste shots on poor returns. He had to make sure his hits counted.

"Aye, Captain."

"Word from Keflavik, Captain," an officer said. "They've tracked the origin point of Soviet missile fire. Looks like their fleet."

Too late to hit them first, but not too late to hit back, though the paltry dozen long-range, anti-ship missiles *Iowa* carried paled in comparison to the Soviet salvo. Fischer would be damned if he saw *Iowa* through her first missile duel without firing a shot in return. "Relay targeting data to the Tomahawks," he said. "Fire all missiles."

"Tomahawk battery, firing Tomahawk missiles. All weapons standby."

Tactical looked at Fischer who didn't meet his eye. The captain could only stare grimly ahead as the radar pulsed with the ever nearing Soviet volley. "Permission to engage."

"Missile control, commence firing."

"Execute plan."

***

The wave-skimming Granit and Bazalt missile swarms sliced through the darkness toward their target with a howl of jet engines. If the air defense batteries of the *Iowa* task force were reliant on human eyes, then they were doomed in this darkness. However, the electronic gaze of the radar arrays of the task force cut through the night and lit up targets for SAM batteries to engage.

The Soviet missiles flew low, far lower than the air-launched Kh-22 or Kh-32 missiles the Backfires used. What the ship-launched missiles lacked in number, they more than made up for in difficulty to track and hit. And of course, they packed a greater punch.

The swarm coordinated via radio waves, synchronizing their actions and divvying up targets. Half of the swarm was instructed to lock onto the largest radar contact it could find—in this case *Iowa* and her *Ticonderoga*-class escort USS *Lafayette* —while the other half was to engage smaller escort vessels. As SAM fire thinned their ranks, target ratios were adjusted, missiles tasked with new targets as their mechanical brethren fell away.

USS *George Bennings* was the first to be hit. With next to no missiles left to defend herself, she was almost wholly reliant on CIWS guns. She struck down the first two missiles before the third—a Bazalt—ripped into her bow and exploded. The frigate was bathed in a rolling fireball as internal stores combusted and the blaze spread throughout the ship's interior. She was bound for the bottom of the sea, taking all hands with her.

***

Captain Fischer watched the blips of a Soviet missile strike *Bennings* and then disappear. Although it was just one hit, it was a fatal blow. A frantic distress broadcast was made before the ship went off the air forever.

"Vampire, distance twenty miles!" Radar called.

"Does it have us?" Tactical asked.

"Aye, sir!"

Fischer's blood ran cold. It was up to their air defense now. He didn't have to issue any orders, the tactical officer made the ship wide announcement. "Missile inbound, starboard! All hands brace for shock."

The men of the CEC assumed crash positions, ducking, covering their heads and bracing themselves, Fischer was no different. Even as he braced, he watched the radar officer who kept an eye on his instruments.

"Ten miles," he said. "Five."

The bridge was ominously silent as the vampires sprinted toward them out of the dark.

CIWS guns ripped out into the night, illuminating the waves in the flickering yellow of tracer rounds. Where they found targets, fresh fireballs blossomed over the surface of the water, momentarily illuminating the dark like abortive suns.

The Bazalt which slipped through struck *Iowa*'s flank at twice the speed of sound.

Fischer felt the impact as a shudder that ran the length of the ship, vibrating the technical equipment and startling the crew. A moment of tense silence followed. There was no explosion. A faulty warhead.

"Damage report?" Fischer asked.

"Impact on starboard side, Captain. No detonation."

Iowa—unlike every other warship afloat—was built to survive direct hits from high-velocity battleship guns. Modern warships were "tin cans," built to stay afloat and survive combat through their onboard defenses. In comparison, *Iowa* was a fortress, intended to slug it out with other ships like her, shrugging off blows that would cripple a lesser vessel.

"Any penetration?"

"Still assessing, but it doesn't seem so, sir!"

The nine-inch armor band ringing *Iowa* had done its job. Fischer couldn't help but smile. *Iowa*'s designers could have never anticipated the sort of threats she would be facing now. His smile died on his face when the radar operator called out, "Second missile sighted! Starboard side!"

Fischer hardly had time to assume braced position again before the missile was on them. Unlike the Bazalt, it went high, arcing through the night and avoiding *Iowa*'s armor belt, instead taking her in the superstructure, a direct hit on the bridge. The warhead flashed and exploded, ripping apart tempered steel plates and throwing fragments through the air.

The blastwave tore back through Iowa's tower, rocking the CEC nestled beneath the battleship's main mast. Shrapnel ripped into the unarmored compartment, catching men and equipment alike. This metal maelstrom passed over Fischer, leaving him somehow unscathed. The shockwave threw him off balance, first falling to his knees and then his face. With ears ringing, Fischer fought back to his feet, shocked to see he was unharmed. The same couldn't be said for many others in the compartment.

Around him wounded sailors cried out or lay groaning. Dark smoke filled the air, creating a hellish glow from the lights and displays of the control consoles here a moment before the power failed, casting the CEC into darkness. Fischer knew that smoke meant fire. *Iowa* was burning.

"Everyone out!" Fischer called, hardly hearing himself over the ringing in his ears. "Able-bodied carry the wounded!" He knelt by the first fallen sailor he came across, rolling him onto his back. He recognized him as one of the weapons officers, missile control.

The young sailor's eyes were wide, darting around in a panic as blood welled from a shrapnel wound to his chest, staining his shirt a deep purple.

"Hang tight, son," Fischer said, taking off his jacket to drape over the sailor. "We need a corpsman over here!"

It was a call being echoed across what was left of the CEC.

With no functioning detection equipment in the CEC, the third missile hit with no warning.

The deck vibrated with the force of the impact and subsequent explosion. This one hit further ahead, toward the bow of the ship, but without more information Fischer couldn't be sure how much damage it had really done. He needed to get out of the CEC and find somewhere on this ship that still had power—if such a place still existed.

Damage control arrived in the CEC within moments, guiding the survivors and helping the wounded.

"Captain, sir, we need to get you out of here!"

Fischer couldn't argue. Looking around at the smoky carnage here, he felt bitter shame seeing his ship—his crew come to this sorry fate.

Leaving the CEC behind, he passed into an open corridor and was surprised to feel the cold rush of wind. The bridge—previously just forward of the CEC—was gone. Blown away by the impact of the Soviet missile.

Stopping, he gawked out over the fragment-riddled hull and saw flames licking up from a gaping wound in *Iowa*'s deck. A hole had been wrenched in her steel hide, one that was lapping up water. It wasn't enough to sink a behemoth like her, but it left her dead in the water as sailors struggled against the toxic smoke and flames burning within her. Fischer didn't know if he could save her, but he was going to do whatever he could.

For now, *Iowa* floated and burned, ringed by a horizon of burning ships. Those that still lived struggled to aid their stricken companions. Helicopters buzzed around, plucking survivors from the ocean as the battleship dipped lower and lower into the waves. *Iowa* was lost.

***

40

Admiral Zharkov listened to the missile attack warning over the PA system as dispassionately as he could.

Return fire from *Iowa* crossed the horizon at supersonic speeds. A spread of a dozen Tomahawk cruise missiles appeared on Soviet radars, each one equipped with the same terminal guidance system as the Harpoon missile. The tactical crew of *Tashkent* tracked and identified each one, marking its speed and heading.

"American missiles at two hundred kilometers and closing."

"*Yuri Andropov* moving to engage. Firing S-300 missile batteries."

"Tracking missiles."

Zharkov said nothing, silently counting the seconds to—.

"Interception. Second hit."

One by one the Tomahawks fell until only two remained.

Zharkov's heart thundered in his chest. He knew that it would only take one.

The Tomahawks would first have to get past the battlecruiser *Yuri Andropov*. They closed to gun range, racing for the kill. *Yuri Andropov's* CIWS guns ripped out and obliterated the last two Tomahawks within sight of *Tashkent*, peppering the sea with missile debris. The fleet was untouched.

Zharkov exhaled and forced a smile. "Well done. Very well done." He drew himself short. Too much praise would make it sound like he didn't believe they could do it. They'd weathered the anemic American response, now all that remained was to verify the *Iowa* and her escorts had been neutralized.

"Admiral Zharkov." A lieutenant stood anxiously at the entryway to the CIC.

"Yes?"

"High priority transmission from Moscow, Comrade Admiral."

Zharkov's heart missed a beat. Even out here, somehow the Kremlin had a leash on him. He hid his fear behind a mask of machismo. "Well?"

The lieutenant flushed red. "It is encrypted, Comrade. Magma cipher. For your attention only."

Either it was truly important or the old men were flexing their power and meddling.

Zharkov nodded, glancing at the tactical officer. "See to things here."

"Yes, Admiral!"

Leaving the CIC, Zharkov traveled a short distance to the communications room, appearing before a harried junior officer who presented the original message and cipher key. Zharkov fed the data and key into the cipher machine which printed and spit out a sheaf of paper with a metallic clatter. Tearing the sheet off the paper roll, Zharkov read it.

ADM Z- STAVKA EXPECTS REPORT ON FINAL SUCCESS WITHIN 24 HOURS. PROVIDE EXPLANATION FOR LOSS OF ADM Y GROUP AND NOVOSIBIRSK. NO MORE DELAYS. NO MORE SETBACKS. -TARASOV

Zharkov read the note without reaction. He felt faint, his heart racing. Tarasov and the Stavka had lost patience with him. Somehow news of *Novosibirsk* and Yevdokimov had leaked to them early. Either through the West or that worm Olesk.

Zharkov calmly folded the note in half and then into ever smaller squares until it would fold no more. He felt faint, his head swimming. He was short of breath and too warm. Victory was the only path forward for the navy, just as it was now the only path forward for him. The Soviet Union didn't tolerate failure, least of all catastrophic failure. To come back empty handed would certainly spell doom for him. If he were lucky he would be "retired" and forgotten about like Kruschev or Kavinski. If he was unlucky? Execution would be the least of his worries. There would be a monkey trial, public humiliation, his reputation ruined, his loyalty questioned. God forbid, they may determine him "mentally unstable" and lock him away in an asylum to rot. His family might be ostracized. Those closest to him purged from the ranks.

Zharkov thought he might pass out.

The only way out was through.

"Thank you, Lieutenant," Zharkov said. His voice sounded faint, distant, as if someone else were speaking. "Comrade Minister Tarasov sends his compliments. I expect commendations all around when this is over."

The communications officer smiled back, though his eyes failed to hide his concern. If Zharkov couldn't fool him, then he had no chance to fool his command staff. "Return to your work."

"Yes, Admiral!"

Zharkov left the communications room, stopping in the passageway to produce a cigarette from his breast pocket. Hit put it between his lips and started to light it when a breathless ensign emerging from the communications room nearly ran into him.

"Comrade Admiral!" the young man blurted.

"What is it?" His headache threatened to return with a vengeance.

"We've just gotten word from *K-488*, word of the attack."

Zharkov plucked the report from the young man's hand and read, cigarette forgotten.

Zharkov tapped his foot endlessly as he looked over the report from *K-488*. Destruction of the American battleship as well as multiple smaller vessels. He read the report again, forcing himself to believe it—daring to feel a growing sense of confidence.

The path was clear. They'd done it. He'd done it. Victory.

He handed the report back to the ensign, "A grave for a giant," he said. "The West's hopes for victory go down with their ships." His cigarette bobbed as he spoke, delicately perched between his lips.

The subordinate grinned uncertainly as he took the report back.

Zharkov's mind was racing again. They had to act fast so as not to miss their chance. He tapped the communications officer's shoulder. "Transmit to the landing group: the path is clear. Battalions will commence landing operations. Have them increase speed to flank, move between us and *Ulyanovsk* group to begin landing."

"Yes, Comrade Admiral!"

The West had nothing left to stop them.

***

41

Raleigh's sonar plot was alive with returns. Everything from the cavitation of propellers to the active pings of sonar sweeps to the splash of sonobuoys dropping into the water. It was a circus of activity on the surface as the Soviet amphibious landing group shuffled nervously across the water like a flock of spooked sheep. All around them were a collection of Soviet escort frigates and destroyers probing the depths and searching the sky, wary of an ambush.

At first Grier felt like they'd only found the Soviet landing group through dumb luck, but now he felt they were impossible to miss with how much noise they were making. Like all things in warfare, the Soviets had made a tradeoff. They'd forsaken any chance at sneaking through in order to maximize their detection capabilities.

Grier rubbed tired eyes and tried to blink them clear. "Any change in their course?"

"Negative, sir. Straight ahead."

They had been shadowing this group since they found it almost half an hour ago, tailing their prey at the edge of their detection radius like a wolf slinking through tall grass. Hitting them wasn't the problem, surviving the reprisal was. One slip up, one mistake, one unexpected sonobuoy and the wrath of the whole group would fall on them like hammer on nail.

Grier paced to the sonar plot and looked over the host of ships. Those which were positively ID'd were labeled with class-names and sometimes even individual ship names. Others were only marked as possible contacts.

This panoply of weapons systems was troubling enough,

but there were a few key points of contention. Sailing in the midst of the landing ships was the largest of the surface ships, a *Kiev*-class aircraft carrier, the source of the ASW helicopters circling the fleet like hungry scavengers.

That ship alone was more than a match for most submarines. Even if they managed to hit her, her aircraft wouldn't be so easily dispatched and, given the relatively small warhead of the mark 48, it would take more than one hit to put the *Kiev* completely out of action.

Despite that, it wasn't the carrier or its smaller escorts which troubled Grier.

"Have we gotten a positive count on submarines?" he asked.

"No, sir. Two for sure, but we're not sure about a third, plus there's a faint return on the opposite side of the fleet."

"Echoes maybe?"

"Might be, but it could also be a submarine at the edge of detection radius."

"Ours or theirs?" Briggs asked from beside him.

"Could be *Sovereign*," Grier agreed, "or it could be an unwelcome surprise." He had to wonder if *Raleigh* was also showing as a faint echo on the edge of the Soviet sonar plots. If so, how long before a helicopter came out with a dipping sonar to investigate them more closely?

"The two under the fleet are definitely *Victor*-class," Sonar said.

"We're going to have to be surgical about this," Grier said to himself. They would only get one shot. *Raleigh* didn't have nearly enough tubes to fire on every vessel at once. "If we can get—."

"Captain Grier, I mark explosions, sir!"

Grier whirled in surprise to the sonar station. "Say again?"

"One of the *Krivaks* has taken a hit in the stern, sir."

Grier's mind spun but he came to the same conclusion as the XO a moment before Briggs spoke. "That must be *Sovereign* then."

"And she's kicking things off early," Grier said.

The Soviet amphibious group reacted nearly instantly, accelerating and maneuvering. The escorts fanned out and probed for the shooter as the transport ships made a run for it.

"Another explosion, one of the Victors. I've got transients, sir."

Two kills ahead already, and now *Sovereign* had taken all the heat. They wouldn't get a better shot at the transports. It was now or never.

"Third undersea contact identified. Another Victor class. They're accelerating and firing on *Sovereign*."

Forcing away his fear, Grier spoke with confidence. "Alright, let's dance. Weapons, get me a solution on both of the remaining Victors, wire-guided only. We'll stab them in the back, give *Sovereign* a chance."

"Aye, sir!"

Both tubes fired, the sound lost in the ambient chaos as the Soviets pounded the ocean with sonar pings and churned the waters with their screws.

"Make sure we've got two harpoons in the tubes," Grier said. "The second we take those submarines I want to hit the carrier."

"Sir."

He got his chance a minute later.

"Impact! Detonations from torpedoes one and two!"

The Soviet submarines never heard them coming.

"Fire tubes three and four!"

Both harpoon missiles spewed from the tubes and breached the surface, igniting their boosters a moment later, their radar guidance going active.

"Drop a noise maker here and take us to flank." Grier was counting on the Soviets responding quickly, and he wasn't disappointed. A minute later, they made two splashes to their rear rocket-deployed torpedoes right where they'd launched from. The torpedoes locked onto the noise maker straight away, seeing exactly what they wanted to.

Raleigh shook with the shockwave of both torpedoes

detonating against the decoy.

There was no telling if the harpoons had found their target or not, but Grier had to assume they would sow further chaos.

"Do we have status on *Sovereign*?" Grier asked.

"Putting up a hell of a fight," Sonar said.

For now.

If there was going to be a chance to try to slip away, this would be it. Grier felt the weight of that decision pressing down on him. *Sovereign* had taken most of the heat, the Soviet escorts were in chaos. He could leave the *Sovereign* to the wolves and duck out, circle back, and maybe strike again.

"Second chances," he mused aloud. They'd let the carriers slip by once, he wasn't going to lose this chance at the landing group, no matter the cost, not when he had the power to turn the tide.

"Sir?" Briggs asked.

Grier could see the fear in his eyes though his XO fought to hide it. He also saw something else, something that hurt worse. He saw trust. Blind trust in the man who was willing to spend his life—all their lives.

"No second chances in war," Grier said. "Tubes loaded?"

"Yes, sir."

"Good. Weapons, fire full spread, bearing 040. Target the closest assault ships." With all the noise the Soviets were making, there was no need for the torpedoes to ping, they would simply follow their targets' sound signatures straight to them.

"Aye, sir!"

They were truly sailing into the mouth of hell now, and his men didn't hesitate. Grier felt pride, but he also felt sorrow.

The second all four tubes were emptied, the crew began to reload as fast as they could. Grier knew that it would take them about two minutes to reload all the tubes. Two minutes was an eternity with all of the attention of the Soviet group suddenly focused on them.

Shortly after the first salvo the gratifying sounds of

straining metal and rushing water came through the sonar as the cumbersome transport craft capsized and sank one by one. Each one of those targets contained hundreds of troops and their gear. Whole companies were wiped out in minutes.

"*Sovereign* is firing, sir!"

The British sub fired a spread of five torpedoes focused on the convoy transports. Attacking from two different directions as they did, it left the Soviets with nowhere to run. Nine separate torpedo hits thundered through the water.

Grier kept his submarine moving, dropping a string of noisemakers as he did. It was all he could do—it bought them precious minutes, but that bill was coming due. As they fired and maneuvered, he watched *Sovereign*'s own struggle on the tactical plot. The Soviets blanketed her with torpedoes and sonobuoys. There was no escape. All they could do was watch as enemy torpedoes closed on her like jackals.

"That's a hit, sir," Sonar said grimly.

"Transients?"

Sonar nodded.

In a heartbeat, *Sovereign* was dead.

Despite the odds, he had done his job. He'd scattered the convoy and filled the sea with dead. *Sovereign* had paid for it with the lives of her crew. Grier knew that his was next.

"Are those tubes loaded yet?"

"Not yet, sir!"

"Enemy torpedo closing! It's pinging us, confidence high."

This was it. Grier was out of tricks. A cold sweat broke out across his body.

"All hands brace for impact! Brace!"

Grier grabbed a white-knuckled grip on the nearest bulkhead knowing that it likely wouldn't matter.

Distance ticked by until—.

Raleigh rocked with the shockwave of a direct hit, her hull groaning, twisting, fracturing.

Grier hit the bulkhead hard enough to smash his face. He ripped his broken glasses away, feeling blood coursing from his broken nose.

"Damage report!"

Briggs began checking compartments using the ship-wide phone, but Grier could already tell that *Raleigh* was mortally wounded.

"Hit to the bow!" Briggs called. "Flooding in all forward compartments! Damage control is working!"

"Another torpedo in the water! Two hundred meters and pinging!"

It was over. "Blow all tanks!" Grier said "Emergency ascent!" All that remained to him was getting his men out of here, getting them to safety—to the surface.

Raleigh shuddered as air reserves cleared flooded ballast tanks, turning the attack sub buoyant. She rose through the water steadily, slowly. Too slowly.

"Torpedo fifty meters! Forty!"

The surface was an eternity away.

Grier felt he should say something to the crew who had followed him dutifully and bravely to their deaths. But there was nothing to say.

Raleigh imploded, her hull broken by explosive force, taking all one hundred and forty men on board in a rush of fatal pressure and oceanic crush.

***

42

Zharkov's mind was addled with fatigue, but the hope and despair which had warred within him were finally coming to a head. They had paid a terrible price for this victory. The Soviet Navy was shattered. But they had achieved their goal. With a missile base established in Iceland, his ships could operate with more safety under the SAM and anti-ship missile umbrella it provided. Then, in coordination with the naval air regiments, they could systematically drive NATO away from the Norwegian coast, isolate the enclaves and secure the Norwegian Sea. A fulcrum and lever to move the world.

He grinned confidently, ecstatic. It would be a Soviet lake. Another Baltic Sea. Another Black Sea. Another stepping stone toward victory.

Zharkov became aware of another officer standing nearby, *Tashkent*'s captain. The captain looked nervous, his expression grim.

Zharkov's hopes faded to nothing.

The other officer held a print out. Zharkov took it from him and read. He didn't need to bother.

"The amphibious group has been nearly destroyed," the captain said. "*Leningrad* has taken damage. We have lost many of the transport craft and...."

What was left would not be enough. The naval infantry had been decimated before they even touched the shore.

"Comrade Admiral...the landing—."

Zharkov let the paper fall from his grasp and flutter to the floor. He had driven the Soviet Navy to its doom. A death ride in the Norwegian Sea. His dreams of a sweeping victory here mocked him. They were just as illusory as ever. "There will be no landing," Zharkov said. No landing, and nothing to return to at home but shame, humiliation, and misery. Exile or execution. Imprisonment and isolation. Torture and death.

Zharkov patted his uniform pockets down until he found his lighter, at last, lighting the cigarette he'd been craving all this time.

The smoke was sweet and he breathed deeply.

"Comrade Admiral, what will we do?"

Zharkov put the lighter back in his pocket and thought. "We will bring the fleet around," he said at last. "North. Coordinate with the naval air forces to cover our retreat."

"Comrade Admiral, surely—."

Zharkov held up a hand to silence him. "Captain, I will be in my quarters. Come see me in ten minutes. Then inform Olesk."

The captain only watched in mute shock as the Admiral left the CIC without a word to anyone. Minutes later, there was a gunshot from his cabin.

***

43

Morris and the other pilots of the bombing raid flew toward the spreading golden crescent of the sunrise. Sunrise over the ocean was nothing compared to the vivid colors of sunset. It was gray, cold, and dim. Still, the light was a welcome change, heralding a new day. It was better than the pitch darkness they'd flown in through.

Ahead, just out of view, was the Norwegian coast. It was strange to think that just days ago he'd been down there, on the ground, among the trees slogging through the wilderness. He'd never imagined he'd make it back. Still, in the forest or in the cockpit he was far from home and far from safe.

Morris kept an eye on his instrument panel, watching for indications of enemy activity or interceptors climbing to face them. None came. It was possible that none were even available if the rumors he'd heard about an impending naval battle were true.

Morris's radio buzzed. "Anvil, this is Camelot. Peepshow confirms Backfires have touched back down."

"Copy, Camelot. Anvil commencing bombing run."

Movement to his left caught Morris's eye.

In the faint light of dawn, he saw the large gray-hulled B-52 bombers his squadron escorted open their bomb bay doors nearly in unison. Built to shuttle atomic bombs from bases in the United States over the North Pole into targets in Russia, they were just as capable of carrying other ordinance.

A flock of cruise missiles dropped free from the bombers and ignited their engines, hurrying off for their date with destiny. Each one had been fed the precise coordinates of a bomber parking spot or other critical infrastructure like fuel depots and repair sheds. Between the half dozen B-52s in the strike group, they unleashed enough explosive force to level the airbase twice over. One stroke to eliminate the threat the Backfires posed.

"Wyvern, package delivered. We're headed home."

"Copy, Anvil," Morris said. "Nice flying with you."

"Nice will be when we're wheels down again. Anvil out."

Morris couldn't disagree. He and his squadron turned in behind the B-52s, trailing them back toward Scotland.

**

Fedorovich had never been so cold before in his entire life. His body shivered so hard that he hurt all over. Salt spray stung his face, but as time wore on he was increasingly numb to the pain. The thin survival blanket he was wrapped in did next to nothing to ward off the icy gales blowing over the surface of the Norwegian Sea.

It was dark and wet in the blaze orange survival dinghy he and Babayev floated in.

Babayev had reached the dinghy first after they bailed out. He'd swam hard, struggling in the surging tide, fighting his way to their only chance of survival.

When their parachutes were falling toward the ocean, Fedorovich had kept his eyes on his co-pilot's chute, half-visible in the dark, never once losing sight of him, determined not to die alone.

When he hit the water, it was like being punched in the gut. All the air left his lungs in a single, involuntary exhalation as the intense, bone-aching cold sapped the life from his body. Somehow he'd fought through it, staying conscious and on top of the waves through force of will. He'd decoupled his parachute and then kicked and paddled. It felt more like fighting than swimming as he traversed the waves, struggling steadily toward Babayev's falling parachute. Through sheer dumb luck, when Fedorovich found Babayev he also found the inflatable dinghy.

The co-pilot had hoisted him into the rubber life raft where they now both sat, shaking and shivering.

They never found Alekseev.

They'd called out for him for a few minutes, their voices lost to the wind. They pretended to continue searching for him for a few minutes more to soothe their consciences, before they no longer had the strength to care. He would be long dead by now, his life vest keeping his body afloat.

Fedorovich kept his arms wrapped tightly around his legs, his knees to his chest, watching some captive sea water sloshing to and fro in the bottom of the inflatable raft.

The radio beacon chirped and flashed, ignorant to his suffering.

They were going to die here.

It was madness to imagine that anyone would mount a rescue operation for them out here in the middle of a war. The sea was no-man's-land and no one had the time or inclination to go looking for a single lost bomber crew.

"The others."

"What?" Babayev looked at him.

Fedorovich was startled to realize he'd said that out loud. He struggled to keep his teeth from chattering, reminding himself that feeling cold was a good thing, it meant his body hadn't yet started to shut down. "The others went down here too," he said. "Other planes. Other crews."

"Even if they survived, we have no way to reach them," Babyev said. "A few seconds of flight time could be kilometers of distance."

Of course Fedorovich knew all this, but he couldn't bring himself to admit it. It was painful to imagine his squadron downed across the sea, scattered, alone and freezing. His men. Men he'd failed.

Babayev kept watch, scanning the sea in the dim twilight as gray dawn broke on the horizon. That promise of the sun kept

Fedorovich going. The idea that things might warm up was all he needed right now.

"It would have been quick," Fedorovich said.

The co-pilot looked at him, his expression troubled.

"For Alekseev," Fedorovich said. "It's painless. The cold."

Babayev nodded, but looked distant.

"It could have been any of us," Fedorovich said, voice as soft as he could allow it while still being heard.

"But it wasn't."

"No," Fedorovich agreed.

Together they listened to the waves and wind. He thought about Alekseev and Pavlov. He thought about home, his friends and family. He thought about death and the endless cold eating into his face and hands.

"If this is it," Fedorovich said, "then let's at least do it the Russian way."

Babayev looked at him curiously while Fedorovich dug through the small survival pouch inside the raft. At last, he pulled out what he was looking for, a small glass bottle of clear liquid.

The co-pilot looked at it in astonishment. "Stolichnaya?"

Fedorovich offered the bottle of smuggled vodka. "If we're to die, we might as well die drunk, yes?"

Babayev took the bottle and uncapped it before taking a swill. "Might as well." He passed it back.

The warmth of the alcohol helped to cut down the chill in Fedorovich's body just as it helped him to care a little less that he found his hands getting stiff. The two of them passed the minutes by drinking and watching the sunrise to split the horizon. All the while the radio beacon flashed and chirped.

When half the bottle was gone, it slipped from Fedorovich's numb hand as he went to pass it to Babayev.

The vodka spilled out across the rubber floor of the dingy as both men scrambled to save it, fumbling and swearing. When at last Babayev seized it, only a single mouthful remained.

He looked at Fedorovich and offered the bottle. "For you,

Major."

"No," Fedorovich said. "I've had enough I think. Enough to sleep."

Babayev looked at the bottle mournfully. "I think so too."

Fedorovich looked up. "Listen."

Babayev tilted his head. "What is—."

"Shhh! Listen!"

This time they both heard it. The thumping of helicopter blades.

Fedorovich practically dove for the survival bag, this time clawing out the bright orange flare gun. The plastic release catch tore at his numb fingertips as he opened it and checked that it was loaded.

Babayev laid a hand over it to stop him. "Wait. Is it ours? What if it's the enemy?"

Fedorovich looked at his co-pilot blankly. "What does it matter?"

Babayev had no answer.

Rising to his knees in the pitching rescue raft, Fedorovich peered into the twilight, searching for the source of the sound. He couldn't be sure if they were attracted to the beacon or they were simply in the right place at the right time.

A glimmer of movement on the horizon, a speck fluttering by.

It might be their only chance.

He raised the gun overhead and fired. A meteoric flare climbed into the sky, bathing the ocean around them a bloody red.

After a few moments, the flare fell back into the ocean and was extinguished.

Both men listened intently, straining over the surging waves and listened as the noise grew fainter. They traded a look of understanding. That was it.

Fedorovich dropped the empty flare gun and slumped against the edge of the raft. He laid his head back and closed his eyes. He was ready to sleep after all.

A moment later, the sound of the helicopter returned, this time growing louder.

***

44

Before there was any sign of the bombing raid, a siren went off in the air base.

Landvick hunkered down on the high ground overlooking the base, binoculars in hand, and watched as tiny figures scrambled for cover. A large, silver-hulled fighter rolled to the head of the runway and took off with a roar of engines.

A second later, a Soviet SAM battery fired, throwing missiles into the sky. They streaked out west, vanishing up into the clouds and leaving only plumes of white smoke.

Landvik counted eight of these launches before the first of the cruise missiles came in like a bolt from Zeus himself. There was no warning. Landvick heard the shriek of the missile only after it had already exploded.

Its target was a crude earthen aircraft shelter that the Soviets had built with stolen bulldozers after claiming the airfield as their own. The shelter did nothing to protect the Backfire bomber it housed as the cruise missile detonated directly overhead.

A picture-perfect mushroom cloud of smoke rolled into the sky from the smoldering skeleton of the Backfire. It would have been impressive enough on its own, but the show was far from over.

The first missile was only a hint of the sheer volume of death that rained down on the base.

Landvik saw the tiny, toy-like forms of airmen and ground crew scatter as more cruise missiles struck bombers and blew up. One by one the Backfires burst like fiery balloons and soon the missiles went to work on the rest of the base. Depots and hangars went up in flames and men ran screaming in all directions, crawling on hands and knees for cover.

The destruction went on and on but was over in seconds.

Smoldering wrecks and billowing smoke was all that remained. The echoing, sympathetic booms of explosions receded to nothing and the chirp of early morning birds replaced it. Smoke rose from the south and east, more strikes against the airport and nearby bases, Landvik guessed.

For a few minutes, Landvik was shocked to inaction by the ferocity of the attack before he picked up the phone handset. "Camelot, this is Peepshow. Target is neutralized."

***

45

Rear Admiral Olesk sat in his quarters onboard *Ulyanovsk* and slowly read over the report in his hands. It was only a few words long, but each one held weight.

Comrade Admiral Zharkov has perished. Command of the fleet has passed to you.

Olesk sniffed once and rubbed his nose. The arrogant bastard had done himself in, no doubt. With deliberate slowness, Olesk folded the paper in half and set about systematically tearing it up.

The officers gathered on the opposite side of his desk only watched in silence.

Once it was shredded, Olesk dropped the papers into an ashtray and lit them on fire with his lighter. He watched the paper curl and blacken as it was consumed.

Olesk snuffed the flames out with an empty glass. "He died facing the enemy. A hero's death." He looked up. "You understand?"

"Yes, Comrade Admiral."

Olesk nodded and dumped the cooling ashes into his waste bin. The golden light of dawn came in through the small porthole his rank afforded. The fleet—what was left of it —steamed north, away from the carnage they'd just been through. He set the glass down on his desk and uncapped a bottle of vodka, pouring himself a healthy dose.

"Destroy all paper communications regarding this," Olesk said. He knew the sort of damage this kind of news could do for morale, especially at a time when things were already grim. Zharkov's ill-planned gambit had failed, but the price wasn't as bad as it could have been. "And make a fleet-wide announcement that Admiral Zharkov was killed in the line of duty." He drained the glass.

Olesk's subordinate saluted and retreated, closing the door softly behind him, leaving him with his thoughts.

Olesk knew that his career was relatively safe. His opposition to Zharkov's plan was well known, and now his position no longer looked defeatist, but reasonable. In fact, with Zharkov and his lackey Yevdokimov out of the way, Olesk was free to spin whatever story he wanted about this whole operation. Not a failed gamble for Iceland, no. This was a successful sortie to weaken Western naval assets. Olesk nodded to himself. Yes. This thing had begun as Zharkov's misbegotten operation but Olesk had salvaged it. Zharkov and Yevdokimov had their uses in life, Olesk mused, and so would they in death. He started pouring himself a second glass as he considered his next moves to save the fleet, and his career. All that remained was getting back home.

***

Admiral Alderman sipped coffee with his left hand and paged through printouts with his right. Between the caffeine and the reports of the destruction of the Soviet Backfire regiments on the ground, his mood improved incrementally.

F-117 stealth fighters had savaged airbases in Soviet-occupied Denmark—ironically the same airfields NATO had been using only weeks prior. Further bombardment of Baltic airfields had been conducted with precision Tomahawk strikes. Both were masterful applications of precision airpower, but they paled in comparison to the total annihilation of the Backfires in Norway. From Peepshow's first hand observation, not one of the remaining Backfires posed any sort of threat, and the airbase infrastructure had been put to the torch.

"Good riddance," Alderman said, sipping the last of his

coffee. With the Backfires out of the picture, they were free to maneuver against the Soviet carrier fleet, at last able to concentrate their superior numbers—what they had left of them, anyway.

The toll on NATO's Norwegian Sea forces was appalling. Three carriers—*Antietam*, *Anzio*, and *Inchon*—were all out of action for the foreseeable future and the surviving carrier's air wings had suffered grievous losses. *Shiloh* at the hands of *Novosibirsk*, and *Belleau Wood* and *Bastogne* from their previous close air support missions over Norway. *Iowa* and her battlegroup were all but destroyed, and they'd finally received confirmation that both *Raleigh* and *Sovereign* had been lost in the action to cripple the Soviet amphibious group.

It was bitter news, but there was some consolation that these losses had built to this moment, allowing him to strike back. Alderman was staggered at the volume of life lost, the loss of ships, sailors, and airmen at a scale not seen since the war in the Pacific fifty years prior.

So many fathers, brothers, husbands, and sons lost to the cold, black seas. And the butcher's work wasn't over yet. The Soviets had damaged three American carriers, but he aimed to destroy their entire navy.

So what was left to do the job?

Though Alderman knew numbers and ships by heart, he forced himself to review the files collected on his desk, leaving no detail unchecked.

With the Backfires out of the picture, *Chancellorsville* and *Shiloh* were free to recommit to the enemy. Likewise, *Belleau Wood* and *Bastogne* were freed up from escort duty.

The British carrier group was spreading out and moving south to fill gaps opened in the GIUK line after the Soviet attacks. They held the Denmark Straits and soon would defend all the waters around Iceland, stepping in where *Iowa* had been. Further to the south, the French carriers *Foch* and *Clemenceau* were moving at flank up from the English Channel. Their carriers wouldn't be able to link up with the American fleet for at least twenty-four hours.

Alderman reviewed these details one by one, double checking speeds, ranges and distances before he committed each facet of information to memory. Once satisfied with his findings, he moved on to the next, collating facts and building a plan of action item by item. There was one advantage Alderman held over the Soviets that they may not have been aware of. Reconnaissance satellites had been put in orbit to replace the last batch lost, this time unmolested by the Soviets.

The admiral took the stack of photographs from its manila folder and laid them across the table, creating a tableau of high-resolution satellite photographs of the Norwegian Sea, each helpfully marked with labels indicating Soviet surface vessels, their classes, and even their names where it could be positively ID'd.

The Soviets were regrouping, drawing up on themselves, and turning east. The remnants of *Novosibirsk* group, the amphibious landing group, as well as the untouched groups around *Tashkent* and *Ulyanovsk*. Four carriers—only two of them peers to the Americans—and their escorts.

Their goal was obvious. They were running for the Norwegian coast. The closer they got, the more they could rely on friendly air cover—from land-based aircraft as well as long-range SAM batteries. Once they reached Norway's fjords they could sail up the coast, sticking to shallow waters where Western submarines would be hesitant to operate. A clean escape.

Alderman hardened his expression. There wouldn't be another shot at this, no better chance to excise the Soviet Navy before it had a chance to withdraw once again into the relative safety of the Barents Sea.

"They can't hide from us," Alderman said to himself, "but they might just get away."

Whoever the Soviets had running the show had to know they were in a corner. From their bold, almost suicidal deathride they'd transitioned very quickly into a far more conservative strategy. Had they realized just how hopelessly screwed they were? Or had their plan just gone belly up, leaving them with no other option? Whatever the case, Alderman knew he had them cornered, and he suspected his Soviet adversary knew that too.

Alderman wasn't as happy with that fact as he could have been. After all, a cornered animal fights twice as hard. Outnumbered, outgunned, the Soviets could still take a lot of people down with them if he didn't play his cards right.

The admiral looked at the clock. It was just past noon and daylight was burning. Alderman had a showdown to orchestrate and little time to do it.

***

All the planning in the world was useless with no one to execute it. That task fell to the pilots and crew of *Bastogne* and *Belleau Wood*. The sailors of the battlegroup were professionals and seasoned ones at that. They'd honed their skills to a fine edge in peacetime and had only improved since then. Aircraft were refueled, missiles locked to pylons, the flight deck cleared and aircraft queued up. This work—though graceless on the surface—required intense coordination, focus, and cooperation. Men raced the clock, pushing beyond fatigue to get their air wings ready for battle.

With all the apprehension and excitement that came with it, they prepared for battle. Just as before, it was a battle in which men were a small part of a larger equation. Supersonic trans-horizon warfare seemed to rely more on machines than men, but the human factor could make all the difference.

The sun dipped toward the horizon off their portside as the carriers turned in sync into the wind and accelerated, readying for launch. With everything in place, they scrambled their air wings, fighters taking to the skies in waves.

The pilots were exhausted, their airframes overtaxed. Both had been pushed to their limits by relentless operational tempo. A round-the-clock pattern of ground attack and intercept operations over Norway had stopped the Bergen-Oslo line from collapsing, but it had wreaked a terrible toll on the men of the fleet.

They'd only just finished sorties against the Soviet Backfire attack, and now were once again being thrown into the fray with fewer aircraft than they would have liked. There would be no stopping though, no rest until the job was done.

After reaching the prescribed altitude, the aircraft formed into squadrons—a staggered arrowhead of fighters and attack craft. Once assembled, they turned north, moving like a wedge between the Soviet fleet and the Norwegian coast. A spread out picket line of Tomcats watched the horizon as Hornets and Intruders followed on, shielding the AWACS craft at the center of the formation. This strike group moved to cut off the Soviets with all the speed they could muster, racing toward contact with the enemy and the uncertainty of combat.

**

Four hundred miles away, *Chancellorsville* and *Shiloh* put their own wings in the air in nearly identical formations.

"Looking good," Gomez said from the back. "Hold this course and straight on."

Rabbit shook his head. His flight helmet seemed heavier than it had been just a few hours ago, his movements more sluggish. He wouldn't admit it, but he was slowing down. Fatigue ate away at his mind like some kind of voracious parasite. Eventually it would wear him down to the point of uselessness. But not now. Not yet.

He flew in the shadow of a large KC-10 tanker plane lit orange by the setting sun. The tanker's fueling drogue trailed a long hose behind it, currently coupled with Ducky's Tomcat. The hose fed vital fuel to the F-14, topping off its internal tanks. Mid-flight refueling was the only way this sortie could reach engagement range as the pilots of both carrier wings were going to be flying well beyond standard range, burning through even what they could carry in drop tanks. It was a long way out, but not so long that it was beyond the reach of the United States Navy.

Rabbit shook his head again, stifling a yawn. He told himself this was the last one before he got real sleep. If they tried to send him up again, he'd tell Hendricks he couldn't do it. Even as he thought it, he knew it was a lie. If they needed him, he'd go up as many times as he had to.

"You good, man?"

"All good," Rabbit lied. Everyone else was just as tired as he was, what could they do? There was no sense bitching about it. "Just ready to be done with this and get some rack time."

"I hear that. Just make sure you get us there, yeah?"

"No problem there."

"You do the flying and I'll—."

"Do the RIO shit?" Rabbit teased.

Gomez chuckled. "Yeah. I'll be the guy in back."

"Works for me."

Just a few days ago, Rabbit had been invincible—a pilot of the world's best naval interceptor in the world's best navy. Now he felt pretty far from invincible. He'd seen friends go down in flames, Metcalf was never coming back and his own number could be next. There were no guarantees in war. It seemed like a lifetime ago he was fantasizing about golf and women. The Grand Old Lady seemed farther away than ever. Now he was just hoping to come back from this mission alive.

Rabbit looked to his left, toward the horizon. He could just about see *Chancellorsville*'s own air wing paralleling their course. They were fresh, having avoided the intense fighting of the past few days. Fresh, but also inexperienced. Rabbit and Gomez had drawn blood, they'd stood toe-to-toe with the best the Soviet Union had to offer and had come out on top. Those guys from *Chancellorsville* were about to get their first taste of battle. He had to have faith they would hold true.

"How long on this course?" Rabbit asked.

"About another hour," Gomez said.

Just as before, the wing was taking a circuitous route to reach the Soviets, this time less to conceal their origin and more to attack from an unexpected axis. They would be coming in opposite of the first attack group from *Bastogne* and *Belleau Wood* in a grand pincer attack. Striking from the sinking sun, if they got lucky, the Soviets would be so busy focused on the air wing between them and their destination that Rabbit and the others could walk right up and stick them with Harpoons again.

This time *Shiloh*'s pilots would be coming in high, avoiding the dangers of flying at low altitude, but in exchange gaining a whole new set of problems. Not the least of these was the increased likelihood the Soviets would pick them up at long range and be waiting for them.

Rabbit could only hope that the Soviets took the bait.

"103, you're up."

Rabbit saw Ducky's Tomcat back away from the tanker with a light spray of spilled fuel.

"Copy." Rabbit put his mind on the task at hand. They had a long way to go yet and he needed to stay sharp.

***

46

The air wings of *Bastogne* and *Belleau Wood* flew in total radio silence. Any stray broadcast could reveal their presence early and doom the operation before it had a chance. The operation was risky enough as it was. Their flight path skimmed the edge of land-based radar coverage from Soviet-occupied Norway. If they weren't careful—or if they were plain unlucky—they could be detected and spoil the plan.

They'd been flying silently for well over an hour, relying on visuals alone to keep the strike group together. Each pilot, RIO, and crewmen was a tight bundle of nerves, alone with their thoughts and their fears. The threat of combat loomed larger by the minute. It was a moment they all dreaded and welcomed. This silence was broken as the wings reached the next waypoint in their flight path. It was time.

The radio crackled to life and set things in motion. "Scepter 100 to all elements. Come about 280, maintain speed and altitude."

The attack force turned as one, drawing up into lines and fanning out as fighters assumed combat spacing. The formation unfolded like a flower blooming. Squadrons spread out and adjusted position to ensure that each plane had clear space to maneuver without risk of collision. No sooner had they finished setting up then they reached the next stage of the operation.

"Scepter 100. Midnight, commence jamming sweep."

"Midnight 200 copies."

The Prowers flying at the forward edge of the strike group powered on their jammers and flooded the airwaves with junk radar returns, blotting out any possibility of long range observation.

To their west, Soviet Merit AWACS planes picked up this jamming clear as day. The enemy was here.

***

"Heavy jamming to our front, Comrade Admiral."

Olesk sat up straighter in his command chair. A jolt of electric fear shot through his body. "Distance?"

"Three hundred kilometers and closing."

The range was too far out to do more than mask the exact composition of the force. That and alert him to their presence. Straight away Olesk knew it was a feint. There was no reason to activate jamming so far in advance other than to light up his scopes and compel him to panic and do something stupid. The Americans were goading him.

"Shall we scramble fighters, Admiral?"

Olesk considered his options. Doing nothing wasn't a possibility, but racing into an obvious trap was just as foolish. He wouldn't fall for the same ploy that Yevdokimov did. "Launch all fighters and move them into a holding pattern around the fleet with orders *not* to close range. If the Americans want to fight, they will need to come to us." He wasn't keen to engage the enemy in range of his own twitchy anti-air gunners, but it was a risk he would have to take. With a little luck, the Americans would be just as afraid of his air defense batteries as his own pilots were.

As his orders were carried out, echoed through the CIC, Olesk formulated his next step. No doubt the Americans knew they outmatched his carrier wings, but they weren't counting on the other assets at his disposal. The Red Banner Northern Fleet was no longer as alone as it had been. Olesk turned to the nearby communications officer. "Contact our comrades in the air force and relay the coordinates of the jamming. Make this a priority target. Any fighters they have should be put in the air without delay."

"Yes, Admiral."

"Anything," Oleks repeated for emphasis.

Olesk was certain, given the air force's staggering losses, that nothing newer than a MiG-23 would be available. Losses would be horrendous, but he didn't care about that. All that mattered was saving the fleet—or as much of it as he could—and by extension also saving his career. Zharkov had put them in this mess, but Olesk was going to get them out.

"Confirmation from aviation group Scandinavia, Admiral. Standby interceptor squadrons will scramble at once."

By positioning themselves between his fleet and the shore, the Americans had walked into a trap. The only question was whether or not they realized it. If they didn't turn back, their fighters would be caught in a vice between his air wings and the land-based interceptors flying out of northern Norway. Even if the air force failed to destroy them, they would be easier targets for his own fighter wings after being softened up.

In minutes, data from the circling Yak-44 AWACS showed the arrowhead shapes of interceptor formations launching from improvised road bases in Norway and Sweden, closing on the American strike group.

***

47

Vlasov kept his Su-27K banking in a slow orbit around the surface fleet. From this distance, the ships below looked like bathtub toys—gray boats with red-brown decks bobbing on an endless sea. It was easy to forget each was a home— or a grave—to hundreds. The ships traveled at close to stop speed—nothing next to the speeds his Sukhoi was capable of —hurrying to the safety of the coast. Vlasov didn't pretend to understand the operational elements at play here. He knew only what he needed too—what his commanders told him— but it was clear that something had gone terribly wrong with this operation. They'd turned back after taking severe losses. Whatever damage they'd done to the West couldn't have been enough to justify the cost. Vlasov tried not to dwell on it. Winning the war wasn't his responsibility. He just followed orders and had to trust that those in charge knew what they were doing. What else could he do?

"When are they going to send us out?" The pilot who spoke didn't bother to identify himself by callsign. In peacetime this would be a serious oversight. Vlasov continued to be stunned by how different things were in war.

"Orders are clear. Stay within air defense range of the fleet." Hydra leader spoke. He sounded subdued, perhaps still shaken over his pilots' lack of discipline when they fired early on *Iowa*.

He shouldn't have expected anything else, Vlasov thought. He and his fellow pilots weren't stupid and they certainly weren't suicidal. There was a difference between bravery and foolhardiness. All men—even the elite pilots of the Soviet Navy —had their limits. Surely the Americans were close to theirs.

"And do our gunners know that?" the insubordinate pilot shot back. "If I'm going to die, I don't want it to be from some drunk, trigger-happy sailor on our side."

"Clear the channel," Hydra leader replied acidly.

There was no reply.

Vlasov had discipline enough not to sass the squadron leader, but he didn't disagree with his comrade. Soviet air defense was trained to shoot first and ask questions never. Enthusiasm and volume of fire would—it was thought—offset NATO air superiority and make them think twice about coming into range. In practice, it often left the skies unsafe for pilots of both sides. He'd heard horror stories of friendly fire incidents, men shot down well behind the lines because some SAM operator got spooked by a radar return.

There was also something inherently demoralizing about waiting to be attacked. Friendly SAM cover or not, Vlasov wasn't keen to wait for the enemy to come to them. Even though his stomach was tied in knots, all he wanted was some positive radar contact, something to shoot at.

***

Olesk gave a tight grin as he stared down at the flashing radar plot. A second attack wave, just as he expected.

"Second group approaching from the west. Altitude seven thousand meters. Seventy aircraft. Radar returns suggest F-18s and F-14s."

The Americans had hoped to pincer him. They hadn't yet realized he was wise to their game. "That trick won't work twice," he chided his enemy. To his tactical officer he said: "Let them come close. We'll engage them with SAMs and fighters simultaneously. The fleet's defense batteries can screen our fighters from the American's long range missiles. Hold nothing back, I won't have anything getting through."

"Right away, Comrade Admiral!"

The American fighters only had one shot at this. If they

failed and were forced back, it would take them time to return to their carriers and re-arm, time they couldn't spare. Once they were ready to try again, his fleet would be within the safety of the shore-based SAM and fighter network. This was their one shot.

What was it that Zharkov had said about the West? Olesk racked his memory back to the pre-mission briefing. Before they set out on this foolish crusade. A joust. That was it. His lips pulled back in a humorless smile. Zharkov had said the West loved a joust. Well here it was and here they came, galloping on.

**

"Griffon to all pilots. Enemy contacts to the west." The voice of the AWACS flight officer carried strong and clear over Vlasov's radio. "Close range and engage. Repeat, all weapons clear. Close range and engage. Acknowledge."

"Hydra acknowledge."

Vlasov's heart started racing. They were here. He pulled his stick over, banking his Sukhoi in a tight turn, coming about to face the enemy. The moment he had them in his sights, he goosed the throttle, spurring his aircraft on, charging forward.

**

Olesk watched the radar plot as land-based interceptors closed and engaged with the first American attack wave to their east. Simultaneously, his own fighter squadrons circled the fleet and drew up lines before turning west and preparing to meet their enemy. Olesk imagined he could almost hear the thunder of hooves as both waves of aircraft closed on one another, plunging towards certain death. Seconds slipped by, minutes running like water through his fingers as the distance closed at the speed of sound. The Americans inched nearer and nearer to the outer edges of his picket ship's engagement range until, at last, they crossed it.

"SAM batteries," his tactical officer said, "commence firing. Free to fire." *Ulyanovsk*'s escorts fired a staccato barrage of anti-air missiles aimed at the heart of the approaching American formation. The missiles passed under his aircraft as they climbed to meet the enemy.

***

Vlasov kept his eyes fixed to his radar, clenching his teeth and willing the Americans to close to range faster. His aircraft wasn't burdened with the dead weight of drop tanks, but it was heavy with missiles, missiles he was eager to be free of.

Even within SAM range of the fleet, Phoenix missiles were still a top concern. The Americans had likely already fired their first volley. It was just a matter of time.

Vlasov's eyes flicked from his radar to his RWR, checking for any evidence of an enemy missile activating terminal guidance radar. Once that happened, his lifespan could reasonably be measured in seconds if he didn't out maneuver them.

Cold sweat broke out across his body and rolled down his neck. The Su-27K vibrated subtly under its own jet thrusters as kilometers flashed by. Then—.

The RWR chirped. Enemy missile lock. The Phoenix.

"Hydra 1-2, I'm breaking!" Vlasov turned hard, setting himself perpendicular to the enemy missiles. Looking starboard, he saw them. Burning white trails cut across the afternoon sky, stabbing directly toward him. One of those missiles had him in its unfeeling sights, burning hard for him. Vlasov's stomach twisted with fear. "God protect me," he whispered. Checking his flight path with the missile's course, desperate to find the 'notch' so his aircraft would disappear in the motionless background clutter. If he could just hit that mark....

All around him, the others in the squadron were likewise defending, maneuvering to break radar locks and dropping clouds of chaff to clutter the enemy radar.

Beneath them, a salvo of anti-air missiles climbed up from the fleet, streaking by to intercept the Phoenixes.

Vlasov watched missiles explode in the distance, popping and flashing to nothingness. Clouds of flaming fuel scattered to the winds, debris tumbling toward the ocean.

The RWR stopped chirping, he'd lost the radar lock. Either he'd notched it or a SAM from the fleet had struck it down. Maybe his comrades in the navy knew what they were doing after all.

To his left, Vlasov saw the flash of a missile detonation.

His radio erupted with a panicked cry. "Hydra 2-5 hit! Going in! Ejecting!"

A billowing white parachute deployed off to port, drifting gracefully down toward the ocean below. It carried a dead man. No helicopter would be foolhardy enough to attempt to mount a rescue during active combat and the water was cold enough that no one would survive in it for more than a few minutes. Vlasov swallowed dryly.

"All craft recommit," Hydra Leader said, sounding winded from the evasive maneuvers. "Fire when you have the range."

"Hydra 1-2 acknowledged," Vlasov said as he banked back to face the oncoming Americans. He gripped his controls tighter and tried to ignore the sharp, icy terror in his chest.

***

48

Rabbit felt the roar of the engines through the vibration of the airframe as he followed the other planes in his squadron into battle. A thin line of Tomcats closed at supersonic speed in the wake of their Phoenix salvo, Rabbit's among them.

"Nails. Twelve o'clock," Gomez said. Enemy targeting radars had them in sight.

"I think we made them mad," Rabbit said, checking his instruments. With no anti-ship weapons there was nothing he could do about the multiple surface contacts he had, but it wasn't his job to worry about the enemy ships.

"We're getting pinged by air and surface radar arrays. Watch for SAMs," Gomez said from behind him. He sounded distracted, preoccupied with keeping the targets in sight, locked up with radar, ready to unleash hell.

"More targets means more chances for glory," Rabbit said with bravado he didn't feel.

Gomez snorted. "Yeah. Right. If there's going to be a plaque for all this I'd just as soon keep my name off it."

Before Rabbit could retort, his squadron leader came over the radio. "Lancer squadron, this is Lancer 100. We've got the go-code from Chancey's CAG. Orders are not to get sucked into a dogfight. Hit and fade. We trade salvos and then go cold. Confirm."

Rabbit felt a small amount of relief at that. Diving headfirst into that hornet's nest of SAM batteries and enemy fighters would be suicide and, once they got into enemy R-77 range, it would be difficult to get back out of it if the Soviets didn't want to let them go.

"Lancer 103 copies," Rabbit said as the others chimed in, then to Gomez he added, "See? No heroics today."

"Yipee."

They'd already fired off their Phoenixes at maximum range, leaving them little chance of scoring hard kills. Still, Rabbit was glad to be rid of the extra weight now that he was coming into range for fox ones.

Off to his port, the Hornets of Banshee Squadron fired a spread of Harpoon missiles and broke, diving for the ocean and turning away from oncoming return fire. They fired on the outer picket ships at extreme range. Hits were a long shot, but it was the best they could manage given the ferocity of the enemy defense.

Now it was up to Lancer to hold the line a minute longer to ensure Banshee Squadron and the other strike craft got away clean. With Lancer left holding the door, Soviet fighters barreled toward them at top speed. Contact came a minute later.

"Spike!" Gomez called, voice cracking. "Twelve o'clock, Flanker!"

They were in it again. It was time to earn that pay.

"Lancer 103 defending!" Rabbit dove and felt his stomach fall out. "Gomez—."

"Countermeasures," Gomez finished.

Their Tomcat sprayed a trail of flares and chaff as it ran for safety. The airframe shook, protesting against the G-forces Rabbit subjected it to. His vision grayed at the edges before he saw a missile contrail flash by above them a moment after the RWR stopped its panicked cries.

Rabbit was too out of breath to swear.

"Dodged it!" Gomez said.

Standing on his rudder pedal, Rabbit pulled the stick back as the horizon spun away, laboriously dragging the F-14's nose up and back on target. His best hope was to get the Flanker running before he had a chance to take another shot at them. "Get me a lock!" Rabbit tried not to think about any heatseekers which might now be racing toward him.

"Locked, get him!"

"Fox one!" Rabbit said. He squeezed the trigger and a sparrow streaked away from beneath them, chasing the radar return.

The Flanker which had fired on them broke away. Rabbit saw it on radar as it pulled defensive maneuvers in an attempt to evade the Sparrow. The radar return went fuzzy—enemy countermeasures.

"Stay on him!" Gomez said.

Rabbit gritted his teeth and focused on keeping the Flanker pinned in his radar.

All around them, the fighters of Lancer swirled and traded missiles with the oncoming Flankers. Once neatly ordered formations fell to chaos as aircraft wheeled and dove. Rabbit hardly noticed any of it, all of his attention was on the enemy. His every thought urged his sparrow on, willing it to find the mark. "Come on," said through clenched teeth. "Get him."

**

Vlasov's RWR chirped and twittered its frantic warning as the enemy missile closed in on him. He hadn't expected the American to fire back so quickly. The maneuverability of the Tomcat had caught him off guard, a mistake he would never repeat.

Inverting his aircraft, Vlasov pulled back on the stick and dove for the ocean. He looked up at the ocean below. Amber waves rolled across its surface, seeming to glow in the dying light of the sun. His breaths came hard, rasping in his facemask. Vlasov fought against the forces draining the blood from his head, his sight dimming. He tensed his core muscles, an old trick to slow the drain of blood. He held the turn as hard as he could, feeling the cold tendrils of unconsciousness caressing the back of his mind. If he passed out now he would die for sure, but if he could dodge this missile then he would be able to recommit. The Tomcat had surprised him, but his

Sukhoi had surprises of its own. Given half a chance he could drive that Tomcat into the ocean. If he could only lose this missile....

Vlassov dropped a trail of countermeasures behind his aircraft. Chaff and flares fluttered down, falling into the waves below.

Just a little further, just a little further.

He caught sight of the horizon climbing back into his field of view a moment before the Sparrow struck his fighter's spine and detonated. Shrapnel perforated the cockpit with metal fragments, tearing through metal and flesh with equal impunity. Vlasov only had a handful of seconds to be aware of both burning pain throughout his body and the sickening spin of his out of control aircraft before he lost consciousness forever.

***

"Splash one!" Gomez said.

Rabbit looked out of his canopy toward the enemy and saw a faint puff of smoke against the red backdrop of the sky. It was too far out to see a parachute, but not his problem either way. It was one less Russian to worry about.

No sooner had they splashed the Flanker than the RWR trilled for a lock by two separate air-defense radars.

"Spike!" Gomez said. "Surface band. We're taking SAM fire."

Rabbit forced himself out of his tunnel vision, craning his neck to scan the sky. There was no sign of the strike aircraft from his wing. The Hornets and Intruders had already launched their harpoons and gone for home.

There was nothing more for them to do here. It was time to run for it.

"Lancer 103 going cold," Rabbit said. He executed a wide bank, dropping a spray of chaff just to be on the safe side and then dove again. Trading what little altitude he had left for some extra speed he went to afterburners. It would be hell on their fuel, but right now all he cared about was getting out from under the Soviet SAM umbrella. He'd worry about running out of fuel after he could stop worrying about getting blown out of the sky.

Ahead of him, Rabbit saw an aging A-6 Intruder fleeing west, ordnance expended. It was there one moment and gone the next as a Soviet missile caught it in the tail. Aircraft and missile exploded in a flash of fire and debris. Flaming wrecking plummeted, scattering over the ocean's surface.

"Shit!" Gomez blurted. Both he and Rabbit knew they could be next.

Rabbit dropped a few flares in case there was a heatseeker on their tail and held course. The burning sun filled the cockpit ahead of him. The promise of safety. If they could just get away.

***

49

"Second attack group is turning back," Olesks's radar operator said.

The mood in the CIC was tense but growing more confident. The first American raid was wrapped up in an ongoing dogfight with the approaching land-based interceptors. Until the Americans cleared the skies—*if* they cleared the skies—they would be unable to attack his fleet directly. If the enemy tried for him now, they'd risk being caught from behind. Even if they did break free, their numbers were thin enough that Olesk felt confident that his air defenses could ward them off, or at least defend the core of the fleet. His ships had expended a significant amount of ammunition intercepting the American Phoenix volley and picking off enemy aircraft that strayed into their sights.

"Losses?" Olesk asked.

"Losses are significant on both sides," Radar said without missing a beat.

Olesk looked to his KAG for confirmation. The air wing commander failed to completely hide his grief at seeing his pilots brutalized. "They've done well," he said of their pilots.

"We have enough numbers to continue combat?" Olesk asked.

"Yes, Comrade Admiral. My recommendation is pursuit." The grief was gone, replaced in an instant by cold fury. "We can catch them and wipe the bastards out." When Olesk failed to answer right away, the KAG added: "If we do not pursue them then they will be back. This may be our best chance to destroy their air wing."

Even if they succeeded in catching the Americans, Olesk doubted how true that would be. Every fighter exchange they'd experienced so far had ended heavily in favor of the Americans. Instead of replying, Olesk glanced at the navigational chart nearby. A junior officer marked the fleet's position relative to land with a grease pen. Not far now.

Finally, Olesk spoke. "I think not. We will be well within ground-based air coverage by the time they are ready to try again."

The KAG grimaced, eager to pay the Americans back for his losses.

"What about the ammunition situation for our fighters?" Olesk asked, gently reminding the air group commander of the realities of war.

"Low," the KAG admitted reluctantly.

Olesk knew that the situation had to be the same for the Americans. Even if both sides wanted to continue the fight, it was going to have to end soon. No, the Americans to the west were escaping, but those to the east were still tangled in a dogfight with the Soviet air force. Olesk saw no harm in securing one more victory before his return to the mainland.

"Have a squadron pursue and harass the withdrawing group," Olesk said, "but avoid a general engagement. We will bring the rest of the wing across to the east and smash the enemy first attack group."

The KAG's eyes flashed. It was welcome news. "Yes, Admiral!"

"Then we've beaten them?" The hope in the tactical officer's tone sickened Olesk. Who could look at this debacle and see a victory? A third of the Northern Red Banner Fleet was in ruins. So many ships were sunk or crippled, or simply broken down with no chance of recovery. Victory? Another "victory" like this and they would be undone.

But, Olesk reminded himself, survival was a sort of victory. They'd sallied out and fought the Americans at their own game, toe-to-toe, and managed to walk away afterwards. Let the Politburo find a way to get water from the stone—to wring a victory from the Norwegian Sea campaign. Olesk simply needed to continue to survive.

Before Olesk could answer the officer, a warning bell sounded through the CIC. A death knell which seemed to reach the bones of every man here.

"Enemy anti-ship missiles detected!"

The Harpoons were here.

The shipwide PA blared to life. "*Missile attack port. Damage control teams standby.*"

Olesk looked to his tactical officer. His expression morose. "Not quite yet."

***

The Harpoons launched by *Shiloh* and *Chancellorsvile*'s air wings dropped down to wavetop level shortly after being fired and were only sporadically visible on Soviet radar systems. They closed in at high speed, shortening the distance to their prey by supersonic leaps and bounds, onboard radars fixed hungrily on their targets.

At such low level SAMs had little hope of firm locks, so the Soviet weapons operators overcame this shortcoming through quantity, which has been said to have a quality all its own.

The Harpoons reached the outlying picket ships first, sprinting in like ravenous wolves.

SAM fire spewed from frigates and destroyers at the edges of the fleet, swatting Harpoons from the sky, thinning their numbers. Handfuls of Harpoons emerged from this barrage and closed into gun range of the outer escorts.

CIWS fire swept across the ocean, shredding missiles as they entered range. Targets were identified, selected, tracked, and destroyed with machine precision.

The first Harpoon to slip past this wall of fire struck a *Udaloy*-class anti-submarine destroyer in its superstructure. The tower exploded in a spray of twisted metal, rippling across the sea.

A second missile found the *Udaloy*'s rear helicopter hangar, punching into the structure before exploding, setting the brand new vessel ablaze as onboard aviation fuel caught fire. The *Udaloy*'s flanks rolled with black smoke.

Kilometers away, a *Krivak*-class took three harpoon hits at the waterline, each tearing into his side like a knife into ribs. While only one exploded, it was enough to rip a gash in his hull which began greedily sucking in seawater. Smoke bled from the holes in his side as rocket fuel burned insatiably. The *Krivak*'s tail dipped lower in the water, his bow lifting up, sealing its inevitable doom.

A smaller, second wave of Harpoons passed by and through the escort ring, following pre-programmed guidance into the center of the Soviet formation. Once past the outlying defenses, the Harpoon's onboard radars burned to life, scanning for the core of the enemy formation and finding a handful of carriers and cruisers.

Now under direct attack, the core ships in the fleet powered on their search radars, hunting for threats.

Olesk watched all this through the sterile lens of *Ulyanovsk*'s radar display. His pickets had gotten off relatively lightly, but what really mattered were the carriers.

"How long?" he asked, watching the sporadic blips of the Harpoons closing on them.

"Sixty seconds," Radar said, voice hushed.

"Have the carriers turn hard to starboard," Olesk said. A hard right turn—east, away from the salvo—would present the stern of his ships to the oncoming attack. A narrower target was more difficult to hit and a stern-on impact would have a harder time breaching into sensitive areas.

As his communications officer relayed the order to the carriers and the helmsman carried it out, Olesk looked toward his tactical officer who didn't meet his gaze, he was already acting.

"SAM batteries target anti-ship missiles. Commence firing!"

The carriers and the cruisers of their inner escort opened fire with every missile battery available to them. Vertical launchers disgorged their contents in seconds, ships were momentarily blanketed by clouds of smoke as SAMs streaked out to intercept the enemy Harpoons.

Even with poor radar acquisition, volume of fire ensured that few missiles came within sight of the ships. The horizon was dotted with flashes and puffs of smoke.

"Missile sighted to aft! Brace! Brace!" the PA barked.

Olesk assumed brace position, teeth clenched so tightly his jaw ached.

Each ship deployed chaff, launching the shells with onboard mortars to surround them with radar-reflective clouds.

"CIWS engaged," Tactical said breathlessly.

As soon as the guns were engaged, they began tracking radar targets, watching for threats.

The moment *Ulyanovsk*'s CIWS guns were given automatic target acquisition they locked onto nearby radar signatures. A computer signaled permission to fire and they opened up.

The *Slava*-class cruiser *Oktyabrskaya Revolutsiya* cruised to *Ulyanovsk*'s port side, carefully positioned between the carrier and the American missile wave. As the missiles closed, *Oktyabrskaya Revolutsiya,* like the other ships in the core group, surrounded himself with clouds of chaff, chaff that now played off *Ulyanovsk*'s CIWS guns' radar.

The rotary cannons on the aircraft carrier opened fire on this intangible cloud of metal ribbons. The shells passed harmlessly through the smoke and punched into *Oktyabrskaya Revolutsiya*'s superstructure, shearing away his large radar array and peppering the bridge. A second burst came moments before the weapons operators could shut the guns down, ripping into the starboard missile tubes. Mercifully, the tubes were empty, having already been fired on the USS *Iowa* the night before.

In the midst of this chaos, the Harpoons arrived—the few of them that had survived the SAM volley.

Ulyanovsk, Tashkent, and their escorts fired, scything missiles from the sky.

A sea-skimming Harpoon caught the battlecruiser *Kalinin* in his flank, exploding on impact. The twisted metal hole roiled with seawater as compartments flooded. Somehow the impact had failed to wrench open enough compartments to sink the ship, but did succeed in flooding small portions of him.

Tashkent's guns cut a Harpoon from the sky meters away from impact. As the missile exploded prematurely, it showered the carrier with a spray of deadly fragments, perforating a parked helicopter on his deck with holes, but otherwise failing to secure a hit.

With that, the American missile wave had finally subsided.

Now it was finally over.

Olesk forced himself to unclench his teeth. The Americans had fired their last shot.

Ulyanovsk's CIC crew recited damage control reports and checked to ensure radar plots were clear before powering down the search radars again.

Olesk hardly listened to all this, focusing instead of his breathing. They'd done it. They'd survived.

"Status on the attack group to our east?" he asked.

"Withdrawing south, Comrade Admiral," the KAG said triumphantly.

The Americans had been sandwiched between two Soviet air wings and were left with no choice but to withdraw to avoid destruction. They'd never even had a chance to launch their Harpoons, and now they never would.

The Northern Fleet had fended off the Americans. Survival had cost them heavily though. Ammunition was scarce across the fleet, virtually depleted. Casualties among his airwing were severe, and two of his picket ships were crippled, a battlecruiser damaged. None of this was irreplaceable, however. Once they reached Polyarny they could begin the process of restocking and repairing.

Somehow, against the odds, he'd done it. The Red Banner fleet lived.

"Begin recovering fighters," Olesk said. "Ensure that gap in our picket line is closed." There was no chance he was going to remain here and wait for those stricken vessels to finish dying. He had to worry about the rest of the fleet, and two ships was a small price to pay for that safety. Now he only had to worry about how he was going to spin these events to the Kremlin.

"Comrade Admiral," Tactical said, sounding confused. He held one headphone to his ear, listening intently. As he listened, his expression fell, color draining from his face.

The tactical officer's growing horror mirrored in Olesk's own expression. He felt his heart skip a beat.

"A fresh group of returns from south west—no, two groups! Sixty aircraft in total. Distance is three hundred kilometers and closing.

Olesk was speechless. It wasn't possible. They'd accounted for every American carrier wing. Had the enemy managed to drag fighters away from the ground war on the mainland? Olesk shook his head. No, it had to be a trick of some kind. It just wasn't possible.

His tactical officer was ghastly pale and starting to sweat. They both had the same thing in mind: they'd spent nearly everything they had to stop the first two attacks.

Olesk ground his teeth. He wasn't going to give up. Not yet.

"Ready air defense! Scramble fighters. Intercept the Americans and destroy them."

But he hadn't yet realized that these fresh contacts weren't Americans.

***

50

Fashionably late like the cavalry in an American western, the fighters of *Foch* and *Clemenceau*'s air wings climbed from their wavetop approach, rising to attack altitude.

A mix of aircraft rode in two attack echelons, first those from *Foch* followed by *Clemenceau*. Super Entenards flew alongside aged F-8FN Crusaders. The pilots of these craft pushed them to their limits, throttles maxed, afterburners flaring, thirsty for blood. Coming in as low as they had had eaten their fuel reserves to nothing. Operating at the extreme edge of their range, they didn't have long. There was no time for niceties like dogfighting. They were here to do one job with time only for one salvo.

At the head of this attack formation, Falchion Leader finally heard the transmission he was waiting for from the trailing Étendard IVP reconnaissance aircraft.

"Falchion leader, this is *Miroir* One. we've confirmed Top Plate band radiation."

Top Plate was the NATO designation for the Soviet MR-750 target acquisition radar which happened to be exactly the type of radar system carried by *Kirov*-class battlecruisers.

Falchion Leader felt a small sense of relief. The American attack had forced the Soviet inner escorts to light their radars. It wasn't strictly necessary for his mission to proceed, but it ensured they had an accurate aimpoint for the missiles they carried.

"Affirmative. Good work, *Miroir*. Hold back and verify the results of our attack run."

"Copy. Good luck, *Falchion*."

Falchion Leader relayed this data and the coordinates to the fighters in his wing, his pilot's feeding the guidance data into their weapons.

Each attack craft carried the infamous French-made AM-39 Exocet missile. It was the same missile which had sunk the HMS *Sheffield* in the Falklands war and damaged the USS *Stark* during the Iran-Iraq war. Strangely, through some fluke of history, this would be the first time the Exocet would be used by the French against the enemies of NATO. Whatever else could be said about the Exocet, it could be said that it was proven to work.

As they drew up to combat altitude, the lead fighters of the French wing were spotted by Soviet air defense radars, sending the aircrafts' RWRs wailing.

Falchion Leader grimaced behind his oxygen mask as his RWR reported a hostile missile lock from a SAM battery. Likewise, he noted enemy aircraft turning to race toward them, desperate to intercept them out of range of the fleet and ward off the inevitable anti-ship attack.

They wouldn't have that chance.

Falchion Leader verified the coordinates were fed into his Exocet before checking the same with the rest of his squadron. Before Falchion and the rest of *Clemenceau*'s air wing could fire, *Foch*'s wing volleyed, their Exocets targeting the outlying Soviet picket ships between them and the carrier. The moment they'd fired, they broke south, fleeing for their own carriers and friendly skies.

Clemenceau's wing passed over *Foch*'s, Falchion Leader among them.

"On my mark," Falchion leader said, watching his instruments, ensuring they were close enough. "Mark."

He squeezed the trigger and the Exocet launched, racing toward the horizon and its prey.

"Falchion, breaking." Weapons in the air, the wing turned cold and fled, leaving two waves of missiles closing on the enemy.

***

Once again, electronics dueled in the sky as missiles chased radar returns. SAMs struck Exocets and tore them from the sky, touching off their warheads kilometers from their targets. A scant half-dozen Exocets lived to reach gun range and, of them, half found their mark, torching three more Soviet escorts in short order.

Olesk could do nothing but watch in mute terror as the first volley of enemy missiles savaged his picket line again. With their SAM ammunition already virtually depleted, they stood little chance. With the outer escorts floundering and burning, a gap had been torn in his defenses that thirty more wave-skimming Exocet missiles eagerly exploited.

The warning bell sounded again in *Ulyanosvk*'s CIC, ringing like the trumpet of Armageddon in Olesks's ears.

"Missile attack starboard! Damage control teams standby."

"Helm come about, hard to port, set heading 360!" Again, the carriers turned, presenting their sterns to the threat.

"Just thirty," Olesk said, feeling outside himself as frantic orders were called back and forth in the CIC. Missiles vanished and appeared from radar. SAMs intercepted them in ones and twos, whittling their numbers.

"Twenty."

Even if only a small fraction of the remaining missiles made it in, they would be enough to ravage the carriers. One hit could prove fatal. Multiple hits would be enough to doom everything.

Olesk's heart felt like it wasn't beating. He didn't dare breathe. He could only watch in sweating silence as the twenty returns became fifteen, drawing ever closer, dropping toward his ships like a guillotine blade.

"Missile sighted aft! Brace for impact!"

Olesk couldn't force himself to move or look away from the radar. A heartbeat later, the blips reached him.

CIWS guns cut loose, unleashing a spray of shells into the path of the enemy missiles. Each one had fixed on the largest radar return it could find. In the lead missile's case, it was *Ulyanovsk*. The carrier's close defense guns swept the skies, shells peppered over the ocean casting up a trail of impact splashes as they tried to blast the missile from the sky—and failed.

Olesk felt the hit like a blow to his gut.

The Exocet punched into *Ulyanovsk*'s aft section and spread a burning cloud of rocket fuel through the engine room. Sailors died in droves as flames filled the compartment, igniting everything that would burn. More deadly than the flames was the deadly wave of smoke that rolled forward through the ship, not quite contained by the water-tight doors.

A second missile struck his rear elevator, punching into the hangar below the flight deck before exploding. Ammunition stores exploded deep within the bowels of the carrier, adding to the growing list of the dead.

Olesk felt both hits as viscerally as if he had personally taken them.

"Damage report!" he shouted.

An answer was not fast in coming. The damage control officer frantically shouted into his headset, demanding clear answers. One thing was clear enough, the flagship of the Northern Red Banner Fleet was burning.

Outside of *Ulyanovsk*, the butchery continued.

Another missile caught the already damaged battlecruiser *Kalinin* in the helicopter hangar just behind the anti-air gun battery with a pyrotechnic flash. Flames licked up from the open elevator. Damage control teams were hastily diverted from his flank damage to contain the flames in the helicopter hangar. If the fires spread to the aviation fuel or ammunition storage, the battlecruiser would be finished.

Arcs of CIWS fire cut through the air, flashing back and forth as they caught the last few Exocets one by one. The last surviving missile streaked through the hail of gunfire and decoys to catch *Tashkent* in the stern and into the hangar deck without exploding, throwing a trail of burning rocket fuel across the aircraft and men inside.

And then it was over.

Admiral Olesk saw the radar scope was clear of enemy missiles a moment before main power to the CIC failed, switching over to battery backup in a heartbeat. The subtle thrum of his engines fell silent forever. *Ulyanovsk* was dead, and Olesks's hopes of salvaging this disaster went with him.

The Soviet carrier group had been decimated. *Ulyanovsk* was lost in billowing plumes of black smoke and licking flames. *Kalinin* stood balanced on a razor's edge between survival and destruction. It was a battle that damage control teams could win given enough time, but time was one resource the Soviets didn't have.

"Admiral, we've lost communication with engineering. Main power failure reported across the ship. Fire suppression systems are non-functional. I think we have a break in the water main. Damage control teams are responding."

Olesk sensed an unsaid "but" at the end of the sentence.

"*Tashkent*?"

"Fire in his hangar deck, but still under his own power."

Olesk only had as much time as it would take NATO to re-arm and mount another sortie to come back and finish them off. It was time he could spend trying to get power restored in his carrier, or time he could use to evacuate what crew remained. Damn that coward Zharkov! Damn this whole operation.

Olesk felt numb as he spoke. "Begin the process to transfer flag command to *Tashkent*. Give orders to scuttle any ship which cannot be restored to power in an hour." As he spoke, he knew full well that included his own flagship.

No one spoke.

Olesk wouldn't wait around for NATO to come back and finish him off. "Start procedures to abandon ship."

The Red Banner Northern Fleet was gutted, burning and

sinking, a defeat had been turned into near total destruction. All that remained, Olesk mused, was to see what would become of him when he made it back to shore.

***

51

When the RWR—which had been trilling near constantly—suddenly fell silent, it took Rabbit a moment to realize he was no longer being hunted.

"Gomez?"

"Flankers breaking off," his RIO said, twisted around in his seat in a vain effort to see behind them. "They're going cold, man. Pulling east."

"East?" Rabbit asked. That was toward land—not back toward the Soviet fleet. The only reason they could break east, as far as Rabbit could tell, was if they were running for land.

"Holy shit, dude," he said, feeling a surreal calm come over him. "I think we did it."

"You think we nailed their fleet?" Gomez asked, incredulous.

Rabbit nodded, "At least part of it. Their birds don't have a carrier to run back to. They're going for air bases inland. That's the only thing I can think of."

"God damn," Gomez said before repeating himself with more enthusiasm, "God *damn*!" He whooped in triumph, releasing all his pent up tension with a laugh. "Game over!"

Rabbit felt his shoulders relax. They were headed back for *Shiloh*. He smiled behind his mask, his fear subsiding in the face of hope. It was over.

***

"We've got confirmation from *Richmond*, Admiral. One Soviet flat top burning, another damaged. Looks like we also struck one of their battlecruisers."

Alderman hardly looked at the reconnaissance photo—

a pillar of black smoke on a dark horizon. *Novosibirsk* and *Ulyanovsk* had been sent down in flames, *Tashkent* damaged, not to mention damage and losses to numerous escorting ships from destroyers to the huge *Kirovs*. It was about as clear a victory as he could ask for. The Soviet Northern Fleet was far from exterminated, but it had lost what offensive capability it had, burned away in a blaze of glory, a death ride across the Norwegian Sea.

There was a temptation to finish the job, a strong temptation. Alderman had the aircraft to try again certainly and there may be no better chance. A concerted attack from three carrier groups on the remains of the Soviet fleet would likely spell doom for them. But what would it cost?

Alderman felt fatigue creeping up on him. How much worse would this feeling be for the men on the cutting edge of the navy—pilots and sailors? They'd fought like hell and suffered for it. The United States Navy had proved its martial supremacy through blood and fire, and they'd just as surely proved that they couldn't do it alone. The Dutch, French, and British had all bled for this. NATO ruled the waves.

Victors or not, they'd suffered for this win.

Let the Soviets run back to their sea bastions. They would still be there when the time came to finish them off. There would be other battles, other chances.

"Start recovering aircraft," Alderman said. "Good work. Damn fine work."

The men of the CIC allowed themselves a taste of levity, smiling in relief. The Battle of the Norwegian Sea was over.

Alderman only half listened to the recovery operations. He left the CIC once he was certain all his pilots were out of harm's way and had verified the strike craft of *Foch* and *Clemenceau* were en route back to their carriers. After ensuring the remainder of the operation was under control, Alderman left the CIC, walking through *Bastogne*'s passageways and ladderways, working his way steadily back to his office. Once inside, he closed the door behind himself softly and savored the sound of silence here. It felt almost expectant, as though this quiet were just the prelude to a new chapter. What was it Churchill had said? Not the end, not the beginning of the end, but perhaps the end of the beginning. Something like that. Alderman hoped like hell that wasn't true. What other possible carnage waited on their future? If he never had to see another battle, he would die a happy man.

He sat at his desk, picking up the picture frame which held the photo of his family. Exhaustion buzzed in his head, singing the siren song of sleep. Soon enough.

Alderman picked up the phone. "Connect me with Admiral Gideon."

"Right away, Admiral."

The sailor stretched the meaning of "right away" as the call was connected and redirected via satellite, bounced across the globe back to Washington DC.

"Gideon."

"We stopped them," Alderman said. "Butt-cold. We stopped them."

"You're sure?"

"As can be. Two burning *Ulyanovsk*s, one damaged. Last I checked, the Soviets only ever made three."

"Then that's all she wrote," Gideon said, sounding equal parts relieved and impressed. "Probably too late to rename *Khe Sahn*."

"*Khe Sahn*?"

"You thought USS *Norwegian Sea* was an idle threat?" Gideon teased. "If we named carriers for people then you'd be on the list I'm sure, right after Nimitz."

"We've got enough heroes to name a fleet of *Spruances* and *Perrys*," Alderman said dryly.

"Too many," Gideon replied, tone more subdued. "Too God damn many."

"But it's over."

"The battle is over," Gideon corrected. "The war isn't. We stopped them here, but now we've got to roll them up."

"End of the beginning," Alderman said.

"Sounds about right," Gideon said. "I'll let the Joint Chiefs know. Get your people together, rested, and refit. I know we've got a hell of a tough fight ahead of us."

Alderman closed his eyes and let out a breath. "I know." But he also knew that they could handle it.

***

52

The skies overhead were crystal clear, bluer than blue, not a puff of clouds in sight. Perfect hunting weather.

Corporal Karlsdotter sat on an empty ammo crate staring up at the sky. NATO aircraft had been flying to and fro all day now, conducting air strikes on Soviet positions. The whistle and howl of straining jet engines presaged the inevitable bass rumble of bombs exploding further away. Almost as quickly as it had come, the Soviet offensive had come undone. Like waking from some terrible nightmare, that inexorable enemy pressure had slackened and fallen away.

Her eyes went from sky to ground where she saw visceral proof of that in the form of twenty Soviet prisoners of war sitting in a nervous huddle, hands on their heads waiting to be processed, watched over by eagle-eyed Swedish reservists. The Soviets were dirty, ragged, and exhausted. Their war was over.

"Corporal?"

"I'm still here, Bucht," she said.

The platoon's machine gunner looked so much smaller without ammo belts looped over him or an FN MAG on his shoulder. Thick white gauze wrapped his bare chest, covering a shrapnel wound. His eyes were half-lidded, drowsy, the eyes of someone in the warm embrace of morphine. "Karlsdotter?" he reached out weakly with his good hand.

Karlsdotter took his hand in hers, feeling a little self conscious, but no one else at the recovery point paid her any mind. Everyone was just glad to be coming off the line.

He gave a weak smile. "You're beautiful."

Karlsdotter smiled and laughed. "And you are higher than a

kite, Bucht. I think you'll regret saying that tomorrow."

"Am I dying?" he asked, suddenly concerned.

Karlsdotter's expression hardened. "No, you're not dying."

"When do we go home?"

Stockholm felt like a lifetime ago, a paradise lost. Or it had until this morning. With the renewed aerial campaign, the Soviets had been driven back, not just to their start positions, but thrown back by kilometers as the line threatened to come apart at the seams. Exhausted, overworked, undertrained, poorly led reservists and conscripts fled in panic or surrendered in groups wherever Swedish and Norwegian units advanced. If they just had more men, they could break them. Karlsdotter could feel it in her bones. They were so close. "Soon," she said.

"Hellström?"

The sergeant was safe, back in a field hospital or maybe already being transferred to Oslo. "He'll be waiting for us there," Karlsdotter lied. "We'll all be home soon."

"But we held, right? We stopped them?"

Now she didn't have to lie. "We stopped them, Bucht. No more talking. Get some rest." She waited until the drugs slipped Bucht into a deep sleep before she carefully let go of his hand, laying it at his side on the stretcher.

She looked around at the rest of her platoon, sitting like she was on the roadside waiting for transport to take them to the rear. There were fewer of them than there were a week ago, and fewer still than there were when they started. She didn't know what would happen to them yet. Would they be reinforced? Used as replacements in other depleted units? Combined with another half platoon? The future was a mystery, and one she had no energy to worry about. One thing she did know was that they were getting off the line. Hot food, hot showers, phone calls, rest. It seemed almost unreal.

Bergman crossed over to her, coming to sit with her and Bucht.

"How is he?" he asked.

"Well enough to flirt," she said.

Bergman laughed softly. "Good. Then he's feeling better already."

Machine gunner life expectancy was never good in war. They were prime targets for enemy fire and it was a miracle Bucht hadn't been killed by the grenade that caught him.

"I just talked with Sundquist," Bergman said. "He said that the British are taking over for us."

"That's right," Kalrsdotter said.

"British marines." Bergman sounded incredulous.

"Yes."

"Wow."

Karlsdotter gave Bergman a puzzled look.

"For how long we were on our own....I guess I forgot there were other people fighting on our side. British marines....Can you imagine?"

She didn't have to imagine. They saw them in person before long. Lines of mottled green armored vehicles and trucks trundled past them, winding up the road toward the new—rapidly advancing front.

The soldiers she could see looked too young, too clean. They stared back at her, faces unreadable. Maybe they were surprised to see a woman out here, maybe they were astonished with the rough shape of her platoon, maybe they were just trying to get an idea of what was waiting for them ahead.

Bergman lit a cigarette and blew a cloud of smoke. "That's it then?"

"For now," she said. As she sat and watched the British pass, she smiled to herself.

***

53

After so long in the cockpit, Rabbit felt a huge relief in finally returning to his cabin. The thin foam mattress was a godsend, like some kind of unimaginable luxury. He laid down and put his hands behind his head, staring up at the ceiling, feeling... nothing. He expected to feel joy or relief but it wouldn't come. Instead he felt a profound emptiness.

The fleet was re-organizing. Ships and aircraft shuffled commands, holes were plugged in the line—the noose around the Soviet Union's neck. For now, he was off the hook. With the Soviet surface fleet and naval air force devastated, there was little left for a Tomcat pilot to do. It was someone else's fight for now.

Rabbit sighed. Turning his head, he looked at the other half of the cramped living space, Metcalf's side. Metcalf's things were still here. Clothes, toiletries, books—it was like he'd just stepped out, like he could be back at any minute. Only he wouldn't.

Rabbit sat up, unable to rest. He'd never been particularly close with Metcalf. They were bunkmates, they were on good terms, but they were never what he would call "friends." Different jobs, different interests, different generations. Metcalf was a good man, but that was all Rabbit could say of him.

He'd never known anyone to die in the Navy before, so he really wasn't sure what would happen next. Presumably someone would come by to collect his things at some point.

As Rabbit looked over the pitiful remains of Metcalf's life, his eyes stopped on a slip of white paper, folded with geometric precision. A letter.

Before he could stop himself, Rabbit stood and picked it up, unfolding it to read. As he read, his heart broke.

Metcalf's letter to his daughter.

Rabbit read it over twice.

Unfinished. A life interrupted, cut short.

He sat back down on the bunk and stared at the letter. What a monstrously unfair outcome for Metcalf, to be robbed of everything so suddenly. His family was going to learn that it was too late. Too late for Metcalf to make things right with his daughter. But it didn't have to be. Rabbit knew, if the roles were reversed, what he would want Metcalf to do for him. He didn't hesitate.

Finding a paper and pen was no object. Rabbit sat down to write.

My name is David Barlow. You don't know me, but I flew with your father. I didn't know him long, but I know that he wanted to patch things up between the two of you. I'm sorry that he never got the chance to tell you that in person.

Rabbit stared at his writing, precise block letters in neat rows. Satisfied it was legible, he continued.

I wanted to tell you about him and what he was like while I knew him.

***

EPILOGUE

Pen scratched paper in the otherwise dead silence of the conference room. Gradenko didn't watch as the paper was signed, the outcome was already a given. Instead he kept his eyes fixed on the window beyond the signatories which overlooked Tbilisi's Communard Garden park. It was small by the standards Gradenko was used to. Everything in Tbilisi was smaller in scale than the grandiose buildings, avenues, parks, and plazas of Moscow, but it had charm all the same.

His trip to Georgia SSR had been swift and uneventful, marred only by the news of the Northern Fleet's near total defeat. Of course, it hadn't been presented to the public that way. In fact, there was almost no discussion of the titanic naval battle across the Norwegian Sea. The only news was of a "difficult situation" and "heroic sacrifices." Gradenko didn't need to be the foreign minister to see through that thin lie to the grim truth beyond.

Tbilisi itself was beyond tense. People seemed even more subdued than in Moscow. The city was scarcely one hundred and fifty kilometers from the frontlines in the Caucasus where Soviet and Turkish troops traded desultory barrages of artillery fire and occasionally engaged in sporadic raids. It was strange, Gradenko thought, to see the old battlegrounds of the Russian and Ottoman empires once again watered with blood.

While rough mountain terrain prevented either side from securing any kind of shocking breakthrough, it kept people on edge. It wasn't inconceivable for setbacks and "difficult situations" to drive the Soviet lines back, closer to the city. With the staggering ranges of modern weapons, very few places were truly safely away from the fighting.

In fact, if it weren't for strict travel controls being enforced by internal security troops and police, Gradenko was certain the city would have emptied out by now.

Soldiers stood on every street corner and defensive missile batteries kept a close watch on the skies. It felt like an occupied city, and in many ways Gradenko supposed it was. The Georgians, like so many of the other SSRs of the Union, had a turbulent past with their Russian overlords. Uprising, protests, and riots had all broken the peace at one time or another. Gradenko couldn't help but wonder how loyal the separate SSRs might remain to the Soviet cause if the central government's power began to wane. What sort of chaos and bloodshed might spring up from that fresh hell? Would the social and political turmoil wracking China be the USSR's fate as well? Gradenko didn't even want to consider it.

"Comrade Minister?"

Gradenko turned from the window to smile blandly toward his opposite number from Bulgaria. Rising from his seat, he picked up the signed document and looked it over.

A memorandum of understanding regarding the war, a resolution concerning the fate of Turkey, Greece, and—most interestingly—a promise of Iraqi and Syrian cooperation. The lease of air bases in exchange for a fresh round of economic aid and more slots for guest workers across the Soviet Union. Another expansion of the war he was desperate to end.

Gradenko soothed his conscience by reminding himself that the stronger the Soviet position the sooner this war could be brought to a conclusion. Besides, even if the military side of things didn't pan out, this sort of maneuvering only strengthened his own position in the Politburo in his political struggle with Karamazov. Tarasov claimed to back him against Karamazov and the KGB; all that remained was to move the pieces into position.

"Comrades, thank you," Gradenko said. "With this document we have secured our future against NATO aggression and take another step closer toward true communism."

Gradenko signed his own name at the bottom of the paper, noting in turn the signatures from Bulgaria, Romania, Yugoslavia, Syria, and Iraq.

The men who provided these signatures sat around him at the table, their faces grave. None were pleased, after all the future was still uncertain. Events were in motion to decide the fate of the Soviet Union, the fate of the war, the fate of the world. It remained to be seen if they had backed the winning horse or shackled themselves to a dying giant.

None of these concerns showed on Gradenko's placid features. The war would move south, to the shores of the Black and Aegean Seas and—if Gradenko was correct—to the streets of Moscow, the halls of the Kremlin. Karamazov's days were numbered.

Gradenko closed the folio and, at last, smiled.

AFTERWORD

Thanks so much for reading! Please be sure to leave a review and let other people know what you thought about it.

https://www.amazon.com/dp/B0C6R5M65B

Also consider following me on Twitter to be kept aware of upcoming releases or feel free to drop me a line on email.

TKBlackwoodWrites@Gmail.com
https://twitter.com/TkBlackwood

ABOUT THE AUTHOR

T.k. Blackwood

T.K. Blackwood is a full time IT professional and part time writer who lives in North Carolina with his wife, child, and too many reptiles.

IRON CRUCIBLE

A conflict nearly fifty years in the making spills from boardrooms and back alleys into open battle on land, sea, and the air. The showdown of the century is here, East versus West with the fate of the world at stake.

Blue Masquerade

The year is 1992. Over twenty years have passed since Soviet General Secretary Leonid Brezhnev was assassinated by a crazed gunman. Since that time, the Soviet Union has been put on a course toward economic success—and war.

In the Balkans, Yugoslavia's collapse into ethnic violence draws NATO and the Warsaw Pact to the brink of Armageddon. Armies deploy and fleets maneuver. Political intrigue engulfs Moscow and Washington, and paranoia radiates from the Iron Curtain. In the zero-sum game of Cold War, neither side can afford to blink or back down.

A conflict nearly fifty years in the making spills from boardrooms and back alleys and explodes into open battle on land, air and sea

Red Front

The year is 1992.

The unthinkable has happened. East and West are on a crash

course for war, and the battlefield will be Germany. Peace is no longer an option and all bets are off as the Free World and the Communist Bloc descend into war. NATO forces scramble to grapple with the Soviet juggernaut, as the Reds pull out all the stops - and engineer a secret plan - to crush them in a single mighty blow. The future of humanity tilts in the balance.

Welcome to World War III.

White Horizon

The year is 1992.

The Soviet Blitzkrieg in Germany has been beaten to a bloody halt along the Rhine River. The Reds rush masses of teenage conscripts and rusty reservists to the front, while NATO scrambles to mount a killing blow against their reeling nemesis.

The flames of war spread north to Scandinavia, embroiling Sweden and threatening Norway. In this grinding war of attrition, both sides endure, and the death toll mounts. Is a breakthrough at hand or has the carnage only begun?

Black Seas

The year is 1992. Europe is in flames. Scandinavia is under siege. Only Norway holds out against the Soviet war machine. And now the pride of the Soviet Navy, the Red Banner Northern Fleet, sallies out to finish the job.

With their armies facing annihilation, and World War III at a tipping point, the combined navies of NATO stand ready to receive their enemy. Europe's greatest naval battle since Jutland, the first carrier battle since World War II, is about to begin.

BOOKS BY THIS AUTHOR

Shadow Fury

The year is 199X and the world is rebuilding after the devastating First-Strike War between East and West. Lawlessness has descended over vast stretches of the globe and only two things are respected: money and violence. In this new and uncertain world, life is cheap and mercenary companies like Kobracom make a killing selling their services to the highest bidder.

This time Kobracom has turned on one of their own: Adrian Blank, a special forces operator turned mercenary, and veteran of the First-Strike War. Kobracom has taken his girlfriend, Kitsune, and left him for dead. Now, Adrian has tracked them to the refugee metropolis of New Saigon where he and Kobracom will undertake an action-packed, high-stakes, and spectacularly deadly cat-and-mouse game through the rain-slick streets of the city.

Dive into this blood-soaked vision of the 1980s retro-future and experience T.K. Blackwood's debut novel now!

The Great War Of 189- : A Forecast (Annotated By Liam Rook) - Foreword By T.k. Blackwood

In an age where we cannot help but try to predict the next great war, it's instructive to see what prophets of the past got wrong...and what they got right.

Written by Rear-Admiral Philip Colomb in 1892, the Great War of 189– captures the spirit of the age, channeling growing fears of a general European war and painting a picture of industrialized societies going to war.

A chilling vision of a future to come, written over twenty years before the events of 1914 plunged Europe into four years of bloody conflict, the Great War of 189– captures the heart of "invasion literature" and through newspaper articles and firsthand accounts of observers tells the tale of the next Great War. With pre-dreadnought fleet engagements in the Mediterranean and massed cavalry charges in Belgium, Colomb describes a World War that looks more like Waterloo than the Somme.

This annotated edition includes footnotes that provide invaluable insight into the events of this era and how Colomb's predictions shaped up. Coupled with newly illustrated maps of the battles and events of the Great War, this is the definitive version of this classic novel.

Printed in Great Britain
by Amazon

27634614R00209